MW01136909

Reawakening

A Regent Vampire Lords Novel

By

K.L. Kreig

ISBN-13: 978-1511992695

ISBN-10: 1511992697

Dedication

For my mom, Linda. Thanks for instilling a love of fantasies so great that I had the courage to pen my own.

Reawakening

Prologue

Running late, Sarah ran across the dark snowy lawn to Swift Hall, pulling her coat tighter against the harsh winter wind. One look at the streetlights showed flurries in the air. The forecast was for another six inches of snow before morning. The winter in Illinois had been brutal this year and she couldn't wait until spring finally arrived in a couple of months.

She ran faster, *hating* to be late, but had been so caught up in her research paper, she'd lost track of time. Not being on time was rude and disrespectful. Over her four years at Northwestern, she'd sat in class many a day waiting for a professor or TA to show up, only to leave after the requisite 'ten minute rule.'

She was meeting Professor Bailey, head of the Psychology department, and that was the one person she did not want to keep waiting. He detested lateness more than she did. His mantra was 'if you're not on time, don't bother.' He'd turned more than one person away for a scheduled meeting because they'd shown up one minute late.

They'd met in her second year when she'd taken a psychology class taught by one of his TA's, who was perpetually late. She'd complained to the professor about him and they'd struck up an unusual friendship. He'd been a great mentor and she really liked him, even if he was nerdy and a little skittish.

So a few short months ago when he'd asked her to be part of his dream study, she was thrilled. She hadn't even known about the study until the end of last semester when they were having lunch and she'd discussed a particularly disturbing dream. He made the offer and she readily accepted.

If there were a perfect candidate, it was Sarah. Having been plagued with strange dreams on and off all her life, she was anxious to understand more about what they represented and why she had them. The study would evaluate underlying things like dream repetition, mental stability, primitive conscience and hidden messages. Of course, her main goal was dream translation. Like most people can and do, she carries on conversations with others in her dreams, except in her instance they were *real* conversations ... remembered quite clearly by her the next day but not by the person she'd dreamt about.

At first, she'd thought everyone else was crazy, and then she began thinking perhaps she was the one with a screw loose. But she knew things she shouldn't and couldn't know otherwise, so they had to be real. Other than

2

her parents, Professor Bailey was the only one she'd talked to about this strange phenomenon. She often didn't know what she should and shouldn't discuss so when she'd slip up and mention a fact she shouldn't know, she played it off. *"Oh, so-and-so must have told me"*, or *"I must have overheard a conversation you were having with so-and-so"* or *"You don't remember telling me that?"* It was a pain in the ass, quite frankly.

Pulling the door open to Swift Hall, she hustled down the long, quiet hallway to the professor's office, melted snow leaving a wet trail behind her. Although the meeting time was unusually late in the evening, he'd said this was the only time he could see her in the next two weeks and needed her notes before the scheduled submission date. She'd offered to email them as usual, but he'd said he had questions from her last set, which needed to be reviewed in person.

Knocking on his closed office door, she entered when she heard "come in."

"Hi Professor. I'm so sorry I'm late, I—"

"No apologies necessary, Sarah. Sit, sit. Take off your coat."

She wrinkled her brows in confusion. He'd never been so forgiving the handful of times she'd been late before.

"Okay." She sat, after removing her wet, heavy coat and placing it on the back of the chair opposite his desk. She handed over the thumb drive that held all of her notes.

"Thank you, Sarah." He took it and simply placed it on the desk in front of him, never taking his eyes from hers.

A twinge of fear made her stomach clench. Something felt very off about this situation. Professor Bailey wasn't acting *at all* like himself. When he rose and walked around the front of the desk and sat on the edge, knees almost touching hers, alarm bells rang loudly in her ears.

Suddenly she questioned whether his intentions for this meeting had been less than honorable. She'd never gotten that vibe from him in all these years, but she knew that didn't really matter. This sort of thing happened all the time. She'd heard that most sexual attacks on women were by someone they knew.

Right before he grabbed her, she swore a twinge of regret flashed in his small, dark eyes. Opening her mouth to scream, nothing came out as her world spun and churned. Moments later, the dizziness passed, but everything was dark. As her eyes adjusted and she got her bearings, she looked around at her new surroundings through blurry, tear-filled eyes.

What in the hell had just happened?

She was alone, in a very dimly lit, small non-descript white room. The only thing that stood between her and freedom was a door with no handle. A filthy thin mattress sat directly on the cold concrete floor, the only other thing in the small area besides herself. She ran to the door, pounding and screaming

4

and crying. Yelling into the silence until her voice was hoarse, she eventually stopped and stood there, not knowing what to do next.

Panic gripped her and she sunk to the cold floor, against the cool wall in the corner of the room and watched the door, waiting for the other shoe to drop. She wanted to be brave and put on a good front, but fear got the best of her and she sobbed uncontrollably.

Questions ran through her head at a rapid speed. What the hell *was* Professor Bailey that he could do something like this? How was she in his office one minute and somewhere else entirely the next? *Where* was she? What did they want from her? She couldn't wrap her mind around what had just happened.

Little did Sarah know, at the time, that this small, lonely, terrifying room is where she would spend the next thirty-three days of her life. And as bad as she'd thought her captivity had been, she had no idea that unknown forces on the inside worked to protect her, or the days would have been far, far worse.

Chapter 1

"How did you learn to make such great sugar cookies?" Analise asked.

"From my mother," Sarah answered, rolling out another lump of chilled dough. "Sugar cookies are one of her specialties, but she'd only make them at Christmastime because they're *too labor intensive.*"

This felt nice. Drinking wine, listening to music and baking with her sisters. Except Kate had sparkling cider instead of wine, due to the baby. Too bad she couldn't keep her mind on the task at hand, however, because of a certain icy blue-eyed vampire she'd crossed paths with last week. She'd already burned two batches of the buttery confection.

"Mmmm. I'm going to get fat if I keep eating like this," Kate moaned, taking a bite of her third warm cookie. She closed her eyes in sheer pleasure.

"You're preggers. You're supposed to get good and fat," Analise quipped, pulling a fresh batch from the hot oven.

"Easy for you to say. Just wait until you get pregnant," Kate said to Analise.

Analise smiled a little sadly and Sarah didn't know why, but decided it was time to change subjects.

"This is the last of it, girls." Having cut the last bit of dough into a candy cane shape, she began to clean up.

Christmas in July, they'd dubbed it— minus the brightly wrapped presents and the decorated pine tree and the brandy-laced eggnog. Okay, so they only had Christmas-shaped cookie cutters on hand, but the reason didn't matter. Kate said she'd woken with a craving for cookies, since it was one of many topics of conversation last week at dinner, and she insisted Sarah make her 'to-die-for' recipe. And pregnant women always got what they wanted.

One would think that given the ordeal she'd been through, and the sick way she'd discovered vampires were real, that she'd be frightened to live in a house full of them, but one would be wrong.

The truth was she didn't feel safe anywhere else, knowing that every vampire here would protect her with their lives and that's why she stayed. Not that she had a choice now that it'd been discovered she was Xavier's third daughter. But all that was beside the point. She felt like part of a family and didn't want to leave anyway, so it was irrelevant that she couldn't.

Ever since she'd been brought here, she had a deep-seated feeling it was for a specific reason. The events that had happened, as horrible as they were, happened for a reason. Was it to find her sisters, Kate and Analise? Was it to perfect her dreamwalking skills? Was it to help others like her? Or was it for a bigger purpose that had yet to identify itself?

Was it perhaps to meet an intense blue-eyed vampire whom she now couldn't stop thinking about, but who clearly didn't return the feeling?

And once again her thoughts circled around to *him*. Romaric Dietrich. The man— *correction, vampire*—whose gaze was so piercing when their eyes connected last week she thought she'd burst into flames and disintegrate on the spot. She'd actually felt the gush of desire between her thighs and her underwear had become most uncomfortable.

Even though she wasn't that experienced, she knew when a man wanted her. Passionate desire had been etched over every inch of his hungry face and his eyes had devoured her like she'd been standing naked and exposed before him for the first time. And she'd *wanted* to be. She'd never been so captivated by anyone. In fact, now she couldn't be sure she'd ever actually *been* attracted to a man before with the unfamiliar feelings Romaric had evoked in her. He reminded her of a wicked, avenging angel.

Sarah now knew he was the man, *er* vampire, who'd haunted her dreams all her life. Even though he'd never shown his face, she *knew* it was him once she'd laid eyes on his face. The face he'd always kept hidden for some reason.

"Earth to Sarah ..." Analise gently shook her.

"Sorry, what were you saying?" She turned to check on the cookies, but they were cooling on the rack and everything was already cleaned and put away. When she turned back around, Analise and Kate were exchanging knowing glances.

"Sarah—" Kate started.

"I don't want to talk about it."

She filled her glass with the last of the wine and headed into the sitting room. The last thing she wanted to reminisce on was the embarrassment of what had happened after she and Rom eye fucked each other over the dinner table. And make no mistake, that's most definitely what they'd done.

She flopped into the comfortable paisley armchair and stared out the window into the sultry evening, taking a big gulp of the buttery Chardonnay. It was still so steamy that heat rose in waves from the blacktop and the cool liquid running down her throat was exactly what she needed to take her mind off things. Focus on that instead of the panty-wetting vampire who'd fled five days ago and hadn't been back since.

Kate and Analise followed her, of course, settling on the couch across from where she sat. She knew they wouldn't let this topic go. They'd pestered her yesterday until she'd finally retreated to the safety of her room where she could again replay the bizarre encounter alone, trying to make sense of it. She'd dreamt of *him* again last night, but as usual, he stayed in the shadows, his face hidden. It was frustratingly confusing.

"Are you hot for him?" Analise asked, taking a sip of her own cocktail.

"Analise!" Kate scolded.

"What? It's a valid question. I'm surprised he didn't throw her on the table and do her right there."

Sarah shot her best 'younger sister' glare at Analise. Now she finally understood what it was like to have older, protective siblings and while slightly irritating, it was somewhat endearing as well.

"It wasn't like that," she hedged, glancing back out the window to cover her lie. Oh, it most certainly *was* like that. And the scary part was, if he had thrown her down on the table, she would have let him.

"Did Damian say anything?"

Kate's question got her attention and she shifted her gaze back to Analise, anxiously awaiting the answer, but pretending it didn't matter at the same time. Sarah knew that Damian and Romaric had some sort of close bond, so if anyone knew the details of what happened, it would be Damian.

Analise glanced quickly at her, before answering Kate. "No, Rom didn't say a word. In fact, he postponed their strategy meeting, spouting some emergency bullshit back at home and returned to Washington with no explanation."

"Well, there must be some interest there, because he asked Dev what your name was. And ..." Kate left the word dangling, hanging in midair like a kite caught on a stiff breeze.

"And what?" she finally asked, not able to help herself.

"And he asked what happened to you when you were captive."

Great. He thought she was damaged goods since she'd been kidnapped by those rogue vampires. She may still be recovering emotionally from the whole ordeal, but having heard what some of the other women had gone through, Sarah knew that, while traumatizing, it could have ended far, far worse for her. She knew she'd be in a far different place had she been repeatedly raped, or, God forbid, pregnant, like many of the women rescued.

Sarah tried not to let her heart, or her ego, take a hit, but damn if it didn't feel like both had just been splattered all over the sizzling hot driveway out front. Taking another large gulp of her wine, she decided it was time to call it a night. Besides, Kate and Analise were probably anxious to get back to their mates. They'd been here for hours and while she enjoyed spending time with them, she didn't need a babysitter. Which is exactly what this whole 'Christmas in July' ruse had been about. She wasn't as naïve as everyone seemed to think she was.

"I think this wine has made me tired. I'm going to hit the hay." They all rose and made their way to the kitchen.

Besides, she had things to do. When her brother died, she'd ended up delaying college for a year, so just turning twenty-four, she was a little older than most grads. Except, she hadn't graduated yet and she'd decided that she really wanted to. Only six credits shy of her Human Development and Psychological Services Bachelor's degree when she'd been kidnapped, since it wasn't safe to leave the house, Kate had found a way to get her enrolled in the remaining two classes via Skype, which she started in a few weeks.

After her Bachelor's, she'd been planning to get an advanced degree in clinical and counseling psychology, but now she wasn't sure what she'd do. It was her intent to start as a counselor at the shelter when she finished her degree and while her original path leaned toward children, she knew these women needed her far more. She found it fascinating that both Kate and Analise studied in the same field she was interested in, but she supposed now that it was all meant to be. That *this* is where she was meant to be.

"I'll let you know if I hear anything, okay?" Analise hugged her tightly and she squeezed her eyes together to hold back tears. She would not cry over some stupid vampire who wouldn't give her the time of day. She wasn't even really sure she wanted his attentions. He was so extreme it bordered on scary.

"It doesn't matter, Analise."

"Uh huh." Winking as she waved goodbye, she turned and left for the main house. "We're headed back to Boston, but I'll talk to you tomorrow, okay?"

"Yes, sure," Sarah mumbled.

"Goodnight sweetie. See you tomorrow." Luckily Kate didn't say another word on the subject, which was good. Either she was going to blow up or cry. At this point, she may do both.

Finishing her wine, she retreated to her room, after checking on a couple of the girls, including Beth. Beth had slowly started to come around, talking a bit more about what had happened and so she'd made it habit to stop by her room every night before going to bed to insure she didn't need anything. The night before last they'd ended up talking for two hours, mostly about mundane things, but it was the first time she'd cracked the door open enough for Sarah to learn about the real Beth. Sarah began to see how Analise and Beth had become so close.

But Beth was already sleeping, so she reluctantly went to her room, pulled up the university website and ordered the two books she'd need for classes, sending them to the university, where Thane would graciously pick them up.

It was still too early for bed, so she puttered around online for a while. Although she hadn't been one for social media prior to ending up here, unfortunately with Xavier on the loose she was forbidden from using any of it for fear they would be able to trace her back here, even with the technological security they had in place.

Much to her dismay, Xavier, her psychotic-biological-sperm-donor-vampire father, wasn't killed in that raid and, after five months, still remained on the loose. And was still trying to find the daughters he'd ordered dead, but were very much alive, so he could turn his twisted empire-building into a *family* business and take over the world.

Thanks, but no thanks ... Dad.

Try as she might not to, once again, she thought of the fear and despair she'd felt during those thirty-three days.

She thought of the terror she'd felt the first time she realized her captors were real life vampires. She thought of the day, two weeks into her captivity that she was saved from a horrific fate by an unknown vampire, who was true to his word that she would be safe. For the first several weeks after her rescue, whenever she closed her eyes, she'd relive that day. The day she was stripped naked, tied down and almost raped by a horde of rogue vampires. Thankfully, those nightmares now came few and far between.

She thought about how if it hadn't been for Kate's dreams of her and Dev's heroic efforts to save her, Sarah simply knew she would have become another statistic. Another tragedy. Another lost soul.

And she thought back to how she'd come to this place. A sanctuary. Her salvation. A shelter that Kate and her mate, Devon Fallinsworth, Midwest Regent Vampire Lord, had created after Dev rescued the first set of kidnapped women from Xavier's clutches, which included Sarah.

Kate had been her rock, getting her through every single tough day. Analise had been a breath of fresh air, making her constantly laugh with her quick wit. And the last couple of months, she'd finally found a purpose in staying. To help others.

Sarah had gotten to know most everyone at the shelter pretty well, even the vampires that lived here, and she quickly discovered, just like humans, there were good and evil vampires. And everyone here was innately good.

Since Dev never left Kate unprotected, and Manny was her guardian shadow, Sarah had gotten to know him quite well. He was funny and kind and flirty. He made her feel normal and she'd needed normal these past several months.

She'd only seen Ren a handful of times and while she could admit she found him very attractive, he was more like an older brother.

Teasing him was her favorite pastime and she'd even begun calling him 'pretty boy' just to get under his skin.

And Thane was quiet, but extremely considerate; going out of his way to help her get anything she needed from town. He frequently accompanied her when she needed to escape the house and go for a walk outdoors. With the boy-next-door good looks and quiet charm, she found him appealing, but he was fast becoming a very good friend and she thoroughly enjoyed his company.

The only vampire she didn't really care for was Giselle. But Giselle also tried very hard to get people *not* to like her for some reason. A reason she'd really like to figure out, so she'd made it her mission to be extra nice to her. Kate had warned her away, saying Giselle was like a 'twisted M&M.' She had a hard outer shell, but instead of mouthwatering chocolate on the inside, she was filled with sour toxic candy. That was a pretty harsh analogy, even for Kate, but they'd also had a less than stellar beginning to their still rocky relationship. While the hard outer shell may be true, Sarah knew it was only a protective measure and what lay underneath was someone who wanted love and companionship, just like every other being on the planet.

As she'd slowly gotten to know everyone who'd been responsible for her rescue, she came to see them as normal. Sure, they had extraordinary abilities. Sure, blood was their main sustenance. Sure, they lived a hell of a lot longer than a human.

But they also had normal lives and normal families and normal businesses. They had hopes and dreams and aspirations, just like humans. And their worries may be greater than the average human, but if there were anyone she'd want protecting the world from evilness like the rogues that held her prisoner, it would be the Vampire Lords and those that worked under them. They were scary and dangerous and a force to be reckoned with, but she felt ridiculously safe.

So yes, after being kidnapped, drugged and almost raped by the stuff that horror movies are made of, she shouldn't have wanted to stay here. But she did.

And the truth of it was, she belonged here. *She* was one of them, even if she didn't really have any true vampire powers. She'd learned that since she was born of a vampire, but was never blooded the three required times to activate her vampiric powers, she was just simply a regular human being. And she'd finally come to learn her very realistic dreams actually had a name in the vampire community.

Sarah was a dreamwalker, as were her two sisters, Kate and Analise. Sisters she didn't even know about until just a few short weeks ago when her appendix burst and only Analise's blood was a unique match to save her. Well, there were two others, but Kate was on her honeymoon at the time, and the only other one

17

was her biological vampire father, Xavier, whom everyone wanted dead. Including her.

But upon his death, that would also mean that she was free to leave the shelter and return home, the threat eliminated. That would mean leaving her sisters and her new friends. And that would mean probably never seeing the enigmatic Romaric Dietrich again.

Not that he wants to see you, silly girl.

Sighing, she decided to take a quick bath and then readied for bed, but not wanting the sting of rejection by Romaric Dietrich in her dreams too, she settled in with the latest romance novel Kate had given her. Not having been a fan of either romance or vampire novels before, it bordered on obsession now. She couldn't devour them fast enough. After finishing a story, she always had more questions for Kate and Analise, which their mates patiently debunked. Sarah and Manny had laughed more than once about the ridiculous vampire world authors created. But at least it was something entertaining to pass the time.

In the last week alone, she'd read three full-length novels. Of course, that had nothing to do with the fact she was trying to keep her mind off the magnetic vampire who'd weaved his way into every one of her waking and sleeping moments.

Turning on her reading lamp, she had only a quarter of the book left. The heroine was missing and the hero just arrived to save her, but the villain had her in his evil clutches.

It sounded eerily similar to the world she now found herself immersed in.

Chapter 2

Rom

Emotional agony. That place where despair and pain and hopelessness boil together in a toxic concoction, which threatens to suck you under with its poisonous vapors.

That's where Rom was. Although he was tethered to earth, his mind and soul felt adrift. He was a goddamned mess and had been for the last five days. Ever since he'd laid eyes on *her*.

Sarah Hill.

Her name rolled off his tongue like the smoothest, finest of silk. He'd had to use every ounce of his stalwart willpower to keep from jumping across that table and disappearing with her until he could figure out this fucking mess.

Sitting in his living room, Rom stared at the lush green forest ripe with wildlife outside his thick, bulletproof glass windows. It was drizzling again, as it generally did in northern Washington. Just the way he liked it. It was the perfect complement to his usually somber mood.

He owned almost two thousand secluded, wooded acres close to the Canadian border, which was where he'd called home since he became Regent Lord of the West close to three hundred years ago now. He monitored every single inch of it with top of the line security and a staff whose sole job it was to handle trespassers, which were frequent, given the propensity of humans to hunt animals and fowl.

As the West Regent Vampire Lord, he had weighty obligations. Ones he'd been woefully neglecting for the last several days. Being in this position of power was never something Rom had aspired to, especially given his complicated history. However, as the population of the Northern Americas grew several hundred years ago, it became too great for one Vampire Lord to handle and three hundred years earlier, the country was split into three Regents. Dev had practically coerced Rom to take the responsibility and Rom initially declined, but was forced to take the role when he saw the other pool of pathetically inexperienced candidates, whom he easily overpowered.

But since he'd taken on this role, he'd never once shirked his responsibilities. Not one day. Until now. And those under his command didn't know what to make of Rom's current state of mind. Circo, his lieutenant, had checked on him several times, but he'd sent him away and last time threatened to decapitate him if he bothered Rom again. Circo's flat response had been that he'd be back in a few hours. Guess it Circo's sorry ass he was putting on the line.

His mind wandered back to Sarah. *How could she possibly be his Moira? His Fate? His Destiny?*

She couldn't. Plain and simple. Every vampire had only one Moira and his had been callously ripped from him before they'd even had a chance to bond. Somehow fate was fucking with him yet again and he had to wonder what he'd done so wrong to be dealt such a blow. It was the same question he'd asked every single day of his lonely life since he'd lost Seraphina.

Losing her had emotionally annihilated him. No one would believe he'd been a rather easy-going vampire before those two weeks that'd changed his life so very, very long ago. It had taken him hundreds of years to regain any semblance of humanity, to master the art of appropriate emotion in the appropriate situations, when he felt none, and to this day, it was still challenging for him to genuinely care about those close to him.

But seeing Sarah flared *something* deep within his soul. It was just an ember, but it was there nonetheless. He felt a spark of ... something he couldn't even dare put a name to yet for fear of jinxing it.

He cared for Damian, Devon and Circo in his own twisted way, but it still wasn't the same as it could have been had his heart not been ripped out five hundred, sixty years ago. They were loyal friends that had been through thick and thin and yet ... yet he'd kept this a secret from them all.

None of them had any idea he'd lost his Moira, as that'd happened well before they knew each other. It was still too painful to talk about, let alone think about, yet that's all he'd done in the last one hundred and twenty hours. He couldn't even escape it in sleep. Embarrassingly, he'd even had to flee Dev's before they could discuss

Geoffrey and that was not at all like him, but he had to get his fucked up head on straight first.

He was a rock. He was swift, decisive and always calm. He was a problem solver, but he had to admit this one stumped him. If his friends could see him now ... well, that's why he'd had to get the hell out of there before he slipped and shared something he wasn't yet ready to. Making the excuse that an emergency came up, he begged his leave and flashed back home, assuring them he'd reschedule soon. Which he had yet to do.

He'd vacillated between memories of Seraphina and the realness of Sarah. The similarities between them were uncanny. But was he simply twisting faded memories into his own version of reality? He'd spent days trying to convince himself he'd merely overreacted with Sarah, but he *knew* that to be untrue. His cock violently ached for her and the lure of her blood was nearly unbearable even thousands of miles away. Adjusting his perpetual hard on, he let his mind drift once again to his agonizing past.

1 June, 1452

Tonight was Romaric's fifth visit with Seraphina and he hoped it would be his last before she finally agreed to be his. He'd spotted her in a village north of Esme's home. Esme was a regular and generous donor, but he frequently looked for fresh flesh and new blood. A vampire had to keep his options open, after all. It would do him no good to lead a human female into believing she had a 'forever' kind of chance with him and he'd seen too much longing in Esme's eyes, so he'd promptly left her bed and scouted other possibilities.

He couldn't believe his luck when he'd spotted Seraphina walking down a dark dirt road, alone. As he approached quietly from behind, his initial thought was 'foolish female' and although he'd intended no harm, as he didn't kill his donors, there were surely others that would readily take advantage of such a young, beautiful, vulnerable girl.

But one look in her golden brown eyes would change everything. He'd found his Moira, his Destiny, and her name was Seraphina. At a mere eighty-years old, he couldn't believe his luck at finding his Moira so young in life. He hadn't even come into his full vampiric powers yet, for that didn't happen until age one hundred. The few vampires he knew back in his homeland hadn't found their Moira's until hundreds of years into their lives.

While the physical attraction with your Moira was strong, almost irresistible, it wasn't always easy to convince her to bond, leaving behind her family and life as she knew it. 'Twas the challenge he'd faced with Seraphina. As the eldest in a family of nine children, her mother and father relied heavily upon her. Seraphina was waffling in her decision. He'd convinced her ties didn't need to be cut immediately. They'd transition into their life gradually, but that, in no uncertain terms, she was to be with him. To bond with him and be his in every way.

He thirsted for both her body and blood and tonight he would have both. She was to meet him this eve on the outskirts of her village, shortly before dark. He was loath to let her wander alone, but she'd refused him to meet at her home. Hiding his vampiric skills was crucial in order to blend with humans, which meant no flashing, so he was forced to wait on the outskirts. But a fool he was not. He knew where she lived and kept a watchful eye.

Several minutes past dusk now, he was getting anxious when he spotted her in the distance. It had been a rather warm day, but as the sun set, the temperature cooled and his Moira wasn't properly dressed wearing only a thin, flimsy blouse. He would make sure she was properly clothed and fed when she became his.

Rushing them into the woods, Romaric peeled off the long sleeve wool shirt he'd worn specifically with Seraphina in mind and slipped it over her head. She was petite and it swallowed her whole, coming nearly to her knees. Once they were enough distance away for his comfort, he backed her up against a large oak tree. The leaves and foliage would provide them well enough coverage, while his keen hearing would sense any interlopers.

"Hello," he whispered against her lips. Lips he'd only had the pleasure of kissing twice, for she'd refused until three nights past. Last eve he'd enjoyed a most realistic erotic dream starring Seraphina, who was expertly riding his cock, as he directed her movements with his hands. How he longed for that dream to be real.

"Hello back." Her breaths were labored, like she'd run a mile to get to him. Maybe she had. Maybe she was as desperate for him as he was for her.

"Are you feeling well? You're warm."

"Yes I am well. I rushed and your shirt is rather heavy."

He was thankful. Medical care was scarce and humans died regularly and easily from vile diseases. He was staying far away from Europe these days, as the stink of death due to Black Plague was toxic.

He easily lifted her slight frame and her legs wrapped firmly around his waist. This brought her mouth level with his. As leverage, he rested her back against the rough bark, hoping his shirt protected her fair skin. He took her mouth in a gentle, soft kiss. Taking her face between his hands, he deepened it and they both groaned their mutual desire.

He couldn't help how his body responded to her breathy moans. Hips thrusting of their own accord, his hard shaft was surely digging into her center. She put her small hands on his shoulders and when he hoped she'd pull him closer, she pushed him away instead.

"Romaric, stop. Please."

Resting his forehead on hers, he spoke softly, "What's wrong Seraphina?"

"I am not ready. I am sorry, Romaric." She was young, only sixteen. He could smell her arousal, so there was no hiding the fact she wanted him, but her body and mind were at war.

"Seraphina ..." He inwardly groaned. While he didn't want to put pressure upon her, he wasn't sure how long he could keep from taking her. His patience was worn thin. She was his and he wanted her with him.

"I thought I would be ready this eve. Meet me night after morrow at my home. Meet Father. Then I'll come with you."

Two more long, godforsaken days. He had to feed. It'd been too long already, but he could wait two more days. The thought of another woman's essence in his veins was repugnant.

"Yes," he reluctantly agreed before taking her lips again. She pulled back all too soon.

"I need to return. Hirum and Clara have fallen ill and mother needs my help."

He selfishly wished he were her priority instead. "I will walk you."

As he left her at the outskirts, watching her walk away, he'd already begun to count down the hours until he'd bring her to his home. To his bed. He'd meet her family day after morrow for evening meal and then she would be his. No more excuses.

Two days passed like ten, and as Romaric neared Seraphina's meager family home, he sensed a life-altering change.

Walking through the small village, the putrid stench of death hung thickly and almost visibly in the air. He burst into her home, uncaring whether he was a trespasser. A young female, whom he assumed was her mother, sat at a small wooden table, crying uncontrollably.

"Where's Seraphina?" he growled. A sick, panicky feeling built in the pit of his stomach.

She seemed unable to focus on him, twisted in her own grief instead. It took two more tries before she finally responded. And when she did, it tried his razor thin patience even more.

"Who are you?"

"I am Romaric. Now. Where. Is. Seraphina?" If he had to repeat himself again, fuck his manners. He would ransack the goddamned house in search of her.

She stared at him with glassy, bloodshot eyes. "She's gone. Dead. She fell ill night before last and passed this morning. Three of my babies are now dead and two more are ill."

His heart died. Or maybe it bled out inside his empty chest. Either way it didn't matter. It was gone, along with his mate. Correction, he could never call her his mate, for they had not bonded. She was never his and now never would be.

Even through his unimaginable grief, Romaric had enough sense not to show his true self to these humans. After he'd discovered they'd already buried Seraphina's body, and he'd never get a final chance to look upon her beautiful pixie face, he turned and left without a word. Without explanation. He'd later learn that a deadly strain of influenza killed almost half of her small village in a matter of weeks.

When he returned home, Romaric roared his unholy wrath so loudly those within one-hundred miles heard his certain agony. Stories would be told for centuries to come in both human and vampire *communities, passed down from generation to generation, about the unearthly sounds heard that cool summer evening.*

Until this past week, Romaric had not fully reminisced on those painful events since her death and now he couldn't stop. It only served to remind him of his one colossal failure. Had he simply taken what was his, without waiting for her acquiescence, they'd be together this day. He would be a completely different male.

Happy perhaps.

Maybe even fun.

Fun may be pushing it. Less impenetrable was probably more accurate.

He kept returning to the one thought that niggled the edges of his brain for days, and what could be the only plausible explanation for a possible *second* Moira. It sounded far-fetched and impossible, but ...

He'd never actually *bonded* with Seraphina. She *was* his Moira, of that there was no doubt. But there was equally no doubt that Sarah Hill *was* his Moira. He'd never heard of such a thing, but perhaps, just perhaps, the Fates had given him a second chance.

It was time to get off his ass and take action. He'd already wasted enough time. He'd been putting this off, but there was only one vampire in the world he knew of that may have access to the answers he sought. One he'd intentionally avoided over the last six hundred years.

Looked like it was time to pay his father a visit.

Chapter 3

Sarah

"How did you sleep last night?" her sister asked as Sarah shoveled another scoopful of the best risotto she'd ever tasted into her mouth.

"Good." Although it came out muffled around the thick rice. Her answer wasn't entirely untrue, but the dream she'd had still disturbed her even this afternoon. As with so many things lately, she wasn't really quite sure what to make of it.

Kate laughed. "I'm glad you're enjoying that. I miss Leo terribly, but Hooker's been a great replacement. Between his cooking and your cookies, I'll probably gain fifty pounds before I have this baby."

Kate looked so happy and Sarah couldn't help the twinge of jealousy she felt, even though it was wrong. She vaguely wondered how she would ever find someone to make her as happy as Dev made Kate if she stayed here long term.

And she *wanted* to find it. She wanted the fairytale ending. She wanted the happily ever after. She wanted a house in the quiet country with three kids, a golden retriever and a dozen horses. She'd wanted that since she was a little girl and had played it out many times with her Barbie Dreamhouse, which had come complete with three stories and rope-activated elevator. She'd had so many plastic horses, she'd lost count, but her favorite was a jet-black Arabian horse, which she'd named Spade.

But she wouldn't find that here because there were no human males wandering around and male vampires only bonded with their Moiras, the one female they were fated to spend eternity with. A concept still a little fuzzy to Sarah. And what were the chances she would find that here with one of the few vampires that Dev allowed into his fortress of an estate?

Umm ... do pigs fly?

No. Here, the only thing, any unmated vampire would be interested in, was a blood donor and a romp in the hay. And while the sexy and enigmatic Romaric may or may not find her attractive enough to fuck her, she had no illusions she'd be anything else but that. An itch to scratch and warm sustenance to fulfill his craving. Vampires were highly sexual and she'd be just another in a bevy of babes. But God help her, she was contemplating it and he hadn't even propositioned her. This vampire had gotten under her skin but good.

"Has the nausea passed?" Sarah needed to get her head out of the clouds and back to reality. Clearly their connection hadn't been as strong for Romaric as it had been for her.

"For the most part. I still get a little queasy in the evenings, but it's much better. I'm not sure why they call it morning sickness if I'm not even sick in the mornings."

"I remember when my mom was pregnant with Jack," she said wistfully. "I was only ten-years old, but I remember her throwing up all day, every day for what seemed like months." She laughed, recalling how she'd felt about her new baby brother. "There was some movie out at the time, *Omen*, about a satanic child. Even though Jack wasn't born yet, I'd already made up my mind that I didn't like him because only a devil baby would make his mother so violently ill."

Kate reached across the table and closed her hand around Sarah's in sympathy. Sarah had told Kate all about Jack, his long battle with leukemia and his tragic death at the young age of eight. Although it was only six years ago, right after she'd graduated high school, it seemed like a lifetime ago but just yesterday at the same time.

Suddenly guilt stabbed Sarah in the heart. Not only had her parents lost her brother so many years ago, but they'd essentially lost her too. She needed to find a way to visit them. Maybe she could convince Thane to take her.

Just then Dev walked into the kitchen, wrapped his arms around Kate from behind and kissed her softly on the crown of her head. Jealousy, that ungrateful beotch, tried rearing her sinful head, but she tamped her down.

"How was lunch with your sister, my love?"

"It was wonderful." Kate turned and captured his mouth and feeling like the third, clunky wheel, Sarah turned away until his next sentence caused her to snap back.

"Rom and Damian will be here this evening for a meeting about Geoffrey." Why he looked directly at Sarah when he spoke, she hadn't a clue.

33

If he was expecting a rise or a reply from her, he was going to be waiting a hell of a long time. Romaric was coming in for business, not with a handful of flowers and chocolates to woo her. She chose not to react, although there were plenty of snide comments just itching to be let loose.

"I would like to see my parents," she responded instead.

Both Dev and Kate looked taken aback.

"Really?" Kate questioned.

Not once had she given a hint that she was ready to see her parents and face their wrath in person. Sarah was a terrible liar, not able to get away with anything as a child or teenager. She was pretty much of a goody two-shoes growing up. She'd gotten good grades, followed the rules and been valedictorian of her class. The times she'd acted out could be counted on one hand, but the one in particular that stood out was when she'd skipped school as a junior. That stunt almost caused her to miss her junior prom.

Someone brilliantly dreamt up junior skip day, their class president if she recalled correctly. They were the coolest class, after all, and there was no way they were going to let the seniors show them up with their skip day. Kids forged excuse notes from their parents, none the wiser that the faculty was already onto them.

Living in a smaller community, they headed out to some abandoned grain bins where several kegs were waiting to be consumed by the under-aged band of merry, clueless teenagers. Sarah hadn't even wanted to go, but she didn't want to look like a prude either. To this day, she thinks the cops were just waiting for everyone to arrive and start drinking so they could write more tickets. Sarah tried profusely lying to her parents when she got home, but of course, they already knew.

So, before she saw them this time, she'd have to practice her fabricated story in front of the mirror until she convinced *herself* that the lies she'd told about why she'd been gone all of these months were the truth. If Thane could accompany her, maybe she could persuade them they'd met in Europe, had fallen in love and she couldn't bear to leave his side.

Yes, that may actually work. Thane would surely be game and with his unruly dark hair and suave good looks, it would be all the more convincing.

"Yes. It's time. It's not fair to them that I've been gone so long and they were terribly disappointed when I told them I wouldn't be home for my birthday a few weeks ago."

"When was your birthday?"

Uh. Oh. Sarah had purposely kept that tidbit of information to herself, not wanting anyone to make a big deal out of it. Besides Kate was out of the country on her honeymoon and that was the time that Analise had been kidnapped and things were in utter chaos. Now Kate would probably be hurt.

"It was July first. Things were kind of crazy around here then anyway." Wanting to change subjects, she added, "So Dev, do you think Thane would be able to take me?"

35

He nodded. "That can be arranged. But Sarah, it will need to be a short visit. It's still too dangerous for you to be out and about."

"Define 'short visit.'"

"A few hours. Half day at most."

Disappointment clearly evident on her face, he quickly apologized it couldn't be longer.

"It's okay. I understand."

Goddamn Xavier and his warped mind. She wished nothing more than for the lords to take him out so she could move forward without the crippling weight of wondering whether he was right around the corner waiting to snatch her or one of her sisters again.

"Call your parents. Arrange a time and place. I'll talk to Thane."

Sarah knew her parents were likely being watched, which is one of the reasons she'd kept contact to a minimum. Dev had graciously given both her and Kate's parents a protective detail, even though neither family had a clue they were being defended against the evils that lurked in the night. Literally.

"Thank you." She smiled tightly. She was grateful, but still angry nonetheless. Not at Dev, but the situation.

Dev gathered Kate by his side indicating he needed her 'fine ass' upstairs for something.

Riiiight.

She'd wanted to talk to Kate about her strange dream, but Dev wouldn't likely take too kindly to her keeping his mate away any longer. They were still very much newlyweds after all and their honeymoon had been cut very short. So yeah, time to get back to the shelter. Because although she loved her sister and her new mate, she *sooo* did not want to hear them doing the nasty. That had already happened once.

Hearing other people have sex—*like strangers*—fine. That could even be somewhat of a turn on and if anyone denies that, well ... just watch their eyes shift as they lie through their teeth. But hearing your sister ... that's just plain awkward. Especially when you saw her less than an hour later at the dinner table with the flush of satisfaction still all over her face.

Just ... eww.

Once again feeling like an interloper, she made her way to the library before returning to her room. She'd finished her steamy novel last night and needed to gather a few more from the plethora of books that Dev owned. Kate had been adding her romances to the collection and the amount of books they had was simply mind-boggling. In her whole lifetime, she'd never be able to get through them all.

Walking into the room with wall-to-wall, floor to ceiling bookshelves, she was taken aback by Giselle sitting on the worn brown leather couch, with a book in her hand.

Huh? Giselle read?

Wow, snotty much, Sarah?

"Hi Giselle." Kill her with kindness, right? That's what her mother used to say.

Instead of replying, Giselle stood and started exiting the room, but not before pinning her with a glare that would make lesser women melt into a puddle of water at her feet. And sweet, innocent Dorothy with a cuddly Toto tucked gently into her picnic basket, Sarah was not. Sarah wondered if Giselle had even seen the Wizard of Oz and saw the resemblance between herself and the wicked witch of the west.

Just as Giselle was about to exit, Sarah called out to her again. She'd been giving this a tremendous amount of thought and she was certain Giselle was the perfect vampire to help her. She simply couldn't ask anyone else. Not even Thane.

"I need your help."

Giselle stopped but didn't turn around, so she continued.

"I want to track my lineage."

At that, the female vampire turned around with the scariest smirk on her face that she'd seen on anyone here to date. *Holy shit, she was seriously intimidating.* Maybe this was a bad idea after all.

"I'm not a fucking genealogist, little girl."

Why ... that bitch.

"My bad. I had heard you were the best investigator Dev had, but I must have heard wrong." She spun on her heels and walked to the closest shelf, not even seeing the books staring her in the face. She was so furious; she could claw that bitch's eyes out. If she wasn't a vampire, she might even try.

At this moment, she admired Kate's cool demeanor and Analise's directness. All she'd apparently inherited was a hair-trigger temper, alien-shaped pinky toes and geographic tongue. *Yes, that's a real thing. Google it.*

When Giselle left without another word, Sarah felt defeated. She'd actually thought of trying to find her birth mother long before she'd been kidnapped, but was far too busy with school to take the time.

Well, that wasn't exactly the truth.

She'd simply been scared. Scared to track down the one person in the world that's supposed to want you and love you unconditionally above all others, but who'd given her away instead. But now that she knew the truth—that her mother had been kidnapped—just like her—but didn't escape with her life—unlike her—she wanted to know more about the maternal side of the family she came from. Because despite her faults and her quick temper, Sarah had goodness in her. And since her father was born from the depths of hell and didn't have a shred of humanity, her goodness had to have come from her mother. And she wanted to learn more.

Her adopted parents *were* her parents as far as she was concerned. She loved them, she truly did, but a person who has grown up with their biological parents can't possibly understand what an enigma an adopted child's biological parents represent. There's always that *mystery*, always the same questions rolling around in her head.

Did she look like her mother?
Did she sound like her mother?
Was her mother a hothead too?

What was her mother like as a child?
Did she have any living blood relatives?

Now, more than ever, she was determined to find out, with or without Giselle's help. Especially after the dream last night where the woman she'd talked to claimed to know Romaric.

A woman who'd looked strikingly like herself.

Chapter 4

Rom

Recalling proper protocol, Rom had arrived in Romania yesterday afternoon. It was customary to announce your visit a minimum of twenty-four hours in advance or risk a stake through your heart by showing up even one minute earlier. While that wouldn't kill him, it would be immensely painful, so he'd rather avoid the offending wood. Or whatever material they were using these days in his homeland for stakings.

Intentionally avoiding his father all these years, he was looking forward to this visit about as much as he was reliving his Moira's death so many years ago. Which was to say, not very fucking much. But to get to *her*, he had to go through *him*.

He stood on the doorstep of the ridiculously clichéd and ostentatious castle, set high in the Alps of Romania and he waited for one of his father's servants to open the heavy, thick oak French doors before him. He rolled his eyes at the hideous copper doorknockers of screaming humans in the throes of agony. He half expected Dracula to come riding around the corner in a horse-drawn carriage being chased by the horde of townspeople carrying torches and pitchforks.

The whole thing was utterly unoriginal, but his father *was* exceedingly melodramatic.

There was no need to knock, as they were expecting him and within a minute, he was ushered inside by one of many who unwillingly served his father.

"Right this way, sire." He was led through several small rooms of the large structure, which had been refurbished inside since he'd been here last. Of course, that was over half a millennia earlier, so without maintenance the home would be in fairly poor shape by now.

They ended in the throne room. This time he had kept his eye rolling internal. Christ, his father hadn't changed one bit in over six hundred years. Still so fucking formal. But if there were any other way to get the answers he sought, he'd have done it. This was truly a last resort, which was his biggest fear. His father would know this and intentionally withhold information.

As the servant scurried away, he walked toward his father, pretentiously sitting on his high throne, a naked whore upon his lap. His father's hands freely roamed her body. Rom's jaw clenched. His father's blatant and callous disgrace of his mate and their bond was one of the many reasons he'd left and never returned.

He inclined his head in the required respect, but that was the very last emotion he held for the vampire before him.

"Makare," he stated simply. He'd not once referred to him as father. He'd not earned it.

"Well, the famous and powerful son returns." As expected, Makare mocked the meaning of Romaric's name. It mattered not. Raina was the end goal here and he'd do well to remember that.

"To what do we all owe the honor of your return?"

"I want to see Raina." Straight and to the point. The least amount of time he had to spend in the presence of his fucking sperm donor, the better. For both of them.

Makare belted out what he assumed was a laugh, but sounded more like a squeal as the horrid sound bounced off the stone walls and reverberated in his ears.

"Do you hear that, whore?" Makare said as he tweaked the nude female's nipple so hard it brought tears to her eyes, but she moaned her fake pleasure anyway. "He doesn't bother to show his face for centuries but when he does, he makes demands, not apologies."

Romaric remained still, regarding Makare with feigned interest. He was the master of hiding emotion and to let any show in the presence of Makare would be a fatal mistake. As strong as Romaric was, his father was still stronger. After several moments, he turned and began to leave. This had been a mistake. He would never be allowed to talk to Raina, so he'd have to just go with his gut.

He was nearly in the hallway when Makare called after him.

"For a price."

Of fucking course. Everything his father 'gave' had strings attached. He turned, but said nothing.

"Actually it's a gift, really. This should be no hardship to you."

His gut clenched. His father never gave of anything freely.

"She's yours." Makare shoved the human woman from his lap and she tumbled down the concrete stairs, landing with a hard thud at the bottom. The scent of her spilled blood filled his nostrils and although it was enticing, it nauseated him at the same time.

When Romaric made no movement, Makare said, "Kill her and you shall see your mother." The female lay whimpering on the cold floor, clearly trying to muffle her cries.

Aaaaand there it was. This was the other reason that he'd left and not returned. His own father regularly broke the no-kill law. He wasn't on Xavier's level of depravity, but he was pretty fucking close. If he thought he could kill Makare without killing himself in the process, he would. But that would also kill his mother, which was why he'd never attempted it. Maybe she'd be better off dead rather than with him as a mate. He'd never understood how the bond between a vampire and mate could be as fucked up as it was with his parents.

But now he had Sarah, his Moira, to think about. He'd been foolish to come here, for he knew in his heart that she was his. The how and the why were irrelevant. He'd wasted too much time already. This venture had taken an entire extra day away from her and now possibly a very dangerous turn. His father didn't like to be told no.

Makare stood to his full imposing six foot seven inch frame, a spiteful smile spreading across his handsome face. A face much like his own. It was a dynamic Romaric could never work out.

"Kill her or die. A simple choice, really," Makare demanded.

To many vampires, it would have been. Their lives or a human female, who could easily be replaced by millions of other human females, but to Romaric, human life was sacred. As sacred as a vampire's life and he would not take hers. Makare knew this. Besides, how could he ever look upon Sarah's exquisite face again if he did? He'd be no better than the monster he stood before. But if he didn't, he may never be *able* to look upon her face again.

Whether it was luck or the Fates intervening, he wouldn't have to make that choice tonight. At the risk of their own life, one of Makare's servants interrupted them.

The young vampire prostrated himself in front of Makare before speaking in Romanian, "Forgive me Oh Great One, Master Taiven has been gravely injured."

Taiven. His younger, *favored* brother to whom he also hadn't spoken to since he left. And that was by design, because in Taiven's case, the apple doth not fall far from the tree.

They exchanged glances and Makare smirked, knowing he would always choose Taiven over Romaric.

"Until we meet again, Romaric." Then Makare was gone.

He should have left, but instead he tended to the injured female and, as if in answer to his prayers, she told him where in the castle he could find his mother.

The fact that Raina, his mother, lived in the oubliette now made his gut churn with unbridled anger. In the medieval days, this is where they left prisoners to die. But that's what his mother was, was she not? A prisoner locked into a loveless bond with a ruthless Vampire Czar for all of eternity.

"Mother," he breathed after finally reaching her small cage through the maze of underground tunnels. He flashed into her cell and pulled her slight, filthy frame into his larger one and she clung to him like a child.

"Romaric. Romaric, is it really you, my son?" Tears drenched his lightweight shirt in a matter of seconds as she openly wept at their reunion. As much as he ached to catch up, time was not his friend. Once Taiven stabilized, his father would be down, checking on his prize mare to be sure she hadn't been spirited away. Romaric wouldn't, but only because his mother forbade it.

"Mother, I'm so sorry, but we don't have much time."

She nodded, knowing all too well the wrath they each faced should Makare catch him here. He quickly spent the next several minutes telling her about Seraphina and Sarah.

"So you never bonded with her? Seraphina?"

"No."

She smiled and that one simple gesture lifted the heaviest of weights from his heart. He felt like he could take a full breath for the first time in centuries.

"I have heard of this. One other time before."

His mother didn't have the specifics, but it mattered not. What mattered was that Sarah was his and he intended to claim her as soon as he could. He would accept no excuses this time around.

It was a bittersweet goodbye and he vowed to continue trying to find a way to break the mating bond so he could free her. He kissed her and flashed back to his home in Washington to shower and change before his meeting this evening with the other lords. And unbeknownst to Sarah, with her.

At over eight hundred years old, his mother was the oldest living vampire mate he knew of that still lived. And regardless of the fact that she now lived in a cage in the dungeon of a two thousand year old castle, she knew amazing things. Things no one else would know. If anyone had heard of such a thing before, it would be her.

The only thing that mattered now was that he'd been given another chance at true happiness. At love. There was no way he would let his Moira slip through his fingers again and, like it or not, Sarah would be in his home, by his side this evening. He would not make that same mistake twice.

He only hoped that his heart hadn't fossilized so hard that it would now be impenetrable.

Chapter 5

Sarah

She was back in the main house library again tonight perusing books and it definitely had *nothing* to do with the fact that Romaric Dietrich was going to be here for a meeting.

Nope.

Nothing. At. All.

Sarah had arranged a meeting with her parents for the day after tomorrow and Thane graciously agreed to accompany her. Of course, they were completely oblivious to the danger they were in, but she was all too aware. Once again she had to put her acting skills to the test, convincing them to meet anywhere but her childhood home in Merrill, Wisconsin, so they agreed to Slade's Lake Mohawksin Bar and Grill, right outside of Tomahawk. It was a favorite place of Sarah's as a child. Many people in Wisconsin had cabins and boats and spent their weekends on the lake. Her family was no exception and she had great memories from those days. Until Jack had gotten sick and they couldn't go anymore.

It was near eleven p.m. and she didn't know what time the meeting between the lords was to take place, and wasn't about to ask Kate or Analise, because then it would appear she was interested. And she most certainly was not.

She could picture Analise's raised eyebrows, silently challenging her—*liar, liar, pants on fire.*

Well ... maybe she was a teeny tiny bit interested.

Tsk, tsk, Sarah. You're about as subtle as a bull in a china shop.

Fiiiiine ... she was a *LOT* interested.

Who wouldn't be? He was the finest specimen of manliness she'd ever seen. Dev and Damian were undeniably gorgeous but, to her, neither held a candle to Romaric. Just thinking of the all-consuming way he'd focused on her was intoxicating. His obvious palpable need had stripped her sexually raw. She was now a tightly wound bundle of want and need and only he could assuage the fevered desire that burned hot and fierce between her thighs. She'd tried to take the edge off herself.

Epic fail.

All she managed to accomplish was to intensify the aching emptiness in her core.

Pandora's Box had been opened and Rom was the Greek God who'd lifted the lid. He was Eros—Greek God of attraction, love and sexuality. He'd brought out a passionate longing in her that she didn't know existed, but couldn't be shoved back in that dark, isolated hole.

Maybe she should switch from romance to history. Clearly the salacious novels had rubbed off on her and only served to fan the flames of her out of control libido. A mind numbing read about the civil war would squash her uncontrollable fantasies for sure.

She *obsessively* thought about him and wasn't that just the shits, because it couldn't be clearer he wasn't interested. If he was, he would have been in contact or back to see her before now. Didn't it figure she'd have to majorly crush on someone who didn't reciprocate?

Her mind played a never-ending game of sabotage between what she'd come to refer to as her Rosie and Nancy alter egos.

Rosie, ever the optimistic rainbow and baby kitty lover, was positive, naïve and idealistic.

Nancy, the sky is falling ho from the wrong side of the tracks, was cynical, distrusting and surly. For the past several days, the conversation between the two had gone something like this:

Rosie: He's a lord. He's probably very busy.

Nancy: Not too 'busy' to satisfy his carnal needs with another bitch's body.

Rosie: But didn't you see the way he stared at me?

Nancy: Duh. You have a beating heart and a pussy. His only two requirements.

Rosie: He looked at me like I was his.

Nancy: Yes, you stupid girl. His next meal.

Rosie: It's only been a week.

Nancy: It's been a week. Time to put on your 'big girl' pants, Sarah. You're just another nameless, faceless piece of ass with all the right proportions, but he's simply not interested.

She wanted to stab Nancy repeatedly with a dull butter knife, but at the same time put a cattle prod to Rosie. Both were extremists and the truth probably fell somewhere in the middle. At the end of the day, she was making excuses for him and like her dad always said, *"Excuses are like assholes. Everyone's got one."*

Ugh. She was acting like a rookie stalker and just needed to go to bed.

Settling on a Harlan Coben novel about a man's missing wife who is really alive, she turned back around to exit the library, but was startled to see Giselle standing in the doorway, watching her. She jumped slightly and didn't miss the slight smirk that had turned up one side of her mouth. *Sour* was the first word that came to mind. Maybe Kate wasn't too off the mark after all.

"Shit, Giselle," she gasped, grabbing her chest. "Announce yourself next time for Christ's sake." And did Giselle's presence mean the meeting was over or hadn't begun yet?

Giselle sauntered into the library, glancing at the book Sarah now held in her hand. "Like a good mystery, do you?"

What. The. Hell?

Giselle had never initiated conversation with Sarah before, choosing to pretend she didn't exist instead. And tonight she was in no mood to play cat and mouse with the ice queen, as Kate so 'lovingly' referred to her. Sarah knew which character she played and wasn't about to be lured into Giselle's trap with sweet smelling, innocuous peanut butter. Which was where this discussion was headed.

"What do you want, Giselle?"

51

"It's not what *I* want, but *you* want, Sarah."

When she was growing up, her family loved games. Cards, chess, board games. You name it, they played it, and so the one thing she'd mastered was the poker face. One summer she'd won fifteen dollars and eighty-three cents from her friends playing poker.

Hey, she was eleven ... that was a lot of money to an eleven year old.

Giselle was dangling something in front of her, but she couldn't figure out what that 'something' was. One thing she did know was that she needed to maintain the upper hand and was suddenly thankful for having such great parents that'd taught her valuable life lessons, whether they'd intended to or not.

"And what do I want?" she asked with contrived interest.

"Information."

"About?"

"Short term memory problems, Sarah?"

Sarah stood silently. Talking in circles was something Giselle was exceptionally talented at. Guess she'd had a lot of years to polish that skill to shiny perfection.

Sarah moved to make her way around Giselle. She wasn't playing her fucking head games tonight. She was halfway to the door when Giselle spoke behind her.

"Have you forgotten our conversation from yesterday already?"

Her heritage. Nope, she hadn't forgotten.

"Why?" she asked as she turned back around.

"Why, what?" Giselle quipped.

Jesus, she was a goddamned infuriating person. She'd love to chip away at that outer layer to see if blood really flowed beneath her flesh or if it was a slushy frosty mixture that fueled her constant rage instead.

"Why are you willing to help me now?"

"Let's just say it's mutually beneficial and leave it at that," she said, turning to leave.

"How is this beneficial for you, Giselle? I have nothing to give you," she called after her. If she thought Sarah would pay her back with something, she was sorely mistaken. She didn't have a penny to her name or anything else of value to barter with.

Giselle stopped and turned back around. "Do you want my help or not?"

"Yes." But at what cost, was the burning question.

"Then you should just say thank you," she replied, eyes singeing her in unspoken challenge.

"Thank you."

And with that, Giselle turned once again and strode out, leaving Sarah to wonder what in the hell just happened and how Giselle had gained the upper hand so damn fast.

As far as Sarah knew, Giselle didn't do anything for *you*; she did it for *herself*. So Giselle's sudden interest in helping Sarah had her wondering. How exactly did this benefit Giselle?

Sarah was quite sure the ice queen wasn't doing this for anyone but herself.

Chapter 6

Rom

This was the longest meeting he'd ever been party to. Since Rom had been the one to interrogate Geoffrey, due to Damian's propensity to burn his captives alive if he didn't care for their answer, and Dev's desire to torture Geoffrey indefinitely, he was the only one now privy to the facts. And the facts certainly led one to believe that Geoffrey was not exactly the traitorous vampire they'd all suspected him to be.

Instead of sitting here, discussing what to do with Geoffrey and Xavier, the only thing Rom wanted to do was claim his mate, return to his home and spend the next month fucking her in every position, in every room, in every way. His sexual appetite had returned with a vengeance the moment he'd laid eyes on Sarah and it hadn't subsided one iota in a week.

Unlike many vampires, since the loss of his Moira, he didn't frequently partake in sexual activity when feeding. Of course, he had imbibed over his long life, but it wasn't an itch he needed scratched often. Even though he'd indicated otherwise, he hadn't actually taken any of the women at Dragonfly. Damian had good intentions, so a little harmless white lie to throw him off track wouldn't hurt anybody.

Now, however, his rock hard erection hadn't abated in days. And it wouldn't until it was buried deep inside Sarah's hot, wet and willing sweet little body. The connection between them was already so powerful, he could feel her somewhere in the main house and he had only one singular focus. To make her *his*. He was discreetly adjusting himself when Dev asked him to repeat himself.

"You need to go over this again, Rom, because I'm just not fucking getting it. Are you trying to convince us that Geoffrey has been *helping* us all along? And that he was kidnapped as a baby from *my* village that Xavier burned to the ground and raised to be a sadistic, unfeeling killing machine, but now he's suddenly grown a conscience and wants to be redeemed by the lords?"

Jesus. Fucking. Christ. His excruciatingly thin patience was ready to snap like a taut rubber band.

"Make no mistake. He's done vile and inhumane things, inexcusable things, but what I'm saying is that the underlying *reasons* are not what we'd originally thought."

He sighed, continuing, "Yes, he's grown up with Xavier and was unaware of his true origin until a decade ago when he overheard Xavier bragging to some new recruits about how he'd slaughtered his entire village, with the exception of yourself, Dev, and a few babies he'd spared to start his army. It was a story he'd told often, but in this particular case, he'd called Geoffrey out as an example of how much better off he was than if he'd been left to hide in the shadows with humans.

"Geoffrey further claims that prior to this knowledge, he'd already begun trying to find a way out and in the meantime, was saving as many of the kidnapped women as he possibly could from their intended fate.

"He was also in bed with the human doctor, Shelton, and, together, they falsified documentation and released women when possible. They were unable to save many, but where they could, they did. And although Xavier thinks no one knew, Geoffrey knew of Xavier's inability to produce a male offspring."

He paused, looking at Dev and Damian carefully.

"He was responsible for the fact that your mates are with you on this day." And *mine*, he thought silently.

"Bullshit," Damian shouted. "He was responsible for putting *my* mate's *life* in danger. How can you believe his fucking lies, Rom? Does he have a super-secret brainwashing skill that we aren't aware of too?"

Rom almost laughed. Almost. And *that* most definitely wasn't like him. Ignoring Damian's outburst, he continued.

"There is a rogue whose skill is sensing a vampire's Moira, so when your Moiras were born, Geoffrey found out. And together, with the human doctor, they got them out." He kept the fact secret for now that they'd also been responsible for saving his.

"He also protected your mates when they were captive. As much as he could, without

57

revealing himself to Xavier and putting his own life, and theirs, in jeopardy. His methods don't always make sense, I'll give you that, but Dev, he was the one responsible for the lapse in shrouding on the day you saved Kate. While he didn't orchestrate that kidnapping, he wanted the lords to take the entire compound, Xavier with it. And Damian, he took your mate because his was being threatened. He knew you would come for her and had he not returned with Analise, his own Moira would have perished."

"I don't believe a fucking word you're saying," Damian mumbled.

He did, he just didn't like it. Because of Rom's incredible array of powers, he had the ability to sense when one spoke truth.

"How many others are like Geoffrey within Xavier's ranks, ready to stage a coup?" Damian asked.

"He doesn't know, but suspects there may be several others. It wasn't something they discussed at the water cooler, per se."

"What's his endgame here? Why not just tell us all of this when Damian captured him, instead of kidnapping his mate?" Dev asked, genuinely confused.

"He would not put his own Moira in danger. I think I can honestly say any of us would have done the same thing in his position. As far as his endgame, he wants the same thing we want—to wipe Xavier, his rogues and his minions out. But he needs our help."

"How much intel does he have?" Dev asked.

"A lot, but not everything. As you can imagine, Xavier keeps things buttoned up pretty tight, so it's taken years to gain the knowledge he has now. He believes he knows where all of the kidnapped women are being held. Xavier doesn't think anyone knows where the children are kept, but Geoffrey has identified five locations. He thinks there may be a few more. He's also been trying to download records on a thumb drive when possible, but that's risky. So, he has some of what we need, but not all."

"Then he goes back in," Damian snapped. "And he stays there until he has every fucking shred of information we need to destroy Xavier and every fucking compound and save every single innocent man, woman and child. And if he gets himself murdered in the process, well ... karma's an evil bitch."

"Agreed," Rom replied.

After two hours of heated discussion, they had a plan and Rom was chomping at the bit to get to Sarah.

"Take me to Sarah," Rom demanded as they all stood to depart. He would not wait one more minute to be with his Moira.

After regarding him for several beats, Dev responded, "No."

"No?" Rom growled in disbelief. If Devon thought he would stop him from being with his soon-to-be mate, he was sorely, and painfully, mistaken.

"That's right. No. I won't let you use her, or hurt her."

"I would *never* hurt her." Fuck, he would *kill* anyone who tried to hurt her.

"Rom, I love you like a brother. But you can be ... harsh and intense. And Sarah is delicate and fragile. I don't know what went on between you two last week, but you need to just find another female. She's not the one for you."

"She. Is. Mine," Rom thundered. There was not one vampire in this house who would keep him away from Sarah and Dev was treading on very thin ice, which unbeknownst to Dev, was cracking under the heavy weight of his feeble protests. Sarah was anything but delicate and fragile. While he didn't know much about her, *that* much he did know. In her eyes, he saw strength and bravery and tenacity.

Damian was quiet, but if the broad, knowing smile on the asshole's face was any indication, he was obviously enjoying the show. Hell, it wouldn't surprise Rom if Damian ran and got some hot buttery popcorn and a box of Milk Duds and kicked back to see who threw the first punch.

Damian's comments last month now echoed through his head, *"Go ahead, yuck it up man. I won't forget this when you find your Moira. Then I'll be the one in the wings laughing my ass off. You're bound to get one that will give you a run for your money."*

"She's yours? As in ... your Moira?" Dev asked disbelievingly.

He nodded tightly.

"She's your Moira? Then how could you fucking leave and not come back for almost a week, Rom?"

He said nothing. Now was not the time to get into the whys of what he'd done over the past several days and he didn't owe either of them a damn explanation.

"Fuck," Dev breathed at the same time Damian started laughing.

"Okay then. Let's go."

Smart vampire.

"I'm tagging along," Damian jibed behind him as they started for the door. Rom would give anything to wipe that irritating smile off Damian's face. He turned back around.

"No. You're not. You're going to go back to your own mate and prepare her. I'll be taking Sarah back to Washington with me. Tonight."

"Rom, you're not fucking serious. You can't just waltz in there, claim her as yours and flash her away to your secluded haunted house in the hills. Jesus, do you have any sense or self-preservation at all? Women do *not* like that shit."

"It matters not what she wants. That's what will happen. I will not let her out of my sight for one single second." He *couldn't.*

"I have to agree with Damian on this, Rom," Dev chimed in, coming to face him. "That's a very bad idea. Just because she's your Moira, doesn't mean she'll want to bond with you and you know that."

In one ear and out the other. Rom didn't give a rat's ass what these two thought. They didn't have a goddamned clue what he'd been through. He'd been down this road before and wouldn't wade down it again. It was too painful and too dangerous.

Dev's face turned serious. "Rom, I know what you're going through." *He didn't have the slightest clue.* "But if you take her against her will, in her mind you're no better than Xavier, even though your intentions are entirely honorable."

Damian interrupted with his two cents of course, "Well, I'm quite sure your intentions are not *that* honorable ... but that's beside the point."

Dev glared at Damian and he just shrugged his shoulders before Dev continued, "And, Moira or not, Sarah might never recover enough from that betrayal to give you a chance. You know I'm right."

"He's right, Rom. I know from experience ... I almost lost Analise because I betrayed her trust."

"Fuck," he yelled, walking to the far side of Dev's office. He was utterly torn. Goddamn Devon and his fucking common sense. Rom was not used to this roller coaster of emotions and quite frankly, it was pissing him off. Suddenly his swift and concise decision making skills had turned on him and he couldn't make a choice to save his soul. He stood there several minutes before making up his mind.

Spinning around, he said, "I'm staying until she agrees to leave with me. But if I have my way, it will be this evening."

Dev nodded, clearly trying to hide his smirk. "The north wing is empty. I'll make sure a couple of rooms are set up for you there."

"I'll just need one. If we stay, Sarah will stay with me."

Damian chuckled and rolled his eyes, not even bothering to try hiding it. "You've got a lot to learn, my friend. A. *Lot*. To. Learn."

"Kate's bringing Sarah back over. She'd gone to bed," Dev announced. Christ ... he was acting like an unmitigated lunatic who needed a straightjacket to keep from harming himself or others. In his case, it was definitely others. Namely the two standing in front of him.

"No. Let her sleep. I'll see her first thing in the morning, instead."

"You're sure?" Dev asked, confusion written all over his face.

They were onto him. His calm, cool façade was quickly cracking. He was acting *way* out of character, though finding one's Moira tended to make a vampire more alpha and unpredictable than normal. But for him, this erratic behavior was extreme. He'd tell them eventually, but Sarah was his first, and only, priority right now.

"Yes. I'll take care of Geoffrey tonight and return immediately afterwards."

He planned to do that as quickly as possible and if he couldn't be with Sarah physically tonight, he would camp outside of her room and guard her against anything, and anyone, that could cause her harm.

"Until morning, my beauty," he uttered, before he flashed to Wyoming to free his captive.

Chapter 7

Mike

He'd fallen asleep on the couch, watching Jimmy Kimmel, when a noise on the porch woke him. Grabbing his Glock 22 from the coffee table drawer, he inched toward the bay window. There had been a rash of burglaries in his neighborhood over the past few weeks and he'd wanted nothing more than to take those fucking crack head thugs down. If one happened to get shot in the scuffle ... oh well. One less shithead roaming the earth.

Two weeks ago, they'd held his poor elderly neighbor at gunpoint, taking the little cash she'd had on hand. She'd ended up having a heart attack and had now gone to live with her daughter in Texas. He expected to see a *For Sale* sign in her yard any day now. What kind of pussies prey on an old woman? Fuckers. He hoped they were on the porch right now with a gun, so he could claim self-defense because he would be the last man standing.

Opening the blinds slightly with the tip of his weapon he was relieved, but confused at the same time, to see Giselle standing at his front door. *What was she doing here?*

Although they'd texted a few times, he hadn't seen her since the last time he was at Dev's, when he'd talked to Jamie. Which was also the day

Giselle had comforted him. That one simple act seemed to change the course of their relationship. She'd not been as frigid as she usually was; therefore he'd kept his barbs to a minimum. He never did say anything to Dev about not working with her, but they'd had no assignments together either and he had to admit that he'd missed her.

Stowing the gun in the back waistband of his jeans, he opened the door. Regardless of the reason she was here, she was incredibly stunning as always. The deep purple corset that pushed her breasts together and barely covered her nipples made him instantly hard. He swore she did that on purpose.

"Giselle. You do realize humans sleep at this time of night, right?" he jibed as he stood back and waived her in.

"Sleeping is for pussies. And old people."

"You couldn't have called first? You have my number," he countered as he made his way back to the couch, sitting down. He flipped off the TV, not caring for the background noise, wanting to focus only on the vision of loveliness before him.

Ignoring his question, she continued, "And you're not old. So ... does that make you a pussy, detective?"

He smirked, stood and closed the short distance between them. Along with that sinful corset, she wore dark black jeans that looked painted on and short animal print boots, which brought her mouth nearly to his height. Some men may be intimidated by a woman who was the same height, but not him. He fucking loved it. It made capturing her lips that much easier.

He reached up, cupping her face, his left thumb skimming her full bottom lip. Which she began to nervously chew on.

"Why don't you check, Giselle?"

Her breath quickened, if the heaving of her nearly exposed chest was any indication. She hadn't taken her eyes from his mouth since her verbal challenge. Even though she'd die before she admitted it, she'd missed him too. He was painfully hard and swore he could smell her arousal. Fuck, he wanted to kiss her.

She swallowed hard, before flicking her eyes to his in silent challenge.

Do it, they begged.

That's the only green light he needed before he took her lower lip between his teeth, dragging it through harshly. She closed her eyes and sighed softly. Her upper lip was next and he paid it the same treatment, relishing in her breathy moans. He finally took her full mouth in a soul-stealing kiss, palming the back of her neck to hold her exactly where he wanted.

Breaking away from her mouth, his lips trailed across her cheek to her ear.

"Christ, I want you so fucking much, Giselle," he murmured in her ear before taking the lobe between his teeth and biting down hard. She sucked in a sharp breath, as he predicted. The one thing he'd come to learn about her over these last several months is how much she loved the sting of his bite, even if it was with dull human teeth.

Kissing his way down her neck, he traced the top of her exposed breast lightly with his index finger, dipping it inside to feel her hard nub. "I want to be buried so deep inside you, you'll feel me even when I'm not there."

She turned her head kissing his neck, dragging her sharp teeth along his thin, sensitive flesh. His ministrations stopped as he enjoyed the kisses and nicks she peppered along his skin.

Fuck, he wanted to be inside her more than his next breath, but he'd pushed her too hard, too fast before, and he would not do that again. This time, if they weren't completely in the same story and on the same fucking page, he'd bookmark it again for another day. As agonizingly hard as that would be. If she wasn't ready yet, he would not pressure her.

He gently grabbed her head, holding it tightly against him, forcing her to stop.

"I want this, Giselle. I want you, but I need you to be all in with me. And if you're not ready yet, that's okay. I'll wait. I'll wait for as long as it takes, baby." And he meant it.

She was silent, but listening.

"I don't know why you're here, baby, but stay. Spend the night with me. Please. I want to hold your body against mine." He placed a soft kiss on her temple and had to force his hands not to roam the body she'd so teasingly put on display. Some may call Giselle a cock tease, but he knew better. She was a confused, traumatized woman and he would not add to that.

"I have a pet project I wanted your help with," she whispered.

He was unable to contain the broad smile that spread across his face. So she wasn't here on assignment, but because she *wanted* to be? Very good to know.

"Stay," he firmly demanded.

"The project ..."

He had her. She wanted to stay, but he'd get her to admit it, because he'd be damned if she'd turn this around on him come the morning when she may be feeling less vulnerable.

"We'll work on it first thing tomorrow. Stay." His lips trailed across her temple. "Stay. I promise to behave," he whispered. He hadn't promised not to take a cold shower and pump the junk a few times to relieve the ache he now felt deep in his balls.

"Yes," she breathed.

Thank fuck. He wasn't sure he could handle her walking out the door, not knowing when he'd see her again.

He'd finally gotten Giselle in his bed, not exactly the way he'd wanted, but it was a start. Now, he just needed to figure out how to keep her there, because against everything he'd ever believed could have happened ... he was in love with this female, a *vampire*, and he didn't want to let her go.

Ever.

Chapter 8

Sarah

His hands traveled lightly down her exposed arms. She wanted them to thread underneath her pajama top and palm her aching breasts. She wanted his lips to take her pebbled nipple into his mouth, but he frustratingly kept his touch light, teasing. Hot breath skated along her neck, but his mouth never touched her skin.

She didn't want to wake, but consciousness beckoned her. *Just a few more minutes, she pleaded.*

"More," she begged.

This was the first time he'd ever touched her in a dream. After all these years of aching for him, he finally had his hands on her but it wasn't enough. And why did it feel so right, yet so weirdly wrong at the same time?

It was *him*, but he'd yet to show his face. It was *him*, but every time she tried to look into his icy blues, they became concealed again. *Gah*! Why was he hiding from her?

Morning rays spilled in around the closed shades and the last images of her erotic dream faded away. She whipped off the covers, her body in agony with unfulfilled need. Her hand snaked down under her panties, finding her pussy completely drenched. She had to relieve some of the pressure that'd built to volcanic proportions. She'd never been so turned on.

And it was just a dream. Imagine how the real flesh and blood Romaric would feel against your skin, in your body.

Spreading her moisture, she reached climax in record time and lay panting on sweat soaked sheets. Once wasn't enough and after the second release, she finally felt a small amount of the heaviness subside. If she did happen to see Romaric, she wasn't sure she'd be able to keep from jumping him on the spot. And wouldn't that be embarrassing, throwing yourself at someone who didn't bother to give you the time of day.

Pushing down her disappointment that she hadn't seen him last night, she headed for the shower. Thirty minutes later, hair slightly damp and curly, with a light coat of mascara and some powder to cover her shiny pores, she dressed in jean shorts and a navy blue tank. Slipping on her flip-flops, she opened her bedroom door and froze.

Standing in her doorway—no, more like taking up her *entire* doorway—was Romaric Dietrich.

Romaric, Greek God of sex.

In.

The.

Flesh.

Sweet. Holy. Mother.

With his sexy goatee and light hair so closely cropped to his head that he almost appeared bald, he *was* god-like perfection and scary intimidating all at the same time. The entire package was rounded out with his clear blue penetrating eyes, and shoulders so broad he'd put any NFL linebacker to shame.

And his scrutiny of her now was as, if not more, piercing as that night at dinner seven long days ago. His eyes raked over every inch of her exposed flesh, lingering on the swell of her breasts, before snapping back to hers. She suddenly wished she'd worn wedges, not only to make her taller, but to lengthen her less than model short legs.

Sweet. Holy. Mother. Yes, she was repeating herself, but *Jesus*, it was worth repeating.

"Hello Sarah," he drawled. The deep timbre of his voice echoed in her ears long after he'd stopped talking.

"Uhhhhh ..."

He chuckled and it was the first time she'd seen a hint of a smile on his oh so serious face. She *loved* it. If he would full on smile, she was sure she'd drop to her knees and kiss his feet. Or something else.

Sarah ... stop.

"It's customary to say hello back."

Not knowing what else to do, she complied. "Uh, hello." But it came out choppy and breathless, instead of sexy and confident.

Groan.

To her surprise, he grabbed her hand—her *rubbin' the nubbin'* one—and brought it to his mouth, brushing his lips across her knuckles before inhaling deeply.

A knowing grin spread across his face and she wasn't sure if she should die of mortification on the spot or kneel at his feet, as she'd earlier thought. His smile lit up the entire room, brighter than the sunlight streaming in her now open window.

Oh. My. Gawd.

He was the sexiest damn thing she had ever seen.

"Accompany me to breakfast."

Was that a demand or a question? She wasn't really sure it mattered at the moment because her answer was yes, yes, *hell* yes.

"Sure," she replied nonchalantly. His grin spread even further, knowing she was anything but unaffected by him. Jesus, instead of acting like the grown ass woman she was, she was acting like a crushing schoolgirl who liked a boy, but for some dumb reason didn't want him to know.

Never letting her hand go, he silently led her through the shelter back to the main house and into the smaller of the dining rooms. The table in here could still easily hold twenty guests. Dev really did like the finer things in life.

"Sit." He pulled out a chair and gestured for her to take a seat. Surprisingly, he pulled out the chair right next to hers and sat, but not before scooting it closer to hers. He had nineteen other chairs to choose from but chose the one right next to hers instead.

Suddenly she was very nervous. And kind of pissed off, actually. After seeing him again, she *knew* she hadn't dreamt up their mutual attraction, so why hadn't she heard from him before now? Why didn't he stop by last night? Why hadn't he called her before now? Why hadn't he made even a shred of an attempt to let her know that she wasn't concocting this insane connection in her own sometimes-crazy head?

"How did you sleep?" he asked.

How did she sleep? That was his first question? He hadn't seen her in a week, ignoring this raging sexual inferno between them, and he wanted to talk about how she'd slept? Why not just ask her what she thought of this ungodly hot summer they'd been having or her thoughts on global warming or hey, what do you think of North Korea's nuclear warhead threat?

How did she sleep?

Nancy: because he was with another ho ... I thought I already went over this with you, Sarah.

She turned in her chair to face him, tucking her right leg beneath her left.

"What are you doing?"

"Having breakfast," he replied flatly. All traces of humor had vanished and the insanely intense Romaric had resurfaced.

Kate and Analise had warned her against Romaric. Analise thought he was 'scary as fuck.' Kate just thought he was lonely. Both agreed he was stoic, calm and calculating. Almost unfeeling, like an emotional lever had simply been flipped off.

She observed him for a few moments. As much as she wanted to have sex with the sex-god himself—and she *really, really* did—she suddenly didn't want to be added to a very long list of women that came before her. And if she stayed here, she'd have to see him occasionally, and

74

wouldn't that just be awkward. She could just imagine that conversation.

Hello Sarah, how are you today?

Great, are you in town long?

Just tonight, I'm afraid.

Oh … are you interested in maybe … coming back to my room?

Thank you for the offer, Sarah. I have someone else lined up this evening.

Yah … that would *so* not work for her. She would get insanely jealous and lash out and probably be asked to immediately leave the premises. Can't have a psycho ex living here, verbally threatening a Vampire Lord.

"I'm not talking about food. I'm talking about what are you doing with *me*?"

"I thought I made that clear."

Uh … what?

"Breakfast?" she asked.

"No, Sarah. You."

He was so serious she almost laughed. Maybe Giselle learned her tail chasing from Romaric, because he was making no fucking sense whatsoever.

"What the hell are you talking about?"

"I want you, Sarah. I'm not sure how much clearer I need to make it."

His intensity suddenly increased twentyfold. His cheekbones became more defined, sharper; his eyes glowed, making them appear almost crystalized; his sinewy body went completely taut and she could see the flex of his

75

muscles underneath the tightness of his stuffy button down shirt.

"But if you need me to spell it out for you, I will."

He pushed his chair back and stood. He was already a good foot taller than her short five foot six frame, but with him looming large over her sitting form, he seemed almost like a daunting mythical warrior that had risen from the ashes. If he suddenly brandished a medieval longsword, it wouldn't surprise her in the least.

Gently taking her hand in his, he pulled her to her feet. His piercing stare was so ripe with longing she almost couldn't catch her breath and the reasons she shouldn't have sex with him vanished like they'd never existed at all. He walked her backward until her back was flush to the dark blue wall.

She swallowed hard, not knowing what to expect next, but waiting for it on pins and needles all the same. Romaric's eyes never left hers as his hands came to the wall on either side of her head, caging her in. His feet came on either side of hers, his thighs pressing against hers, which allowed him to unashamedly push his rock hard erection into her stomach. She was well and truly trapped and *so* incredibly turned on by his blatant display of ownership over her body that she thought she could possibly climax from this physical contact alone.

"What I want, Sarah—no, what I *crave* more than my next breath—is to bury my aching cock deep inside your hot, tight, soaked pussy and fuck you until your throat is raw from screaming my name. I'm going to fuck you until you've come so many times you think you can't come again, but you will because I will demand it. I'm going to fuck you every way I can until you crave me on a subconscious level and can't live without my cock. Then I'm going to make love to you until you agree to be mine."

Fucking. A. Well ... let's get right to that, then.

"Is that clear enough for you now, my beauty?"

Yes. Yes, that was as clear as the Caribbean Sea. But his words had robbed her lungs of air and apparently severed the connection between her brain and mouth, so she could only nod her understanding.

"Good."

She expected him to kiss her next. Christ, she *wanted* him to kiss her next. One would think after a guy verbally fucked you like that, they'd follow it up with a soul-sucking kiss to prove they weren't all talk.

But not Romaric.

He pushed away from the wall, which also pushed him away from her body, and she swore every single nerve ending he'd touched while leaning against her was burning out of control.

Once again, his stony mask snapped into place. He held out his hand to hers, escorting her back to the table, resuming the same positions they'd had before. She was stunned speechless and pinched herself to wake up from this most bizarre dream, but the sting proved she wasn't sleeping. She dared a sideways glance at Romaric, who was staring at her with open interest.

She felt like a science experiment and opened her mouth to demand he stop it, when Hooker entered, rolling an entire cart full of food. He always, always went overboard and she felt bad for all the food that went to waste.

"That will be all," Romaric rudely replied when Hooker placed all the items on the table.

Hooker started to leave when Sarah called, "Thank you, Hooker."

His lips turned up and he inclined his head slightly in acknowledgement. He would never say, but she knew he appreciated the kindness. Just because these vampires were lords and all powerful, didn't mean they needed to be assholes. A nice 'please' and 'thank you' went a long way as far as she was concerned. Maybe that was the Midwest girl in her.

After he was gone, Sarah turned to Romaric. "You didn't need to be so rude, you know."

He set his fork down on his plate, which had been halfway to his mouth filled to the brim with scrambled eggs.

"Rude?" He seemed genuinely confused by her accusation.

"Yes, rude. He works hard cooking and cleaning and doing whatever else it is that Dev demands of him. It's not too much to ask to say thank you for all the work he went to making breakfast."

She turned back to her plate, but her appetite had vanished. Both her physical and sexual one. Romaric may be a hottie, but who was she kidding? He was *waaay* out of her league and she was still very much intimidated by him. He may think he wants her now, but he would quickly tire of her. She would never fit into his world. Into *this* world. And she'd been naïve to think otherwise.

They were complete opposites.

She had manners. He clearly didn't.

She wanted happily ever after. He just wanted to fuck her brains out.

She was sympathetic and empathetic. He was emotionally closed off.

She had a hair-trigger temper. He was calm, cool and collected.

He intrigued her on so many levels and what she wouldn't give to be able to peel away his protective layers one by one. To *really* get to know the untainted soul she saw hiding underneath his gruff exterior. He put on a very good front for everyone else, but the second she'd looked into his eyes, she knew there was so much more to Romaric Dietrich than he would ever let on to the outside world. She'd seen a deep wound that she'd foolishly wanted to uncover and heal.

But it would never work between them. She was far better off keeping him in her dreams, where he belonged. Where he'd always been.

"I'm not hungry after all."

Placing her napkin on top of her untouched food, she stood and walked toward the door. She didn't make it five steps before running smack into a solid, immovable object, which threw her off balance and she began to fall backward. Strong arms reached out and swept her off her feet before she could hit the ground.

"Where do you think you're going, Sarah?" Romaric said, holding her tightly in his oh so strong arms. She had no choice but to put her own arms around his neck for support.

Okay, so she did, but her momma didn't raise no fool.

"I'm going back to my room," she retorted. She didn't owe him anything, certainly not an explanation. And she'd be damned if she would give him one.

"I don't think so."

He didn't think so? What?

Me Tarzan.

You Jane.

If his hands were free, he'd probably be pounding his chest with his melon-sized fists trying to convince her of his male worthiness.

"Um, I *think* so, buddy. Let me go." She now used her arms in a fruitless attempt to push out his iron grip hold.

"We've already been through this. You're mine, Sarah. You're not going anywhere."

She stopped her futile efforts and gawked at him in disbelief. *Wow.* He needed a lesson in twenty-first century courting, because he was sorely behind the times.

"I'm *yours*?" She couldn't have kept the biting sarcasm out of her voice if she'd tried. Which she didn't.

"Yes." The very matter-of-fact way he said that word burrowed under her skin.

She laughed. *Really* laughed. She couldn't help it. This entire thing was so unbelievably ridiculous and she couldn't wait to gossip to Kate and Analise about how downright preposterous her morning had been.

Me Tarzan, You Jane.

"You're mine, you're not going anywhere."

They'd laugh about it for months and months. She'd just keep his impassioned 'fucking' speech out of the story, however. That was for her ears alone and God knows she'd be pathetically replaying that twenty times a day.

Romaric was gawking at her like she'd gone to crazy town and maybe she had. She finally got control of her laughter enough to speak.

"I'm not a piece of property that you can just claim, Romaric. And I'm not *yours*. I belong to no one except for myself. Now, kindly put me down. This has been … interesting, but I have a very busy day."

She didn't.

At her tirade, a devilish grin ate up his entire face and a terrible sense of foreboding wormed its way into the pit of her stomach.

"Ah, but that's where you're wrong, my beauty. You *are* mine and I've come to do exactly that. Claim you. For you see, Sarah, *you* are my

Destiny. My Fate. *You*, my insolent beauty, are my
Moira, which makes *you One. Hundred. Percent.*
Mine."

     Oh.
     My.
     Holy.
     God.

Chapter 9

Geoffrey

He'd been back with Xavier for all of twelve hours and it already felt like twelve fucking thousand. Xavier would never believe the lords—especially Romaric—had captured Geoffrey and let him escape unscathed, so he'd been forced to endure hours of agonizing torture at the hands of the lord before being set free. Which Romaric certainly enjoyed.

But he was recovering fairly well and would be completely healed by tomorrow at this time. And although it'd repulsed him, he'd had to feed as he'd needed blood to recover, but he'd wanted nothing more than to take the sweet blood of his Moira instead.

He'd taken a huge risk being captured by Romaric, but it'd been the only way. He'd told Romaric the entire truth ... and was surprised that he'd been believed. In hindsight, being captured by Romaric was the only reason he was still breathing. Had one of the other lords captured him, particularly Damian, he'd be dead.

The rumors about Romaric had been true, and then some. He was powerful, calculating and strategic. He was a formidable opponent, one that Geoffrey didn't feel Xavier could best. Although he didn't deserve it, he hoped to make an ally out of Romaric, instead of an enemy. If he could bring the lords what they needed to wipe that sick fuck out of existence, he stood at least a *chance* to make it back to his Moira alive.

"And how is my loyal lieutenant recovering?" Xavier mocked, as he strode unannounced into one of the small, bare rooms in the Kentucky compound that Geoffrey now occupied. He had a bed, a chair, a desk and a small closest that housed a few items of clothing and that was it. It was all he'd needed until he could get the fuck out of this hellhole.

He sat up, as agonizing as it was to bend at the waist. He was not about to be in a vulnerable prone position with the devil incarnate standing over him, waiting to decapitate him any second.

"Better, my liege." The knife wounds in his midsection were the worst as several had punctured his lungs. The strips of flesh that Romaric had so enjoyably removed from his back were far better and laying down wasn't nearly as painful as it was when he'd first arrived.

"Good. I'd hate to have to *replace* you."

He fucking wouldn't. Xavier loved nothing better than breaking in new servants, as he'd so intimately learned his first sixty years on the job.

"So, tell me again how you escaped with your life? Romaric Dietrich isn't one to make such a grave mistake."

This had been the tricky part. Xavier was right. No one escaped the lords with their life intact. They were lords for a reason. If they wanted you dead, you were dead. Especially Romaric.

"As I said, I had the amulet on me you'd procured from the last witch. It wouldn't work with Romaric, but he was called away. I overheard his minions say that it was for some sort of strategy meeting with the other lords in their fruitless efforts to end your life, my liege. That gave me the opportunity to use its negating ability on a lesser vampire so I could take his form. I barely escaped with my life."

Geoffrey added, "I would never betray you, my liege. I would gladly give my life to protect you and your righteous mission." *Or he'd gladly give it bringing Xavier's evil sorry ass down to hell along with him.*

Xavier scrutinized him closely. He was very good at detecting subterfuge, but Geoffrey had also mastered that skill many years ago. It was the only way to keep his head.

"I have an assignment for you tomorrow," Xavier simply said, turning to leave without another word.

Whatever the assignment was, he'd follow orders to the letter. He needed to regain Xavier's confidence and trust and prove that he remained his undyingly loyal servant, even if that had been the furthest thing from the truth for years.

The only question was, how long would that take and how much longer would he have to live in this hell on earth?

Chapter 10

Rom

They'd been sitting here over fifteen minutes in a silent showdown. After he'd dropped his big bomb, his little firecracker's cheeky comments suddenly evaporated and she hadn't said one word since. He'd carried her into the library and deposited her on the well-worn leather couch, taking up residence in the ivory armchair sitting opposite her. Their eyes were locked in some unspoken duel and neither of them would give. He could do this all day.

But what he *wanted* to do instead was haul her to his home and spend the next several days, or months, ravaging her. Every word he'd spoken earlier was true. He could think of nothing else other than repeatedly burying his painfully hard cock into her sweet, willing body until she cried uncle and acquiesced to be his. And she was very willing, despite how she was currently behaving.

This morning when he'd heard her pleasuring herself, he'd almost broke down her door with the burning need to watch. He'd wanted to watch her wet fingers circle her clit, going faster as she neared the peak. He'd wanted to see the ecstasy on her face in the throes of orgasm. He'd wanted to lap up every single drop of her come, which he'd been able to smell through the thin drywall. His cock had throbbed so hard he swore it had its own heartbeat. And with the way she'd eyed him like her favorite treat after she'd open the door, he knew *exactly* who'd been the cause of such arousal.

"How do you know I'm your Moira?" she finally asked.

"It's undeniable, Sarah."

She laughed, shaking her head. "You know, this would be a whole lot easier if you'd just answer a goddamned question straight up instead of being so damn obstinate."

Now it was his turn to laugh. "*I'm* the obstinate one?" He'd wanted to tell her to look in the mirror, but he didn't think *that* would serve him well during this particular conversation.

"Yes. *You're* the obstinate one. I ask a question and you give me half-assed answers, which aren't really even answers at all. They're more like riddles that I'm expected to solve or magically understand. I feel like I'm a kid again when my parents would tell me *'just because'* or *'because I said so.'* Those are not answers and neither is the crap you're feeding me."

Damian's words again rattled around in his head, not for the first time this morning. '*You're bound to get one that will give you a run for your money.*'

And boy, did he ever.

She'd crossed her arms, which only served to press her mouthwateringly plump breasts up. They were practically spilling out the top of her barely-there tank. It was very distracting.

"I guess I just don't speak *Romaric*, so you're going to have to speak *Sarah* instead."

He was being a bastard, and he knew it. The problem was, he really didn't know any other way to act. He hadn't explained his actions to anyone else in hundreds of years. He hadn't needed to. As a powerful vampire and a lord, no one questioned him or his actions without repercussion. He said. They did. End of.

Suddenly he was now faced with this tiny, fiery, simply mesmerizing woman who was demanding something from him that no one else dared. Yes, he'd wanted her to accept their fate simply because it was, with no additional explanation. For him, there was no explanation. It simply was. But she needed more than that. She deserved more than that. So for her, he'd try.

"Okay Sarah. What specifically do you want to know?"

She visibly relaxed, but kept the protective layer of her arms across her torso.

"How *exactly* do you know I'm your Moira? I mean, could it be just a case of mistaken identity?"

Why did it piss him off that she thought this pairing could be a mistake? More than that, why did those words physically *hurt,* like a knife sunk deep in his chest?

"It's instinctive, is the best way I can describe it. Just as you know to instinctively eat or breathe or sleep in order to live and thrive, a vampire instinctively knows when he meets his Moira, his Destiny. There are no mistakes, my beauty. You are my Moira."

"Why did you leave for a week? I mean, if you knew I was your Moira, why did you leave and not even call me?"

Her feelings had been hurt and that made him feel like a bigger bastard than he did before. He'd only been thinking of himself and how *he* felt, not how she would take his silenced absence.

"I had some things to take care of. It took longer than I expected."

Her eyes narrowed in skepticism, but he would not reveal more. Seraphina was his past and Sarah was his future. It would serve no purpose to bring her into the discussion.

"Do I get a choice to bond with you?" she asked.

The question momentarily stunned him. What he wanted to say was *fuck no*, she did not get a choice. She was his and he would *not* let her go. But what he said instead was, "Do you want a choice?"

"Yes," she responded immediately and another emotion he hadn't felt in so very long reared up. Disappointment. It's amazing how three little letters could cause such crushing disappointment. He wanted her and he wanted her to want him in return.

Fierce possessiveness roared through him and he had to fight the near feral urge to flash her back to his home and tie her to his bed. But Dev's words of last night came rushing back and he now knew that would be the single biggest mistake he could make with this stubborn, independent

89

female. *'Just because she's your Moira, doesn't mean she'll want to bond with you and you know that.'*

Fuck.

If he wanted to win Sarah—and Jesus, he *did*—he would have to travel into a space that was completely foreign to him.

Rom was skilled at many things.

Battle.

Strategy.

Leadership.

Business.

But the one area he had no earthly clue about was relationships. He wasn't warm and fuzzy. He wasn't an open book. He didn't negotiate or compromise. He didn't 'talk about his feelings.' But all of those things were required to build a successful, long-term partnership. And regardless of the intense physical attraction that burned hot between them, he desperately wanted a relationship with the woman now sitting in front of him, because she would demand no less.

The thing was ... he had no goddamned clue how to go about opening himself up. Building trust, building a relationship takes time and he felt a foreboding sense of déjà vu. This was exactly what Seraphina had done and he'd lost her before they could bond. He simply knew he wouldn't survive losing a second Moira. His mind and his animalistic nature were at complete odds with each other on how to move forward. He had to convince her to spend time with him, get to know him, persuade her that she belonged with him.

He had to get her back to Washington.

Realizing he'd been introspective for too long, he rose and joined her on the couch. He sat next to her, legs touching. He uncrossed her arms and took her hands in his.

"Do you feel that?" The electricity arching between them singed his skin. Her breath quickened the instant he'd touched her, and he knew she felt it too.

"Yes," she whispered, moistening her lips.

He let a smile tease his lips. Another thing he'd rarely done before meeting Sarah. He'd smiled more today than he had in twenty years.

"Good."

He easily lifted her slight frame and settled her on his lap facing him. She looked ready to protest, but he set a finger to her soft lips, effectively silencing her. He couldn't help his growing erection at her nearness and merely shrugged when she glanced down at his pants then back to his eyes. She wasn't unaffected either, if the intoxicating scent of her arousal was any indication.

"The physical attraction between a vampire and his Moira is powerful and passionate and all-consuming. That's what's happening between us now. You are drawn to me as fiercely as I to you, Sarah. Your body knows you're mine and recognizes its mate, just as mine does. Soon, the physical need will become too great for either of us to ignore. And there is no shame in that. It's simple biologics."

She started to speak, but another finger to her mouth stopped whatever she'd been ready to say. He wanted to set the ground rules and let her know, in no uncertain terms that she would be his. It would be her choice, but he intended to make it an easy one.

"I meant every single word I said earlier in the dining room. I am in agony with want for you, but I want more than a physical release. I want to connect with you on every single level possible. I want you to crave me in the way I crave you. Yes, you are my Moira and it's true *I* have no choice in what the Fates have decided for me. But, my beauty, I couldn't have chosen better myself, for you are everything I need.

"Do you have a choice to bond with me? Unfortunately for me, the answer is yes. If you gave the word, I'd bond with you this very instant, making you permanently mine. And I want that with every animalistic fiber of my being. But it's your choice. You have the power. You get to say when."

Jesus, those words had been excruciating to say.

Grabbing her around the waist, he pulled her flush against his throbbing shaft, then cupped her face. The heat of her pussy just about made him come undone and he had to force his hips to stay still.

"But know this, Sarah. I will do Every. Single. Thing in my power to convince you that bonding with me is the best, and only, decision you can make because you won't be able to live without me, as I cannot without you."

Unable to deny what he'd been waiting a whole week for; he took her mouth in a heated, undeniably passionate kiss. His Moira responded just as he'd expected. Fiery, enthusiastic and wanton.

And now that his mouth was upon hers, he didn't know how in God's name he would hold back from making her his ... with or without her consent.

He was so screwed.

Chapter 11

Sarah

Every cell was ablaze.
Every nerve ending ultra-sensitive.
Every thought gone.
There was only him. His touch. His kiss.

In her wildest fantasies and dreams, it hadn't been like this. It was like she'd been kissed—*really* kissed—for the first time ever. Definitely far superior to that little make-out session with Tommy Barber behind the high school in the fifth grade. And a hundred times better than her last boyfriend, Hunter Graber. He had so much excess saliva pooling in his mouth, she was sure he had an overactive gland issue. Kissing him had been like making out with a sopping wet sponge. Gross, sloppy and just plain disgusting. So ... that relationship didn't last long.

But Rom ... he knew precisely how much pressure to put on her lips. He knew precisely the right angle to tip her head. He knew precisely how to duel his tongue with hers. And he knew precisely how to make her act like a shamelessly carnal woman, who maybe hadn't had sex in well over a year.

His left hand had now slipped to her waist, his thumb lightly grazing the exposed flesh between her tank and shorts. Each slow pass of his skin on hers went directly to her hot, wet center. He may as well be stroking her sex directly because it felt almost that good. As his hand slipped fully under her shirt and began a slow ascent up her side, she lost her breath. And she almost forgot where they were. Which was right smack in the middle of Dev's library. Where anyone could walk on by and stop for the show, she was so freely giving.

With great effort, she broke the kiss and stopped his hand from going any further, even though what she wanted was to set it directly on her aching breast. Or between her legs so she could verify if his fingers felt as good as she imagined they would.

For purely scientific reasons only, of course.

"Sarah ..." he choked.

He'd grabbed her face again, gently running his thumb across her wet, swollen bottom lip. His vulnerable eyes flicked between hers and her mouth. She wanted him so badly her entire body ached with unfulfilled desire and voracious yearning. But she had to slow down. *They* had to slow down. They'd talked for all of fifteen minutes total, maybe. And half of those words had been sexually charged. She knew nothing about him and vice versa. As attracted as she was to him, she wasn't about to open her legs without a little conversation first.

"We can't do this here," she finally croaked out, once she could string a sentence together.

"My room." He made a move to get up before she stopped him.

"No." At his confusion, she added, "We can't do this period, is what I meant to say."

Freudian slip?

"We can't do what, Sarah?" His voice had hardened, his soft blue eyes icing over once again.

"I just met you, Rom. I can't have sex with someone I just met." And she'd just keep trying to convince herself of that.

"Sarah," he sighed. "I told you this is simple biologics. Neither of us can resist our magnetic physical attraction to each other. Why fight it?"

Anger blasted its way through her lust-filled haze as she scrambled from his lap. "Why fight it? Because I'm not some wanton hussy who will spread her legs for just anyone, asshole. And, yes, I may be attracted to you, but I don't even know you, and unlike all the hundreds, or probably thousands, of women you've undoubtedly charmed and then left heartbroken in your wake with your callous disregard for their feelings, I won't be one of them."

She jumped beyond his reach and headed quickly to the door, but knew she wouldn't get far. A hand on her upper arm pulled her up short and turned her back toward its furious owner. His clenched jaw ticked hard, pinching the bridge of his nose in frustration.

God, why did it make her feel so bad to upset him? She wanted to apologize, and she had absolutely nothing to be sorry for. But just as she thought it, she knew why. The vulnerability on his face when he'd told her she had a choice to bond with him and the passion she'd seen right before he'd kissed her were so much more appealing than the hard, dominating, controlling version of the male that now stood before her.

He was silent so long, she didn't know if he was going to speak or just whisk her away somewhere without her consent. Which she would *not* put past him for a minute. He wanted her to just agree to be his. Period.

No questions.

No discussion.

Nothing but submissive obedience.

Well, fuck that. Submissive was not a word used to describe Sarah and never would be. If he expected that in a mate, then he might as well keep looking because if he forced her to bond with him, they would be two of the most miserable people on the planet. Mainly him ... because she would make his life a daily living hell.

He fingered her diamond encrusted horseshoe necklace, which hung on a thin silver chain around her neck. It was a present from her parents for graduation and she was very surprised she'd been allowed to keep it when she'd been in a dungeon for over a month. Surprised, but relieved nonetheless.

"You like horses?"

"Yes," she responded flatly.

A slight smile curved his lips. "Come home with me," he demanded. And it was most definitely a demand. Not a question, or even a suggestion.

A red haze fell over her vision.

Breathe, Sarah. Think yoga. Center yourself before you say something you'll regret.

"Are you *fucking* kidding me?" she yelled. She maybe should have taken a bit more time for the centering to *really* take effect.

"Why must you be so obstinate?"

"Why must you be so pushy?"

"Sarah ..."

"Rom ..." she countered. "Look. I told you I'm not just going to jump into bed with you. I'm not like that, so if you're looking for someone easy to poke your impressively large stick into and nourish your body with, you've barked up the wrong tree."

The corner of his sensual mouth turned up and for a fleeting moment, she saw a glimpse into the real Romaric.

"Impressive, huh?" He actually chuckled. And it was the best sound she'd heard pass his lips.

"Oh my God ... *really*?" She shook her head, trying to understand why he was pushing so hard, so fast. She knew Analise had bonded with Damian in pretty short order, but Kate and Dev had taken at least a little bit of time. Against Dev's wishes, of course, but he still gave her the space she needed to make her own decision. To ask questions. To be *sure.*

"Rom, why are you pushing this so fast? If we're meant to be together, like you said, then why must we rush things? Can't we take some time to get to know each other first? I mean ... this is permanent, right?"

A look crossed his face that she swore was pain. How could her words have hurt him? She felt like there was something going on here she wasn't privy to. Did he think she didn't want him? She *sooo* did. Badly. Her body throbbed for his. She felt almost in physical agony by not having him inside of her right now. And he had to know it.

"I admit it, okay? I'm insanely, unreasonably, frighteningly attracted to you. I *want* you to fuck my brains out. Right now. I want you to do everything you promised earlier. But ... first I just need to get to know the real Rom you're hiding underneath that hard, tough exterior. And I don't think that's too much to ask."

Once again he cupped her face, the heat in his now burning eyes unmistakable, but he silently regarded her for several long moments before speaking.

"Fine," he said softly, but firmly added, "But I want you to come home with me. We need uninterrupted time together and there's no better place than my home. *Our* home."

Why did that one little stupid word send flutters through her belly? *Our.*

"I—"

"Sarah, don't say no."

She sighed. "I'm not saying no. I'm just saying ... not today." His eyes hardened again and she quickly added, "I have plans to see my parents tomorrow up in northern Wisconsin. I haven't seen them since the ... kidnapping, and I'm not cancelling."

He nodded; his eyes alight in understanding. "I'll take you."

"That's a kind offer, but Thane is taking me. It's all been arranged."

Fury flashed in his eyes and his grasp on her tightened slightly. Before she knew what was happening, his lips crashed upon hers again. They were bruising, possessive and claiming. While it should scare her, instead it sent an unexpected thrill zinging through her blood. As quickly as his mouth was on hers, it wasn't.

"You will not be accompanied by another male. Ever. Again. You're mine to protect, beauty. I will take you and that is *not* up for discussion."

As much as she already hated the domineering, controlling Rom, she liked the fact that she felt equally as safe with him. However, she wasn't sure she'd be able to convince her parents she'd fallen for someone as militant as Rom, versus how easy it would have been with the laid-back Thane. Mind made up, she did the only thing she could. The only thing she really wanted to.

"Okay," she whispered.

Chapter 12

Sarah

Desperately needing the advice of her sisters, she'd convinced Rom to give her a few hours of breathing room. He insisted this evening they have a private dinner brought to the bedroom he was using in the main house and she'd reluctantly agreed. She wasn't sure it was really wise to spend time alone in a cozy secluded room complete with a king-sized fluffy bed and a deep-seated Jacuzzi tub, when these erotic and sexual feelings she had for him swirled around like an EF5 tornado. Of course, she wasn't really sure that the location mattered. Time alone with Rom was just a little unnerving altogether. But she'd said yes, and there was no way he'd let her back out now.

Sarah and Kate sat in her bedroom and they'd patched Analise in via FaceTime. She'd told them about her morning, but was no longer laughing. Quite frankly, she was scared shitless. Rom was intense to the 'nth' degree and the fact that she was his Moira was more than unsettling. It was downright petrifying.

"I'm not surprised, sweetie," Analise quipped. "I told you he wanted to throw you down on the table and fuck your brains out right there last week. I haven't spent a lot of time around Rom, but I do know that vamp doesn't react like that to any woman. He's cold ... like a machine. I hadn't seen one emotion cross his stony features before that day."

She thought about that last comment. Rom was anything but cold, nothing like a machine. More and more she was convinced that something happened in his past to make him emotionally barren. Or make him *want* to be anyway. This morning she'd seen a plethora of emotions. Passion, lust, fury, disappointment, frustration. And even pain. Those aren't the reactions of an emotionally absent person.

"He looked at you like Dev looks at me, or Damian looks at Analise. I knew it was only a matter of time," Kate added.

And that was the thing. The one thing that had bugged Sarah about all of this was that Rom had simply vanished. For an entire week. From what Kate and Analise had both said, their mates wouldn't let them out of their sights for a moment. Dev even later confessed to Kate that he'd followed her all over the city for several days, never taking his eyes off her for a single second.

"What did he say when you asked him why he left?" Analise asked.

"He hedged. He just said he had some things to take care of is all."

Kate added, "Why he left for a week without returning is certainly a puzzle, but I'm sure he had good reason, Sarah. It doesn't really matter anyway, because he's back and from what you said, he's not letting you out of his sight now."

Still … something was off. "He's just so … intense," Sarah uttered, more to herself than anyone else.

"They all are, sweetie," Kate replied in empathy. "Honestly, it's exhausting sometimes."

"And suffocating. I feel like I can't even go to the goddamned bathroom without the third degree. And sometimes a girl just needs a few minutes by herself to breathe. Or fart." Analise chimed in.

They all laughed. Analise had once again effectively lightened the mood. She excelled at that.

"He wants me to go back to Washington with him."

And Sarah was torn here as well. She *wanted* to spend time with Rom. Saying no wasn't much of an option, because she knew how difficult it was to get her mouth to form that word when it came to him, but she was scared to leave the safety of the mansion. It's not that she didn't feel safe with Rom, just the opposite. But she felt comfortable here, like she had purpose. What would her purpose be in Washington, so far away from her sisters? She knew she couldn't stay here forever, but at the same time, she couldn't be somewhere where she had nothing to do.

"You should go," Kate cajoled.

"Absolutely," Analise agreed.

"I know, but what about the shelter? What about the girls? They need me."

Kate grabbed Sarah's hands in hers. "Sarah, you're attracted to Rom, right?"

103

"God yes." No point denying the obvious. Both of her sisters knew exactly what she was going through, hormones and emotions being put through the ringer.

"Then you owe it to yourself, and Rom, to go. Besides, if he's anything like Dev or Damian, he may act like it, but he's not really going to give you a choice. Yes, the intensity of the attraction is unnerving and doesn't make sense, but does it really need to? It is what it is. Embrace it. Go with it. We'll work something out with the shelter. Analise makes it work from Boston. Stop making excuses and go be with your man."

"And let him fuck you until you pass out," Analise laughed, but Sarah's thighs clenched at the thought.

"Is that all you think about Analise?" Sarah asked.

"Has there ever been a stupider question?" she replied seriously. "You *have* seen my mate, right?"

Just then Damian's face appeared on the screen behind Analise's and she squealed as he did something to her neither of them could see. Not that Sarah wanted to.

"And with that ladies, I'd like to reclaim my mate so I can grant her wish and fuck her until she passes out." The screen went black as Analise laughed.

Well then.

"I'd better get back to Dev. He has something top secret planned for tonight and I need to get ready. Not that I can look sexy in anything with this growing belly." Kate got off the bed and started for the door.

"Kate, can I bother you for just a couple more minutes?" She'd really wanted to talk to Kate about her strange dream.

"Sure sweetie." She came and sat back down on the bed.

"So ... I had a very strange dream the other night and I'm not really sure what to make of it. I had a conversation with a woman about Romaric."

"Really? What did she say?"

"Well ... that's the strange part. She wanted me to tell Rom that she was sorry."

"Sorry for what? Who was she?"

"I don't know. I woke up before I could ask any of those questions. But that's not really the part that bothered me."

Sarah stalled so long, Kate prodded, "What is it, Sarah?"

"Looking at her was almost like looking into a mirror. Except for her hair color, which was darker, we could have been sisters."

And what exactly did that mean? Because Sarah knew dreaming of this girl wasn't simply coincidence.

Mystery girl was somehow tied to Rom's past.

Chapter 13

Mike

Waking up with Giselle in his arms was unlike any feeling he'd ever had before. After cleaning the pipes in an ice-cold shower, he'd thrown on a pair of sweatpants because his normal buck-naked nighttime attire would definitely make it hard to honor his word of simply holding her.

As it was, having her almost naked form pressed up against his all night had been fucking excruciating. He'd given her one of his t-shirts to sleep in and it barely covered her firm, toned, black lace clad ass. Which she'd so generously gifted him a nice glimpse of when she bent over, neatly placing her clothes on the chair in the corner.

Glancing at the clock, he noticed it was already well after noon. He wasn't sure if Giselle was awake or asleep, so he lay quietly, lightly running his fingers up and down her back. A back he wished was bare so he could feel her soft skin under his rough hands. His dick was painfully hard, so it looked like another cold shower was in the cards this morning. Correction, this afternoon. He couldn't remember the last time he'd slept this late when it hadn't been courtesy of the brown bottle.

He really had to piss, but he wasn't about to move. He was afraid to break this peaceful spell that had been woven around them. Would Giselle wake up with regret, or had they finally moved past all of that shit? Would she admit she wanted him as badly as he wanted her? Would she trust him enough to let him into her complex mind? Or her heart? Or would she wake up, piss, moan and yell and walk out on him again, all the while trying to convince herself that he'd tried taking advantage of her vulnerability.

She stirred and he tightened his grip on her. If she was going to Mrs. Hyde on him again, he wouldn't make it easy on her. It was time they talked and figured out where this fucked up relationship was going, because he was done trying to convince himself that he didn't want her. He *did.* God help him, but he so did. And it was time *he* made himself vulnerable for once and let her know it. He wanted more than her body. He wanted her affection. He wanted her *love.*

Her body was sprawled across his, like he was her own personal body pillow. Her bare leg was thrown over his polyester covered one. It was precariously close to his hard on, so much so that if she moved just slightly there was no way she wouldn't notice his raging want for her. Of course, he could just blame it on morning wood, but they both would know that for the lie it would be.

He knew she was awake when her fingers started lightly moving against his bare chest. The moment a nail grazed his oversensitive skin, his cock jumped and, noticing, her head tipped up, eyes meeting his.

"Hi beautiful," he rasped thickly. In the next thirty seconds, he'd better either get out of bed or breaking his promise, she would end up underneath him and filled to the brim.

"Hi yourself," she whispered.

Their gaze was smoldering and he felt her heart beat faster against his chest.

"Jesus, I want you Giselle," he mumbled, unable to help the lust-filled words that tumbled freely out of his mouth.

At that, she closed the small gap between their mouths and kissed him with a hunger that matched his own. As hard as it was, he let her take the lead, but he wasn't going to sit idly by either. His right hand cupped her cheek as his left ran lightly over her naked torso, which was now bared thanks to the tee that had ridden up.

Never breaking their fused mouths, she climbed on top of him, straddling his hips. Her hot pussy was now perfectly positioned over his throbbing cock and he just about blew when she began to gently roll her hips. His hands now roamed over her trim thighs, making their way underneath his t-shirt she wore so fucking well. Slowly, giving her time to stop him if she wanted, he made the long ascent to her perfect, weighty bare breasts.

Testing the shape and feel in his palms, they both moaned and she increased the tempo of her pelvis. He rolled her erect nipples between his thumbs and forefingers and his mouth actually hurt with the need to taste them. He wanted his lips and his tongue and his hands all over her tight, toned body.

Breaking the kiss, she sat up, gripping his gaze with hers. Reaching down, she slowly removed the shirt, leaving her completely naked, save for the supremely sexy jet-black panties she wore. His breath caught at how fucking beautiful she was and the longing he saw in her bright blue eyes. Surprising him, she took one of his hands and placed it over her lace-covered sex.

"Touch me," she pleaded. Didn't have to fucking ask him twice.

He desperately wanted her under him, but it was clear she was directing this show and he was simply happy to be the star. Slipping underneath the drenched fabric, he ran a thumb through her soaked slit, which caused her head to fall back on her exquisitely exposed shoulders.

"Fuck, Giselle. You're so wet," he groaned.

He circled her engorged clit lightly with his wet digit before taking another pass through her liquid center. She rolled her hips faster and he was as close to coming outside of a woman's body as he'd ever been. And at this point he didn't even care. He angled his hand so he could slip two fingers inside her snug pussy, while increasing the pressure on her most sensitive nub. Feeling her tight walls clamp down on his fingers, he knew she was close.

Her hands reached up, displacing his remaining one with hers as she cupped her ample breasts and began plucking her nipples. *Jesus, that was hot.* He felt his balls tighten and the telltale tingling at the base of his spine. He was seconds away from coming and he was not going to do it without her.

Directing her hips with his free hand, he uttered, "Fuck my fingers, baby. I want you to come all over my hand."

At his command, she exploded. Her body shook and convulsed, her thighs quivered and his name never sounded sweeter than it did falling from her in the throes of pleasure. Seconds later, his own hot release followed and white heat raced at lightning speed through his veins. Low curses fell from his mouth. He wasn't even inside her and already this was the best, most intense, orgasm he'd ever experienced.

Her body fell heavily against his and his arms immediately wrapped around her, fingers feathering up and down her spine. The feeling of her skin on his was heaven. The feeling of her lips nibbling his naked flesh was nirvana. The feeling of her in his arms was ... *right.*

Mike was hit with a sudden and voracious need to completely claim this woman. Demand that she fuck only *him* and take only *his* blood and love only *him.*

He loved her and wanted to demand that she be only *his.* Forever. After all these months of fighting it, what he longed for rang loud and with clarity.

The unanswered question was ... what did Giselle want?

Chapter 14

Rom

His cock hadn't ached this bad in over half a millennia. Whether he'd consciously suppressed it or not, he hadn't thought about fucking a woman this much since Seraphina. And now he could think of absolutely *nothing* else. A thousand ways to take Sarah raced through his mind, each more carnal.

Her taste lingered on his tongue. Her smell permeated his senses. A vision of her was permanently burned into his retinas and the shape of her hips seared into his palms. And now he could think of nothing else but how the feel of her tight sheath surrounding his cock would be as he lost himself in her. For days.

To keep from going to her room and simply taking what he wanted—what was *his*—he'd spent the afternoon making plans to take his Moira home with him instead, which he would promptly do tomorrow after they'd visited her parents. Having watched Dev and Damian and the mistakes they'd made with their Moiras, he'd tasked Circo and Sulley with readying his place for her. He'd beefed up security, he'd assigned Jaz to get her a complete wardrobe and her own computer and he'd demanded Cyri ensure the stables were cleaned and the horses groomed.

A thrill ran through him when Sarah said she liked horses. In total, he owned eighteen of them. Most were Arabian or Friesians, but he also owned several wild Mustangs. At one time, he'd had two Thoroughbreds, but couldn't devote the time to training, so he'd sold them for a pretty penny. He didn't ride as much as he once had, and was actually quite looking forward to taking Sarah out.

He'd asked Dev's chef to prepare an exquisite French menu for dinner this evening. He'd skipped the traditional seven courses and the five to six hours eating a fine French meal would generally take, because he hadn't wanted to be interrupted that many times. They'd start with Escargots Bourguignon, followed by the main course, Carre d'Agneau, a delicious lamb dish. He'd still have a nice cheese board, however, and chocolate profiteroles for dessert. A fine Krug NV Grande Cuvee Brut Champagne would round out the meal.

Satisfied with the set up in his room, he headed to get Sarah. She'd wanted to just meet him in the mansion, but Rom insisted on 'picking her up'. If it was a courting Sarah wanted, that's exactly what she'd get. It was balls to the wall and he would put the full court press on her. And surprisingly, he *wanted* to. He hadn't been interested in what a woman thought or cared about in hundreds of years. Sarah had hit the nail directly on the head there. But he cared now. He *cared* ... and that was unquestionably a unique, and unsettling feeling.

He'd half thought about talking to Dev or Damian this afternoon, seeking advice, but if he thought his feelings for Sarah put him out of his comfort zone, *that* was outside the realm of thought right now. Surely he could muddle through if those two had done it.

Knocking on Sarah's door, he was anxious. And that was another emotion Rom did *not* do. He felt completely out of control and needed to pull his shit together, getting back to the confident, arrogant male he'd been just a short week ago. A male who didn't ask, but commanded.

But all those thoughts fled when Sarah opened the door, standing there in a soft blue strapless sundress that cupped her flawless perky breasts. The simple outfit was rounded out with strappy heels and her reddish blond locks flowed soft and seductively around her shoulders. On any other woman, it would be casual but on Sarah, it was sexy as hell. He could only wonder what type of lingerie lay underneath and was determined to find out later. His eyes raked over her slowly and deliberately and he not only heard her sharp intake of breath, but he smelled her unerring desire for him. It was inebriating.

She'd put on a bit more makeup than he'd previously seen her with and was pleased that she wanted to look good for him. Unfortunately, the light cherry gloss she'd swiped on her lips, was about to come off.

He pulled her firmly into his arms. "Hello, beauty. You look stunning," he sighed against her full, shiny mouth before taking it in a searing kiss. She opened for him immediately and wound her arms around his neck, straining on her toes to reach his lips.

Fuck dinner. He wanted to dine on her instead.

He started walking them backward into her room, but she broke their lip lock. "I thought we were eating?" she said breathlessly. Her chest was flush and her soft caramel eyes were dilated with need. Her swollen lips begged for his return.

"That's what I was trying to do." He winked, which garnered him a laugh. And the sound wrapped around his heart like a fist, squeezing until it beat a little faster, a little stronger.

"Wow ... and he can even joke." She smiled so bright his heart swelled this time. Like the Grinch, except his had just increased ten times the size. "Well, I was quite looking forward to eating *actual* food and talking."

Shoving down his disappointment, he kissed her chastely on the lips. "Your wish is my command, beauty."

Making their way back to his private quarters, his only thought was of stripping that flimsy fabric from her body and spending all night worshipping her.

Now, he just had to convince her that's what she wanted as well.

Chapter 15

Sarah

Jesus, she was nervous. When Rom insinuated staying in her room, eating her instead, her whole being raged with blistering need and animal lust. *Yes* had been on the tip of her tongue, so why something entirely different—which sounded an awful lot like *no*—came out instead, she was baffled. Square Rosie had decided to make an appearance.

Buttoned-up bitch. That was the last of her she'd see tonight.

When they walked into Rom's room, Sarah's steps faltered. Dozens of flickering candles lit nearly every surface, throwing supple dancing shadows on the taupe-colored walls. Soft, romantic music played in the background. Champagne bubbled in flutes on the white linen covered table, which sat in the middle of the large, open space. To the right of the table was a tall king-sized four-poster bed, covered in a cream comforter and a mountain of silk throw pillows. She saw French doors to what appeared to be a balcony straight ahead, but the blinds had been drawn to set the most romantic scene she'd ever witnessed.

Wow ... jokes *and* romance? Rom was definitely an enigma she wanted to solve. She sensed she was being watched and peered at Rom, who was gauging her reaction with keen interest.

He was trying to hide it, but she saw the same nervousness mirrored in his eyes.

"You did this for me?"

A small smile turned his lips. "Everything I do from now on will be for you, Sarah," he said with such sincerity and such conviction, she had no choice but to believe him.

"Come, have a seat." He ushered her to the table and gallantly pulled out her chair.

"Thank you," she replied as she sat. "So—"

Just as she spoke, a knock sounded at the door. Rom barked 'come in' and in walked Hooker with a dome covered silver tray. He sat it down at the table and uncovered what appeared to be some type of stuffed snail dish. *Yuck.* He quietly exited and Sarah just stared in silence at the table.

"What's wrong?" Rom asked.

"Hmm ... nothing."

He dished them up each a couple of the unsightly slugs and she picked at it a bit before Rom spoke up.

"Not a snail fan, I take it?"

"Not really," she laughed. "I'm more of a meat and potatoes kind of girl."

His wicked smirk shot a jolt of lust straight between her legs. "What kind of *meat* do you prefer?"

Not missing a beat, returning a devilish smile of her own, Sarah replied, "The salty kind."

"Jesus, Sarah ..." Rom's icy eyes began to glow and lust tightened every one of his chiseled features. She wanted to swipe the dishes from the table, bend over and beg him to take her right now. And he knew it.

She laughed nervously. "You made that too easy."

"As did you."

The sexual tension swirling in the room was thick and almost suffocating. If Sarah didn't get things back on track, and quickly, she would end up in bed with the irresistible Romaric Dietrich tonight and as much as she wanted that, she also wanted to wait.

"You can go ahead and have the snails. I think I'll wait until the next course. There is a *next* course, right?"

"Yes. And if you don't like that, we'll get you something you do like, beauty." He winked. His words were laced with promise and double-entendre. Of course, she was likely just turning them into that with her own dirty thoughts.

And whenever he referred to her with that verbal caress, it twisted her insides in the most delicious of ways.

Rom finished the escargot as Sarah regarded him silently, sipping the most delicious champagne she'd ever tasted. Another knock and Hooker entered with a second covered silver tray. She cringed at what would be underneath this one. She quickly discovered that it was lamb and some little fried potato croquets, which turned out to be very tasty.

"So, what do you do for fun?" she asked between bites.

"Fun?" His thick brows drew together, causing her to laugh.

"Yes, fun. You know, activities or hobbies you have that make you happy or laugh. Things you enjoy doing outside of work?"

He sat back in his chair and gazed at her seriously. "I don't have time for fun, Sarah. I am very busy."

A smile teased the corner of her mouth until she realized he was serious. "You don't have a hobby or anything? Painting? Exercise? Video games? Reading? Body-building?" she asked as she took in his fine physique.

"I work. That's it. That's all I need."

Well ... how sad and utterly depressing.

"What do you do for fun?" he asked, clearly interested in her answer.

"I love to read. I really enjoyed my classes at the university. I'm a huge fan of Real Housewives. Atlanta, of course. And I really love horses. But you already know that."

"Yes." He smiled. "I do."

During dinner, while it didn't dissipate, they kept the sexual tension to a minimum and talked about mundane, but interesting things. She told him about her studies and finishing her degree. Talked about her family, leaving out the painful death of her brother for now, as to not bring down the mood. She learned that Rom had been a lord for over three hundred years and that he owned various nightclubs, just as Dev and Damian did, but was surprised to hear he owned over twenty and had expansion plans in the works

118

for eight more. He talked a bit about his home and land in Washington, but refrained from saying too much because he 'wanted to surprise her.' And her mind was absolutely blown when she also found out he was over six hundred years old.

But the one thing he wouldn't talk about was his past. When she asked questions about parents or siblings, he easily diverted the subject back to her. When she asked about friends, he simply said the lords didn't have the luxury of friends, except those they trusted with their lives, which were a proven few. And when she asked about other women, he merely growled, telling her he refused to talk about such things that were completely irrelevant.

As she suspected he would, he asked several questions about her captivity, but like her brother, she didn't want to talk about it. He'd reluctantly accepted, but told her they were not done with that conversation. If she had her way, she'd never talk to him about it. Guess they both had things they didn't want to discuss.

Two hours, two bottles of champagne and too much food later, Rom escorted them to the balcony where they sat on a double chaise lounge underneath the inky, moonlit sky. To control her libido, she'd tried to keep a respectable amount of distance between them, but just as he'd done at breakfast that morning, he moved directly into her personal space. Their bodies touched from shoulder to foot and the warmth of his bare forearm sunk deeply into her skin.

He'd worn another button down shirt this evening. This time it was a stunning royal blue that complemented the iciness of his eyes. He'd paired it with black dress slacks. Trying to go for casual, the top two buttons were undone and his shirtsleeves were rolled up several times. Every time she'd seen him, he was dressed to the nines. She wondered if he ever relaxed and hung around in jeans and a t-shirt. God, would she love to see his ass molded in a pair of faded denims.

The alcohol coursing through her veins made it easier to ask the question plaguing her mind since she'd discovered his age. Turning her head, she asked, "Is it unusual to not find your mate for so long?"

Rom's entire body stiffened like he'd just been electrocuted and he refused to meet her eyes, staring at the night sky instead. "Some vampires never find their Moira," he answered tautly.

Now she was absolutely convinced there was a story there, a personal one, but she didn't push. She longed to ask him what the girl in her dream was sorry for, but was equally not sure she wanted to know.

Needing to bring back the relaxed Rom she'd just spent a most enjoyable evening with, she did the only thing she could think of. Only inches separated their hands, so she reached over, taking his in hers. At that gesture, he turned his head toward hers and they lay there quietly gazing into each other's eyes.

"I'm sorry," she whispered.

"Why are you sorry, Sarah?" His voice didn't hold quite as much vinegar as just a minute ago and she knew she'd made the right move. She longed to know the pain life had thrown at him, which he'd buried so deep. Whatever it was, she was convinced it had to do with this girl she'd dreamt about and an uneasy feeling crept over her.

"For whatever I said to upset you."

His demeanor softened significantly and he reached his free hand to cup her cheek. "You didn't upset me, beauty."

Secrets. They were like a slow growing cancer eating you from the inside out until the growth was so big, so noxious, it refused to be ignored anymore.

They were quite the pair. They both held secrets they didn't want the other to uncover. And *that* both upset and hurt her feelings. The fact that she was being a hypocrite wasn't lost on her. She expected him to open up, but wouldn't do the same.

"I think I should go to bed." She moved to get up, but found herself pinned underneath a heavy, hard vampire instead, his thick shaft pressing into her belly.

Oh my.

"Stay."

"No." Guess she *could* say no to him after all.

"Sarah ..." he growled.

"This sounds oddly repetitive," she retorted.

He exhaled heavily, putting his forehead to hers. "I don't want to be parted from you."

"Why?" She instinctively felt this was more than the Moira thing and was acutely important to him. He seemed almost *afraid* to let her out of his sight. Did this have to do with Xavier?

"I've been safe here, Rom. Nothing will happen to me."

His voice and face hardened and she saw an almost cruel side of him she hadn't before. "Nothing will happen because you will be under my watch at all times, Sarah. That is not up for debate or negotiation. You will stay."

And with that little announcement, he rose and strode back into the room, leaving her lying alone in the dark of night to wonder what the fuck just happened.

Chapter 16

Geoffrey

Sitting in this sleazy, low-life human bar was grating on his very last fucking nerve. Xavier had sent him back into the lion's den, aka Milwaukee, to do some further recon on the clubs the lord's owned and search for additional clues on the whereabouts of his daughters. More likely he wanted him recaptured and killed by the lords. Too bad for him taking his sorry ass down was the number one priority on Geoffrey's list, and he wasn't going to spend eternity burning without Xavier in his hip pocket.

The easiest way to find further information on Xavier's offspring would be to go back to Dragonfly and hit up a few of the slutty women who prostituted themselves all in the name of pleasure. Or a buck. But he couldn't stomach the thought of looking at another woman, let alone touching one. So here he sat, nursing a bitter rum and Coke, trying to plot his next chess move.

He was well and truly fucked. On one hand, he was an infiltrator in his own organization. On the other, were powerful death-wielding lords just waiting to slaughter him if he made one wrong move. Hand over information to Xavier about their whereabouts ... die. Don't ... die. Pretty fucking bad choices all around. He'd have to walk a fine line if he wanted to make it out of this alive, which looked bleaker by the minute.

His mind drifted to Beth. The fact that he'd found his Moira under such heinous circumstances was not only inconvenient, but distressing. But the fact that he'd been unable to protect her from the ravagings of the monsters under Xavier's boot made him murderous.

She'd been taken captive while he'd been on another assignment, so by the time he'd returned she'd been there for almost a week. And while he didn't know everything that had happened during that time, he had a pretty fucking good idea. He'd managed to protect her when he returned, but by then the damage had already been done. He only hoped she'd be able to emotionally heal, move forward and live a happy life. He'd like nothing more than that life to be with him. He craved it, but she'd likely never want to see his face after what she'd been put through.

A voluptuous, striking blonde, who was clearly vampire, walked into the dimly lit bar and his radar immediately pinged. The vampire community wasn't necessarily a small one, but it wasn't all that large either. And the female vampire population was even smaller. Geoffrey had been around for over five hundred years, so he knew most of the female vamps running around the United States. And this was not one of them.

She had sharp cheekbones, arresting green eyes and long hair so pale it was almost white. Her fair skin stood starkly against her all black attire.

And her painted on black leather pants and tight fitting Henley didn't leave much to the imagination. If he hadn't found his Moira already, he might be trying to tap that, but there was absolutely no spark of desire, just ... interest. Who was she and what was she doing in the heartland of the US?

She scanned the bleak place with a look of disgust on her dainty features and was just turning to leave when she spotted him. Not hesitating a moment, she made a beeline straight toward him, nonchalantly taking the seat opposite of him, like they were old friends meeting for a night of chitchat.

"I'm looking for someone." She spoke English, but with a heavy accent, waving off the waitress who had scurried over to take her drink order.

Not breaking eye contact, Geoffrey took another sip of his unpleasant cocktail, the cheap rum lingering far too long on his tongue. "And what makes you think I would help you?"

She sneered. Geoffrey knew a predator when he saw one. He'd grown up around the worst kind all his life. Hell, he *was* one.

"I could make it mutually beneficial," she purred.

"I highly doubt that, sweetheart." A month ago he would have been all over that shit, whether he'd decided to help or not.

She regarded him contemplatively, trying to figure out her next play. Yep... takes a player to know a player. But she was on his playground now and he was the motherfucking king of the hill, so she'd better bring her "A" game.

"I'm sure you're well aware of the hierarchy in this country, yes?"

"Meaning?"

She tried very hard to hide the fury boiling underneath her china doll façade. Unsuccessfully. "Don't be obtuse, asshole."

"Get to the point, sweetheart. This is boring the fuck out of me."

"One of your lords is in danger."

He laughed mockingly. "And this is newsworthy?" The lords were always in danger. If not from Xavier and his minions, then from many other foolish vamps who thought they could overthrow them. But okay, he'd play along. "Which one?"

"Romaric Dietrich."

"And you care ... why?" Romaric could take any vamp blindfolded. Probably even in his fucking sleep. Of any lords being threatened, he was the one Geoffrey would be the least concerned about.

"Let's just say, it's personal."

Personal? "And who might you be, exactly."

"An old friend." She smirked.

Riiiight. A scorned lover perhaps.

"An old friend with or without a name?"

She leaned back, crossed her arms and smiled silently. She wanted to play like that, fine by him. He threw a twenty on the table and got up to leave. It was twenty too much. Fuck, they should have paid *him* to drink that pigswill.

He'd just stepped foot outside when he heard her call after him. "Do you know where I might find him? It really is life or death."

He turned, pinning her with his glare and baring his sharp teeth in what anyone who had a functioning brain cell would understand was a threat.

"No." Truth. "And even if I did, I'm not inclined to get into the middle of a lover's spat. Or hand over his whereabouts to a groupie stalker simply because I have a cock and she batted her long eyelashes and dressed to show off her assets to their greatest advantage."

She looked genuinely torn. He'd discuss this with Rom the next time they connected, which was in a week's time, at a place that Rom would disclose an hour before the meeting. He'd picked up several burner phones, provided all numbers to Rom and had left them at various locations so Xavier wouldn't catch on. He had no doubt he was on a short leash and Xavier would be tracking every movement he made, which was all the more stupid that he was here and not at Dragonfly, which was where he was headed next.

He turned again, intending to head around the side of this shithole and flash to a conveniently inconspicuous spot outside of Dragonfly when what she said caused him to freeze in his tracks.

"It's his father."

His father? Rom's father lived? Where? Why had he not heard of this before?

He slowly faced her and for the first time, she let the grimness of the situation show on her concerned face. Vampires grew stronger with age and if Rom's father lived, as powerful as Rom was, he would be more so. So if there was a riff between Rom and his father ... well, that was very fucking bad. And that put his own plans very much in jeopardy.

"Who are you?"

"I told you. I'm an old friend."

"You'd better give me a fucking name or I'm walking."

The silence was deafening. Finally, she spoke. "Ainsley. Romaric will know who I am."

"And how do I know *you* aren't the threat, *Ainsley*?"

Her patience snapped. "Are you going to tell me where I can find him or not?"

"No. But, I will get a message to him and if he's interested, he'll find you."

This time, he flashed away without the cover of dark, uncaring whether a drunk-ass human saw him or not. Once inside Dragonfly, he made his way to whom he'd seen Damian with several weeks ago. He assumed he was the manager of Dragonfly UG.

He only hoped that he wouldn't get his head severed before he had a chance to deliver the dire message from Rom's very beautiful, very sexy, and very foreign old *friend*.

Chapter 17

Sarah

He'd locked her in the bedroom.
Fucking.
Locked.
Her.
In.
Like a goddamned prisoner. After several minutes of fuming on the balcony, she'd made her way back into the quiet, still candlelit empty room, intending on returning to her own bedroom, despite Rom's caveman demands. But when she made it to the door, the handle wouldn't turn. She'd pounded and yelled for Rom for fifteen minutes before making her way back out to the balcony to see if she could escape there.

Unfortunately they were four stories up, so dropping from a hundred feet in the air was probably only a good idea in the event of a fire, because she'd likely break both of her legs. Or her neck.

Because there was no phone in the room, she couldn't even call for help and since they were in a wing of the house where only Rom was staying, the chances of anyone else coming to her rescue were slim to none.

Fucking hell. That bastard.

Her own supposed mate was keeping her prisoner. How could he do that to her after all that she'd been through? She'd been a hostage for thirty-three goddamned days, locked in a room she could never leave. They decided when she ate. They decided when she drank. They decided when she slept. They decided when they'd take her blood. They'd decided *everything*. She had no control over her decisions or her life or her body for over an entire month and she swore she'd never put herself in that position again.

She'd *never* forgive him. He could forget taking her to his house because that would happen when hell froze over. And if he tried against her will, she'd just call Kate or Analise and surely Dev or Damian would come to her rescue. Or if he didn't let her call, which was the more likely scenario, they'd know she was missing within very short order and send the calvary. They wouldn't let Rom do this to her.

And he could also forget accompanying her to her parents tomorrow too. The minute she got out of here, she was tracking down Thane to see if he would still be available. Screw what Rom wanted. Despite his prehistoric view of women, he did not *own* her.

She decided what she wanted, when she wanted and how she wanted. *She* was master of her own domain. Never again would she be a prisoner to what someone else wanted.

Hours later she knew he wasn't coming back for her tonight, so she crawled on top of the plush bedding, gave into her exhaustion and fell into a fitful sleep. As always, the impenetrable shadow was there, hovering, watching, protecting. And while still in the dark, blending into the

130

background, he was also more prominent. His stony, impassive face was still concealed, but she knew it was Rom.

Even in sleep she was pissed and tried to banish him from her thoughts, but he remained stubbornly still. And even through the darkness she could see the bastard even had a smirk on his face. She dreamt of several crazy things, like the fiery pits of hell icing over, before the mystery girl reappeared. All the while Romaric was there, following her from one bizarre scene to the other. Until *she* came. Then he was suddenly and conspicuously absent.

She was beautiful, but very young. Innocence and sincerity oozed from her and she made Sarah feel instantly at ease.

"He cares for you. I am glad," said mystery girl.

"Who are you?" And why do you look so much like me, she wanted to ask, but didn't.

"I am but a memory long passed. You are his future."

"Why do I feel like I know you?"

"Because you know yourself."

Huh?

"Romaric has been through more than you can imagine, Sarah."

"What? Please tell me," Sarah begged.

"It is not my story to tell. It is his. And he will tell you in his own time."

"Who are you?"

Mystery girl simply smiled. "Give him a chance, Sarah. He is exactly what you need. And you are exactly who he's been waiting for. Who he was always waiting for." Then she vanished.

As soon as mystery girl evaporated into thin air, Sarah woke. She bolted up in bed, taking in her surroundings.

Ah yes, her very own prison.

This time she had fluffy pillows, a down comforter, and fresh air, but it was still a prison nonetheless.

It was early. Only a little after 6:00 a.m., but she was now wide awake, so she got up. Doing her business in the bathroom and finger brushing her teeth and hair, she smoothed the wrinkles out of her sundress as much as possible before heading out to the balcony.

She loved the crisp mornings of summer. It was July and the temperature didn't get as cool in the evenings as she would like. This morning it was already sultry, the air heavy with unshed moisture. There would likely be a nice afternoon thunderstorm later and she dreaded thinking about having to be on the road in driving rain.

God, she wanted a coffee. With three heaps of sugar and half a cup of cream. Okay, so she wanted a little coffee with her cream and sugar.

Flopping on the dew-covered chaise, she thought about mystery girl's even more mysterious words. What *story* had she been talking about? What had happened in Rom's past? Was it with this girl? And who the hell was she? Was she a sister, a friend, a *lover*? That thought made her unreasonably jealous. So many questions and no one to ask.

One thing was certain. She wanted Sarah to give Rom a chance... but why? And *should* she after this little stunt he'd pulled? She wanted to tell him to take a hike off a tall mountain almost as much as she wanted to fix whatever was wrong with him. It was all so confusing.

A noise tore her from her thoughts. Even from outside she heard the door scrape open. A few moments later, she felt his presence in the doorway but didn't turn. She was still very much full of piss and vinegar.

"Did you sleep well?"

What was it with him and her sleep?

She snorted. Very unladylike and unattractive, but tough shit. She got up and tried to brush past him without making eye contact, but he gently grabbed her arm with his steely hand.

Christ, every time he touched her, desire pooled in her stomach and headed south like a flash fire. Her breaths quickened and her pulse shot up so fast, it bordered on high blood pressure. Her body may be flashing slutty green, but her mind was a solid go-to-hell red.

"If the next words out of your mouth are not I'm sorry, then you can just fuck off."

She wrenched her arm free, knowing that she only could because he allowed it. She walked quickly to the door, but stopped short when he called behind her.

"I went about things in the wrong manner."

Sarah shook her head. Rom's version of a mea culpa. An apology ... yet *noooot* quite. Yep, he'd definitely taught Giselle a thing or two. Anger morphed quickly into hurt and she couldn't help the tears that unwillingly stung her eyes.

With her back to him, her voice cracked. "How could you do that to me knowing what I've been through?" He may not know the details because she'd refused to talk about it, but he knew she'd been held against her will by savages.

Before she knew it, she was wrapped in his hard, sinewy arms. Pressed against his sculpted chest. Not willing to give in, she let her arms hang stiffly at her side, trying hard not to cling to the male who had caused her such pain, even though wrapping herself around him was stupidly all she wanted to do.

"Sarah, I reacted badly. I am truly regretful."

Mystery girl's words rang in her ears. *"Romaric has been through more than you can imagine."*

Her arms moved of their own accord and wrapped around his thick waist. He stroked her back and whispered his apologies. She cried.

"Why?" she croaked, her voice muffled against his chest. She simply had to know why he'd done it. They'd had a fantastic night and he'd ruined it.

He stilled. "I ..." He was quiet so long she didn't think he'd answer. And so help him if he didn't. "It ... I don't ... I don't suppose you'd accept that I'd gone temporarily insane?"

Laughing, she pulled away, mascara likely streaking her face. She probably looked like a raccoon.

"Well, insanity was a given. I was just wondering what triggered it."

He cupped her face, wiping the tears and running makeup away. "Sarah ... I don't want anything to happen to you."

Was this fear for her safety natural? She'd have to talk to Kate and Analise about it. It seemed to her it bordered on irrationally obsessive. Who keeps someone locked in a bedroom all night because they are afraid something will happen to them?

"What are you worried will happen to me?"

"Anything and everything. I can't lose you before I even have you, my beauty." His eyes were full of torment and sincerity and the fury she'd worn like a protective coat of arms almost vanished. *Almost.*

"Don't do it again or I can assure you, we're through." Saying those words sent a jolt of physical pain to her heart. She badly wanted to act on this magnetic pull to Rom, but she wouldn't be at his mercy either. Moira or not.

He nodded tightly. His pained look quickly turned to one of hunger as he eyed her mouth. Every look from him like that felt like a physical caress and she couldn't help the way her body responded, just like she couldn't help breathing.

Yes, she was still mad. Yes, she was still hurt. And yes, she should punish him a bit longer, as he so rightfully deserved. But she didn't want to. What she wanted was his lips on hers, tongues dueling, breaths mingling.

Don't judge.

When his eyes drew back to hers, they couldn't deny what she desired and his mouth descended. His kiss was soft, gentle and reverent. A physical and emotional apology, which she greedily accepted. He held her still as he switched angles, deepening the kiss, deepening the connection between them. Her hands roamed up his back over his broad, powerful shoulders and the low rasp in the back of his throat shot straight to her sex.

Their mouths continued to battle as a hand traveled down her torso, over her hip to the bottom of her wrinkled sundress. Cool air hit her butt when he bunched the fabric to her waist. She'd worn an ivory-colored thong, which matched her strapless bra. And yes, she'd selected them with only him in mind.

At the first touch of his palm to her bare ass, she felt a gush of liquid seep from her core. His fingers lightly traced the outline of her panties from the top of her bottom, down to the very inside of her cheeks and directly to her pussy before slipping underneath the flimsy material.

"Christ, Sarah," he groaned as he slipped easily through her wet folds. His lips traveled the length of her neck, brushing her ear. "Let me make you feel good, beauty."

"Yes," she managed to choke through the lack of oxygen currently *not* circulating through her lungs.

He easily picked her up and carried her to the messy bed, laying her down gently. He stood to his full six and a half foot frame and feasted on her body with his starving eyes. He was so beautiful. A specimen of perfect, raw masculinity. And he was *hers*.

He wasn't looking at her face, his eyes instead focused on his hands as they slowly made their way up her bare, splayed thighs. He silently reached underneath her dress, which was almost inappropriately around her waist now. Not that it mattered, for he was about to see far more than just her barely-there underwear.

As he drew down her panties, she felt the cool air hit her sex but it did little to ease the fire burning there. His blue eyes now locked on hers as his palms caressed her legs, slowly making their way back up to her aching flesh. His fingers spread her thighs as far apart as he could before the heat of his stare reverted south. He sucked in a breath and cursed low and soft.

"Rom." His name was a breathy entreaty falling from her lips.

"Perfect," he worshipfully whispered. "Jesus, you're perfect, Sarah."

His thumbs spread her wetness around, lightly grazing her engorged clit with each pass. He pulled her to the edge of the bed until her bottom nearly hung off. He knelt on the floor, grazing her inner thigh with his sharp teeth.

"You're mine," he rasped in between nips.

"Oh God," she moaned. She was afraid of his bite but craved it all the same.

"Not today, beauty," he uttered as he nipped and nuzzled her sex, inhaling deep. "But soon."

Hot breath feathered across her skin, leaving goose bumps in its wake. At the first feel of his fiery tongue, her hips involuntarily bucked and he reached one arm up across them to hold her still. Two fingers slowly slipped into her tight sheath and she swore she'd died and gone to heaven. The pleasure ricocheting through her body was searing and fierce and unchartered.

Rom wasted no time devouring her like his next meal. His fingers curved, hitting just the right spot and pumped ruthlessly while his tongue lashed her clit furiously, bringing her to an almost embarrassingly quick and red-hot, mind-blowing orgasm.

"Rom," she panted, holding him in place as if he would stop otherwise. Hot streaks of pleasure radiated throughout her body and she shook uncontrollably with her release. As her legs quivered and her body intermittently convulsed, he brought her down soft and slow, pressing gentle kisses on her inner thighs and lightly curled mound.

"I found my new favorite place to be," he whispered against her sensitive flesh.

With one lingering kiss, he stood and climbed onto the bed with her, bringing them both to lie in the fluffy mound of pillows. Completely sated and boneless, she snuggled into his side. She loved the possessive feel of his arm around her. They were silent for several minutes, while her breathing regulated and she tried wrapping her mind around her uncharacteristic reaction to him. A half hour ago she'd been ready to rip his head off. Now she wanted his *head* other places. *Wink.*

He broke the silence first. "What time are we meeting your parents?"

"You still want to take me?" she asked, knowing full well what his answer would be since he wouldn't even let her return to her own bedroom last night.

"Sarah ..."

She had a feeling she'd better get used to him saying her name with exasperation. A. Lot.

"Just asking. Noon." She looked at the clock and it was already past seven. "I need to shower and we should hit the road. It's a long drive."

"We're not driving four hours, Sarah. That's asinine."

She sat up, looking down at his lounging, composed form, one arm flung underneath his head. He looked... relaxed. Well, except for the mammoth erection straining the front of his tan dress pants. Her fingers itched to run down its impressive length and take care of him the way he'd just taken care of her. God, he was a sexual menace to women everywhere.

Clearing her throat, she prompted, "And just how are we going to get there?"

A sly smile upturned the corners of his sensuous mouth, still shiny from her juices. *Jesus, that's hot.*

"Surely you're aware of flashing, aren't you? And I'm not talking about a pervert in a tan trench coat jumping out from the bushes to show his junk to a bunch of school-aged kids."

She couldn't help the laugh that escaped her. She could fall hard and fast for this lightened up version of Rom.

"Yes, I'm well aware of the speedy way you vampires get around, but we can't just pop out of thin air into Slade's and nonchalantly make our way to a booth. I think that would arouse suspicion and my parents are already skeptical of why I've been away so long."

He regarded her quietly and she could tell he wanted to argue. "We'll compromise." He sat against the headboard and pulled her astride his lap, settling her firmly against his hard shaft. "And so you know that I'm trying, that's a new action for me."

Squirming a bit, he grabbed her hips, holding her still. "Don't tempt me, beauty. I want you with a voracious need that I am *barely* in control of right now. But I understand your need to wait and I'll respect that. For now." He winked and smiled.

Sarah couldn't help leaning forward and placing a chaste kiss on his lips, tasting herself in the process. She may be tempting the beast, but it felt like the right response to his words. Sitting back, she ran her fingers lightly over his broad shoulders. "What sort of compromise?"

"The kind that involves me not entirely getting my way. That's what kind."

Her fingers halted. One step forward, two steps back. "You're exasperating. Do you ever actually *answer* a question with a straight response?"

He sighed deeply, his hands tightening on her hips. "Sarah, understand I'm not used to answering to anyone about anything. Ever. I make the rules. I enforce the rules. I say jump and people not only ask how high, they ask what else they can do to fucking please me. It will take some time getting used to having to explain myself to someone. To *you*."

She thought on his words for a moment, understanding his point of view but wanting to make hers heard. "I'm not a pushover, Rom. I'm not one of your lackeys that will do whatever you say, whenever you say it. I've had my control stripped from me before and I will *not* be in that place ever again. You need to understand that."

He held her face in his strong, safe hands. "I'm so sorry, Sarah. And I do understand. Please allow me time to adjust my long-set ways." Unwelcome tears sprang to her eyes and she nodded. He pulled her head to his shoulder and held her tightly.

"As much as it will pain me, I'd like to hear about it." She knew what *it* he was referring to.

"Someday."

"It's a good thing all those who had a hand in your abduction and subsequent events are dead, or my first mission would be to wipe them from the face of this fucking earth. Xavier will soon no longer be a threat. Don't doubt that. Then you'll be completely out of any madman's crosshairs, beauty. And we can live a long and happy life together."

He pulled her back; his icy gaze bore into her eyes so she would feel every word he uttered. "After we bond, of course."

It felt so very right to say the next two words. "Of course."

Chapter 18

Rom

He'd fucked up. Colossally. The Titanic of all fuck ups. Last night did not end at all like he'd hoped, with Sarah writhing in passion underneath him. Instead, he'd spent it next door in the room Dev had made up for Sarah, listening to her scream and cry, feeling like a low-life piece of shit the entire time, but unwilling to come back and make it right. Unwilling to be no more than a few feet from her, even if Sheetrock and plywood separated them.

When Sarah said she was leaving, he'd lost control and reacted impulsively and irrationally. He was lucky that she'd forgiven him, because what he'd done was almost unforgivable. Her words stabbed him deep and piercing when she asked how he could have done it. He'd been asking himself the same exact question since the minute he'd walked out on her. It's not like she was going to contract a deadly virus between the mansion and the shelter and be dead in the morning.

Oh wait ... that *had* happened before.
Christ.

She deserved better than an emotionally unstable male for a mate, but fuck if he would give her up. He'd protect her. He'd rid the world of Xavier and any other threat to her, because she was it for him.

He only hoped he'd be able to control himself in the future, because Sarah was a strong, independent woman and she would not tolerate another such screw up. She spoke true when she said she would walk and that terrified the hell out of him. Because he wasn't sure that he wouldn't massively screw up again. In fact ... it was a one-hundred percent certainty he *would*.

She was right. He couldn't command her the way he could everyone else and that scared him shitless. No, he didn't want a spineless puppet for a mate, but he also wasn't sure how he felt about this little wisp of a woman challenging him at every single turn either.

She pushed every one of his buttons, completely eviscerating his calm, cool and in-control demeanor. If he said black, she said white. If he said up, she said down. If he begged her to stay the night, she asked why.

He should just tell her about Seraphina. Make her understand the anguish and suffering he'd been through in losing one Moira. Beg her to bond with him now so her fragile human life would become strong, powerful and virtually invincible. He couldn't lose her. It would *ruin* him. Permanently. But he also couldn't bring himself to talk about Seraphina either.

Because knowing she wasn't the first ... he had a feeling *that* may ruin Sarah.

Chapter 19

Sarah

"This is your compromise?"

"Yes."

"This is a stretch limousine, Rom."

"Yes."

Ugh.

"You do realize we're going to a dive restaurant on the lake, right?"

"Yes."

UGH!

They were driving north on Highway 51, about ten minutes out from Slade's. *That* was his compromise. Jeannie them to Wausau, and have one of his staff drive them the rest of the forty-five minutes in a completely inconspicuous black stretch limo. What the hell would her parents think?

Brilliant.

She simply sighed and turned to watch the fields fly by through the tinted glass windows. Suddenly she was being pulled across the leather seats and set across one stubborn vampire's lap, both legs dangling over his and a strong arm snaking up to cup her nape.

He nuzzled the thin, sensitive skin right underneath her ear. "Did I tell you how delicious those jean shorts mold to your fine ass, beauty?"

Instantly, embarrassingly wet.

"Ah ... no," she replied, breathless.

Kisses were being scattered now. Hot, wet, scalding kisses. And she *might* have shamelessly angled her head to give him better access.

"Rom ..." He'd leaned her back slightly, running his sharp teeth against her collarbone. They were going to arrive any minute and she would be a flush, hot mess.

He snared her mouth in a wicked kiss that rose her body temperature ten degrees. His left hand palmed her head, while his right traveled underneath her white bohemian blouse, but stopped short of touching her where she craved.

For the next five minutes, they made out like teenagers going to their senior prom. It was fun. It was sweet. It was refreshing. And it filled her heart in places she didn't know were achingly empty.

When the car slowed and turned a corner, Rom stopped their little make-out session and the need and emotion she saw as his eyes bored into hers stripped her raw. It was too early for love, but she could feel something close to that bleeding from him into her. It filled her mind with a fuzzy, dreamlike haze and her body with a rush of sweet, addicting adrenaline.

How he could go from infuriating her to infatuating her literally one second to the next was dizzying.

"We're here." The words tickled her lips.

"Okay," she responded. *Lame. Very lame.*

The car stopped and their driver opened the door. Rom hadn't let her off his lap and she scurried to move, but he kept her tight against his stiff erection. One last chaste kiss later, he held her in his arms as he exited the car, finally setting her down on the gravel parking lot.

She spun and after fixing her hair and shirt, began walking quickly to the entrance. Rom let her get about four steps before he was at her side, her hand now ensconced in his.

Yep, *everyone* was looking at the showy couple who'd just arrived in a flashy, ostentatious car. *Great*. Her parents were probably watching them walk across the parking lot right now wondering what kind of scary monster kidnapped their daughter. If they only knew how close to the truth they were, but it wasn't the male now walking beside her. No, the monsters that had kidnapped her were far, far worse.

As they walked, he leaned down to whisper, "And those fucking little boots are a male's wet dream."

Gah! First stop, bathroom.

"Behave," she hissed.

Her stomach was in knots. She'd been so pissed last night and distracted this morning that she hadn't even practiced what she was going to tell them and would have to wing it. *Wing. It.*

So not her strong suit. Sarah studied. Sarah prepared. Sarah did *not* wing.

Walking into the restaurant, she spotted her parents at the far end, sitting impatiently at a booth. And from their vantage point, there was no doubt they'd seen the vehicle she arrived in and the possessive, intimidating man—*vampire*—hanging from her arm.

Shit. Shit. Shit.

Taking a deep breath, and digging deep for her Meryl Streep Oscar skills, she pulled Rom along with a big, fake smile plastered on her face. In truth, she was so nervous she wanted to vomit.

Rom squeezed her hand in a show of solidarity and a tiny bit of relief flooded through her. He would have her back. He would help her through this. He would deflect any heat her parents heaped on her. She looked back and smiled gratefully, mouthing *"thanks."* His gentle, sweet smile in return would help her make it through this difficult conversation.

Her parents anxiously rose from their seats and her mother enveloped her in a hug so strong, it almost took her breath away. She was sobbing and Sarah was barely holding it together, tears hanging precariously on her eyelashes. Her dad's hug was similar and after what seemed like several minutes, and one very public family reunion later, they all sat.

Rom had somehow moved to the side of the booth her parents had occupied and quickly ushered her to sit, where he promptly took his place beside her. She was confused until he eyed the door and she understood exactly what he'd done. He wanted an unobstructed view of the restaurant and wasn't about to put his back to the crowd, endangering them.

"Mom, Dad, this is Romaric Dietrich. Rom, this is my dad, Henry, and my mom, Linda."

"Pleased to meet you, Mr. and Mrs. Hill." He extended his hand and her parents tentatively took turns shaking it. Her dad looked nearly murderous, her mom was somewhere between awe and fear.

Ha! She knew *exactly* how they felt. Awkward silence had echoed for several beats before her dad started the grilling.

Aimed at Rom.

She mentally slapped her palm to her forehead. Her dad had done this with every single boy she'd ever brought home. He was the quintessential father cleaning the shotgun, except in his case ... he *really* did. He scared off any potential boyfriend she may have ever had and in sixth grade when her next door neighbor and best friend, David, started paying attention to her in a *'girl, I just noticed those aren't mosquito bites'* kind of way, her dad promptly stomped over to have a "come to Jesus" meeting with David's parents.

And that didn't end well. For *her*. David avoided her for the rest of the summer and she ended up having to hang out with Tiffany Finnegan, who was a little ho and lost her virginity in the back end of a clichéd Chevy Camaro to a fifteen-year-old high school pothead in the skating rink parking lot. If her dad only knew what kind of person he'd driven Sarah to, he'd only have *wished* David had still been ogling her boobs. Because despite his early fascination, he turned out to be gayer than a three-dollar bill.

"So ... how did you meet my Sarah?" her dad peppered.

My Sarah? Kill her now. Please.

"Dad ..." she spat.

"No, it's okay Sarah. It's a valid question," Rom calmly responded, as he blatantly put his arm around her shoulder in a very public display of ownership. *Lovely.* Now her boyfriend, future mate, whateverthefuck he was, and her father were getting in a pissing match. And she knew exactly who would win.

In retrospect, she should have spent those five minutes they'd sucked face in the car explaining the lies she'd told her parents about her absence. Weaving your accomplices into your web of lies is surely the first and most important bullet in *Deceit For Dummies.*

"We met at a class I was taking at Richmond, Daddy."

"I believe I asked your friend, Sarah."

Seriously ... kill her now.

"Stop it," she hissed across the table. "I'm a grown woman."

Her dad pinned her with a stare that used to have her shaking in her ballet shoes when she was younger. Now it was just almost funny.

"Yes, who left the country unexpectedly without telling a single soul where she was going. Without a phone call or a goddamn text for an entire month, Sarah. Forgive me if I'm having a hard time buying this *cockamamie* story you're telling."

Or not.

Rom spoke up. "You're right, sir. That's not exactly how it happened."

Sarah whipped her head around so fast, her brains rattled. And if eyes could shoot sharp pointy objects, Rom would be full of them right now. Her glare was full of heat and fire and if he felt it, he didn't give any indication. Instead, Rom never broke eye contact with her father and Sarah had to stifle a gasp when he squeezed her shoulder and pulled her even closer, bringing her flush against his side.

"In fact, that's what we wanted to talk to you about today. I met my beauty several months ago, and ..." he turned to look at her before continuing, "... we fell madly in love and were married in secret. I'm afraid I whisked her away on an extended honeymoon and we've only just returned."

He. Did. NOT. Just. Do. That!

She opened her mouth to speak, but Rom squeezed her shoulder—hard. So in retaliation, her left hand clamped down on his rock hard thigh and squeezed as tightly as it could. *Fail.* He was unfazed and she only succeeded at cramping her fingers.

"Sarah knew you two would be upset about the lack of a proper family wedding, so you'll forgive me that it was my idea to make up the small white lie about overseas study until we could return to tell you in person."

If she thought her dad looked murderous before, if his beet-red face was any indication, he was outright homicidal now. She wouldn't be surprised if he excused himself to get the shotgun she knew he kept in his truck.

And she didn't miss her mom's attempted glance at her left hand, checking for a wedding ring, no doubt, but it was still hidden safely under the table. So instead, she slid her eyes to Rom's empty finger and then back to his face.

"We have a private appointment early this evening in Milwaukee to pick up a piece I had commissioned especially for Sarah and a matching one I had made for myself. Not that any precious metal or gem could compare to, or demonstrate, the depth of my love for your daughter."

Wow. He was goooood. He even had her damn near fooled.

His smoldering eyes shifted to hers and there was no way her parents didn't feel the chemistry. The air around them snapped and crackled and popped. *Yes, a lot like Rice Krispies, except this was deafening. And shot straight to her groin.*

Did it suddenly get hot in here?

"W – Well, honey ... that's ... wonderful," her mother finally stuttered.

Her dad said nothing, his face a stony mask of fury. And it was all aimed at Rom. Anyone else she knew would be cowering at Rom's feet by now, but not her dad. She loved her dad for loving *her* so much. Not for the first time, she was so grateful for her parents.

"Daddy, I—"

Rom interrupted. *Again.* He was simply maddening. "Henry ... may I call you Henry?" Without waiting for a response, he continued, "Henry, I know this may seem sudden to you, but I assure you, Sarah and I are *destined* to be together." Once again his molten eyes locked on

152

hers. "I've waited a lifetime for her and I didn't intend to wait a moment longer to make her mine."

Ah ... check please.

Everyone melted away, including her parents. The words were said for her parents benefit, but he meant *every single one* of them for her. Only her. And because of his obvious inability to discuss his feelings, he took advantage of this roundabout to do not only that, but give her a plausible excuse for her long absence.

"Well then ... welcome to the family. I guess," her dad reluctantly snapped. Even her overprotective father couldn't deny the passion that arched live between them and that the daunting and possessive Romaric Dietrich would do *anything* for his little girl.

He was still infuriating and dominant and challenging. But in that moment as their eyes held, that blurred line between crush and love became a little clearer. A little more defined.

And a lot more precarious.

Chapter 20

Sarah

Two hours later, they were back in the limo, returning to Wausau. This time, she couldn't get close enough to him. After a rocky start to their reunion, her dad warmed up to Rom enough so that at least the scowl he'd had plastered on his face for most of their time together had *nearly* disappeared by the time they'd left.

And color her surprised to discover Rom could be quite the charmer when he wanted to be. She wondered why he kept that persona buried, because that would work wonders in his efforts to woo her, versus his *Me Tarzan, You Jane* approach. Unbeknownst to him, or maybe it was intentional, he'd made up tremendous ground with her in these last two hours. So much so that she was no longer worried about going to Washington with him. She couldn't wait to discover the many complex layers that made up Romaric Dietrich, because there were many.

"Security, huh?" That's what he'd told her parents he did for a living.

"Yes. At the highest level, that is what I do, my beauty."

Huh? "I suppose."

She once again sat on his lap, but this time her head lay on his shoulder, nimble fingers stroking her long hair.

"Thank you," she mumbled.

"For?"

"For all the nice things you said. I know you did it for my parents' benefit, but I appreciate the kind words nonetheless." *Yes, she was unashamedly fishing ...*

Strong steely hands gripped her waist and suddenly her back met the cool leather seat, her prone body covered with a thick, large, muscular frame. Intense, burning eyes bored into hers as strong hands cupped her face.

"Jesus, Sarah. Is that what you think? That I said those things for *their* benefit? I don't waste words saying something I don't mean. Ever. My only regret is that we've not yet bonded and you are not yet *mine*. Fuck, I want you to be mine."

With that passion-filled statement, their lips crashed brutally together in a clash of teeth, tongue and lust as they both fought for dominance, which Rom easily won. And for once she didn't care. Every fiber of her being craved him and everything he could give her. Their hands frantically roamed each other's bodies and his erection pressed almost exactly where she needed it. She wished they had no barriers between them.

She suddenly wanted nothing more than to live a deep-seated fantasy of hers before they arrived at their destination, so as much as she didn't want to, she broke the kiss, because his tongue wasn't exactly what she wanted in her mouth. She wasn't sure when she'd have another opportunity and she unequivocally knew she wanted to live out this fantasy with Rom.

155

"Stop," she breathed. She couldn't help but smile when his hands froze. His chest heaved and he buried his face in her neck, teeth erotically scraping the fragile skin. *Holy balls that felt good.*

"Sit up." At her demand, he raised his head to look at her and must have seen the pleading in her eyes. He slowly, reluctantly rose and leaned back like a regal king. His arms spanned the back of the long seat and his legs fell apart in the way only a hot man can do while still looking ultra-sexy. God, she could scour a thesaurus for hours and not find an adequate adjective to describe how erotic this male before her was.

Never looking away from his burning gaze, she moved in front of him and knelt on the thin black carpet. The thick bulge straining his pants had her mouth watering and she couldn't wait to taste him, like she'd wanted to do this morning.

Running her hands up his brawny thighs, which could have passed as tree trunks, he tensed when they converged on his groin, but didn't quite touch his cock. His icy blues lit bright with undisguised lust and silently egged her on. She'd never felt more empowered or brazen in her life.

Taking her left hand, she lightly ran her fingernail down his steely shaft through his trousers, while undoing his belt buckle with the other. Making quick work of his button and zipper, she finally broke eye contact and peeled apart the expensive fabric to reveal the largest, thickest cock she'd ever laid eyes on.

Holy ... Holy. There were no words.

Again … she may not have a lot of experience, but what twenty-four year old hasn't had a gander, or two, or ten, at Playgirl? She used to think there was quite a bit of photo doctoring at play in those magazines, because surely no male could be *that* big. But if they *were* adjusted, then the editors may want to aim a *lot* higher, because Rom put every single one of those well-endowed male models to shame.

He already had several drops of pre-cum shining on his purplish bulbous head and her glands salivated to lap it up. She was so primed, if she put a finger to her clit, she'd instantly explode, but this wasn't about her. It was about him.

Not waiting a second longer, she grabbed his massive, veiny erection in both hands and brought him into her mouth, greedily licking his salty, manly goodness. Releasing him with a pop, she ran her tongue up and down his impressive length before taking him back in and swirling the head, paying attention to his sensitive underside.

"Fuuuuck, Sarah," Rom rumbled in agonizing pleasure. His hand wound almost painfully in her long mane, and he thrust deeply, hitting the back of her throat, causing her to gag slightly, but once again she didn't care. She wanted to give herself over to him. Completely.

She should have probably thought this through a bit more, because she'd only done this one other time and it hadn't exactly been her finest sexual moment. But she didn't need to worry because Rom, as usual, took the reins and fucked her mouth with intent and purpose. When she

157

looked up, he was openly watching her, desire glazed eyes at half-mast.

Damn, her man was hot.

"Your mouth is sin," he rasped. He had swelled even more right before he picked up the pace. She looked back down, until his next words had her eyes flicking back to his.

"Watch me, beauty. Watch what you do to me," he thickly demanded.

Low curses spilled under his breath and his head fell back as seconds later his hot release spurted violently at the back of her throat. His orgasm seemed to go on forever and she luxuriated in her feminine prowess to bring him to such a blissful state. Worshipfully, she brought him down from his euphoric high. His hands loosened their death grip on her hair follicles and he scooped her off the floor to straddle his lap, not bothering to tuck himself away.

"I need to watch you fall apart," he murmured against her swollen lips. Undoing her shorts, he pushed them down, but she had to climb off his lap to remove them completely. Instead of staying seated, Rom slid onto the floor and laid on his back, right between her now spread legs and bared sex, all the while holding her gaze with a devilish gleam in his eye.

"What are you doing?" she whispered breathlessly.

"I'm hungry," he replied, grabbing her hips and pulling her down onto his waiting mouth.

"Ahhh, Rom," she cried out, throwing her head back as he speared his tongue deep in her slick channel. Holding her firm, he impaled her on his mouth over and over again. He relentlessly drove her higher, and she was already wound so tight from having him in her mouth that the second his thumb circled her clit she exploded on a wail and shamelessly ground her pelvis into his face.

This was the second time today that he'd given her a mind-melting orgasm and although it should be enough, it almost wasn't. She'd never wanted a man to take her as much as she did at this moment. And she didn't care that they were in a clichéd limousine that you wouldn't want to take a black light to, or that the driver surely heard her just scream like a banshee.

"Sarah …" He whispered her name on a long reverent breath before sliding her down his body and taking her mouth in a soft, slow kiss. God, she never loved her name more than when it fell like a prayer from his wicked tongue.

And in a dozen lifetimes she knew she would never tire of it.

Chapter 21

Rom

Love. The all-consuming act of caring for another person so profoundly, so fiercely, so *bone-deep*, it wasn't even in the terrifying realm of possibility to imagine your life without them walking beside you every day of your life.

Love. The emotion he could finally admit he'd felt blossoming from the second he laid eyes upon Sarah.

Love. What he madly, achingly wanted from *her* in return.

She was his life.

His savior.

His redemption.

And he was falling hard for her. Desperately, terrifyingly, head-over-heels in love. What he'd felt for Seraphina wasn't a thousandth of what he felt for Sarah. He felt reborn, reawakened.

Whole.

Spending the last two hours with Sarah and her parents was surreal. He hadn't intended to say the things he did, but they flowed without thought from somewhere deep inside him. The words felt right and by the end of their visit, he knew that their relationship had turned a corner.

When they'd gotten in the car, she'd climbed on his lap and snuggled of her own accord. That one little action warmed his soul.

They were still ten minutes outside of Wausau and after the sweetest mouth to ever wrap around him, his cock was still throbbing. He wanted nothing more than to shove down her shorts again and bury it inside her slick heat. Her scent was driving him out of his fucking mind.

"Are you ready to go back to our home, my beauty?"

She smiled and nodded. "Yes. But I think I need to pack a bag."

"Everything has been taken care of. You won't need a thing."

His phone rang for the fourth time in the last three hours. It was just Dev and he didn't want to do anything but spend uninterrupted time with Sarah, so he silenced it again and turned it off for the rest of the day.

"Shouldn't you get that?"

"No." He kissed the tip of her nose. "You can call your sisters when we get there, but we'll go directly from Wausau."

"Okay." Her eyes shifted down and he lifted her chin with his finger.

"What's wrong, beauty?"

"Nothing." At his arched brows, she added, "I'm just nervous, that's all."

"Are you afraid of me, Sarah?" Jesus, he hoped not.

"No, no. That's not it. I just … I don't know."

"I'm nervous, too," he confessed. And damn if that wasn't the truth. He was exhilarated and terrified at the same time.

A shy smile turned her lips. "You? Nervous?"

He snickered. "Yes. I don't want to fuck up again," he admitted.

Placing her hands on his cheeks, she pressed her lips to his. "You will. You're a guy." She winked. "But as long as you don't lock me up, we'll work through it."

Putting his forehead to hers, he confessed, "I don't want to lose you, Sarah."

"You won't, Romaric."

She wrapped herself around him. Nothing had ever felt as good as she did in his arms. He clung to her fiercely until they arrived at the dealership, where they returned the rented limo.

Then he flashed them to his palatial estate in northern Washington, where he planned to ramp up his courting and convince her to bond with him as soon as possible.

Chapter 22

Mike

They'd spent the last forty-eight hours together and it was sheer bliss. He couldn't remember being happier in his whole life. Giselle had been able to procure quite a bit of information from the records recovered during the raid on Xavier, so they at least had a starting point, albeit full of holes, to begin researching Sarah Hill's lineage. Giselle could have easily done this on her own, but the fact that she *wanted* his help filled him with all sorts of very unmanly, mushy thoughts. And he didn't give a flying fuck.

They'd split their time between research and doing normal 'couple' things, like watching TV, taking walks, talking and cooking. He even taught—or *tried* to teach—her how to play *Destiny*, his new favorite Xbox game. He was quite sure she was better at killing in real life than she was with a controller. She just plain sucked. And since she was ultra-competitive, she'd finally gotten so mad she refused to play anymore.

And though she'd slept in his bed for the last two nights, always letting her take the lead, they never did anything more than heavy petting. He wanted her with a voracious need—*all* of her— but he would wait until she gave the green light. He'd also debated asking her questions about her past, about what happened when Xavier took her, but he hadn't wanted to shatter the fragile comradery they'd developed. He'd rather not know and keep her here, than ask and have her run.

They'd each spent the afternoon doing research and making phone calls. Since these women would have been missing before the Internet, they had to do most of this the old fashioned way. Giselle had retrieved her laptop, so they were pulling double duty. They had a surprising amount of information to go on, as the medical staff serving that sick motherfucker had kept very detailed records of each woman taken. Pictures. Blood work. Area of the country from which they were abducted. Even DNA, once that became available in the late 70s and early 80s.

But the critical pieces of information they didn't have were specifically related to Xavier's fertilizations, as those records were a lot less accurate. Guess he'd wanted all traces of his inadequacies eradicated. And, they had no names of the missing. Each woman was assigned a number instead, like the sick little science experiments they were. It was disgusting.

So because they had no names and were still missing many records, they had their work cut out for them. This puzzle could take months to solve, if they ever could, but he also didn't care. As long as it allowed him time to spend with Giselle, he, quite frankly, hoped it took years. Or decades.

Yesterday they'd narrowed down the women that were still captive around the time Sarah was born and with the pictures, could clearly remove those women that, due to nationality differences, couldn't have possibly been her biological mother.

That left them with four. Three of the four were from the Midwest and the other's origin was just general East Coast. They'd both agreed to concentrate first on the local three, as it made more sense they would have been taken to the closest holding facility. And two of those three were fairly strong possibilities, both with features that were similar to Sarah's.

"Okay, I've emailed all three pictures to about two dozen major PD's in the Midwest. Let's see if we get any hits on those, then we'll start moving to smaller communities next," he said, yawning and cracking his sore neck.

They needed names. Their plan after that was to hack into medical records to see if they could get a hit on blood types, or at least exclude any, and if they were really lucky, DNA. It was all a long shot and he wasn't hopeful they'd have any success.

"You hungry?" he asked, turning toward her. It was after 6:00 p.m. and they'd only had a light lunch. He was starved. For more than just food if he was honest.

She froze, swallowing thickly. When she turned toward him, there was a glow in her bright blues that he'd only seen when she was aroused. Quicker than he could process, she was out of her chair and headed toward the front door, without a word.

"Hey, where the hell are you going?" he yelled, jumping up to follow.

She had the front door half way open by the time he reached her and he slammed it shut with his right hand, while spinning her to face him with his left, her back now flush with the wood.

"What the fuck, Giselle?"

"I ... I need to go out for while."

The vibe she threw off was disturbing. "What for?" he growled through gritted teeth, even though he had a good goddamn idea.

And that would happen over his dead body.

"I'll be back in a bit," she countered.

"What is this really about, Giselle?" Anger rose by the second, until her eyes strayed to his neck. Fury quickly morphed to white-hot lust and his cock turned hard as a steel rod.

Still holding onto her arm, he drug her to the couch, sat and pulled her astride his lap.

"It will be me or no one," he gritted out. He couldn't even believe he was saying this, or— *Jesus*—how *much* he wanted it, but the thought that she would take another man's blood made him shake with unbridled rage.

"I ... I don't th—"

"Be quiet, Giselle." He grabbed her face firmly between his hands. "The thought of your mouth anywhere near another man, let alone *on* him, makes me fucking murderous."

Her breathing sped up. Her eyes shifted between his throbbing pulse and lust-glazed eyes, checking for the truth of his words. Moving her head to his neck, he muttered, "God help me. I want this, baby."

Then her hot mouth was upon his, her kiss ravenous. They were a flurry of hands and heat and passion. Before he knew it, his shirt was off and his cock was out of its denim confines, being stroked from root to tip for the first time in her strong grip. *Fuck.* If it was like this every time, he'd gladly serve her three square liquid meals a day.

Wet lips trailed eagerly up his neck, sucking hard on his carotid. What he wouldn't give to have that suction on his aching shaft instead. She struck so quick, all he felt was a fleeting sting before the most intense, euphoric pleasure ever known to mankind flooded his body, setting off an instant and violent orgasm.

"Jesus Christ, Giselle," he cursed, his hips bucking uncontrollably.

His left hand held her head in place, her lips tightly to his flesh as his right joined hers in milking his cock of every last drop of seed. All too soon he felt the forceful pulls stop and then she erotically ran her tongue across his skin. If men were multiple orgasm creatures that would have set him off again.

Completely spent, his head fell back against the couch and his heavy eyes drifted shut. Giselle's lips feathered across his jawline up to his mouth and he barely had the energy to kiss her back.

"Are you okay," she asked tentatively and he laughed.

"Ah, yah. Fucking brilliant."

Resting her head on his shoulder, they sat in contented silence. He felt the beat of her heart against his chest and the heat of her breath against his skin and was suddenly completely overwhelmed with the love he felt for her. So much so that he couldn't keep it in if he'd tried. He braced himself for her reaction as he bared his vulnerable soul for only the second time in his life.

"I love you, Giselle," he whispered.

Chapter 23

Sarah

She couldn't believe her eyes. Rom's house was simply incredible. It wasn't nearly as big as Dev's, but it felt more like a home. While the house was set high on a hill, trees as far as the eye could see surrounded it entirely as if it'd simply been dropped from the sky directly in the middle of the thick forest. The floor plan was open, with a large kitchen, main room and dining area all sharing the same enormous space. All four walls were made up entirely of windows, which made for an absurd sight.

"The view here is stunning," she said as she stared into the multi-faceted green gorge.

"It is." His words feathered against her nape causing goose bumps to spread like wildfire in dry brush. She hadn't realized he stood so close, craning her neck to look at him. He watched her with blatant desire and she knew the view he was referring to wasn't Mother Nature.

"Oh." No smart or flip retort would come fast enough.

"Come. Let's finish the tour."

So far they'd been through two levels of the three-story house, which she'd put at about ten-thousand-square feet. The lower level consisted of a typical male's dream. A giant game room held a pool table, massive big screen TV and a huge bar. The workout room had every piece of equipment ever made, an indoor pool and sauna rounded out that level. The main floor simply held the kitchen, main living and dining spaces, Rom's office, a bedroom and two bathrooms.

"What, no super-secret underground tunnels to show me?" she asked as he ushered her upstairs. According to Kate, both Dev's old estate and new one had massive underground tunnels and that's where he held the majority of his meetings with the lords.

"No, beauty. Unlike Dev, I do not like to conduct business in my personal space. No one is allowed here except my staff and security detail." As they reached the top of the stairs, his large frame pinned her smaller one solidly against the wall. "And you, my Moira," he breathed, nuzzling her check.

Heady desire drowned all common sense as she turned her head to capture his mouth.

"Christ, Sarah," he murmured against her swollen lips when they'd come up for air a couple of minutes later. "You're going to be the death of me."

Stepping back, he looked unsure of what he wanted to do next. Shred her clothes and take her hard against the wall *(for the record, her vote at this point would be hell yes)*, or ... well taking her against the wall was all he really looked like he wanted to do *(still voting yes)*.

Instead, he grabbed her hand and walked so fast, she practically had to run to keep up.

"Bedroom," he uttered as he opened the door closest to their right, not even stopping so she could actually *see* it.

"Bedroom," he clipped as he opened the next door up the hallway. Again not stopping. "Bathroom." He pointed to a third closed door on their right as they traveled a bit further down.

That's it. There were only four doors on this level and they stood before the last set of cream-colored closed French doors to their left, about two thirds of the way down. As Rom opened them, he stood back for her to enter first and the sight before her was nothing she could have possibly imagined.

The master suite clearly took up half of the upstairs space and was so spacious, even the oversized king bed straight ahead looked small from here. The left wall was once again floor to ceiling windows and she didn't see any blinds, so she wondered how Rom slept because even the moonlight would be very bright.

A sitting area lay just to the right. Also with floor to ceiling windows, it was a cozy nook area that was half walled off from the rest of the room. On the half wall was a large bookcase that was stuffed and clearly in no order, as Dev's library was. Which surprised her. As organized as she imagined Rom would be, clutter didn't seem to be his thing. An overstuffed black leather chair and sofa completed the area. That seemed to be a theme with Rom. His house was done almost entirely in black and white.

As they walked further into the showy room, he took her into the first room on the right, which turned out to be a giant walk-in closet, probably the size of the living room in her childhood home. Both sides clearly held Rom's clothes and she couldn't help but notice not one pair of jeans in sight. *Damn.*

"Do you own anything but stuffy dress clothes?"

"You don't like the way I dress?" Surprise laced his voice.

Turning around, she quickly added, "Oh no. I mean, yes. Yes, I love the way you dress, but I just didn't know if you ever did casual, you know? Jeans, tight, stretchy t-shirts, gym shorts?"

"No. I'm in a position of power, Sarah. I must dress the part."

She couldn't help the laughter that escaped.

"What's so funny?"

"Nothing," she giggled. "Okay, that's not true. Do you really think a pair of denims and a t-shirt will diminish the power and danger and control that rolls off you in terrifying, almost paralyzing, waves?"

Confusion drew his brows together.

"The answer is no." She winked. Turning, she walked further into the spacious area and was surprised when there was a left turn. What she saw pulled her up short. There were hundreds of shoes lining the lengthy wall from top to bottom. And not just men's shoes. There were women's shoes as well. She turned back toward Rom, knowing she looked perplexed.

"They are yours."

"Mine?" Tears gathered in her eyes at his completely over-the-top gesture.

"Yes. I told you that you'd have everything you need here."

He grabbed her hand and led her through the second part of the walk-in, reserved just for her. She even had her own entrance. The entire space was filled with more shirts, pants, jeans, dresses, skirts and lingerie than she could ever wear.

"Rom, this is too much. I don't need all this," she rasped through the thick lump now residing smack in the middle of her throat.

"It's non-refundable. You must keep it." He pulled her into his arms, kissing the top of her head.

"Thank you." It didn't seem like nearly the right thing to say, but she had no words.

"Come. We're not done with the tour."

Pulling her out of the closet, he showed her the bathroom, which was also ridiculously big. He could throw a huge party in this bathroom alone. A large black tiled walk-in shower was to her left and a long black marble counter with a double sink was to her right. And at the far end of the room was a large white sunken tub with four black pillars that ran to the ceiling. You had to walk up three steps to get into the monstrosity. She could imagine sitting in that tub with a glass of champagne, leaning naked against Rom in the

173

warm bubbly water after they'd made love in it, gazing out the grand glass lined wall into the black inky, star-lit night.

"Sarah, stop," he growled, sounding as if he was in pain.

She turned. "Stop what?"

"Stop your lurid thoughts. You're making this very difficult for me to follow your pacing when you think such things."

"You can hear what I'm thinking? *Every* thought?" she asked incredulously. He was *shitting* her.

A low rumble sounded in his back of his throat. "Many. From the moment we met."

"How?" *This was so bad.*

He cupped her cheek. "Because you are my Moira and our bodies and souls are bound tightly."

"Oh." She frowned. "What if I don't want you to hear me?"

"I'd like to say when we bond that you'll get stronger and may be able to shield your thoughts, but I don't know if that's the case. I'm very old and very powerful."

She took a few steps back, out of his reach. "Well, that's not fair. I want to hear your thoughts too then." *That's not fair? What was she, a whiny little sissy girl?*

A dark, lascivious, wicked grin turned his beautifully sharp features even more so. "Are you sure you want to hear my thoughts, beauty. Because they are not clean. They are not flowery. And they are definitely *not* G-fucking-rated."

He stalked toward her and she moved back until her butt hit the cold countertop. She could hardly breathe. Standing so close she had to crane her neck to maintain eye contact, he ran a single finger down her cheek, her skin tingling in its wake.

"You want to know what I'm thinking, Sarah? Hmmm?"

Hmm ... it was a coin flip, really.

He smirked, leaning down so he was inches from her now flaming face. "I'm thinking so many lewd and lascivious things."

Their bodies were but a hair's breadth from each other, yet all that touched were his lips to the shell of her ear as he spoke. Every wicked word made her panties drip more and they were already pretty uncomfortable from earlier in the day.

"I want to fuck you stupid while I take my fill of your sweet, honeyed blood that's driving me absolutely mad. I want to take you in *every single way* a male can, Sarah. I want to bury my fingers in your soaking pussy, which is intoxicating me even now, and have you ride them until you come harder than you ever have in your life."

His tongue snaked out, startling like a bite.

"I want you sobbing and begging to be mine when I'm fucking you on this cold marble counter, taking my essence into your body so you're tied to me for all of eternity. And I want all of that Right. Fucking. Now."

Oh. My. God. Yeeees.

Every word he uttered caused the flutters in her stomach and pussy to go wild with want. Grabbing her hips firmly, he slowly ground his hardened erection into her midsection.

"But I won't do any of that until you are sure. Until you are ready. You will not get my *impressive* cock inside your sweet, tight body until you agree to be mine, my beauty."

Throwing her words back at her? So not cool.

His restraint must be ironclad, because after that over-sharing he simply nipped her earlobe—hard—and took a step back. A smug, knowing smirk turned up his dirty-talking lips as they stared at each other.

Clearing her throat, she asked, "So, um ... where's *my* room?"

Really Sarah? Really?

His eyebrows arched and she knew. *This* was her room. The room she was sharing with Rom.

Oh boy.

Chapter 24

Rom

Lying beside her all night had been excruciating. His dick was so hard it throbbed in angry retribution. She'd protested the fact that they were sleeping in the same bed, but he promised to "be a good boy, leaving her virtue intact until she was ready to gift it to him." That earned him a slug to the arm. Although it hadn't hurt, she had a pretty damn good right hook. He even went to bed fully clothed, for fuck's sake. He'd eventually convinced her to just lay with him and after she relaxed, she quickly fell asleep in his arms. It was both sublime heaven and torturous hell and he'd had to force himself not to reach for his cock many times throughout the night.

He should have gotten up to work, as he was sorely behind, but he couldn't bear to leave her side. Jaz had purchased Sarah several little sleep sets that were far too conservative for his liking. He'd have to scold her later. If he had it his way, she would have been naked. If he had it his way, she'd be naked *all* the time when they were in their home.

He was so close to the prize he could *taste* it. He'd already worked out his plans for today. Horseback riding. He wanted her to envision this as her home. What was his was now hers.

He'd give her two days, tops.

Then she would be his. Until death parted them.

"Is the security detail in place?"

"Yes, my lord," Circo replied. "Exactly as ordered."

He'd gotten up early to meet with Circo, leaving Sarah to sleep. He should have checked his voice mails, but he'd leave that until this evening. If anything urgent had arisen, Circo would know.

"Anytime I cannot be with Sarah, then Jareth and Elliot are not to leave her side."

"Yes, my lord," Circo replied. "I have a couple of updates that I've been managing since you've been … otherwise detained." Otherwise detained … interesting choice of words. Circo was always very politically correct. One of the many reasons he was Rom's second for so long. Rom simply didn't have either the patience or inclination to be PC.

"The San Francisco Bay location has a two-week delay on construction. There was an issue with the granite order. The Las Cruces build is running a bit ahead of schedule. Opening is still on track for November first and I've selected several resumes for management that look promising. Those are on your desk for review. There was also a security issue at the local Seattle club last week, but the offender had been taken care of and banned from that premises, as well as all others."

Christ. Generally he spent several hours a day in his office and visited each of his clubs at least once per week. Showing your face in your own establishments was not only good business, but kept those in his employ in line. All of whom had to be wondering what the fuck was going on with him, but clearly Circo had been taking care of things in his stead. And he was grateful.

"Anything else?"

"No, my lord."

Rom nodded and Circo wordlessly departed.

He was at the kitchen counter with his laptop, responding to his many overdue work emails when Sarah walked in about an hour later.

"Good morning," he said, closing his computer. Now that she was awake, she would receive his full attention.

"Good morning."

She wore a robe over her pajamas. Damn Jaz. Why would she buy garments that cover up Sarah's beauty? He would find and burn them all.

"How did you sleep?" He held out a hand and was happy when she walked around the island, letting him draw her into his arms.

"Better than I have in a long time."

He smiled inwardly. "I'm glad," he said, kissing her temple. "I have something I'd like to show you after breakfast."

"What?" She pulled back and he could sense her trepidation.

"It's a surprise. Go shower and then we'll eat." He swatted her fine, pert ass and she squealed, heading back toward the stairs. He loved this Sarah. She was sweet and compliant. Why couldn't she be like that all the time?

179

An hour later they were at the stables and Sarah's mouth wouldn't close.

"You have horses. A *lot* of horses," she mumbled.

"Yes."

"I love horses."

"I know."

She smiled brightly and it filled his heart with light and goodness and joy. Jesus, she was perfect for him and he couldn't keep his eyes off her.

They walked from stall to stall where the horses were kept. As soon as they were done here, he'd have them taken to the pasture. She stopped to feed, pet and talk softly to each one, getting to know them individually. His Moira was simply the most magnificent creature he'd ever encountered.

When they reached the last stall, to his most prized possession, his nerves tingled. Vampires didn't have traditional wedding bands, like humans. They used their mating marks to identify ownership, and when he'd told her parents he'd commissioned a piece for her, it got him thinking. He didn't want to give her meaningless jewelry, and he didn't think Sarah was the blood diamond type anyway. He wanted to give her something of *meaning*. Something that was dear to him. And there was nothing better than his favorite pure black Arabian, Frumusețe.

After but minutes, Frumusețe was as in love with Sarah as she was with him. And he understood why. Sarah had an undeniable magnetism that simply drew in any creature in that came in contact with her. In her presence, they basked in light and warmth and kindness. They pulled their strength from hers.

"He's magnificent," she gushed.

"He's yours."

"What? Rom, no. He's too much."

"Sarah. No arguments. He's yours." When it looked like she would continue her fruitless efforts, he put a finger to her lips. "I *want* to do this. *Let* me do this. Please."

Delight emanated from her face. "Okay. Thank you. What's his name?"

"Frumusețe."

"Wow. That's beautiful. What does it mean?" She couldn't look away from the magnificent animal in front of her and he couldn't tear his eyes from *her*.

"It means beauty."

At that, he heard her sharp intake of breath. She slowly tilted her head to him. "He's yours, isn't he?"

"They are all mine, Sarah."

Turning fully toward him now, she'd completely forgotten about the horse. "No. I mean he's your favorite."

He nodded slightly.

"Why would you give me your favorite horse?"

He backed her against the rustic wood planks of the empty stall next to Frumusețe and held her face in his hands. As her breaths became ragged, he let his thumb brush her parted, full bottom lip.

"The better question is what *wouldn't* I give you, my beauty?"

He leaned down, skimming his nose along her jawline, inhaling her heady scent, which went straight to his pounding cock. After their little encounter in the bathroom yesterday, he was ready to explode. He'd never wanted to bed a female more than Sarah.

"Rom ... you're making this very hard," she said breathlessly.

Grabbing her hand, he entwined their fingers and placed them together on his steely shaft, rubbing firmly down his length. "I would concur." Nipping the sensitive flesh beneath her ear, her breathy moan sounded an awful lot like *yes*.

Christ, he'd never felt pleasure like he had at her hands and mouth yesterday in the car. He longed to rip her clothes off and take her right here, right now.

Never stopping the up and down movement with their locked hands, he whispered, "I told you I would do everything in my power to make you mine. And I intend to keep my word."

He slowly traced her lobe with his tongue before pulling back and removing their hands from his cock. It was cruel to them both, but he needed to leave her wanting, aching, unfulfilled. Like him. When he finally took her body, he would take all of her. He wouldn't be able to hold back from bonding and in the heat of passion she would agree, only later to regret it. The need was *that* fierce, *that* strong, *that* overpowering that once he slid home, he wouldn't be able to control his animal nature that had been clawing to break free since the moment he laid eyes on her.

Mine, mine, mine, it clamored, louder with each passing second he was denied his mate. Sarah had no fucking idea how violently he'd been battling his beast. He swore he wouldn't lock her up again, but that's all he could think about. He wanted to lock her up and take her repeatedly until she acquiesced to bond with him. But the man in him, the one that'd listened to Dev and Damian, knew doing so would be a fatal blow to their future, so he would bide his time and battle his demon. For her.

And as much torture as it may be for Sarah, it was a hundredfold for him. Tonight, he would, once again, lie in bed beside her sweet, sexy sleeping form and have to keep his hands and cock to himself. He ought to win some fucking prize for his restraint. Like a Pulitzer.

She's your prize, his beast roared. How right he was. A throat cleared and he turned his head.

"My apologies, my lord," Cyri said, head slightly lowered. He'd asked him to meet them in the stables, but damn if he just didn't want to send him away instead. He wasn't ready to share Sarah with anyone.

"Cyri. This is Sarah. Sarah, Cyri. He works for me, mostly keeping these fine animals in tip top shape."

Sarah moved around him, extending her hand. "Nice to meet you Cyri."

183

"Yes, my lady."

"Oh God, please do *not* call me that. Sarah is just fine."

Cyri shifted his eyes to Rom, waiting for his approval. He shrugged his shoulders. It didn't really matter what Sarah requested. She was his intended mate and Cyri was very old school. He would never refer to Sarah by name. It would always be ma'am or my lady. It almost made him laugh, because he could envision Sarah getting very bent out of shape about something so inconsequential.

"Yes ma'am."

Sarah opened her mouth, but Rom intervened. "Cyri, we'd like to go riding. Saddle Zephyr for me and Frumuseţe for Sarah. He is hers now."

Cyri's eyes widened slightly, but quickly recovered, slightly smiling. "Yes, my lord. Right away."

Rom had pulled his entire staff together early this morning when he woke and made sure they were all aware he'd found his Moira and she was to be treated with the respect and reverence she deserved. She was to be given anything she desired and above anything else, she was to be protected with their lives, as they would give for his. Cyri was particularly happy for him, having been with Rom nearly as long as Circo, over three hundred years. And he knew how much Rom treasured Frumuseţe, so he understood how much his gift really meant.

Today, Rom would spend the day showing Sarah his life here in Washington. What *her* life would be like when she agreed to bond. They'd talk, they'd ride and they'd learn more about each other.

But tomorrow all bets were off, because by tomorrow at nightfall ... he wouldn't take no for an answer any longer.

Chapter 25

Sarah

They'd spent several hours riding and her ass and thighs were protesting. It had been many years since she'd ridden and she hadn't realized how much she really missed it. When she was a teenager, she'd begged her parents for a horse, but horses were expensive, as were stabling them. So she did the next best thing, volunteered at a horse ranch just outside of town.

She'd spend hours there every Saturday and Sunday, grooming, brushing and exercising them. She loved it. Then Jack became sick and both money and time were scarce. And after he died, it suddenly didn't seem so important any more. Once she headed off to college, she became entrenched in college life, her love of horses all but forgotten.

When they'd returned from riding, Rom insisted they watch a movie.

"What do you like?" she'd asked.

"I don't watch movies. You pick." He played with her hair, tickling her shoulders as he watched her.

"Help me out a little. You at least have to know the genre of movie you like. Horror? Mystery? Shoot'em-up? Fantasy?"

"Hmm … definitely fantasy," he replied in a low murmur before her back was on the couch and his mouth was on hers.

Just like in the limo, they made out for several minutes, but he never took things further. Finally, he sat back up and made her select a movie.

So to get him back, she'd selected Basic Instinct, which had sorely backfired for her, because now she couldn't get sex off the brain. Not that it had been that far anyway, but she'd blown her chance to divert her thoughts for at least a couple of hours.

He'd teased her all day and subsequently denied her. And he wasn't as sly as he thought. She knew exactly what he was up to. Leave her aching with raging desire until she not only gave him her body, but her soul as well. Until she agreed to bond with him.

And damn him ... it was working! Every single raunchy word he'd spewed rattled around in her brain. Every look set her body on fire anew. Every caress left her breathless and needy. Every part of her ached to be possessed and owned by him. She could literally think of nothing else.

Gah! She'd turned into a nympho and she hadn't even had sex with him yet.

Her world had turned completely on its ear and she felt like she'd lived a lifetime in just the last two weeks alone since she'd met Rom. And for some reason, for the last several days her kidnapping was never too far from her thoughts and it bugged her. Because that's also what led her here, to this magnificent male.

Feeling very overwhelmed, after they finished eating dinner, she'd called Kate and talked to her for over an hour. Kate grounded her. In addition to being her sister, she'd been her counselor over the last several months. There was no way Sarah would be where she was today without her. She'd probably still be locked in her room, trying to fight the nightmares on her own.

After finishing her call, she now sat alone on the expansive balcony, off the master bedroom. A covered hot tub was just steps outside the glass doors and her glass of Merlot sat untouched on the table beside her. She listened to the sounds nature made and enjoyed watching the thousands of fireflies lighting up the night sky. Sarah had never seen anything so beautiful in all her life and she instantly knew why Rom lived here. It was peaceful and serene and soothing.

Surprisingly, her impromptu counseling session tonight actually centered on her kidnapping and not the current situation she found herself in. She knew she'd give into Rom. Eventually. Well ... soon probably. The pull was simply too strong and she was too enthralled with him to deny her feelings much longer. He'd been nothing but attentive the last couple of days. Regardless of his sometimes gruff, commanding and downright scary demeanor, his soft, giving and fiercely loyal side had stolen her heart and she was more than falling in love with him already. When she thought of the future, it was him.

Picking up her wine, she took a sip, thinking back to the night she was saved from a horrific fate by an unlikely, and still unknown, ally.

Her cell door opened and a large, imposing man stepped in. Only this time, he didn't have a tray of food with him. He stood there, gazing at her with unmistakable lust in his eyes. Oh God. She began to sob uncontrollably.

"Come," he barked.

Shaking her head, she crouched further into the corner, wishing she could melt into the concrete wall. Nonononono. This cannot be happening. He took two steps before he was on her, dragging her over his shoulder in a fireman's carry. She screamed and fought, hitting and scratching his back. She kicked her feet, trying to ram her knees into his chest. Suddenly, calm flooded her and her body went limp. Deep within she was still petrified and wanted to fight back, but couldn't get her body to respond in kind.

He carried her down a series of hallways, leading into what looked to be a sterile, surgical room of some sort. There were several other men milling about, getting equipment ready, checking monitors. There was a covered surgical tray next to a steel table, to which her captor deposited her upon. The steel table had a cutout on the lower half, which would allow someone to step in directly between her legs. Holy Jesus. This was not happening.

The men began to restrain her hands and feet. Fear broke through the calm façade and she began screaming and fighting once again, managing to kick one of the men in the mouth, causing him to bleed. Yet again, she was overcome with a sense of calm and stopped writhing. They finished tying her down, even though her mind was pleading with her to fight.

"What the fuck, John. Keep the whore under control," said the man with a hideous scar running from the corner of his right eye to the top of his clavicle; who was now bleeding profusely from his mouth, thanks to her.

"I am, fuckwad. She's strong and keeps fighting it."

After they had her completely restrained, at their mercy, they went back to ready themselves for whatever they'd planned to do. One of the men suddenly came at her with a large knife and a cruel smirk on his otherwise handsome face.

Oh, God.

Inside, she cried and pleaded with them not to hurt her. Outside, she said nothing, sickened with her compliance. He lowered the tip of the sharp knife to her breast and circled her areola through the dirty tank. She held her breath, paralyzed with terror.

He teased the knife dragging it down her stomach to the top of her plain cotton panties. His eyes were dark with lust. Tears ran unbidden down her face, into her ears. All of a sudden he flicked the knife expertly upwards and sliced her tank in half, taking her bra with it. There wasn't a nick on her that she could tell, or feel. He removed her underwear in the same manner, pulling the shreds of clothing out from beneath her prone body.

She was completely naked now, strapped spread eagle on a steel surgical table. She had lain like this for what seemed like an eternity, but probably hadn't been more than ten or fifteen minutes, before a short, pudgy, balding man with black-rimmed glasses entered the room. He carried a clipboard and was furiously taking notes on it. He looked at her with no emotion, or lust, like the other men. Walking around the table, he regarded her body like she was nothing more than a science experiment.

"Hello. I'm Dr. Marcus Shelton. There's no reason to be afraid, dear. You are very special to our cause. Cooperate and it won't hurt. Much."

Tears flowed freely down her face like a river. "Please just let me go. I won't tell anyone what happened. I promise."

"Aw, I'm afraid I can't do that. We need you."

The other men in the room started gathering around the table where she was bound. There were five in total. They all began to undress.

"No!!! Please, please ... no!!!"

One of them held a syringe of some sort, giving it to the doctor. "John, if you can't control her, I'm going to have to drug her."

"I can't help it, Doc. Bitch keeps breaking through my compulsion."

"Very well, then."

Looking at her with what she thought was a slight twinge of sympathy in his eyes, it was quickly gone. Maybe she'd imagined it.

"It's okay. This will make you feel all better." He came toward her with the needle and she tried futilely to thrash and fight, but the needle painfully stabbed her arm and warmth spread from the puncture site throughout her bloodstream.

191

The doctor softly spoke to her again, circling the head of the table. He stroked her hair, whispering in her ear.

"You have been chosen by our Master for a very special cause. Vampire babies can only be conceived and carried in the human female womb." He sighed and sounded regretful in his next comment. "Unfortunately conception can't happen through any artificial means. Believe me ... I've tried."

As the drug worked its way through her system, she felt herself calm, even with the horrific things he was telling her. Vampires? Babies? What was this psycho talking about?

She now knew she would be brutally raped by several men, and there was nothing she could do to stop it. There was no white knight in shining armor coming to her rescue, like in romance novels. She would be horrifically violated in the worst possible way a woman could be, yet as the drug took hold, she stopped crying and thrashing. She felt fuzzy. Numb. Oddly detached.

He continued to whisper in her ear.

"I hear that sex with a vampire can be very pleasurable, if you let it be. This drug should let you relax enough to enjoy the pleasures these males have to offer you, dear. Let's just hope that you conceive this month. For your sake. I've been preparing you since your arrival here for this very moment. It's a kindness, actually. Without it, our chances of conception would be virtually nil and this would be far less merciful."

He continued with his babbling, as if she cared. *Conceive? None of it made any sense to her jumbled, drug-hazed brain. This was happening to someone* else, not her. Looking around the table, she noticed all of the men, except for the doctor, were now completely nude, their excitement evident. A small, pathetic sob escaped her once again.

The doctor moved to the foot of the table and nodded to scarface, who stepped between her spread legs, his thick erection bobbing.

"Take no blood," the doctor barked.

As scarface stepped closer, what she saw completely shocked and horrified her even more than what was happening to her body. Scarface's eyes glowed bright, his incisors long and sharp. Oh God. He is *a vampire. She looked at the ceiling, closed her eyes and began to pray. They may be able to take her body, but they would take nothing else from her.*

When she felt him grab onto her hips, she tried to drift to a place far, far away.

Then she heard commotion and yelling in the background and suddenly scarface's hands were gone and she was being released from her bonds by one of the largest and most handsome men she'd ever seen. What was happening? Was he taking her for himself? The drugs coursing through her system made it too hard to think. Too hard to care.

Throwing a baggy t-shirt over her naked body, the large man, whom she just knew was also vampire, carried her back to her room and placed her gently on the thin mattress.

"You'll be safe soon." He whispered the words so softly she wasn't sure if he'd actually said it or she'd made it up.

That was the last time anyone attempted to hurt her and two weeks later she was rescued by Dev's team. To this day, she didn't know who it was that'd saved her or what had become of him. Yes, he was with the bad guys, but his actions were a definite contradiction to that of someone evil. She wished she'd have gotten the opportunity to thank him but never saw him again.

Guilt ate her insides every day that she was saved and so many others weren't. Why her? What made her so special that this unknown vampire chose to save her? Why was it that she was now afforded an opportunity to be with this incredible male who so clearly cared for her and most of the other women rescued wouldn't ever be able to move past the horrific things done to them to even think about a relationship?

That's what she'd spent the last hour discussing with Kate. Survivor's guilt, Kate called it. Or a form of it anyway. They'd talked about it often during their sessions over the last few months, and she'd made tremendous progress moving past it. But after meeting Rom, all of those unwelcome feelings came roaring back with an almost suffocating vengeance and she had a difficult time putting the situation into perspective. Kate told her she wasn't allowing herself to be happy and she was spot on. Why did she deserve happiness?

Did she?

God, she *wanted* it. Happiness stood right in front of her, in the form of a sinfully handsome, intimidating and erotic warrior. And the irony that she was so drawn to a vampire, when those same creatures were responsible for the worst month of her existence was hard to wrap her head around. While she had no doubt Rom could be a monster if provoked, he was nothing like the ones that had kidnapped her. His heart was pure. His intent to protect, not hurt.

"How was your call with Kate?" The low timbre of his voice penetrated through every pore like a blossoming flower, burrowing deep and taking root within her wounded soul. She smiled inwardly. Just hearing his voice made her feel better.

"It was good." She hadn't turned to look at him standing in the doorway, afraid that if she did she'd crumble into a million pieces. The emotional razor blade she balanced on was precarious. One wrong slip and she'd be sliced open, exposing her fragile state to the one person she needed to keep it hidden from.

He walked around in front of the cushioned loveseat where she sat and held out his hand. "Let's go to bed," he said softly.

She took a deep breath, turning her head upward to meet his gaze. Instead of the heated pools of desire she thought she'd find, his eyes were filled with so much kindness and love that it was almost her undoing. She fought to control her tears, putting her hand in his and he pulled her gently into his warmth.

"Rom, I—"

"*Shhh*. Tonight I just want to hold you in my arms, my beauty."

She could only nod. Overwhelming emotions constricted her throat so tight words couldn't possibly pass. A lone tear escaped, quickly absorbed by his shirt, and that glimmer of happiness she'd seen dancing before her since she'd met Rom suddenly didn't seem so unattainable after all.

Chapter 26

Rom

He'd held her in his arms until she fell asleep, then extricated himself to get some work done, which he'd long been neglecting over the past week. If she stirred, he'd hear and be immediately by her side.

He couldn't hear her every thought, but he'd heard enough that he was in utter emotional turmoil. If every one of those fuckers was not dead, he'd be out for blood, damn any consequences. And the fact that she thought she didn't deserve happiness because she'd fared better than the other women was simply ludicrous. He'd just have to convince her of that tomorrow, because he still planned to end the day by making her his.

He had a meeting with Geoffrey in five days' time to get an update. And he'd better come through with some very comprehensive intel on Xavier's operation, because Rom's infamous patience was wearing very thin. The fact that all of the lords' mates were in danger because of that psychotic son-of-a-bitch was simply unacceptable. But the fact that Xavier had actually been the one to create each of their mates ... well ... that was something he couldn't get out of his mind and he didn't know what to make of it.

Was it some cosmic fuck-you? He didn't know. But now that he'd found his Moira, and she was in danger from him, he'd done a complete about-face. Once a proponent of imprisoning Xavier, he was now aligned with Dev and Damian to mow that fucker down once and for all. He'd never heard of a vampire being able to sire females only and it was most certainly not a coincidence that every one of the living females he had sired were dreamwalkers. Not all three of their Moiras' mothers could have been dreamwalkers, for that was far too rare.

He didn't know if anyone else had caught onto that little factoid yet, but again, it was irrelevant. Xavier's life must end. And he didn't give a flying fuck if Xavier sired both Moiras and dreamwalkers ... his life would end. They didn't need him alive to determine what made his DNA so special ... they just needed his blood. Which he'd gladly be on point to retrieve. After he cut off the fucker's head.

After two hours spent replying to emails and setting up several meetings for the following week, he reached for his cell; powering it up to check for missed calls. Rom hated cell phones. They were a necessary evil, given his responsibilities and he reluctantly admitted they made doing business much easier, but he detested being able to be reached twenty-four seven.

Checking his messages, he had a dozen, but several more missed calls. Dev had tried reaching him three times throughout the last two days, but there was only one voice message from him earlier today. That's the one he clicked on first.

"Rom, call me when you get this message. It's urgent."

Now what?

Forgoing the rest of his messages, which were also probably considered urgent by the sender, he dialed Dev instead. On the second ring, he answered.

"Rom. How's Sarah?"

"My Moira is fine. Is that what was *so* urgent?" Rom didn't need Dev or Damian shadowing him around like some prepubescent teenage nerd who needed advice every five seconds while trying to get into some female's pants. Jesus, he *did* have more moves than that.

Dev just chuckled on the other end. "No. Ronson called. Apparently Geoffrey came into Dragonfly the other night trying to get you a message since he has no other way to reach you. He asked you to meet him at Dragonfly. He'll be there at midnight each evening until you arrive. He said it's life or death."

Rom laughed. "Whose death? Because it will be his if he's not careful."

Dev was silent for several beats and a bad feeling began stirring in Rom's gut. "He asked me to mention the name Ainsley. I thought it best not to give him your number since I don't trust the fucker."

His blood froze.

"I'll take care of it."

"Everything okay?"

"Sarah and I will be back tomorrow evening. I hope I can leave her under your care while I meet with Geoffrey."

"Of course. Kate will be happy."

He disconnected the call, fear freezing him in place. Ainsley was a childhood friend of Rom's. His best friend, until he chose to leave his homeland so long ago. He'd tried convincing her to come with him, but she'd refused, claiming she couldn't leave her family behind. It was really because her family was in bed deep with his father and if she'd left, they would have suffered the price.

He'd seen her twice in the last six hundred years, both times she'd sought him out, trying to convince him to return and unseat his father. Both times, he'd adamantly refused.

The fact that Ainsley was here now, just days after he'd returned to Romania was *not* a coincidence. By not listening to his gut all along, he'd put not only *his* life in danger, but that of his Moira. Now not only did they have Xavier to contend with, but he had his mentally deranged, narcissist of a father as well.

Fuck! *What had he done?*

Chapter 27

Sarah

"Sarah, you must complete the bonding. Time is running out."

"Time's running out? What does that mean? Who are you? How do you know him?"

"That is not important now. What's important is completing the bonding. You are the only one that can save him."

"Save him? Is he in danger?" She didn't know much about Rom's skills, but she'd heard he was very powerful. The most powerful of all the lords. She doubted he could be in danger from anyone or anything.

"Yes, Sarah. Romaric is in grave danger. Your special abilities will be the key to saving him. But only if the bonding is complete."

Mystery girl started fading away. "No. No, don't go. Tell me who you are. Tell me how Romaric's in danger. Please!"

Mystery girl faded to black and Sarah bolted up in bed, a thin layer of sweat coating her skin.

"What the hell?" she whispered. She must bond with Romaric because he was in danger and she's the only one that can save him? Who the hell was this damn girl and why wouldn't she just tell Sarah? Why did she feel like every dream about her was a puzzle she was supposed to solve? And why did Sarah feel like she'd spoken the truth?

Mystery girl's words sat like a boulder in the pit of her stomach.

She just noticed Rom wasn't in bed with her. Looking at the digital clock on the nightstand, it read 5:02 a.m. Throwing back the covers, she padded quietly out of the room, down the hall and descended the stairs to the second level. To her right, she noticed a light shining from Rom's office. He was probably working and she should leave him alone, but she had this visceral need to be with him. To make sure he was all right. Which was crazy stupid, but she couldn't ignore it.

Making her way to his office, she stood quietly in the doorway, watching. Sitting in a large black leather office chair, his back was to her and it appeared he was staring out into the darkness. She listened for a few moments to be sure he wasn't on the phone and when she heard nothing, she entered.

Not waiting for an invitation, she walked in and around his desk. His eyes raised to hers and her breath caught at the fury—and *fear*—emanating from them. He silently held out his hand and not wasting a second, she grabbed on like it was her only lifeline in a choppy, unforgiving ocean. She climbed silently into his lap and curled up into his strong arms, which he'd wrapped around her.

"What happened?" Mystery girl was right. Something was terribly wrong and suddenly she was very afraid. He remained silent and she didn't think he would answer. Typical male ... trying to protect his woman.

"We need to return to Milwaukee tomorrow evening. I have an impromptu business meeting that I must attend."

"Is everything okay?"

He squeezed her tightly, stroking her bed-ravaged hair. *Lovely.* In her haste to get to him, she probably should have walked by a mirror first.

"Yes," he murmured. "Come. Let's get you back to bed."

"Will you stay with me?" She could hear the pleading in her voice, but didn't care. She'd beg him if that's what it took. She needed to be in the safety of his arms.

"Of course." Soft lips pressed gently against her temple.

Minutes later they were snuggled back in his bed, her body wrapped around his.

"Sleep, my beauty. I'll be here when you wake."

As her eyes drifted shut again, Sarah couldn't shove down the feeling that a series of events had been set into motion the second their eyes met that neither could prevent from coming to fruition.

But how would it end and what would *her* role be?

Chapter 28

Sarah

Consciousness slowly claimed her, but it took several moments to remember where she was. In Rom's bed. *With* Rom. She'd rolled away from his hard body in sleep, now facing the wall. Eyes glancing up, she noticed it was now just after 8:00 a.m. And unfortunately she'd remained dreamless. Mystery girl hadn't returned.

Dammit!

She needed more answers on this danger that awaited Rom so she could warn him. Maybe she should try anyway. That bitch, Nancy, reared her ugly head again. *"Right, Sarah. And what will you say? Some mystery girl who looks exactly like me, told me I had to bond with you to save your all-powerful ass? Oh...and tick-tock, time's a wastin'."*

Why didn't Rosie choose to appear at these times instead of that ho? Probably because that beotch usually made more sense. *Ugh*. Of course she couldn't say anything about that dream, because just like the other two, neither made a lick of sense.

Sarah thought back to Rom's tenderness last night, both on the balcony and again in his office. Did he know that those actions were the ones that endeared her to him? That each time he uttered a compassionate word, or touched her with such reverence and genuine caring, it became almost impossible to deny what her heart wanted, but what her mind fought. Her body knew, and had since day one. But her mind ... her stubborn mind had been fighting it every blessed step of the way.

She knew very few people, if any, had really seen the true Rom underneath all of his multi-faceted, complex layers. It hadn't taken her but minutes. She'd immediately seen his depth, his compassion, his sensitivity. It was there. It was just buried underneath heartache and loss and pain. And she knew *that* had everything to do with mystery girl. She just didn't understand why.

Was she falling for Rom, despite the fact her common sense urged her to slow down? *Yes.* Could she envision her life without him? *No.* Did she want to? *Hell* no. Was she ready to make a lifelong commitment when there was still so much she didn't know about him? After last night, she was much closer to the *yes* line than she had been just yesterday. And if mystery girl was right? If Sarah's stubbornness in bonding until she knew every nit and nat about him caused her to lose the one person she knew was meant for her ... would *that* push her over the yes line? Unequivocally yes.

No, she may not know every single thing about him, like his shoe size or his favorite toothpaste or whether he liked pepperoni or ham pizza best, but she knew what kind of male he was. And she knew she wanted to wake up next to him every single day she lived.

Turning over, she noticed Rom gazing at her, a pensive look creasing his oh-so-handsome features. He reached a hand out, slowly running the back of his fingers down her cheek.

"I can hardly breathe when you look at me," he rasped. "I feel like you're a figment of my imagination and if I blink you'll be gone."

Her breath caught and a sudden, ravenous hunger assailed her.

Hunger for his body.

Hunger for his blood.

Hunger to be *his*.

Not because of mystery girl. Because of Rom. Because, notwithstanding the fact that normal people didn't fall in love in less than two weeks, they weren't normal. They never were and never would be. And despite what Rom had said the other day about this being simple biologics … he couldn't be more wrong. This was so much more than physical. This was *soooo* much more than girl meets boy, kisses in a tree, falls in love, marries and lives happily ever after.

This was raw, visceral and irrefutable. They belonged together. They belonged to each other.

Not caring that she hadn't brushed her teeth or how her hair looked or even if the makeup she wore to bed was smudged, she rolled onto all fours and closed the short distance between them.

Rom's pensiveness turned to raging desire. His glacial blues dilated and began to glow. His shirt was off and her breath stopped. Her mouth went bone-dry. Holy mother … he was sin personified and sex incarnate. Imagine your masturbation fantasy came to life … and it would be him.

God, she loved ink on a man. Thick, sexy tats swirled over his right pec, down his bicep, but other than that he was free of ink, free of scars, free of a single imperfection. There was not one hidden ounce of fat on his muscular, sinewy body. The sheet he'd draped over his lower half couldn't hide the chiseled V, which led to the most perfect cock she'd ever seen ... or tasted. And it couldn't hide the fact that he was, indeed, aroused.

He watched her, watching him. She didn't miss his intake of breath when her hands traced his six-pack abs. She didn't miss his moan when her lips sucked a hard flat nipple into her mouth. And she didn't miss the hiss that escaped his lips when she told him she wanted him to fuck her.

She straddled him and eyes never leaving his, reached down to remove the little navy blue tank she'd worn to bed, leaving her only in tiny matching shorts.

His eyes raked over her nakedness, heat blazing in their fiery wake. His gaze was so potent, she swore she felt fingers feathering her oversensitive skin everywhere it landed.

"Christ, Sarah ..."

Leaning forward, she brushed his ear with her lips. "Make love to me, Rom. Please."

Her lips left a damp path down his neck and back up his strong jaw until she took his mouth with hers. She felt empowered and in control, but reckless at the same time. His mouth devoured hers as one hand palmed her neck and the other reached for her exposed breasts, tweaking one nipple first, then the other. Her hips undulated against his rock hard cock and she could think of nothing else but being possessed completely by him.

She wanted him to consume her.

Breaking the kiss, she spoke the words that had been on the tip of her tongue since she woke. "I'm ready. Make me yours."

The events that followed those five little words would be something she would reflect back on for days.

His body completely froze. His lips stopped kissing. His hands stopped touching. His hips stopped thrusting. He forced her head to rest on his shoulder. She tried moving, but he restrained her. She was completely and utterly confused.

"I think we should wait. Just a few days."

What.

The.

Fuck?

The last several days he'd been doing nothing but trying to get her to acquiesce to the bonding and now that she was, he thought they should *wait. Why?*

Pulling out of his strong grip, she searched his face for answers. "I don't understand."

He looked away, unable to hold her gaze. "I'm sorry."

Unable to control her emotions, she yelled, "Are you serious?"

"Sarah ..." he started.

Pulling free from his tight grip, she scrambled off the bed, heading for the safety of the bathroom. "No. Forget it. Forget I said a fucking thing."

"Sarah ... let me explain."

Explain? *Explain?* There was no explanation on Earth that could possibly justify the about-face that had just occurred.

"Fuck you," she shouted, slamming and locking the bathroom door. Not that it would stop him if he wanted to enter. Thankfully he didn't. She started the shower, stripped her pajama bottoms and stepped under the hot spray. Tears flowed, mixing with the scalding liquid cascading over her body.

He'd rejected her. She'd finally agreed to be his and he'd rejected her. *Why?* What happened last night that had changed things? Had he heard her thoughts on the kidnapping and what occurred that horrific night? Did he think she was tainted goods? Was he afraid she thought he was the same as those monsters who had kidnapped her? Or was it something else? Was it possibly the danger that mystery girl had referred to?

Whatever the reason, she wasn't really sure it mattered. Sinking to the cold tiled floor, she curled into a ball, letting the hot water rush over her and cried, giving into every single emotion that she'd buried for the past several months.

She cried for her parents.

She cried for herself.

She cried for a future she'd once dreamt of that would never be.

But mostly she cried for the loss of a new future, a new happiness, one she'd come to accept and even embrace with girlish giddiness. For some unknown reason that now seemed to be in jeopardy.

And she had no damn clue how to fix it.

Chapter 29

Rom

He was gutted.
He was heartbroken.
He was tortured.
He was resolved.
He was in hell.

Chapter 30

Sarah

She was lost.
She was sad.
She was confused.
She was pissed.
She was in hell.

Chapter 31

Mike

He'd woken this morning and Giselle was gone. Classic. Totally expected, yet, soul-crushing nonetheless. But surprisingly ... he wasn't mad at her. He was mad at himself. He *knew* he was moving too fast. He knew she may not be in the same place he was emotionally. Hell ... she may *never* be. Maybe he was just a shiny new plaything to her and nothing more. But even as he thought it, he knew it not to be true. The feelings she had for him could not be hidden in her expressive eyes. She just couldn't verbalize them. Therefore, he should have kept his big fucking mouth shut and maybe she'd still be here right now.

She apparently needed space, so he'd decided against texting or calling. Instead, he'd spent the entire day working on their project, contacting additional PD's and faxing pictures of the two missing women. Then about an hour ago ... pay dirt.

Marna Clark was age twenty when she went missing in Des Plains, Illinois in 1969. There were very few leads and her case quickly grew cold and eventually forgotten in favor of the newest missing person. Hundreds of thousands of people go missing each year in the United States alone and Marna quickly became a statistic, like so many others. Mike was able to get her parents' names, number and address. He'd called, but there was no answer.

Fuck it. Des Plains was only an hour and fifteen minutes from Milwaukee and since there was no reason to stick around here, he grabbed his phone, packed an overnight bag and headed to the garage. He'd sleep in a cheap motel close to their house and stop by the Clark's first thing in the morning. Talking to them in person would be better anyway. He could gauge their expressions, and more importantly see their faces. Did either of them resemble Sarah? Did they have other children that did?

He didn't really understand why Giselle was working on this project for Sarah, since Giselle wasn't really the warm and fuzzy type, but the reason didn't matter. Even if she'd decided not to come back, he would continue on his own. He'd do it for Sarah. He'd do it to keep his goddamned mind from spinning and churning.

And he'd do it in hopes that Giselle would come to her fucking senses and return to him. This time for good. Because next time she walked through that door … he wasn't letting her leave. Ever.

Chapter 32

Rom

It was 1:00 a.m. and he sat at *The Bar* waiting for Ainsley to show. His stomach churned at how he'd left things with Sarah. They'd barely spoken since she'd declared she'd wanted to bond this morning. At those words, his heart soared, but quickly crashed. He'd wanted nothing more at that moment but to bury himself deep inside her and take what she'd so freely offered. What he'd been waiting for.

Mine, mine, mine, his beast roared.

No, no, no, his logic countered.

He didn't know the right answer. He wanted her with raw animal need that bordered on insanity. But was it the right choice? Was his decision misguided? Should he confide in her and let her make her own informed choice? Maybe.

Fuck. He didn't know.

Once again, his calm, collected, decisive demeanor had escaped him and he felt truly lost for the first time in his life. And for one as old and formidable as he was, that was not a comfortable place to be.

A stunning blonde dressed all in black entered the bar bringing Rom out of his introspection. He couldn't help but smile as their eyes caught and she hurriedly made her way to him. Standing, he pulled her into his arms.

"Ainsley," he greeted as he swiftly pulled back. Even though they had more history between them than most, he still felt uncomfortable holding another female in his arms. Friend or not. Sarah was, and always would be, the only female he would ever hold again. Christ ... he'd been an absolute idiot earlier today.

"Romaric. You look good." She took a seat at the table he'd selected. Strategically placed, it afforded both of them a view of the entrance and exit, allowing each to quickly react if necessary.

They regarded each other silently until Rom spoke. "What is the plan?"

She snorted. "Your death, of course."

"How?"

"I don't know for sure, but they will surely try to trap you. Trick you using your mother so you return to Romania." She gazed at him quietly before continuing. "He knows you spoke to her. She's already been severely punished. I'm surprised she still lives."

Mother. Fucker. He would so enjoy taking his father's head.

"You look different." Her head cocked. He didn't miss her not so subtle glance at his thumb, looking for a mating mark. A smile crossed her lips. Ainsley was an extremely beautiful and desirable female and when they were children he fancied himself in love with her. The fact that she'd not met her mate to this day saddened him. "You're in love. You found her."

Rom remained quiet, unsure how to respond. Did he trust her enough? *No.*

"When?"

She chuckled, very much onto him. "Within the next month, maybe sooner. He's trying to locate someone who can find you."

"You."

"Yes."

He nodded. He'd suspected as much. So he had two weeks at most to prepare.

"What powers does he possess?"

The only down side to not staying in touch with his father, or anyone from his family, was that he didn't know what skills his father had been able to procure over the years. And since he was a ruthless, callous killer, he imagined it was many. When Rom faced a rare foe more powerful than he, knowing his weaknesses would mean the difference between life and death.

Rom was known as The Reaper in the vampire community. His skills were unmatched, except by his father. His bloodline had the unique ability to absorb and negate vampiric powers. Meaning ... if a vampire used their powers against him, he could either resist theirs or they then became his. If he harvested theirs, the other vampire didn't lose them, per se, but they would weaken permanently. How much, he wasn't sure, because he'd only left one vampire alive who'd tried. And that was his first and only mistake, which he'd quickly remedied. Any vampire who used their skill against him deserved—and was awarded—death.

His father was drunk on power. His mind warped with being the Deity he thought he was, but never would be. Early on, he'd wanted Romaric to join him, rule together, but he'd refused. He couldn't rule with someone whom he didn't have an ounce of respect for, who respected no one but himself. He'd never wanted to rule anything, so the fact that he found himself in a position of leadership in the United States was a hard pill to swallow for many years. And was a pill even more bitter for his father, who took it as a personal slight.

But they'd kept their distance, they'd keep the peace and they'd both kept their heads. But now ... now because of his foolish decision to get self-validation on something he already knew in his heart to be true, he was back on the radar and their centuries' long standoff would come to a head. And the only result would be one of their deaths. Hopefully not his. Which was why he'd rejected Sarah this morning.

Regardless of the position she'd been put in, Ainsley was trying to save his ass and he would pick every nugget of information from her brain before she left. So before he returned home to his very pissed off Moira, they spent the next two hours talking and strategizing.

He agreed to return to Romania in two weeks' time. He would not put Sarah in any more danger than she already was, so he would keep this battle far from her. They agreed to meet at *The Bar* twice in-between in case there was information each needed to share. Exchanging cell phone numbers was far too dangerous.

Much to his dismay, he discovered that he and his father were equally matched in skills and the only way he could possibly beat him was to obtain the power of stasis within the next fourteen days.

And the only vampire that could come from was Xavier.

Chapter 33

Sarah

"I don't understand." Tears she'd thought were under control fought to break free again. *Damn him. He didn't deserve her tears. Hell ... he didn't deserve* her.

"He's a complex creature, Sarah. I'm sure in his own mind he has a very good reason." Kate sat on her right and Analise to her left. When Analise heard what had happened, she demanded that she and Damian return to Milwaukee for the evening.

"Well, I think he's an asshat," Analise declared, holding up her shot glass.

"Here, here," Sarah agreed. "Cheers." They both downed the smooth tequila, sans training wheels. Only pussies took their tequila with salt and lime.

In the last hour and a half, Analise and Sarah had each had at least three margaritas and two shots of tequila. Or was this three shots? Oh, who the hell was counting?

But while her mind was now pleasantly fuzzy, the alcohol hadn't done a damn thing to lessen the crippling pain in her heart. In fact, it made it worse. Whose bright idea had it been to drink when she was already melancholy? Oh ... whoops ... *hers.*

"Damian and Dev will talk to him when he gets back and get to the bottom of this once and for all," Analise snipped. Analise was good and pissed at Rom for hurting her this way. Thank God for sisters. They'd always have her back.

"I don't want them to say anything. If he doesn't want me, he doesn't want me. I don't want or need anyone's goddamned pity, especially Romaric Dietrich's."

She stood and walked on wobbly legs—*okay, so she stumbled*—to the window, gazing out into the night sky. It was incredible how much brighter the evening sky was where Rom lived versus here. A pang of hurt caused the waterworks to start again.

They'd been back in Milwaukee pretty much all day and while she had no idea what Rom had done, Sarah spent it all at the shelter, talking to the girls. Beth seemed a little better today and she'd enjoyed catching up. Of course, she didn't share her own tales of woe. They just talked about mundane things as usual. And even Jamie seemed to be having a good day, but she still had so far to go.

"I dreamt of her again," Sarah murmured, still looking out the window.

"Who?" Analise replied, slurring slightly. Oh … she hadn't told Analise about the dreams she'd been having of mystery girl.

Turning around slowly, so as not to fall, she answered, "Mystery girl. At least that's what I call her because she won't tell me who the hell she is. But she knows Rom. In the first dream, she told me to tell him she was sorry, but wouldn't say for what or how she knew him or even give me her damn name."

She walked—*walked, stumbled...don't judge*—back to the chair across from where Analise and Kate now sat. She leaned her head back and closed her eyes, but continued to talk. "In the second dream she told me it was always me. I think she meant I was always the one for Rom. That one makes no sense at all."

She took a deep breath and tried concentrating on formulating words without slurring. Which was proving to be very challenging.

"And in the dream I had last night she told me that Rom is in danger and the only thing that will save him is me. But only if we're bonded."

"Wow. That's pretty heavy, Sarah," Analise said on a loud exhale.

"Right?" Sleep wanted to take her, but Sarah fought to stay awake. "He meant something to her and I'm pretty sure the feeling was mutual. I don't know how or why, but that's the vibe I get."

"Then why don't you just ask him about it, Sarah?" Kate asked. Kate always had the best advice. Except in this particular instance.

"Because what am I supposed to say, Kate?" She pulled her heavy head off the chair and opened her watery eyes. "Oh hey ... my twin says to tell you she's sorry and you have to bond with me or you're gonna die?"

"Well ... yes."

Sarah laughed, but it was humorless. "Well ... no. Not happening."

222

Kate got up and knelt in front of Sarah, taking Sarah's hands in hers. "Sarah, mystery girl is coming to you for a reason and ignoring her message, however cryptic, is the worst possible thing you can do. For both you and Rom. We all know that we have these dreams for a reason and burying our head in the sand as to their meaning is foolish and dangerous. You *need* to tell Rom. You aren't giving him enough credit. Don't jeopardize your future, or his life, by keeping this from him. If you do and something happens, you'll never be able to forgive yourself."

Every word Kate spoke was like another shallow scalpel wound and tears of shame ran freely. "You're right," she slurred.

Just then Damian and Dev walked into the room. Both stopped to take in the sight in front of them. It was after midnight and Analise had now fallen asleep, or passed out, on the couch, and was snoring pretty loudly. Sarah's face was surely a blotchy red mess and her eyes would barely focus.

Dev walked over to Kate, helped her up and took her into his arms.

"You could have that," Rosie whispered. For once, she agreed with Rainbow Bright.

"But he doesn't want you," Nancy jibed. She was just a vicious, spiteful bitch sometimes.

"The reek of alcohol carries into the other room, love. How are your sisters?"

Kate laughed. "Drunk, as you can clearly see."

By now Damian had Analise scooped into his arms, her small frame hanging limply in his arms. And she was sawing more logs than a flannel-wearing lumberjack. "Awww, Kitten," he whispered against her temple as he silently carried her out.

Dev held his free hand out to Sarah but she declined. "I'll jusss sleep on couch." So much for not slurring. She couldn't even make full sentences. There was no way she could make it all the way back to her room in the shelter and pride prevented her from asking for help.

Dev's brow raised. "I don't think that's a good idea, Sarah."

"No, no. I'm be fine. Really. Thanks you for being concern."

Inclining his head, he laughed, "It's your ass when Rom doesn't find you where you're supposed to be."

She snorted. Because really, that was just about the funniest thing she'd heard today. Rom had avoided her the entire day. She doubted he'd even miss her when, or if, he returned. She knew nothing of his plans, where he'd gone and when he was coming back or how long they'd be here.

Dev shook his head and sighed. He picked Sarah up and laid her on the couch, tucking a blanket over her shorts and t-shirt. "Sleep tight."

He turned off the light as they left the room and Sarah fell into a deep, restless, Rom-filled sleep.

Chapter 34

Rom

It was after 3:00 a.m. before he returned to Dev's estate. Anxiety painfully gnawed his gut like a colony of termites. While he thought he could trust Ainsley, he certainly wouldn't put his life, and that of his Moira, on the line by trusting her implicitly. Which meant he had to return to Romania and do some of his own recon. Since his father was the self-proclaimed fucking king of Europe, there were many vampires who lived under the tyranny of his boot and wished to get out from under it. The question was, would they be willing to put their lives on the line for a revolt, if it came to that? He meant to uncover the answer.

Killing Xavier and taking his power was the best possible plan he could come up with, but that fucker had been elusive for so long, what were the chances the universe would cut them a break and they'd be able to get enough intel to put him down once and for all within the next two weeks? He wasn't going to hold his breath. So, that meant he had to come up with a plan B and a plan C. And going to Romania was just step one. Like it or not, he would have to tell Devon and Damian about his father.

But that could wait until morning, for he desperately wanted to lay his eyes upon Sarah, if even to just stare at her in sleep for the rest of the night. He'd been a foolish ass both this morning and all day and regret had joined anxiety in his belly, making it raw. While he was steadfast in his decision not to bond with her until this danger passed, there was no reason he couldn't still sink inside her sweet body and nourish himself with her essence. It had been over two long weeks since he'd fed and his beast was beginning to clamor.

He felt her in the library, wondering why she would still be up at this late hour. Making his way, he was waylaid by Devon and Damian.

"We need to talk," Dev said.

"Not now." Rom tried pushing past them, intending on retrieving his Moira.

"What the fuck is going on, Rom?" Damian challenged, stepping in his path. "You drop Sarah off here, ignore your Moira like a goddamned leper all day and then take off without telling us what the hell is going on."

Rom cruelly stared his friend down. What he really wanted to do was unleash a little power, putting Damian in his place. "I didn't realize I reported to you, D. My apologies. Next time I'll be sure to review my agenda with you prior to my arrival so I can seek your approval."

He brushed passed the two, heading toward Sarah, but Dev's words stopped him short.

"I can only think of one reason a vampire would refuse to bond with their Moira."

Of course they knew. Damn females and their gossiping. He turned slowly, facing his friends.

"You bond your life to hers. If you die, she dies."

226

He remained silent.

"Sarah's sleeping off a tequila binge, so you have plenty of time to tell us what the fuck is going on and why, if your life is in danger, would you not choose to tell us about it. This is no longer just about you, my friend. With our mates being sisters, we are all intertwined. What affects one, affects all."

This felt like role reversal. *Rom* was always the calm in the eye of a storm. *Rom* always gave sound advice. *Rom* could pierce through the haze and confused emotions caused to make others see reason. But Rom's head was fucked. So many feelings swirled he couldn't make heads or tales of them and he was screwing up at every turn, with every single decision.

"It's a long story."

"We'll make time," Dev replied as they made their way to his office, Rom reluctantly on their heels. All he wanted to do was hold Sarah, but this conversation was long overdue. And the fact that he'd pushed her to drink herself stupid pissed him off.

A half hour later, the room was silent as Dev and Damian processed his information dump.

"So your father lives and wants your head," Damian said.

"I would say that's his preferable outcome, yes." It had been painful to discuss his family, particularly his mother. And to see her in such an oppressive state just a few short days ago caused him considerable guilt.

"How could I not know your parents were alive?" Damian asked rhetorically. The simple answer was, only a handful knew. By leaving his homeland and his father, he'd essentially been disowned. Like he gave a fuck. But by returning like he had, and now having been seen by others under his father's rule, there could be no doubt whose son he was. His father had let him leave once. He wouldn't do it twice. Turncoats did not go unpunished, according to his father. And it would undermine his father's power if he appeared lenient.

"I know we want to burn Xavier's entire organization down to the ground, but I'm not sure that's a realistic goal any longer," Dev started. "I think we simply need to take the information that Geoffrey can pull together within the next few days and find and kill the fucker and be done with him. We'll just have to deal with the fallout."

Without thoughtful planning, there would be many civilian casualties. And Rom struggled with that. How important was one life over another? How important was *his* life over a woman who'd had hers heartlessly and cruelly stripped away from her by a rogue? Didn't *she* deserve a fair chance at life too? And what about the innocent children, who were a complete and total unknown? They all deserved to be rescued and placed with loving families who couldn't have children of their own. They certainly didn't deserve death at the hands of any remaining rogues because he'd been so intent on saving his own ass. It was a moral struggle.

"Let's give him a week or so. Then we'll act," Rom said.

"Rom, that's pushing it too close," Damian pleaded.

"We owe those women and children a chance, Damian. I will not place the value of my life any higher than theirs simply because I am vampire. I'm old. If this is the end of my time on this earth, then I accept that." And wouldn't that just be a big fuck you? With Sarah, he'd got an unexpected second chance at happiness, only to have his own life ended.

Dev regarded him thoughtfully before speaking. "Sarah feels as deeply for you as you do for her, or she wouldn't have drunk herself into a stupor this evening trying to dull the pain you've caused."

Ouch. "And your point?"

"My point is that I know what you're doing. By not bonding, you're trying to protect her life, but she's already in love with you, so your gallant efforts are in vain, my friend. If you do die without bonding, while she may still be here in body, she will be a shell of a woman because her heart and soul will be ripped away with you. There is no one else for her, as there is no one else for you. There is strength in bonding, Rom. Sarah's your Moira for a *reason*. Trust that fate has chosen correctly and, *together*, you will be victorious. Besides ... we have your back and *we* will not let you lose."

"I can't believe I didn't know your parents were alive," Damian mumbled to himself, shaking his head.

229

Rom ignored him and his childishly hurt feelings. Everyone had secrets, even Damian. Get over it.

He felt like Dev was trying to tell him something else, but in his current state of mind, he wasn't reading between the lines very well. "What aren't you telling me?"

Dev laughed. "Sorry. Mate code. I'm sworn to secrecy. That's for you and your Moira to discuss. You should actually try talking to her. You'd be surprised at what you may learn."

"Talk to her about what *specifically*?" he barked. Dev was talking in riddles and rhymes.

Dev stood, walking to the door. "I need to return to Kate. All I can say is maybe you should ask Sarah about her dreams lately." And with that, Dev exited the room, leaving only himself and Damian.

"Rom, I can't believe you never told me about your parents."

"Jesus, get over it already," Rom growled before leaving to find his own Moira to try to make up for his egregious error in judgment today.

Chapter 35

Sarah

A truck was literally sitting on her head. No. A *jackhammer* was blasting its way out from inside her skull. Mother effer, did that hurt. And her mouth felt like someone had cauterized off each and every saliva gland. She wasn't sure there was enough water in the world to quench her unending thirst. But her stomach was declaring outright mutiny. Apparently tequila had well earned its nickname '*to-kill-ya*', because right now, she wanted to kill whoever poured all that poison down her throat.

Which would be her.

Oh. God.

She was going to be sick.

Scrambling from the bed, she ran to the bathroom and worshipped the porcelain god until all that would come up was bitter bile. She'd never understood that stupid phrase. There was no goddamn devotion going on here, unless you counted the plea for mercy and a quick death.

A cool washcloth pressed against her forehead right before she was lifted in strong arms and carried back to bed.

Bed? Had she fallen asleep in a bed?

She was situated against a strong, warm body and knew it was Rom but was in too much agony to open her eyes. The fingers of one hand stroked her arm, while the other gently massaged her scalp, sending her back into a fitful sleep.

She dreamt of mystery girl, but this time she didn't speak and the scene quickly changed to that of the past. Mystery girl was walking on a dirt road with a tall, broad man, holding hands. Their backs were to her. They started to turn, but then evaporated into thin air like a hologram.

The next time she opened her eyes, she felt marginally better. The jackhammer had quieted down to a dull, but almost bearable, throb. Her stomach was no longer in a full-blown riot, but probably wouldn't welcome any visitors, such as crackers or water, any time soon either. And her mouth was still bone-dry. Sleep called to her once again, but before she fell under she registered Rom's gentle and soothing strokes.

Mystery girl again haunted her dreams, but this time she saw the young girl's demise. She was flush with fever and pale as death. Her breaths were shallow, labored and uneven and her bed sheets soaked. The stench of mortality emanated from the entire house. A young woman ran around hysterical and crying. The scene suddenly changed and someone burst through the door, yelling. The young woman now sat at a wooden kitchen table, sobbing.

Bile rising caused her wake again.

She was sick several more times throughout the morning, mostly dry heaves, and Rom was there, caring for her. Holding her hair back, cooling her with a cloth and cuddling her against his broad, firm chest. She dosed on and off and each time she dreamt of mystery girl. And each time she woke, she thought Rom would be gone, but he never was. He didn't leave her side and he didn't scold. He whispered words of comfort. His touch soothed. Sleep pulled her under one last time.

She was back in the young woman's kitchen and the woman was hysterical.

"Where's Seraphina?" a deep voice growled.

That voice. She knew that voice. Sarah's head turned slowly toward it. Taking up the entire small doorway was a larger than life Romaric, but she knew this was of a time very long ago, because his clothes clearly gave it away.

The young woman didn't answer, not even realizing he stood there. He had called to her two more times before she responded.

"Who are you?" she finally asked.

"I am Romaric. Now. Where. Is. Seraphina?"

"She's gone. Dead. She fell ill night before last and passed this morning. Three of my babies are now dead and two more are ill."

Sarah woke again, heart and head pounding. Mystery girl was Seraphina. Seraphina had died. Rom had *loved* her, and not in a sisterly way. The devastation and loss that bled from his eyes at the news of her death was agonizing to watch. But who *was* Seraphina? Did vampires fall in love with normal humans outside of their Moira's?

"How are you feeling, beauty?"

How was she feeling? Better. Yes, better.

"Better, I think." But she *reaaally* needed to brush her teeth. She could smell her own lethal breath and it almost made her gag. "I need the bathroom," she said as she moved to get up.

"Are you going to be sick again?" he called after her.

"No. But I need to shower and clean up. I stink." *And I need to think.*

She shut the bathroom door, hoping he'd give her privacy. He was here and she supposed that was good, but things were far from right between them. He had some explaining to do about the way he'd treated her. Again.

She wanted to rehash her dreams, but didn't want to risk him hearing. She really needed to talk to him about them. Soon. But first she needed to figure out how to approach it, because she knew Rom would shut down. And Sarah knew that this girl had been the cause of the pain that he'd buried so deep. But for now she pushed it to the back of her head to delve into later.

She brushed her teeth and quickly showered, but realized she didn't have a clean change of clothes with her and she was *not* about to put on the vomit splashed tee and shorts she had been wearing. How Rom even let her touch him with that shit on her, she didn't know.

Having no choice, she wrapped a towel around her nude body and opened the bathroom door. Rom now sat against the headboard, long muscular legs crossed at the feet and beefy arms crossed at his chest. Today he'd worn his traditional dress pants, in tan, but instead of a stuffy button down shirt, he wore a black fitted Henley that was pulled tautly against his broad chest. He was so fucking sexy, her mouth watered.

His head turned at the sound of the door opening. Hungry eyes bulged and traveled slowly down her barely covered body. Her nipples beaded and her pussy went wet at his perusal.

God, even after what happened yesterday and how angry she still was, he simply lit her body on fire, without a word or touch to her flesh. Just a look was all it took and she was wet and aching and wanting.

The raging desire to rip his clothes off and sink onto his hard cock was almost too much to ignore. But she willed her feet firmly into the floor instead. There was only so much rejection a girl could take and she'd had her quota for the week. Or month. Or ever.

Besides, even though he'd spent all morning taking care of her, she was still very much pissed and confused at not only his rejection to bond, but also the way he'd ignored her all day.

"I, uh ... need some clean clothes."

"Come here, Sarah." His voice was low, firm and demanding. He held out a hand, expecting her to blindly obey. And her body wanted to. Hell, even Rosie and Nancy were doing cartwheels at both his blatant invitation and the colossal bulge in his pants. But her resolve held firm.

"No. I just need some clothes."

"No?" he asked incredulously. Eyebrows arching high, he swung his feet over the edge of the bed.

His eyes glowed and jaw ticked as he waited for her response. He had some goddamned nerve mocking her after what he'd done yesterday. Fucker.

"Yes. I said no. I mean I realize you're not used to hearing that word, like *ever*, but maybe you should get used to it. Because I plan on saying it. A. Lot."

That felt like the right thing to say until a predatory look overtook Rom's beautifully hard features. Every tightly coiled muscle rippled underneath the fabric of his shirt. *Oh. My.* She'd unknowingly thrown down a verbal gauntlet and there was no way someone like him wouldn't pick it up.

Shit.

"You do realize you've just challenged my beast, don't you, beauty?"

Double shit.

"Life would be pretty boring without a challenge. Wouldn't you agree?" She may sound calm and cool on the outside, but inside she was shitting bricks. Big ones.

"You're mine," he growled, as he pushed slowly from the bed and stalked toward her. Breathing became difficult and *damn* ... what she wouldn't give to have panties on, soaking up the rush of desire that ran between her thighs.

The need to flee was strong, but she stood her ground, crossing her arms, pulling the towel tightly around her. She was woman ... hear her roar, dammit. Gone were the days of letting people intimidate her. Her chin lifted a little higher, her shoulders stood a little taller.

Bring it, vamp boy. You've met your match.

"You do realize you're sending mixed messages, right? Four days ago you said you'd bond with me *that minute* if I agreed and then yesterday, I practically *threw* myself at you, begging you to fuck me and make me yours and you rejected me. Rejected me! So do *not* stand there and give me that *'I am strong vampire, you are mine, do as I say'* bullshit."

Her breathing was ragged, but now it was more due to anger than desire. He'd continued to glide slowly across the room the entire time she ranted, the wolfish look never leaving his face. She should be scared, but she wasn't. She was just plain pissed. When he reached her, their gazes held as he grabbed the towel and tugged it away, dropping it to the floor.

Her arms went to cover herself. "Why you ass—" But she was cut off as he grabbed her, spun them and pinned her against the wall.

"I was wrong," he rasped, holding her naked body solidly in place with his massive, clothed frame. Holding her wrists above her head in one hand, he slowly ran the other down her arm, grazing the outside of her swollen breast, continuing down her torso. When he reached her hip, he palmed the round globe of her bare ass and squeezed, pulling her against his hardness. An involuntary moan escaped her parted lips.

Jesus, Sarah. Stop.

You're angry.

237

You're hurt.

You deserve an explanation.

Reason tried overriding the raging inferno of pent-up desire that had built to now volcanic proportions inside her, but hot flames kept tamping that bitch down. One final attempt to use her brain prevailed.

"Let me—"

Once again he didn't let her finish as his mouth swooped to take hers in a brief promise-filled, panty-melting kiss. *If she had panties on, that was.* Breaking away, he whispered against her now swollen lips. "Jesus, Sarah. I was so fucking wrong. I'm sorry." His lips trailed a wet path to the shell of her ear. "I want my cock inside of you and your blood on my lips. And I want to make you mine. I can't wait another goddamned minute."

God, she wanted to give in. She wanted to scream *'for the love of God, what are you waiting for'?* So why couldn't she just shut off reason and leave well enough alone? He wanted her ... wasn't that all she needed to know?

"Why?" *Apparently not. Sarah, you stupid bitch.*

He groaned, leaning his forehead against hers. "I promise I'll tell you. Tomorrow. We have a lot to talk about, but I'm done talking. I'm done waiting. I need you, Sarah. I must make you mine." He kissed her slow and deep. "Please," he begged.

Rom begging. That's it. Fiery flames burned reason to ash. "Yes."

Holding her tight, he said, "We're not doing this here." The words barely left his mouth before he'd flashed them to his house. A hard wall met her back and his firm unforgiving mouth was once again upon hers. But this time she gave back. She let all the all-consuming desire she'd felt for Rom finally take over.

"God, I want you," he muttered.

Hands trailed down her flushed body, cupping her full breasts. Hot lips drew down her neck, latched onto her flesh and sucked. Her heavy head fell back as her hands flew to his head. The ferocious need to have him take her blood brought tears to her eyes.

"Rom, please. I need you inside me," she croaked. She'd thought of nothing else but this moment for weeks. Her soul and body felt empty and only he could fill both places.

"Not yet, Sarah. I want to enjoy seeing your naked body completely for the first time." Pulling back, he quickly disrobed and all the oxygen was sucked out of the room. *Good Lord Almighty.* A clothed Romaric Dietrich was impossibly sexy. But an entirely naked Romaric Dietrich was downright awe-inspiring. She was speechless.

Brawny muscles rippled with every single movement he made. She wanted to trace each honed inch of tanned flesh with her tongue. His very large, very erect cock stood at attention, begging to be stroked and sucked. She wanted to drop to her knees and be the one to make *him* lose all control.

But instead he was the one on his knees in front of her. His arms wrapped around her waist and he placed slow, reverent kisses to her stomach. Her hands went involuntarily to his head, holding him in place. It was an unusually sweet and poignant gesture in the heat of passion and it was nearly her undoing.

That one little action made her heart almost burst. She was undeniably in love with this wonderfully sweet, caring and loving male. Tipping his head upward so their eyes met, she told him so. "I love you, Romaric. I'm yours. I don't want to wait a minute longer."

"Sarah …" His voice broke and she swore there were tears in this strong male's eyes. "I will spend the rest of my days worshipping you. Making you happy. Loving you."

In one swift move, he stood and scooped her into his arms. She thought he would walk to the bed, but instead he strode through the room and to the balcony, depositing her upon one of the chaise lounges. As it was late afternoon, the sun was beginning to set, casting shade on the private deck. She smiled. They would become irrevocably bound together under the sky unencumbered by clouds that they both loved so much.

"Spread your legs," he demanded.

The sweet and reverent moment was gone, replaced by raw lust and voracious need. And she was miles beyond ready. Holding his eyes, she did as he commanded.

"Wider, Sarah." She heard a low curse when she complied. He'd stepped back into the sun and the rays that shone done on him made him look otherworldly. He stood tall and proud like the sex-god he was.

Controlling.

Commanding.

Domineering.

Cock-sure. *But he'd clearly earned that right.*

"Show me how wet you are for me, beauty."

Ahhh ... embarrassingly. She'd never done anything like this before, but she felt empowered and bold and she wanted to drive him mad with desire for her.

Taking her hand, she ran it slowly down her stomach to her wet folds. Wet was an understatement. Running a finger easily through her drenched slit, she brushed over her swollen clit and, leaving a glistening trail behind, drew it back up her stomach, circling first one pert nipple, then the other. Inspired by how his hungry eyes devoured every move, she brought it up to her mouth and sucked it clean.

"Very," she purred.

The deep rumble emanating from the back of his throat at her brazen move had her smiling. "Oh, Sarah. You naughty, naughty girl."

For the second time, he dropped to his knees in front of her. *A girl could get used to this.* He grabbed her legs, pulled her to the end of the chair and then his tongue was on her, trailing the very same path that her finger had just taken.

"Rom ..." All bravado faded once wet heat circled her hard nipple. All sanity fled when the scrape of his teeth pricked her skin hard enough to draw blood. And unimaginable ecstasy coursed through her when he moaned as he took her essence into his body for the first time.

"I ache," she pleaded. "Please."

Instead of filling her with his cock, thick fingers stretched instead.

He groaned. "You're so damn tight, Sarah. I can't wait to sink my cock inside this pussy. *My* pussy."

Her eyes slammed closed as each sensitive nerve ending was caressed with every movement he made in and out. His name floated repeatedly from her lips.

"Come, beauty," he roughly commanded. The second his thumb circled her firm clit she exploded. Heat burst from her center outward and she felt the path it took all the way out her fingers and toes.

"Fuck. That was beautiful."

Yes. Yes it was.

Chapter 36

Rom

He couldn't be gentle. He couldn't be soft. He couldn't be loving. Next time. Not this time. Kneeling on the chaise between her legs, he palmed his cock, stroking up and down until pre-come dripped onto her soaked mound. Sarah watched each glide of his hand with fascination, licking her lips.

No ... he wouldn't be gentle next time either. He was going to fuck her until both their bodies and voices were raw. And then he was going to fuck her again.

Running his throbbing shaft between her slick folds, Sarah closed her eyes on a breathy plea. Taking some of her juices with his free hand, he ran a wet finger to her forbidden puckered flesh, teasing slightly before pushing it in. Her eyes flew open, latching onto his.

"Rom ..."

"Shhh. I'm going to make you come hard for me again before I make you mine." He loved how close a climax brought blood to the surface of the skin. The pheromones made it that much sweeter. And Sarah's blood tasted like nectar from the Gods themselves.

He slowly eased in and out, getting her used to the foreign sensation. Soon her hips were moving in time with his shallow thrusts. He began circling his shaft on her clit, increasing the tempo of both, as her breathing became choppier, indicating she was close again. She clawed at the fabric beneath her, trying to gain purchase so she could move her pelvis faster and faster.

"Oh God. Rom ... don't stop."

"You're so goddamn sexy. Come undone for me, beauty."

Several seconds later she exploded again, wailing her pleasure into the dusky sky and he was mesmerized. She was a vision with her head thrown back, her back arched, a pink flush on her damp skin and rapture etched onto her angelic face. No woman had ever looked as beautiful during or after an orgasm as Sarah.

Mine.

Unable to wait another second, he found her entrance and with one hard thrust, sunk himself to the hilt, hitting the end of her womb. *Sweet Jesus.* Nothing felt as good as Sarah's pussy. *Nothing* in his six hundred-forty-two years of life felt as good as his Moira. His mate.

"You okay?" he croaked. *Christ, please be okay.*

"Yes," she breathed. "Fuck me."

"God, Sarah. You're perfect for me." He grabbed under her thighs and tilted her sex higher, allowing him to penetrate deeper. "Hold on, beauty."

Withdrawing nearly all the way, he slammed back home, pulling her hips hard toward him at the same time. He repeated the same movement again and again. Each time he buried himself balls deep in her wet heat. Her head thrashed, her nails bit into his thighs and her moans were a constant litany. Her sex was so tight, so hot, so silky and so well lubed from her earlier orgasms that it didn't take him long to feel his own climax racing toward him.

Leaning over, he grabbed beneath her shoulders, lifted her and stood. Never leaving the warmth of her body, he walked a few steps and sat her on the thick railing that ran the length of the balcony.

"Legs around my waist, hands on the banister," he commanded. She immediately complied. Wrapping one thick arm around her back and the other around her nape, he pulled her mouth to his and thrust his hips just as fierce, but not wanting this to be over so soon, he slowed his pace. *Christ, she felt so fucking good.* He never wanted to leave the pleasure of her body.

Breaking free of her lips, he leaned her back slightly to reach the ripe berried nipple that was calling him. Latching onto one hardened nub, Sarah's hands flew to his head, grasping hard.

"Faster," she pleaded.

Releasing it with a pop, he chuckled. "This is a marathon, beauty. Not a sprint." Placing hot, open-mouthed kisses on her moistened flesh, he made his way to her other hardened nub, adding, "I told you I was going to fuck you until your throat was raw from screaming my name. I don't think it's hoarse enough yet."

As he drew her other nipple between his teeth and gently bit, she squeezed her inner muscles, clamping down like a vice on his thick cock.

"Fuck, Sarah ..." he grated. They locked eyes and she did it again. "Do it again," he rasped. She smiled teasingly ... and squeezed. And that was the beginning of the end. He tightened his grip and began fucking her with long punishing strokes.

"I'm going to make you mine, Sarah."

"It's about time, vampire," she taunted breathlessly, but quickly lost her cockiness as he pounded viciously into her sex. Now her walls were clamping with impending climax versus her taunts from seconds ago.

Hips never losing time, his mouth quickly found that perfect spot where neck met collarbone and sucked, priming her for his bite. Her hands were at his head, holding him firmly in place like she was afraid he'd deny her again. But he was too far gone to deny her, or himself, what he so desperately craved. He struck hard and fast and relished in her sharp intake of breath right before she shattered in rapture in his arms.

Her blood ... he'd never tasted anything like it. Her lush, spicy taste was an aphrodisiac on his tongue. It was heady. It was the Promised Land. And it was his. Two more thrusts and he joined her in mindless bliss, coating her insides with his hot seed. Every clench of her sex milked him, until he was empty and spent. One last pull and he closed the wound.

Now they would complete the bonding.

Chapter 37

Sarah

Pure unadulterated ecstasy flowed like hot molten lava through her entire being. She couldn't form a coherent thought. Every brain cell was singed with the most intensely pleasurable orgasm she'd ever experienced.

"Sarah, drink." Rom's voice tried penetrating through her endorphin filled haze, but she didn't understand the words.

Drink? Drink what?

Something warm touched her lips. Warm and coppery and tangy. *And fucking magical.* As the first drop of the thick sustenance touched her tongue, her stomach clenched in pain and she became ravenous. She latched securely onto wherever this enchanting flavor was coming from and drank with fervor, holding it tightly to her lips.

It was decadent.

It was power.

It was life.

"Sarah," Rom growled. He sounded more animal than human. His cock was still hard and his rough thrusts resumed. She loved every single second of his unrestrained lovemaking. She wanted more.

With each swallow sounds became sharper. She could hear the wings of birds fluttering as they flew high overhead. Each cell felt renewed and strengthened. She felt impervious.

Awakened.

Immortal.

The smog of her human life was lifted and she was now perfect and untainted.

She felt Rom's pleasure as clearly as she did hers and it was pure nirvana. This time they crested the precipice together. All too soon, the life giving nourishment was taken from her and she was being carried somewhere. Soft bedding touched her back and within seconds, a warm cloth was being run over her skin, cleansing her.

Undiluted electricity and power coursed through her body, humming deliciously under her skin.

This is what she was always meant to be.

Sleep beckoned and she couldn't resist. Her last thought before she fell under slumber's spell was *I love you.* She swore she had heard a deep "*I love you too, beauty*" before she let the darkness claim her.

Chapter 38

Geoffrey

A week. He had a goddamned week to pull everything together needed to kill Xavier and take out the entire operation. No pressure. But Rom had said Geoffrey couldn't kill Xavier, that pleasure was reserved for him. Well, get in line, fucker. No, he knew he couldn't do this on his own, and he'd sought their help, but he'd still planned on being the one to take Xavier out.

When he'd talked to Rom earlier, they'd agreed to give him bits of information over the course of this next week. Just enough to make it appear he was making progress on both the additional clubs and the whereabouts of Xavier's daughters to throw off the cloud of suspicion that hung like a thick, black fog over his head.

He now sat back in this dingy human bar, nursing a beer, updating Xavier via phone. It was still slop, but far better than the rum and Coke he'd had the other day.

"Devon and his mate will be back in the country in two weeks' time." Lie. They were already here.

"And that's been verified?" Xavier's smarmy voice echoed through the speaker.

"Yes, my lord."

"Any progress on locating his new estate?" The new witch Xavier had found was actually working for Geoffrey, so of course, she hadn't been able to locate shit. Except for two more of the facilities where they'd kept the children. He had six now located. Were there others? Could he find them in time? He hoped so.

But the information he'd uncovered today was actually far more disturbing and needed his immediate attention.

"I have a couple of leads, my lord. But nothing has panned out so far. His subjects are very loyal."

Silence.

"I'm also checking out a lead on another club in the St. Louis area. I'll have an update on that tomorrow."

Also lies. Tomorrow he planned to be in the godforsaken hills of Wyoming where they'd located the newest child facility. He needed to scope it out and get in and out undetected, which shouldn't be a problem.

"You have a week to get me something solid. At the end of those seven days, if you have nothing, I'll have to seriously rethink your position in my ranks, Geoffrey."

Which meant he'd be dead. *Guess what, fucker ... you'll be the one missing his head at the end of seven days.*

"Of course, my lord."

Ending the call, he downed the liquor, waved for another and thought about his conversation with Rom when he'd asked about Ainsley. He was told, in no uncertain terms, to "fuck off and mind his own business". So Ainsley was telling the truth and Rom's life *was* in danger. Christ on a cracker … could this get any worse?

Wanting nothing more than to be with his Moira at the end of this blessed mission, he also felt an overwhelming obligation to repay the favor of trust that Rom had bestowed upon him in letting him live. Rom's friend must be genuinely worried to seek him out, which meant this was a very real threat. So the question was … what was it and how could Geoffrey repay a debt, while keeping his life? *If* he had one after this next week. The last thing he wanted to do was to get out from underneath Xavier's bootstrap only to be under one of the lord's for all of eternity.

Feeling eyes on him, he glanced toward the door. Standing there was none other than the stunning Ainsley. Today she was dressed in a pair of dark blue jeans and some sort of red whimsical, flowy top. Apparently in her world, making eye contact was code for *"don't mind if I do"* because seconds later, she had her ass planted in the chair across from him.

Leaning back, he crossed his arms. "You stalking me?"

"Why? Is your dick hard?" She waived the waitress over and ordered a double whiskey, neat.

"You wish, sweetheart."

Laughing, she said, "I've seen a lot of cock in my days, vampire. I'm sure yours is nothing special."

Geoffrey couldn't help but smile. He liked her. "I beg to differ, but I guess we'll just have to agree to disagree."

Her drink was delivered and she took a healthy swallow, regarding him silently. He had a feeling meeting her here a second time wasn't random in the least.

"So, you know Romaric?"

"You could say that," he replied.

"How well?"

"We don't get together for afternoon tea and fucking biscuits, if that's what you're asking. We have a ... common business interest. So, you talked to Romaric, then?" Of course he knew she did, he just wondered how much she would volunteer.

"Yes." She hesitated before continuing. "It's serious."

"I gathered."

"He could die." She looked genuinely concerned for Romaric's wellbeing and not for the first time he wondered the nature of their relationship. Not that it was really his business, but he was a nosy SOB.

"And you care ...?" He'd asked her this question before and didn't get a straight answer.

Smirking, "I told you. I'm an old friend and I care about him. He's got a good soul."

"You are aware how powerful Romaric is, yes?"

"Yes. But his father is more so. Or at least ... different."

Geoffrey thought on this for a moment. As The Reaper, Romaric could essentially steal another vampire's power and it became his own. Since Romaric's father would also possess the same skill and had lived longer, he'd had the chance to acquire more. Or different, as Ainsley had suggested. A thought crossed his mind.

"Does his father possess the skill of mimicry?"

She cocked her head, studying him. "No."

A plan began formulating. If he lived through the next week, could this be the way he would free himself from any indebtedness to anyone, and finally, for once in his long life, be entirely free?

The simple answer was, yes. But would Romaric accept his help?

He had to. Geoffrey just wouldn't take no for an answer.

Chapter 39

Mike

"Thank you for seeing me on such short notice, Mr. Clark."

"Oh please, call me Bud. Everyone does."

Bud ushered Mike into the house, the screen door clanging loudly behind him as it closed. He followed him through the small, cluttered kitchen and into the living room, where Bud indicated he should take a seat on a heavily pilled, shit-brown couch that looked like it'd been pulled straight from the dump.

"Would you like some coffee or a glass of water?"

After seeing the state the kitchen was in, he'd pass. "No, thank you. I'm fine."

"So, you said you had some information regarding Marna?"

Shit ... he felt like a heel giving this man such false hope when he knew Marna was dead. Well ... since there was no body, he didn't *know* for sure, but there was simply no chance she was still alive.

"Is Mrs. Clark around? I'd rather talk to you both at the same time." *And I'd love to see what she looks like.*

A sad look crossed Bud's face. "I'm afraid Ellie passed last year. Her only wish before she died was that we'd find out what happened to our Marna. But I guess that wasn't meant to be."

You don't want to know what happened to your daughter, Bud. Trust me. "I'm sorry, sir."

"Not your fault, son. Now, what can I help you with?" Bud leaned back in his lounge chair, the kind his dad always used to sit in and watch TV from the time he'd get home from the shop until he stumbled up to bed, drunk, hours later. Mike always hoped his dad would silently pass by his room on his way. Sometimes he was lucky. Other times he wasn't. It didn't take Mike long to learn not to fall asleep before his dad was passed out for the evening.

"Well, I've taken on a couple of cold missing persons cases, your daughter's being one of them. I'd like to ask you a few questions if you don't mind. Maybe look at some old photographs and see if I can get any new leads."

"Of course. Anything I can do to help." He paused, gaining composure before continuing. "I know my baby is dead, but it would sure bring me peace to be able to properly bury her remains before I join Ellie. And Marna."

Mike nodded respectfully. He'd put Bud over eighty-years old and his days were probably numbered. With the pallor, constant smoker's cough and heavy stench of tobacco he'd smelled when Bud opened the door, he'd put him pretty damn close to death's doorstep. And he'd like nothing more than to help this elderly man complete the dream of locating his daughter's remains before he kicked the proverbial bucket. In fact, for some odd reason, that had now become his mission.

They spent the next hour talking about Marna. How she went missing, what she was like growing up and looking through old pictures that were mostly kept in shoeboxes. This man's love for his daughter and his family was profusely apparent in not only every word he spoke, but the tone he used. It made his heart ache, wondering if he'd ever get the opportunity to build his own family. *Love* his own wife and children as much as this man apparently had.

Throughout their conversation, he'd discovered Bud and Ellie had been married for sixty-two years before she died. Incredible really. Living with one person day in and day out and to love them that deeply, that long. Would he ever get that? And while he wasn't exactly sure how a human and vampire mating worked, he'd found the woman. She just needed to stop running.

His phone had buzzed in his pocket several times since he'd arrived at Bud's, but he'd ignored it. Bud had taken the time to meet with him after just a phone call this morning and Mike thought it rude to whip out his cell. Besides, he was genuinely fascinated with Bud and his stories.

A knock on the door halted their conversation and Bud shuffled slowly out of the room, telling him he'd be right back, mumbling something about the damn doorknockers and that he needed to get a No Solicitation sign to hang.

Mike took the opportunity to pull out his phone, checking his messages. Three missed calls and six texts. All from Giselle. He didn't have time to listen to the voice mails, but he quickly scanned the texts and each had gotten progressively nastier. A broad smile was plastered on his face. *Aw*...she *did* care.

Where r u?

Answer ur GD phone.

Is this some sort of childish payback? Grow the fuck up.

If ur fucking some othr whore, I will kill her. Then castrate u.

He didn't get a chance to read the last two because Bud had returned and he couldn't tear his eyes from the person trailing behind him.

"Detective Thatcher, this is my daughter, Brynne. Brynne, this is Detective Thatcher. He's working on Marna's case."

He stood, still in a stupor. "Uh ... Mike. Call me Mike." Extending his hand to hers, she placed her smaller one in his.

"Mike, nice to meet you. I told my father to wait until I could get here, but obviously he ignored my request and went ahead without me."

Mike turned to Bud. "I didn't realize you had another daughter, Mr. Clark. I didn't see Marna with a sister in any of the pictures you showed me."

Bud threw his arm around Brynne, pulling her close. "Well, our Brynne was a surprise that came a little later in life, so there was quite an age difference between the two."

He'd say. In fact, he'd put Brynne at no older than early thirties. Maybe not even thirty yet. So she came well after Marna even went missing.

But the thing that fascinated him most was that Brynne was the spitting image Sarah. They looked so much alike they could practically be twins. Mike didn't need any medical records or blood samples or DNA. Because there was absolutely no doubt that he was standing in this dingy, grungy, messy house with Sarah's maternal grandfather and her aunt Brynne.

And damn if it didn't feel good to finally have at least one tiny win in his corner in this fucked up vampire nightmare he'd found himself mixed up in.

Chapter 40

Sarah

Warm breath skating over her inner thighs woke her. Thick fingers invading her tender, bruised flesh, which had been deliciously used the night before, caused an involuntary moan to escape. Even rousing from sleep, she was already wet and wanting her new mate.

"Rom ... please."

"I'm going to wake you like this every morning, beauty."

What's a girl to say to that? 'Hmm ... no I think I'll pass?'

His tongue flicked her swollen bundle of nerves and her hips jackknifed off the bed. Rom wrapped his left hand under her thigh, and flattened it on her lower stomach, holding her in place while he assaulted her with his mouth and fingers. She was quickly racing to the finish line, only to be thrown over violently when Rom sunk his fangs into her fleshy mound, setting off a brutal, crashing climax.

Her legs still quivered when Rom crawled up her body, twined their fingers above her head and entered her so slowly her breath left her lungs. His large frame covered hers, their kisses languid, mimicking their lower bodies.

"I love you, Sarah," he whispered, pulling back to lock eyes with hers. The truth of his words rang loud and she felt like sunbeams of happiness were bursting out of every pore.

"I love ..." *Gasp* "... God, don't stop."

He chuckled, but it was strained with lust. "Take my blood."

She'd wanted to from the second she woke, but she didn't know how and she didn't want to hurt him.

"You won't hurt me, Sarah. Strike in the same place on my neck as I did yours. It's that simple. Hurry, beauty. I'm close and I want my blood coursing through your veins when I come inside you."

He freed her hands and she wrapped them firmly around his neck, drawing him to her. Once her lips touched his flesh, she instinctively knew what to do and the second she sunk her teeth into his skin, they both rocketed to blinding orgasm.

Seconds, minutes—hell, maybe hours later—they lay recovering and after Rom lovingly cleaned her again, he lay down pulling her back to his chest.

"What's this?" He traced the cross tattoo she'd gotten on her shoulder in remembrance of her brother. He would have loved Rom. Idolized him. Six years was a lifetime, but only yesterday.

"It's in memory of my brother, Jack. He died six years ago. He was eight."

Rom turned her so they were face to face; the sadness in his eyes matched hers. He tucked a wayward hair behind her ear, fingers lingering on her skin. "I'm sorry, Sarah. What happened?"

"The unfairness of life happened." Yes, she was bitter. She would have given anything to take Jack's place, for he was far too young and precious to leave this earth so early. "He had chronic lymphocytic leukemia, or what the medical community refers to as CLL. It's a very rare cancer in children. When he was four, he got sick and they couldn't figure out what it was. He had a constant fever, he lost weight, which he couldn't afford to do because he was already so little, and he slept all the time. It took months for them to make a diagnosis." Months that maybe could have been used to save his life, she'd often thought.

"They tried chemotherapy first and that didn't work. Then they moved to radiation and, for a while, he got better. They even said he went into remission. But then just a few months before he died, he became sick again and they restarted the radiation. They were discussing a stem cell transplant when he took a turn for the worse and just three days later, he was gone."

By now, tears streamed freely down her face. Rom wiped at them, but they came faster than he could keep up with.

"Tell me about him," he whispered against her lips before placing his softly on them.

She laughed, although through the tears it came out choked. "He was magical. I loved him so. I remember how sick my mom was when she was pregnant and so I didn't like him before he was born, but oh my God, after I saw him the first time in the hospital, I was in love with him. I was ten and a little mother hen, so much so, that my mom had to tell me to back off.

"He was a little toe-headed blond with bright blue eyes and literally the cutest human being I'd ever seen. He couldn't pronounce his r's so he called me 'Sawa'." The smile she had thinking of him died. "A part of me died with him."

Rom watched her with such empathy—and understanding—it made her heart ache. His lips found hers in a gentle, chaste kiss before pulling her completely in his arms.

"Do you ever dream of him?"

"No." And she never understood that. She'd dreamt about so many things, she wondered why Jack had never come to her in all this time.

"Maybe he will someday." Fingers massaged her scalp and she moaned. "Here, turn over onto your stomach."

"Hmm ... I think I need a little more recovery time. And maybe a soak first."

Chuckling, he dipped his lips to her shoulder, nipping lightly. "While I'd love to be inside you all day, beauty, I want to massage you and then we'll take a nice hot bath. I need you recovered because I intend to ravage my new mate later."

Massage? Wow. Really? Can we skip that for the ravage part?

He laughed loudly now. She was face down and his hands kneaded firmly her tired, overused muscles. "Yes, Sarah. Really. Although on second thought, with my hands rubbing all over your sexy, sweat-covered skin, all I really want to do is sink my cock back inside your warm body."

"Don't you have to go to work or something?" she murmured, almost unable to string together a coherent sentence because she was so relaxed.

"No. I'm the boss."

A loud moan escaped when he hit a particularly hard knot between her shoulder blades. "God, that feels so good," she groaned.

His hands stilled and he moved her hair all to one side before she felt a hot tongue dragging a path toward her ear. In addition to the bonding, they'd made love twice in the night and again this morning, and she really was sore, but her sex still readied itself for her mate anyway. She imagined if she didn't have his blood running through her body she'd be in agony by now because his cock definitely stretched the limits of her sex. She smiled.

"You're making me so fucking hard with those sounds, Sarah. If you keep moaning like that, I'm not going to be able to help myself from taking you again right now."

She wanted to tell him to do it. Slide it in. She wanted it from behind. Hell, she wanted it any and every way possible. Instead, she muttered, "You're insatiable."

"Fuck, Sarah. You want it any and every way and I'm the insatiable one?" His breath feathered across her flushed skin, causing goose bumps to break out. "You love it. Don't deny it. Your body doesn't lie."

Oh, she wouldn't. Sex with Romaric was unlike any pleasure she thought humanly possible. Now she knew why Kate and Analise had Barbie doll smiles plastered on their faces twenty-four hours a day, seven days a week.

All too soon his hands left her body and she felt the bed dip when he got off.

"Come back," she whined.

His lips touched her temple. "I'm going to draw a bath. I'll be right back."

Massage? Bath? Declarations of love? Who knew the stuffy, enigmatic, buttoned-up Romaric Dietrich had a soft, romantic side? Her sisters would never believe her in a million years. Yet he did. He'd showed it multiple times over the last week.

Several minutes later he returned, scooped her up in his arms, and carried her into the elaborate bathroom, up the three stairs to the sunken tub, which he'd filled to the brim with steaming water and bubbles.

Romaric had bubble bath stashed somewhere? Would wonders never cease?

After he had them settled in the blissful bath, her leaning back against his chest, he pulled their left hands out in front of them to inspect the mating marks spanning their thumbs.

"You're mine, now," he rumbled in her ear. "For all of eternity." Feeling him grow hard against her bottom, she groaned. Something must have happened with the mating, because if she thought she'd been completely consumed with sex before they'd bonded, now she was downright obsessive. Almost feral.

"Yes, I'm afraid you're stuck with me," she retorted, squirming against him.

Grabbing her hips, he growled, "Sit still, beauty."

She huffed. "Tell me why you wouldn't bond with me the other day." If he wouldn't let their bodies get busy, then his mouth had better. He owed her some answers, and if she were honest with herself, his rebuff still stung a little.

Grabbing a loofa, Rom squirted citrusy scented gel on and it began washing her. "Sarah, it's complicated," he hedged.

"Uh uh." Turning around, she moved to the other end of the tub, far away from him. It was so huge their feet almost didn't touch, even with Rom's large frame. "You owe me an explanation and I'm not taking no or, it's too complicated or, it's too dangerous for you to know bullshit responses. We're bonded or mated or whatever you call it and that means I'm your equal. So ... no more dancing around the question, vampire. Start talking."

A slow grin spread over his drop-dead gorgeous face and he lounged back, throwing his beefy arms on either side of the tub. He stared at her so long without speaking she began to get uncomfortable.

"What?" she snapped.

"You are going to test every ounce of patience I possess, beauty."

She laughed, mimicking his casual position. "Well, I guess we're made for each other then."

"That we are." His smile dropped a little and her dream of mystery girl suddenly popped back into her head. Now, in addition to a burning desire to know why she'd been rejected, she desperately wanted to know who they were to each other. Would he tell her? She highly doubted it and that weighed heavily on her heart. But first things first.

"So ... I'm waiting," she said, tapping her fingers against the cold marble.

He sighed heavily. "There are some ... *complications* ... from my past that have resurfaced and I'm afraid they pose a danger not only to you, but myself as well."

A tinge of fear ran through her. If Rom was afraid of something, then this must be very serious. And if he'd refused to bond with her because of it, then the situation was grave. "And it doesn't have to do with Xavier?" She already knew the answer.

"I'm afraid this is a new threat."

Chills caused her to shiver slightly, even though the water was plenty warm. "What happens when we bond? I never did ask you. How long will I live exactly?"

His face turned bleak. She'd hit the nail on the head. "Your life is tied to mine. As long as I live, you live."

She swallowed hard. "And if you die, I die?" she whispered.

He nodded slowly, suddenly looking guilty. "Sarah, I should have talked to you about this before we bonded. Given you a choice. I'm— Fuck, I'm sorry."

Her eyes stung. *He thought she was upset because they'd bonded?* What a goddamned fool. She closed the distance between them and climbed onto his lap, wrapping her arms around his neck, laying her head on his shoulder. He held her tightly, stroking her hair gently.

"I'm sor—"

"Stop," she yelled, pulling back. Grabbing his face, she held tight. "I'm *not* sorry we bonded and if you say that again, I swear I'm going to kick you in the balls." Her mouth met his harshly and when she sat up, she was unable to help the tears that fell down her cheeks. "I don't care about me. I care about *you*. I just found you, Rom." Her voice cracked and she had to choke the next words out. "I can't bear the thought of losing you. Of losing us. Now. Or ever. I love you."

"I love you too, Sarah. I won't let anything happen to you."

And that meant nothing could happen to him. She believed him. He was strong, mighty, and powerful. Drawing on her strength and fortitude, she firmly resolved to herself they would get through this together. "Okay then. Tell me about the threat and let's figure out what we're going to do about it."

He grabbed her shoulders firmly. "*You* won't be doing anything Sarah. It's too dangerous."

Her arms flung up underneath his hold, effectively knocking it away. His eyes bulged. "Yah, that's right, vampire. I may not be as big as you are, but I certainly am not weak. In mind or body. I'm your mate now and I feel your power coursing beneath my skin like a million volts of electricity just waiting to be unleashed. I may not be able to go into a battle with you because I'm inexperienced, but I will be able to hold my own if I'm threatened. I told you that I won't be under anyone's boot again. And that includes yours."

Grabbing her face, he kissed her hard. "Christ, Sarah. I'm so lucky to have found you."

"Yes. Yes, you are." She smiled. Turning serious again, she asked, "Who or what is the threat?"

He sat back, hands on the sides of the tub again and she felt bereft. After several long beats, he finally answered. "My father."

His father?

Grabbing the sponge, he poured fresh soap and began slowly washing her again as he talked. "We hadn't seen each other in over six hundred years. You could say we have very *different* views on life."

"If you haven't seen each other in so long, why is he suddenly a threat now? And how do you even know he is?" She was clearly missing some puzzle pieces.

"The source I have is very credible, and the threat is very real, I'm afraid."

This still wasn't making sense. "Wait a minute. You said *hadn't*. As in you hadn't seen him ... until recently?"

She didn't miss his eyes quickly shift away from hers, returning now with resolve.

"Why did you see him?"

"It matters not. All that matters is that I need to eliminate the threat."

Oh, it mattered. If he'd avoided seeing him for that long and just recently saw him, something must have precipitated their visit. He wasn't exactly lying, but he was hiding something. She knew that with absolute certainty. Sarah thought back to what she'd learned about vampires over the course of her months at the shelter. What she'd learned from Manny, Thane and her sisters. Even from Damian and Dev.

"What does he want?"

"That's simple. He wants me *under his boot*, as you say. And if I refuse, then he wants my head."

"But ... why? Why now? I don't understand."

That thick steel door that Rom liked to use when he didn't feel like answering a question slammed firmly shut. She practically saw it hit the ground and heard the echo reverberating in her ears.

He sighed. "Trust me to protect you."

She knew that each vampire possessed a certain skill or set of skills passed down from their bloodline and they got stronger as they got older. If Rom's father lived, he was most likely stronger

269

than Rom and she'd heard gossip of the West Regent Lord from her sisters long before she'd met him. He had unheard of power, but she didn't know exactly what it was.

"What is your skill, exactly?"

Smirking, he dropped the loofa into the bath with a splash. Gripping her hips, he pulled her firmly against his stiff erection so hard her breath caught. "I'm skilled at many a thing, Sarah." Leaning forward, he nipped her earlobe. "And fucking my mate until her voice is raw is one of them."

Putting her hands on his shoulders, she pushed away. "Rom, do you realize that anytime you don't like the way a conversation is going that you either divert with sex or dirty talk, or you get angry and shut me out?"

"Sarah ..."

"Or you do that. You say my name with exasperation."

"That's because I am exasperated with you. Why can you not trust that I know what I'm doing? Why the third degree?"

"You see? That's the problem right there. This isn't about me trusting you at all. I *do* trust you, Romaric. With my body. With my heart. With my *life*." She should pull away, but instead she rolled her hips slightly, eliciting a groan from him. "This is about *you* not trusting *me*. And when I ask you a question and you divert or you hedge or you simply shut me out, then I have to make up my own shit. And that's not a good place for me to be, because the stuff that I'm coming up with is probably far worse than reality."

"I assure you, it's not," he muttered. Shifting so he was aligned with her entrance, he thrust hard.

Her head fell back in pleasure. "Rom ..." she moaned in both euphoria and frustration.

"You're wrong. I do trust you, Sarah. I just want to protect you." Holding onto hers his hips pushed upward in slow strokes. "I. Love. You." Each word was punctuated by another rough movement. Cool water sloshed everywhere. His hand snaked down and found her swollen bundle. "I love your pussy, beauty. It's always so wet for me."

"You're ... you're doing ... it ... again." She could barely talk. *Damn him.* Damn him for feeling so good she couldn't tell him to stop, even though she knew exactly what he was doing.

"I need to feel you clench around my cock." She squeezed her inner muscles. "Fuuuck. Come hard for me, Sarah. Now."

The control he had over her body was almost scary. It greedily obeyed his every command, each whim. Minutes later, they lay against each other, breathing still ragged, her skin chilled by the cooling water.

"Let's dry off and I'll answer any questions you have, okay?"

"Thank you."

Chapter 41

Rom

Fucking hell. He did not want to tell Sarah about Seraphina, but he didn't want to lie to her either. She would know. His blood was very potent, he could already sense the changes within her. Within less than twenty-four hours, she'd already gotten remarkably strong and would only continue to do so. The fact that she could take his blood on her own without his assistance proved it.

Rom had reaped many powers over his lifetime, both physical and mental. In fact, there wasn't much he couldn't do.

With his vast abilities to manipulate both the body and mind, he could bring even the strongest vampire to their knees with either physical or emotional agony. He could control all of the elements with simply a thought. While vampires could live a very, very long time, they were not immortal. They could be killed. But with his unique powers, Rom was as close to immortal as one gets. And unfortunately so was his father. So the only way to end him was to take his head.

And while Sarah would never match his strength, she would become very powerful, so he needed to prepare her. Things he should have done before he bonded with her.

"How are the eggs?"

"God, they are so good. I'm starving," she mumbled through a mouthful.

A smile crept its way over his face. Christ, he loved this woman so much already it was terrifying. Winning a battle against his father would be difficult, but losing was simply not an option he would consider. The one thing he thought lost to him forever after Seraphina died, was sitting across the table and a thousand years with her wouldn't be enough time, let alone just a few measly days.

He hated to leave her, but he needed to prepare and strategize. He had to return to Romania within the next few days and there was no way he'd take her with him. Even with the beefed up security here, Sarah wouldn't want to stay, so he needed to talk to Dev. Leaving her in his care seemed to be the best option.

"Thank you, Raziel," Sarah said as his chef took their plates. He'd introduced her to his staff this morning, including her security detail, which, surprisingly, she didn't balk at.

"My pleasure, ma'am."

"Please call me Sarah, Raziel."

"I will try, ma'am."

He laughed when she rolled her eyes. "He's very old fashioned, Sarah. In fact, most of my staff is."

"Hmmm ... of course they are. You hired them."

"Touché."

Leaning back in her chair, arms crossed, he knew questions would start coming at him like rapid fire any moment. And he hadn't decided how much he would share with her. She was wrong when she said he didn't trust her. He *did*. Maybe it was old school of him, but as the man, he thought it his duty to protect his woman. And telling her the entire truth would only upset her. He never wanted her to know the entirety of the threat that loomed over both their heads.

"So, let's start with your skills."

Easy enough. "Okay. I am what's known as a reaper. I have the ability to take the powers of other vampires as my own, but only if they use them against me. I can also negate any power they try to use against me, but then I can't procure it. So I have to be selective about the skills that I reap because if I can't absorb it quickly enough, it could be deadly to me."

She sat there stunned, opening and closing her mouth a couple of times before she finally whispered, "Wow."

Rom had never really thought too much about his skills. He was born with them, had them his whole life and yes, they were mighty useful, but he'd be a liar if he didn't admit that his mate's look of awe was ego boosting.

"So, what kinds of things can you do?"

"I have many skills. Too many to count, but I can bend any element on Earth to my will. Fire, water, air. I can also manipulate anything in the physical or mental state."

"Meaning?"

"Meaning, if I want to cause pain, I can. If I want to make someone fall to their knees in emotional agony, I can."

"Can you do those things to me?"

Rising from his chair, he walked around the table and pulled her up into his arms. "No, beauty. Vampires cannot use their skills against their mates." If they could, he was sure his father would have used them against his mother long ago. Instead his father used physical, verbal and emotional abuse as his weapons of choice. The simple, but effective, tools that humans also use against one another.

"And your father has the same powers?"

She was very intuitive. "Yes and no. We have similarly matched skills."

She stepped back, leaning against the back of the couch. "But you can beat him, if it comes to that. Right?"

"I must." There was no other choice.

"You visited him recently. Why?"

He needed to be much more careful with his words around her. One little slip up and she'd already caught it. "I had some ... *business* that I needed to discuss with him."

"But what could be that important to cause you to seek him out after over six hundred years of avoiding him?"

You.

How could he ever make her understand? How could he possibly tell her he'd loved another before her? That she was meant to be here today instead of Sarah, but the Fates had decided differently. It would crush her.

"Sarah ..."

A resigned look on her face, she chose to let it go, whispering instead, "I'm scared." Her soft caramel eyes were bright with unshed tears.

Fuck. So was he. For the first time in his life, he was petrified. And he had no one to blame for this predicament but himself. He'd questioned fate and by doing so, he'd put both his and Sarah's life in jeopardy. He never should have set foot on that godforsaken continent.

"All will be fine, Sarah." It had to be. He would settle for no other option. "But I do have things I need to do and I can't take you with me."

"But—"

"But nothing. Sarah, yes, as my bonded mate you're stronger than you were yesterday, but you are years away from being able to use the full strength of your power. And I need all my wits about me where I'm going. I can't do that if I'm worried about you."

She nodded her head against his chest. "How long will you be gone?"

"Hopefully no more than two or three days."

"Do I have to stay here by myself?"

"No beauty. I'll speak to Dev, but I'm sure you can stay with him and Kate. But Jareth and Elliot will also accompany you."

"Okay." She gripped him tighter. "You'd better make sure you don't get yourself killed or I swear I will spend all of eternity haunting your ghostly ass."

He chuckled. "You're something else, Sarah."

"You haven't seen anything yet," she retorted.

Sarah had so many amazing facets to her personality. He only hoped he had hundreds of years to uncover every single one of them.

Chapter 42

Rom

He turned the flash drive over and over in his hands. Distraction was fatal and he couldn't afford it. He needed to pull his head out of his ass and focus on the tasks at hand for the next few days.

Kill Xavier.

Kill his father.

In that order.

And the sooner, the fucking better. He was tired of this cloud of doom hanging over him, threatening the happiness that had eluded him so long.

"I found some rather disturbing developments at the last compound," Geoffrey stated.

Rom waited for him to continue. It was after one a.m. and he wanted nothing more than to return to Sarah, crawl in bed with her and hold her in his arms all night long.

"The children appear to be growing at an alarming rate."

Well, that got his attention. "Explain."

Geoffrey got a faraway look in his eyes. "They keep these vamps locked up like fucking animals in cages from the time they are born until their last blooding. Even the babes. No touch, no comfort, no love. I had no idea until I stumbled across these last two compounds. I mean, of course I knew how the older ones were treated, but when you're raising monsters, you have to cage the beast until he's housebroken. But I swear I didn't know about the babes."

"You're making no sense."

He sighed heavily. "As you know, after the lords raided Xavier a century ago, he significantly diversified his operation, more than I even realized. All of the compounds I've been to have babes to adult vamps, so it was quite by accident that I discovered he had other compounds for just newborn babes. I found two such locations this week. My intent was a quick in and out to get records, a count of heads and a blueprint of the compound. But when I was downloading the data on the flash drive, I noticed that the birth records and charts do not match at all with normal growth patterns. At first, I thought that something was just wrong with the documentation, so I took a look for myself.

"Fuck. Babes, that were born just weeks, are the size of toddlers. I saw a two-year old who looked like a ten-year old. I've been suspicious over the last few years that something wasn't quite right, because kids were becoming adults so quickly, so I thought maybe more women were kidnapped than I knew about, but never in my wildest dreams could I have imagined this. Xavier does a lot of shit behind my back, some of it I find out about, some obviously I don't. He's harder to keep up with than two-bit whore."

"How does it work?"

"I don't know exactly. Hopefully, some of the records I took will help. But I need to talk to the researchers. Give me a day or two, tops."

Rom thought back to the rogues they'd come across during the last raid on Xavier. They were definitely larger and more powerful than he'd seen before. Too much so for them to be normal vamps. During the heat of battle, he hadn't given it too terribly much thought and of course he'd been otherwise occupied since then, but he should have considered this. And what exactly did it mean? Of course, all adult rogues would have to be destroyed, but was there any chance to save the young ones and give them a better life or did they need to be destroyed as well? That thought made him surprisingly melancholy.

"How is it you didn't know about this until now?" Rom knew Geoffrey was telling the truth, but something wasn't adding up.

"I think I may have pieced together a system that Xavier's been using to give just enough information, but not all, to any one vamp. Each compound works in seclusion from the others so there is no chance of duplicity. From what I've been able to uncover, I believe there are several of these "babes only" locations. I've found five. There may be more. I have some more recon to do before I'm sure exactly what he's doing, but what's clear is that not one person is privy to everything. Including me."

"Are the kids salvageable?"

Geoffrey scrubbed his hand over his chin. "Perhaps some of the very young ones. I really don't know. Who the fuck knows what kind of chemicals may have been pumped into their tiny bodies by the time we rescue them? The vamps coming out of these compounds are ruthless, heartless killing machines. They all need wiped out."

"Would you put yourself into that category?"

Geoffrey laughed. "Of course. But I won't go down easy."

"I would expect no less." Rom hadn't decided whether Geoffrey should live or die at the end of this mission. He fell squarely into the ruthless killing machine category, but he also knew that this life had been forced on Geoffrey and he had attempted to right his wrongs.

Geoffrey leaned back in his chair, balancing precariously on the back two legs. "I want to talk about your father."

"Good for me that I don't give a flying fuck what you want. We'll meet again here in three days' time. Keep your burner on in case I need to reach you earlier." Rom stood to leave, throwing a twenty on the table for his untouched beer.

"I want to offer my services."

He laughed loudly, drawing attention from the humans surrounding them, but they all quickly shifted their attention away when he looked around the room. Most humans weren't dumb. They knew a predator in their midst when they saw one.

"And what makes you think I'm in need of your *services*, vampire?"

"Your friend seems genuinely worried about you."

"She needn't be." Rom shifted around the table to leave.

"I would like to repay you for saving my life. And then we're even," Geoffrey stated flatly.

"You assume that I intend to let you live after we're through with this business endeavor. You put Damian's mate in danger. Both he and Devon want your head on a fucking stake."

"But I also saved her life. And Devon's mate's life," Geoffrey responded.

And my mate, he thought, but Geoffrey didn't know that, and he wasn't about to tell him, or let him anywhere near Sarah for that matter.

Rom always relied on his own skill and it was a tough pill to swallow to think he'd have to rely on anyone or anything else, but even he knew when to shove aside his pride and ego and call in reinforcements. He'd been wracking his brain to figure out how he was going to kill his father without killing himself in the process, and if Geoffrey could be useful to that end, he'd take the stupid fuck up on his offer.

"I'll consider it. Should you live through the coming battle, that is."

Geoffrey nodded once.

And with that, he exited the bar, flashing back to Dev's estate.

"I need you to look at this and have a summary ready by tomorrow afternoon," Rom said as he passed off the flash drive to Circo.

"Yes, my lord."

"There may be a lot of information on that and there have been some new medical developments that we don't have time to dive into right now. By morning I need compound layouts, human and vampire headcount at each facility and the like. Tomorrow evening we have a meeting at eleven thirty to review all intelligence we have so far. I expect you there with a full report."

"Of course, my lord."

Rom turned to head to the room where Sarah was sleeping, but Circo's statement had him turning back.

"Just so you know, my lord, I intend to make the trip to Romania with you." Rom had planned to have Circo stay back and take care of Sarah. He trusted his staff implicitly, but no one more so than Circo. Sarah was by far the most precious thing to him and he would not leave her vulnerable.

"That sounded suspiciously like a command coming from someone who is under mine." Rom took orders from no one and no one dared to do so, except now maybe Sarah. Surprisingly, the thought of that didn't bristle him like it would have a few days ago.

Circo's face remained impassive. "You, and now your mate's, life is my priority. You need me and I will not let you head into the mouth of the lion's den alone. If you take that as me commanding you, then I guess that's what it is. But I won't take no for an answer."

Laughing, Rom said, "Have a death wish, Circo?"

"No, my lord. But I have no death wish for you either."

Well ... *shit.*

"I have no fucking idea why I put up with you," Rom grumbled, turning on his heels to head to his mate so he could climb in bed and hold her until dawn.

"You love my sunny disposition, my killer smile and my mad research skills. Oh, and the fact that I'm the only one with balls enough to stand up to you," Circo called after him.

That was true. Other than the lords, Circo had been the only one to ever verbally challenge Rom and get away with it unscathed. That is until a warm honey-eyed, curvy vixen caught his eye across a dining room table a few weeks ago. Now, he was challenged on a daily basis and had a feeling that he would be every day for the rest of his life. He looked forward to every second of it.

With anyone else that would be enough to get his powers flaring to life, but when Sarah did it, the only thing flaring ... was his cock. Which it was doing right now at the thought of lying next to her sleek, naked body.

Screw holding her until morning. He was going to be buried inside her sweet heat for hours instead.

Chapter 43

Sarah

Two men—no, vampires—who looked like strikingly like Rom were talking in hushed tones in the corner, but she heard every word as clearly as if they were being whispered in her ear.

"She will find him."

"She can't be trusted."

"She can, father. She hasn't seen him since he left over six hundred years ago. She has no allegiance to him now."

"She'd better not. Or it will be her head."

"What will you do once he returns?"

"Give him an ultimatum, like I should have done long ago. Rejoin our family, our life, and restore his, and my, honor and live. Do not, and die."

Who the hell were these people? Was this Rom's father? And did that make the other Rom's brother? He hadn't mentioned that he even had a brother. Why did he look and feel so familiar? The physical resemblance that he, in particular, bore to Rom was eerie and a funny feeling sat hard in the pit of her stomach.

"He will not."

"Then he will die."

"We need to know what powers he has gained, father, so we are victorious. I've heard he is very powerful."

"He won't kill me. If he kills me, he kills his mother and he hasn't had the balls to do that in over

six hundred years. But even if he thinks he can, we have your secret weapon, do we not Taiven?"

Taiven's smile was evil, but there was something else underlying. Something Sarah couldn't quite decipher. Something that was good. Why did she feel like she knew this vampire already? Malevolence rolled off the other vampire in almost visible, potent waves that made her sick, but that same vibe was not present in Taiven. His evilness was a shroud, a cover-up, but it was so evident to Sarah she didn't understand why the other vampire couldn't recognize it.

"When is she to report?" the man, whom Taiven called father, asked.

"She is due home tomorrow with an update. Romaric has remained elusive for all these years, so I suspect it may take some time to locate him."

"For the sake of her own life, she'd better hope her search bears fruit. What of our other project?"

Sarah noticed a visible change in Taiven at that question. He was barely able to control his rage. Again, this was so clear to her, but the other vampire seemed completely oblivious.

"Another shipment is due within the week."

"Good. Good. I would like to sample the wares this time. Make sure they are ... untainted."

A sneer crossed Taiven's face. "They won't be untainted if you sample them."

Anger rolled off the other vampire. "You think to deny me?"

"I do believe that I am in charge of this aspect of our business, father."

286

Suddenly an unknown force hurled Taiven across the room and held him pinned high against the stone wall. He wailed in obvious agony.

"I do believe you have forgotten your place, Taiven," the other vampire stated flatly.

As quickly as Taiven was held to the wall, he was released and now lay panting on the floor.

"I'll expect you to personally escort me." He turned and walked away without waiting for a response.

Taiven stood, brushed himself off and shifted his eyes directly to hers. Sarah sucked in a breath, fear permeating every single muscle. His heated gaze traveled slowly over her, lingering on the swell of her breasts, almost as if he knew her intimately. Something niggled in the back of her brain that made her very uncomfortable. Something she didn't want to examine too closely. She was dreaming, she knew it, and while she could see people in her dreams, they didn't really "see" her, per se, like what was happening now. This was just as real as if she were standing in the flesh before him. And she knew he wouldn't forget their conversation, like everyone else before him.

Wake up, wake up, wake up, she chanted. Over the last few months, Kate had helped Sarah tremendously to have control of her dreams, but waking at will wasn't one she could master. The dream ended when it ended, and not a second before.

"Yes, dreamwalker. I see you. And I've been waiting for you. Sarah."

Holy balls. He knew her name?

287

"Yes, I know who you are, Sarah. I've been watching over you since you were born. You are Romaric's new lovely mate." She didn't miss his eyes as they moved to the intricate mating mark wrapped around her left thumb or the flare of jealousy that was quickly gone. "Lucky him."

Gulp. That nagging sensation picked up speed, refusing to be ignored. The sick feeling in the pit of her stomach intensified. Had it been him all along instead of Rom?

"I need to meet with my brother."

"Who's your brother?" She knew exactly who he was referring to, but they'd never mentioned Rom's name so she wasn't about to.

"Don't play dumb, Sarah. You're far above that."

She snorted, unable to help her reaction and unable to believe this was really happening. "Why? So you can kill him? I think I'll take a pass on delivering that message."

He continued, unfazed by her derision. "Tell him to meet me at the Reverie in four days' time. Midnight."

The uncanny similarities between Rom and Taiven were many. In looks, build and personality. Apparently the Dietrich men thought they could command anyone to do anything at any time and they would jump. No questions asked. Well, just like Rom, Taiven needed someone to knock him down a peg or two. Or a hundred.

"No."

He regarded her with the same cool look that Rom had given her dozens of times already. "You will if you want him to live, female."

Then he was gone.

Sarah woke with a start, heart beating out of her chest, veins swarming with adrenaline. Thoughts and emotions swirled like a violent tornado through her head. Rom had a brother. She'd talked to him. He *knew* her. *He* was the one all along, not Rom. He was the shadow in her dreams. The thought made her sick.

He'd touched her.

He'd wanted her.

Oh God.

Why on Earth would Rom's brother have been the one in her dreams all these years? Yet now that she'd met him, she knew it to be true. Only in this last dream she'd had of him before she'd mated Rom did he ever show any interest in her in a sexual way. All other times she'd felt safe, protected. *Watched over.*

Why did she believe him when he insinuated he was trying to help Rom, even though everything else about him creeped her out?

She thought back to Seraphina's cryptic words. *"You are the only one who can save him."* Was this what she had meant or was it something else? God, she was so confused.

She tried moving but was pinned to the mattress tightly by two solid arms and a heavy leg thrown over hers.

"What's wrong, beauty?" a husky voice rasped in her ear, setting her body on fire in a totally different way. Would his every touch and every word always affect her like this, she wondered. If she was lucky, the answer was yes.

Should she tell him about the dream? Was it a trap? Or was Taiven really trying to help save Rom's life? She believed the latter to be true.

"I had a dream," she replied.

"Mmm," he nibbled on her earlobe. "Did it involve you riding my cock? Because mine did." His left hand was now roaming over her nakedness, leaving tiny goose bumps behind.

She stifled a moan. They needed to talk, not spend hours making love, even though she'd like to simply forget the whole disturbing conversation she'd just had with his brother and do just that. She would leave out the part, however, about how he's haunted her dreams for the last twenty some years and she'd mistaken his brother for him.

Well ... here goes nothing.

"No. It was about Taiven."

Chapter 44

Rom

His hand stilled. His muscles went rigid with fear. "What did you just say?"

She turned in his arms, facing him. "I just had a conversation with your brother, Taiven."

He couldn't breathe. "That's not possible."

"It's not possible because? You know I'm a dreamwalker, Rom."

Fuck.

Jumping out of bed, he began pacing, barely checking the anger and terror washing like icicles through his veins. "Sarah, tell me what the fuck just happened."

Grabbing the sheet, she covered herself and sat against the headboard, concern and anxiety wafting off her.

"I had a dream about your brother and your father. I think."

Double fuck.

It seemed they hadn't talked about a lot before they bonded. They'd not talked about Sarah's dreamwalking skills yet so he didn't really know exactly how hers worked. Each of her sisters had slightly different variations of the talent.

"How does your skill work, exactly?"

"Uh ... I don't really know. I have conversations with people. I learn things that they don't remember telling me because, of course, we talked about it in my dream state and not while awake. It's always been a pain in the ass, honestly."

"So you had a conversation with my brother? Just now?"

She nodded, clearly unnerved by his agitation.

"What about my father?"

"No. Just your brother."

Did they know who she was? If so, he was fucked. They would come after her. Use her as leverage to get to him. She was in terrible danger, and for the first time since they'd bonded, he wished he had waited until he could have taken care of this threat for good. His father would not hesitate to slaughter his mate if he didn't agree to any crazy-ass terms he threw at him. And if they ever found Sarah, Rom would do anything they asked of him to save her. Absolutely fucking anything.

"Tell me exactly, *word for word*, what was said."

"Okay." Sarah spent the next several minutes reiterating what happened and now he was absolutely beside himself. His brother knew who she was. He *knew* she was his mate. He could *see* her and even Sarah knew this dream was different from any she'd had in the past. How could that be? Where on Earth could he have reaped that skill?

Fucking hell. This was bad.

At one time, he and Taiven had been close. Inseparable. Taiven was only thirty years his junior. But as Taiven had become fully blooded, he began to change. He took on his father's evil, malicious qualities and even Romaric couldn't change the path that Taiven had headed down. Another one of the reasons he'd left home and never looked back. How he could be cut from the same cloth as his father and brother were, he didn't know.

He'd obviously been lucky and inherited his mother's kind heart, at least in the aspect of respecting human life. Of any life for that matter. Rom was cold, calculating and deadly when he needed to be. But he did not thrive on killing. He never had. He never would. And that's exactly what his father wanted to make of him.

A heartless, cold-blooded killer. A mini Makare.

"Are you going to go?" she whispered, unshed tears shining bright.

He stood at the end of their bed, unable to take his eyes off the woman that he'd come to love so. His heart swelled so much he thought it would burst and he had a hard time even remembering how incomplete his life was without her. How she could have wormed her way so far into his heart and soul and psyche within such a short period of time, he had no clue. But whenever he laid his eyes upon her, he literally felt the hardness in him melt away, being replaced by the most glorious warmth only love could possibly bring.

She was scared for him, but he thought just as she did. This was not a trap. What it was exactly, he wasn't sure, but he would find out.

He'd planned on going to Romania anyway, but would head out a couple of days earlier than anticipated to do his own investigation. And he needed to meet Ainsley before she returned to Romania.

"Yes. I am."

A stray tear escaped as she tried holding in her sobs. He could feel her anguish and anxiety for him. For *them*. She silently held out a hand and he climbed back onto the bed, taking her into his arms.

"It will be okay, beauty. This is a meeting. Nothing more."

"I'm scared. I just want all of this shit to go away so we can be happy."

"I will make it so. I swear it, Sarah."

And he would. He would do anything it took, use anybody he needed and kill anyone he had to in order to keep Sarah safe. So he could live the happy life he'd fucking earned.

God help anyone who stood in his path. If his father wanted a heartless, cold-blooded killer, he'd get one. Romaric's wrath would know no bounds until every damn threat had been eliminated.

And right now ... outside of the lords and their mates, everything and everyone was fair game.

Chapter 45

Geoffrey

They sat around a very long conference table, a thirty-page report and maps spread out in front of them. All courtesy of Circo, Romaric's lieutenant, who had clearly worked the last twenty-four hours churning data.

Romaric had called an hour ago demanding he attend this strategy meeting and, of course, was blindfolded and 'escorted' personally by Romaric's lieutenant. Very *Mission Impossible*. Quite frankly, he was surprised to be included at all outside of the information he was gathering and handing over. All the lords were present, as well as their respective lieutenants and a few others he hadn't met before, and had it not been for one person in this room, he had no doubt only his head would have been in attendance at this meeting. Probably sitting on a gold-plated platter in the middle of the table like a fucking centerpiece. Or a dartboard. The menace aimed his way by every other member in the room was palpable and unmistakable.

He was an unwelcome interloper.

And he did not miss the power pulsing in the room, reminding him that if he made one false move, he would be dead quicker than he could blink. Of course, the very sharp, very long knife, that Damian had laid in front of him, could have clued him in too.

But right now he held all the cards, which was the only reason he was even present. And alive. And he'd been handing them over slowly to the lords, needing to keep a couple of critical ones in his pocket for the right time, for if he showed them too early, his usefulness would end and he'd likely be a dead vamp. And a few weeks ago, he would have actually welcomed it. Now, however … now, he had every reason to want to live. He was desperate to get his Moira. Not that he deserved her, or ever would.

"So there are twenty-one locations, spread out in twenty different states," Circo stated. Geoffrey hadn't been exposed to Circo much, but in the bit he had, he already had immense respect for his intelligence. And there were twenty-two locations, as he'd found out last night, but he was going to keep that to himself just a tad bit longer until he did some additional research on this very small, very specialized compound.

"Do we have all the records now?" Damian snarled at Geoffrey.

Letting a smirk turn his lip, he retorted, "All electronic records. Not all paper copies. As you know, this has been going on for some time. Well before electronic recordkeeping, and it would look mighty suspicious if I were to back up a fucking truck to each facility and haul out reams of papers."

After several tense seconds, Damian sneered, "You're living on the edge, vampire. And I'm fucking hoping you put one foot over so I can push you the rest of the way."

Geoffrey held the furious vampire's glare and smiled. In another life, he had no doubt Damian would be a friend. But the only thing he could hope now is that any time he was around the powerhouse that Damian wouldn't burn him to a crisp.

He'd taken several liberties at being Damian DiStephano over the years and Damian knew it. Yes, he was responsible for taking Damian's mate's mother into captivity. But that had been the mission. Retrieve a powerful witch. And back then, he did what was commanded of him without question, brainwashed into believing it was all 'for the cause'.

Geoffrey had done countless deplorable and heinous things over his lifetime and he was under no false illusions that his current attempts to right some of the wrongs he'd helped create would absolve him in either the lords' eyes or his own. Since he'd discovered the level of Xavier's depravity, whenever the opportunity presented itself, he'd tried to do the right thing. Shit, there were untold lives he'd tried to save and things he'd done that he hadn't even told the lords about yet. Because a martyr he definitely was not. But he'd spend the rest of his life, what was left of it, trying to atone for his sins. A vamp had to start somewhere, right?

"Damian, we all know your feelings, but we have business to conduct here and like it or not, we need him," Rom stated flatly.

Yes, they did need him.

The last twenty-four hours had been spent tracking down information on not only the inner workings of the transportation system Xavier had so intricately weaved together, but the astonishing revelation around the chemicals used in the vamps bloodings, and he was exhausted. It took a lot of effort to hold someone's form when he mimicked and he'd done it countless times over the last day. So much so, that he'd had to break down and feed from the vein of another female, who was *not* his Moira, so he could continue his efforts. He'd been nearly unable to stomach it. The only way he could get through it was to close his eyes and envision it was Beth's sweet nectar running down his throat.

"Update us," Rom commanded.

He bristled but kept it under wraps. He was fucking tired of being ordered around like a dog, but the last thing he needed to do was piss off an entire room of immensely powerful vamps who would just as sooner see his head severed from his body than leave him breathing.

"The human scientists have created a super growth hormone that not only speeds development of the children at an alarming rate, but also seems to give them the bulk, size and skills of an advanced vampire.

"They were successful at developing this formula fifteen years ago and first started experimenting at fifteen and twenty, the second and third bloodings. Just in the last six years they've extended those experiments to the babes, but only the ones kept in two smaller locations. They've been tweaking the potency to where they can now develop a full-grown vampire within six years' time, but it has less than a thirty-percent success rate, which is why they don't inject all the babes, only a small percentage of them. And most disturbingly, the next iteration, they have developed, are for full-blooded vamps to bring them into full power well before age one hundred."

There was one far more disturbing thing he'd discovered that had been developed decades ago, but he needed to vet that out a bit further before divulging to this group. Because if it were true, it made what he'd just shared seem like a bouquet of freshly cut roses about ready to bloom.

"Christ," Damian breathed. The look he shot Geoffrey would make lesser vampires cower. "You knew about this, didn't you, fucker?"

Geoffrey held his glare with one of his own. "No. I did not. Everyone has a piece of the puzzle, but not one vampire is privy to everything, including me. I suspected something was going on, yes, and that's what I've been working to uncover so I could shut it down. But until this week, I've been unable to find anything concrete.

"Xavier has singlehandedly created a very complex and siloed system. All locations work in isolation from each other and, no one, vamp or human alike, are even aware there are but one or two additional compounds. Babes are taken from their mothers after birth and are moved from place to place. That was all part of the ruse, of course, to throw everyone off."

"And how could children be transported from various places without someone figuring this out before?" Devon asked.

That's what had taken Geoffrey a while to uncover. "Of course Xavier won't let the humans leave the compounds, so vamps have to transport the children. As I said, everyone involved has only a couple pieces of the puzzle. Let's say vamp one moves babe one from location one to location three. Vamp one is only ever privy to locations one and three. When it's time to move babe one to another location, vamp two steps in and moves from location three to location two, for example. Vamp one knows nothing about location two and vamp two knows nothing of location one."

"Unbelievable," Damian muttered.

"There's more. The reason it's taken me so long to piece things together is because Xavier is as paranoid as a conspiracy theorist. He's been moving compounds."

"Christ," Ren spat. "This just keeps getting worse and worse. How are we supposed to catch a fucking ghost?"

"It's complex, yes. But I think we can all agree at this point that we'll simply need to develop a strategy based on what we know *today* and pull the trigger. Cut off the head, the snake will die. So our primary objective is the fucking head, but we'll decimate as much of the body as possible and have to deal with what's left afterward. Circo, review what you've put together," said Romaric.

"There are one hundred twelve women spread out among fourteen locations. Each compound is noted on your maps as W one through W fourteen and as you can see, they are spread out in fourteen different states. The other seven locations are boarding houses for the children, eighty-nine heads in total, if the records are accurate. On your maps, the locations marked I one and I two appear to be only for the infants, as Geoffrey already discussed, and there are only a dozen infants between the two. At some point, they spread them out to the locations marked I three-I seven. Between all twenty-one locations, there are also between two and fifteen other humans. That information is a little more sketchy."

"We have to hit all locations at once in order to take Xavier by surprise," Ren said. "And that's going to be pretty fucking hard to do, given they are all in different states."

"Does Xavier have a witch?" Devon asked, looking at him.

Devon would probably kill him on the spot if he found out who was helping Geoffrey, so he simply nodded. "But she is in *my* pocket and that's all you need to know."

"I decide what I need to know, rogue. And we need to understand how powerful this witch is and if she's going to fuck you, and consequently us, over."

"She won't. She's trying to right as many wrongs as I am."

The tension in the room increased and Geoffrey felt the not too subtle power Devon and Damian painfully threw his way. He internally grimaced, not wanting to show any outward sign of weakness.

"So with all of the intel now gathered, why do we need you any longer?" Damian snarled.

"Who said you have *all* the intel?" Probably not the smartest retort, but, Jesus, that vamp got under his skin. If the lords wanted to ensure Xavier was destroyed, along with the compounds, they'd best keep him alive because only he would know his schedule.

The smile Damian gave him was pure evil. "I'm getting hard at the thought of killing you, rogue."

He scoffed. "I can't wait to see you try."

Romaric interrupted. "Christ, Damian. Set aside your ambivalence for once. Geoffrey's still on the inside and is our best chance at tracking Xavier's whereabouts. We need to be absolutely certain that he's killed in this next raid, because I, for one, am tired of chasing his sick fucking ass all over the goddamn country and worrying about our mates."

Yes, Geoffrey had not missed the brand spanking new mating mark around Rom's left thumb, and now that he'd found his own Moira and could do nothing about it, seeing Rom's made him unreasonably jealous. And he didn't like that feeling one goddamn bit.

"We need a few days to pull together enough resources for the raid," Devon said, looking at Geoffrey pointedly. "And to make sure we have all of the information necessary to kill this fucker once and for all."

Geoffrey nodded sharply. Once his suspicions were confirmed, he'd have no choice but to divulge the other compound, because of anything more critical than destroying Xavier, destroying this place was a close second. And the clock was ticking, because Xavier expected something concrete regarding the lords or his daughters within the next few days, so he was going to have to come up with something creative to buy himself more time.

As they dispersed and he steeled himself to meet with Xavier next. He prayed to a God he didn't believe in that they could end this once and for all.

And he would finally be free.

Chapter 46

Mike

"When are you coming back?" Jake asked. Same question, different day. Since he'd taken his "leave of absence" several months back, they'd met up regularly to shoot the shit and throw back a few beers. They'd hung out occasionally when they were partners, but hadn't socialized too often, and he now had to wonder why he hadn't let Jake in before now.

But he knew. Mike had made a sport out of keeping people from getting too close to him. Jake always tried and Mike always pushed back. And no one had gotten past those roadblocks ... until Giselle. She'd changed him in ways she didn't even realize.

He wanted to be a better man. *For her.*

He wanted to get his shit together. *For her.*

And he desperately wanted to unburden himself from this fucking boulder of revenge that had been weighing him down like a permanent set of cement shoes for the last eleven years. *For both of them.*

He loved being a cop. It was in his blood, but he'd been doing it for all the wrong reasons.

Danger.

Revenge.

Guilt.

Mainly guilt. A feeble attempt to make up for his past transgressions with regards to Jamie. So he wasn't sure he was ever going back.

"I don't know, man," he finally responded.

"What the fuck do you do all day? Eat bon bons and watch soap operas?"

Jake didn't know anything about vampires. There were days he longed for that ignorance again, but those days were now further apart, because had it not been for vamps, he never would have met the woman he was now head-over-heels in love with. Even if she didn't feel the same way.

Not for the first time he had to wonder if what had happened with Jamie had somehow led him to Giselle. And that guilt tore him apart inside because she'd suffered so much at the hands of the devil himself.

"Pretty much. Young and the Restless is getting pretty good. Billy's daughter got killed in a hit and run by none other than his wife's brother, Adam. Now Adam's gone missing, presumed dead, but he's not. They never recovered the body. It's some twisted shit, bro."

Jake gaped at him. "Wow ... you've really gone and grown a pussy."

He laughed. "I've always had one. I'm just embracing it now."

"Waitress!" Jake yelled. When she sauntered over to their table, in her too low cut tiny white tee and almost indecent black skirt, Jake ordered. "Two shots, please. Wild Turkey. This guy's dick clearly needs regrown. And keep 'em comin' sweetheart."

He hated this dingy, dirty bar, which some stupid fuck with absolutely no creativity had named *The Bar*, but it was within three blocks of his house, so it was a quick walk home. Old habits die hard. Cop or not, he wasn't about to get behind the wheel after having even a couple of beers. And definitely not after shooters. Plus, they did have decent live music, which was playing a little too loudly in the background.

He enjoyed his guys' night with Jake, but he was also here avoiding one pissed off female. Giselle had called and texted him several times in the last day, but he'd not returned any of them. And he'd kept conveniently away from his house because he had no doubt she would probably stalk him there. And if he ran into her tonight, he hoped to be too drunk to care if she rebutted him again.

A pussy move? Perhaps. But she'd seriously pissed him off when he'd woken up the other day to find her gone. After he'd laid his soul bare, making himself more vulnerable than he'd ever been in his entire life. And he wanted her to suffer a little, like she'd made him suffer.

Yes, he was a vindictive asshole. Or a fucking fraidy cat. Take your pick.

"To our dicks," Jake toasted, holding up his shot glass.

"May they grow," he cheerfully replied before throwing the burning whiskey back.

Half an hour and four shots later, all heads turned toward the entrance when a simply stunning curvy blonde walked in wearing clothes that were a man's wet dream. And his fuzzy brain was immediately on alert. This beautiful, and deadly, creature with the arresting green eyes and porcelain skin was clearly vampire.

A sharp slap to his pec by his former partner's hand had him wincing. "Holy fuck. Who the hell is that, bro?"

Someone who's looking for a tasty liquid meal.

"How the hell should I know? This isn't fucking *Cheers* where everybody knows your name." Although Charlie, the bartender, and two of the waitresses knew his pretty goddamned well.

"Dude, she's coming over here," Jake whispered excitedly.

Great.

She-vamp sat at their table without invitation. Christ, the gall of vampires irritated the fuck out of him. She may come wrapped in pretty packaging, but she was venomous and deadly as a rattlesnake hiding in the brush, waiting to strike and kill its unsuspecting, innocent victim.

"Buy me a drink," her silken voice purred to Jake. A demand. Not a question.

Before Mike could tell her to pound sand, Jake piped up. Clearly his dick was enjoying the potent whiskey. "What's your poison, doll?"

Mike could hardly contain the eye roll. There were so many things wrong with that question he couldn't even begin to count.

Her gaze flicked to the more than a half dozen empty small glasses sitting in front of them and back to Jake. "Looks like I need to catch up. I'll have what you're having."

Jake tried flagging down the waitress, but she was clearly enjoying the ass fondling currently being given to her by the tatted, wife-beater wearing biker dude two tables over, so Jake went to the bar himself to retrieve the shots.

As soon as he was out of earshot, Mike snapped, "You should look elsewhere for dinner, sweetheart."

He didn't know what to expect for a response, but a broad, shit-eating grin was not it. She-vamp leaned back in her chair, rhythmically tapping her fingers against the worn, sticky table. "Are you offering instead, human?"

Shit ... should he deny his friend the intense pleasure a vampire bite could bring? Just thinking of how hard he'd orgasmed with Giselle's mouth on him made him uncomfortably hard.

Yes. Yes, he was cockblocking his friend. He didn't know this female and while Mike may be more accepting that not all vamps have evil intentions, he was far from blindly trusting them.

"Fuck no. There are plenty of unsuspecting humans—and maybe some *suspecting* ones—you can find. But my friend isn't one of them."

Her nose wrinkled a bit when she answered. "He's a big boy. I think we'll let him decide for himself."

"I— "

He was cut short when Jake returned with a tray of amber-filled glasses, precious liquid sloshing over the sides in his haste to return to the dangerous beauty he thought he would bed tonight.

Shit. Now what?

Just then he felt a charge in the air. It was electric and every hair follicle he had stood on end. His cock hardened painfully and his blood sang. Slowly he turned his head toward the entrance and standing just inside, sights set firmly on him, was the woman he couldn't stop thinking about. In the flesh. Everything and everyone else faded away.

How did she find him here?

He almost didn't care. She'd tracked *him* down and that's all that really mattered. She was here and she was a fucking glorious sight, looking all pissed and shit. He felt fury radiating from her across the twenty-five feet that separated them. Her gaze flicked to the yet unnamed female sitting at their table and he couldn't help the slow smile that turned his lips. Green jealousy swirled with the icy blue of her eyes, making them a mesmerizing jade color that he could clearly see from here.

In a blink, she was standing at their table, hands on her luscious, curvy hips. She looked absolutely ravishing in the skintight, barely-there black dress and leopard print heels she wore. Christ, she was simply amazing. Every cell in his body screamed *mine* when he looked at her. And the possessive vibe and sharp daggers shooting from her eyes echoed the same feeling in her.

"Who the fuck is this?" she fumed. Every ripple of toned muscle she held in check mesmerized him. His cock strained, aching to get to the woman who owned every part of him.

"She's nobody." His eyes never left hers. He was done with this shit. She was coming home with him and she would be his. At the first sight of her standing across the room, his patience snapped. He was done waiting for her to make a decision. It was being made *for* her.

"Why haven't you returned my calls or messages?" Her words were filled with venom, but hurt visibly strained her beautiful pixie features and all of a sudden he felt like a bastard.

Throwing sixty bucks on the table to more than cover his drinks, he stood, grabbed her by the hand and began dragging her protesting ass to the exit. Screw Jake. He was a big boy and could handle himself just fine. Hopefully, Mike didn't find his body in the sparse trees outside this shithole tomorrow, but he wasn't about to waste another minute letting Giselle flounder in the wind.

"What do you think you're doing?" she yelled as they left the shabby building.

Taking her around the corner, where it was dark and private, he pushed her up against the paint chipped wood, trapping her in place with his body. Taking her face in his hands, he pushed his throbbing erection against her perfectly aligned core.

"I'm doing what I should have done a long time ago." Feathering kisses along her jaw, he took her mouth in a bruising kiss. "I'm going to take you home and fuck you stupid until you scream for me, Giselle. I'm going to fuck every other man out of your head and replace every single bad memory with nothing but pleasure. With nothing but love. With nothing but *me*."

Reaching his hands under her short hem, he pushed aside her panties and found her soaking pussy. Without waiting for invitation, he pushed two fingers in, circling his thumb on her swollen clit. He swallowed her moan with his mouth, whispering against her lips, "And don't tell me you don't want this or you're not ready. Your pussy is weeping for me." Not stopping the movement of his fingers, he continued, "You're mine, and tonight I'm going to prove to you that I'm yours. You can trust me with both your body and your heart, Giselle."

His assault was brutal and the clenching of her walls indicated she was close to tipping. Nipping her earlobe hard, she exploded around his fingers, digging her nails into his shoulders so hard, he was sure she'd leave bloody crescent-shaped marks. But he didn't care. *Bring it, babe.* He wasn't taking no for an answer. She was scared and scarred, but she trusted him or she wouldn't be here. She wouldn't have sought him out. She wouldn't keep coming back.

Feathering kisses along her neck, he pulled back and looked into her heavy, sated eyes, once again laying his heart at her feet for the crushing. "God knows I tried to fight this, but I'm done. I'm a complete and total goner and you own me, Giselle. All of me. You've wrecked me for anyone else. I fucking love you. It will *ruin* me if you walk away from me again." Pausing, he murmured, "You are mine. Come home with me." He wanted to say forever but stopped short. He'd already said enough to drink himself into a coma for a month should she turn and abandon him again.

After several tense moments, just when he thought she'd reject him yet again, she grabbed and clung to him instead, and finally whispered the one little word he'd longed to hear for months.

"Okay."

Chapter 47

Sarah

They'd been back in Milwaukee on and off for two days now. Rom had been gone much of the time in strategy meetings with Dev, Damian and others. Things were ramping up and everyone felt the thick, oppressive tension in the air, weighing down on them like an anvil waiting to drop.

And Sarah was scared shitless. Rom would go to Romania later tonight, even though the meeting with his brother wasn't for another two days and she'd been on the edge of a panic attack all morning. Kate and Analise had tried taking her mind off things with a workout, but it was no use. All she could think of was never seeing Rom again and that flat out terrified her. They'd just found each other and it felt very unfair that the universe was endlessly throwing these life altering and threatening situations at them.

Screw Rom's sadistic father.

Fuck her maniacal father.

Give them both a one-way ticket to fire and brimstone.

She just wanted all of this ugliness to go away. If Rom could magically poof them to another alternate plane where fluffy marshmallows were clouds and milk chocolate ran in shallow streams and never made you fat, she'd do it. Yes, it was childishly naïve, but who the hell cared at this point. Looked like sunshiny Rosie hadn't strayed too far.

She also couldn't get the latest dream about Seraphina out of her head, although she tried to temper those thoughts around Rom, because she wasn't quite ready to talk to him about it yet.

Who exactly was she to Rom and why was Sarah so afraid to ask him? Seraphina hadn't returned in a dream since the morning that they'd bonded and she had a feeling she wouldn't. She'd delivered her message and she'd shown Sarah what she wanted her to know. Now it was up to Sarah to do what she would with that information.

And that was the million-dollar question. Did she *want* to know who this girl was? Because Sarah knew that Seraphina had been very important to Rom and that knowledge sat like a hard twisted ball of angry jealousy in the pit of her stomach.

Needing some time to herself, she sat alone in the library. She'd searched for a book to divert her attention and decided on the Gillian Flynn novel *Gone Girl*. Only two chapters in and already riveted, she felt someone staring at her. Looking up, Giselle stood in all her frozen ice-cold glory in the doorway.

"What?" Sarah barked. She just couldn't find it in herself today to be nice to anyone, least of all Giselle, the one person in the world who cared about only herself and what you could do for her. And she had enough of her own damn problems to worry about what Giselle wanted.

"Jesus. What crawled up your ass and died?" Giselle spouted as she sauntered into the room, sitting across from her on the setae.

Hmm ... That was her *line.*

She crossed her very long legs, of which Sarah was insanely jealous. "So you and Rom, huh?" Giselle hedged, picking imaginary lint off the arm of the fancy chair.

Had she landed in an alternate universe? She looked around the room to make sure she wasn't in Kansas or Oz or Hell because those are the only places this conversation would happen. Giselle didn't converse. She didn't ask questions. She didn't answer questions. She certainly didn't give a damn about you, how your day was or your latest OPI nail polish color. She was the vampire version of the stupid childhood game, dizzy bat.

Sarah narrowed her eyes, suspicion bubbling. "What do you want, Giselle?"

Instead of answering, she gestured toward the book Sarah was reading. "Damn brilliant read. Can you believe that wife set up her husband to take the fall for her fake murder and then had the balls to turn back up? That's a mind-fuck right there."

Sarah frowned, throwing the book to the side. She'd purposely avoided reviews and conversations about this book so the ending wouldn't be spoiled.

So ... thanks for that, bitch.

"Did you bring in a pint of Ben and Jerry's and bottle of wine too so we can gossip about the best sex toys and the couple of hotties that Thane

315

is regularly banging at the club?" she asked sarcastically.

Wow ... her snarkiness had reached an all-time epic level. *Rock on Nancy, you callous ho.*

Thinking that would surely send Giselle storming out of the room, imagine her surprise when she busted out laughing instead. *Giselle could laugh?* And the eighth wonder was just discovered.

"I like you, Sarah," she said, wiping a stray tear.

She liked her? What the hell? "Will the real Giselle please stand up?" she muttered.

Raising a brow, Giselle bit out, "Wow ... she knows Eminem too."

"I'm confused at what's going on here."

"Can't a girl just want to talk?"

"Yes ... but ..." She didn't want to say it. It was too cruel, even for her. Even though she was sure a hurtful word or jibe couldn't pierce skin as thick and tough as reinforced steel.

"Yes, but I'm not a *girl*, right?"

A wry smile curled Sarah's lips. "You said it, not me."

Giselle watched her for a few very long moments before speaking softly; like she really had a heart beating in that freezing tundra she called a chest. "I have information about your mother. Your birth mother. I know her name."

Sarah's heart stopped. After all these years of wondering, she was about to find out her mother's name. And if she had other living relatives. Aunts? Uncles? Cousins? Grandparents?

And suddenly it felt almost like a betrayal of the two people that had raised her as their own. Loved her just as much as they'd loved Jack, their natural child. Unlike Analise, Sarah had luckily landed in a very loving home with truly loving parents. Although she'd dreamt of this day for so long, she honestly didn't think that she'd ever be successful at finding a shred of information, especially given the horrific way she'd been conceived.

With Giselle's next intuitive question, Sarah saw a completely different side to the strong, arrogant and cold female vampire. A softer side. A *caring* side, even. One she knew always was locked deep inside, but just couldn't bust through her harsh exterior for fear of being vulnerable.

"Would you like to wait until you're ready?"

Would she? Would it even matter that she had other family out in the world that she didn't know? Who didn't know her? Eventually she would have to spend less and less time with her parents as it was because now that she was bonded to a vampire, she'd never age and after time, that just couldn't be hidden. Would it be fair to start a relationship with others, only to have to cut them out too?

After only seconds of mulling, the answer was clear. It didn't matter how much time she could spend with them. Because the minutes we spend with our loved ones in our time on earth, no matter how short or fleeting, create irreplaceable memories that she believed were carried on into the next life.

She wouldn't take back a second of the time she'd spent with Rom, no matter if their lives ended with these threats looming over them or not. Loving him, no matter if for two weeks or two millennia, was a blessing, and if she decided to not move forward with this, with meeting her family, she'd be doing the same thing he'd tried to do to her by not bonding. And then she'd be a hypocrite.

Decision made, and still trying to get over the fact that Giselle had actually followed through with her request, she willed the butterflies in her stomach to settle down and nodded at Giselle to continue.

"No. I'm ready."

Chapter 48

Sarah

Marna Clark. Marna Clark. Her mother's name echoed off the walls in her head. She was just twenty when she was kidnapped, tortured and forced to have her in horrific conditions. And while her grandmother, Ellie, had recently passed away, she had a grandfather that was alive, still living in Des Plains, Illinois. *Bud.* Just the name made her smile. She also had an aunt, Brynne. Twenty-nine and unmarried. Twenty-nine. She was hardly older than Sarah. She felt giddy thinking about the chance to meet them both and see pictures of her mother.

And what about her mom? Had she been forced to have any other children? If she did, they were rogues by now and according to Rom, all the rogues would be destroyed. That made her sad, even though she knew there could be no other real outcome. But was there a chance that maybe one of the younger kids, who were still untainted, could be saved? Probably not and she just needed to let it go.

Giselle told her that her mother was likely killed after she was born. Apparently bearing barren vampire females were pretty much life ending in their underground prison. And how completely fucked up was that. Males determined the sex, and she didn't think that could be any different in the vampire species, but what the hell did she know.

"Hello, beauty," a raspy voice rumbled in her ear, brushing over her nerve endings like feathers. Rooted to the same spot in the library for the last hour, she'd been so engrossed in her thoughts she hadn't heard Rom approach.

"Hello yourself, my handsome mate."

"What are you contemplating so hard?" He sat down next to her, but immediately pulled her into his lap, straddling him. Her favorite position. Well, one of many, really.

"I received some interesting news this afternoon."

He brushed an errant curl from her face. "You look disturbed. Tell me who upset you and I'll take care of them."

"Really? And what will you do exactly?"

He considered her question for a moment, before answering. "I'll fuck them up, of course."

Laughing, she said, "Oh my God. You are totally serious. What if one of my sisters upset me? Would you *fuck* them up?"

"Well, of course, not. But I'd have a talk with their mates and then their punishment is up to them."

She slapped him on the shoulder. "You need to stop being so protective. You can't shield me from anything or anyone that could make me unhappy, Rom. It's not realistic."

The loving look he gave would have brought her to her knees, had she not been sitting on them. But his words ... his words were so authentic and so sincere they brought tears to her eyes and melted her heart. "But I can try, Sarah."

Anyone, who thought Romaric was cold and heartless, didn't know a damn thing about him. He was scary fierce and frustratingly protective and aggressively dominating, but she'd come to decide those weren't bad qualities, because she knew without them, he wouldn't have the ability to love her as deeply and as strongly as he so clearly did.

"You are simply incredible," she murmured.

A smirk upturned the best lips she'd ever tasted. "Yes. I know."

"Ha! I'm beginning to think your ego is bigger than your cock, vampire."

In the next second, she was pinned underneath his heavy bulk, his evident desire pressing on just the right spot. "I can assure you, beauty, nothing is bigger than my cock," he replied before taking her lips in a soul-sucking kiss.

"Prove it," she said breathlessly when he trailed kisses down her neck to the swell of her breasts. She wanted nothing more than to spend the time they had before he went to Romania in a tangle of hot, sweaty limbs.

"That sounds like a challenge." Nimble fingers dipped inside the top of her blouse, seeking a rigid nipple, making her moan his name. "What about your news?" he rasped against her throat, sucking gently in just the right spot.

News ... what news? Every brain cell banded together with single-minded intention when he did those diabolical things with his mouth and hands and other— *harder*—body parts. And it wasn't to talk.

"Later. Take me home and fuck me."

"As you wish, milady," he chuckled.

Within seconds, they were back in their house in Washington, but in Rom's office instead of their bedroom.

"What are we doing in here?" she asked, chest still heaving from their earlier exertion. She ached for him to fill her and didn't need a pit stop so he could make a phone call or send a damn email for God's sake.

A slow, predatory smile spread across Rom's undeniably beautiful face and that familiar warmth zinged between her legs. His smoldering eyes blazed across every inch of her scantily clad body, and the fire he left behind burned its way straight south between her legs. She couldn't imagine ever tiring of the way he eyed her like she was his favorite meal.

"The only business I'll be conducting in here is to bury myself so far inside your pussy, you'll be begging me to stop."

She smiled lazily back. "Oh, you're wrong there. I'll never beg you to stop. Do your worst."

"Another challenge, beauty?" he said in a low, sensual voice.

"Do you expect anything less?" Taking several steps back, she slowly drew her hands up her torso, cupping her achy breasts through her white fitted tank. She didn't miss his sharp intake of breath or the heat his glowing eyes now threw her way. Whatever plans he had just gone completely by the wayside. This was now *her* show.

Feeling bold and definitely tempting the beast, she reached for the zipper on her short flowery skirt and eyes never leaving his, unzipped and dropped it to the floor. She'd worn a particularly sexy pair of deep blue and barely-there lacy thong panties, with an equally matching skimpy bra.

"You take my breath away, Sarah," he muttered. And without her now keen hearing, she wasn't sure she would have heard it from the distance she had now put between them. Intending to put on a little show, she wanted him riveted to her every movement, but those soft words were almost her undoing.

He was so alpha, but so romantic at the same time and the contrast was mind-blowing. Never knowing if something filthy dirty or heart wrenching was going to come out of his mouth always kept her on her toes.

Deciding to move on with the show, her hands moved to the hem of her shirt, bringing it up inch-by-inch, teasing the fabric against her sensitive flesh, aching for the feel of his fingers on her skin instead of hers, but enjoying too much the way his hungry eyes devoured her to rush this.

Pulling the tank over her head, she now stood in her matching lingerie set and a pair of tall summer wedges. Reaching behind, she undid the clasp of her bra and happily let it join the growing pile of discarded clothes on the floor beside her.

"Jesus," he growled. "I can smell your arousal from here. I could get drunk on your scent." He was now leaning against his desk; gripping it so tightly the knuckles on both hands were white. His breathing had become shallower and she reveled in the fact she could affect him like this.

Unable to help herself, she palmed and kneaded both breasts and closed her eyes, enjoyed the relief touching them gave her. Rolling her pebbled nipples between her fingers, she heard him groan and when she opened her lids, he was stroking his thick and strained erection through his pants, eyes laced with molten desire. His raw masculinity nearly had her running into his arms, begging for him to take her.

Snaking one hand down her stomach, instead, she inched it under her now very wet panties and ran a finger through her drenched folds, unable to help the moan that fell from her lips. Hot sparks of their shared connection now thundered through her veins.

She felt his lust.

It was heady.

Before she knew it, cold wood pressed against her back and cool air hit her naked sex moments before his hot mouth was upon her. "Enough," he rumbled and the vibrations against her aching body ratcheted up her lust tenfold. His thick fingers penetrated her roughly and he began a punishing rhythm as he nipped and licked and used his tongue in wicked ways that should be illegal. As she was about to crest he stopped, nipping everywhere but where she so desperately needed him to in order to send her flying.

"Don't tease," she whined. Sharp teeth pricked particularly hard, but not enough to break the skin. Dammit.

"I'm schooling you. And I have more patience than you can even fathom, beauty."

"Rom ..."

"Mmmm ... I could stay between these beautiful thighs all night." His hand moved again, slowly, dragging his wet digits deliciously along every last internal nerve ending. She shifted her hips trying to gain the pressure and rhythm she needed, but a well-placed arm stopped her flat.

"Please. I need to come."

"Ah, but you challenged the beast, Sarah, and he does so enjoy rising to it."

He brought her to the edge countless times, only to cruelly pull back, leaving her panting; a fine sheen of sweat now covered her straining body. She begged and pleaded until her voice was hoarse and her legs quivered with effort, but he gave her no any quarter.

Nearing orgasm again, she wept with joy and divine ecstasy when she felt the sting of his bite, scattering every thought to the wind. She cried out in sheer bliss, her eyes closed so tight she saw stars. Still in the throes of pleasure, her body flipped, the cold of the desk on her front quickly warming with her body heat.

Without warning, he harshly grabbed her hips and easily thrust his unyielding, silky shaft into her slick sheath and held still. "I'm going to fuck you now, beauty. Hard and fast and rough."

He withdrew until only his thick head remained inside and plunged again so rough her breath rushed out and she had to hang onto the edge of the desk for leverage. "And once I'm done fucking you and making you scream ..." out, in ... out, in ... out, in ..."I'm going to spend hours making love to you, making you moan."

"Oh God ... Rom ... so good."

It was a brutal, punishing coupling. Living up to everything he'd promised, she screamed for him now and moaned for him later as he spent the next several hours wringing unending hedonistic pleasure from every inch of her body.

She gloried in every single second of it, hoping beyond hope it wouldn't be their last.

Chapter 49

Rom

It was just after midnight and he needed to get moving, but he could hardly stomach the thought of leaving his mate, whose every naked limb was currently wrapped snugly around him in peaceful slumber. She gripped him tightly as if she was afraid he would sneak away in the dead of night.

As if.

She needn't worry. He wouldn't ever let her go. And although he wouldn't do anything foolish, he was done worrying that this would be the end. This was just the beginning. He may have a few loose ends to clean up to keep them both safe, but he hadn't lived this long by happenstance. He was confident in his strategic, battle and preternatural skills and he'd accepted the fact he couldn't do it alone. He would let Circo accompany him and he'd even tap Geoffrey, Devon or Damian if necessary. It was time to swallow his pride and just kill these fucks so he could move on.

So they could all be free.

There were so many things he wanted to do with Sarah. So many places he wanted take her and show her and make love to her. And he couldn't do any of those things with these threats hanging over their heads like vicious black thunderclouds. They'd all been hiding and he was tired of it. Sarah had spent the last several months tucked away in a house or a shelter, unable to enjoy the simple joys of going for a coffee or shopping for clothes. She'd told him the only time she'd been allowed out, other than a walk on the grounds, was to see her parents, and that was simply unacceptable.

He'd changed so much in just the short time he'd known Sarah. The vulnerability part he could do without, but he could honestly say she was the only one he would ever be comfortable *showing* vulnerability to. And who knew he had a softer, gentler, even romantic side? He sure as hell didn't. He didn't intend to say half the things he did to her, but when he opened his mouth, they just involuntarily poured out. It was sappy and maybe he needed to get his man card back, but fuck all if he just didn't care. Who knew such simple words could cause light as bright as a thousand suns in her eyes when he spoke them? He'd do and say anything to keep that light burning brilliant now and always.

And he'd do absolutely anything to keep her safe. With that thought, he begrudgingly tried to wake her. It was time.

"Beauty, it's time." Sarah was one of the strongest women he'd ever met, but she'd cried herself to sleep and every tear was like a shallow cut directly to his heart. It pained him to be parted from her as much as it did her.

"Sweetheart, time to wake." He gently shook her, but she was fast asleep. Rolling her onto her back, he extracted himself from her arms and legs. He took several minutes to simply admire not only her outer beauty, but also the inner beauty that shone so brilliantly it dwarfed the outer a hundred times over.

Leaning down, he placed soft kisses to her jaw and her neck downward until he got to the sweetest spot on earth. What the hell, another half hour wouldn't hurt. He'd woken her this way every day since they'd bonded and he wasn't about to break their streak. It was quickly becoming his good luck charm.

Several minutes later she was panting and thrashing and singing his name like a symphony as she came before her eyelids finally fluttered open. "Hi," she said softly.

He just smiled, suddenly not trusting his voice to remain steady.

Shit, pull it together. You're a goddamned lord for Christ's sake.

When she reached down to run a finger along his jaw, he almost lost it. Quickly crawling up her body, he grabbed her and buried his face in her neck. Wrapping her hands around his head, she pulled him closely to her.

"Come home to me or I'll haunt you forever."

He extracted himself from her, kissing her soft lips. "Always so bossy."

"You love it."

"Hmm ... I wouldn't use the word *love*." He would.

She smiled knowingly. She'd heard him. Their mental and emotional connection since bonding was strong, intense and incredibly amazing. Like everything he'd heard of but nothing he could have possibly expected or understood until he'd experienced it for himself. And their physical connection was simply mind-bending, but that was fully expected since it was the mating bond calling to one another.

Her eyes became watery as her face turned serious. "I love you, Romaric Dietrich."

He wasn't sure he could respond in kind without tearing up himself, so instead he said, "Jareth and Elliott will be you with at all times. Do not leave their sights. Understood?"

She nodded.

"I'll be home in forty-eight hours. And I'll have my phone. You can call me anytime, and I'll answer if I can. If I don't, please don't worry. I'll call you back as soon as I'm able."

"And you remember how to use the message feature when you can't answer right?"

Smiling, he pushed an errant hair from her sweaty forehead. "Yes, beauty."

"And you remember how to use the FaceTime feature, too, right?"

"I have absolutely no idea how the world survived over two thousand years without twenty-four seven access to someone."

She huffed. "Yes or no?"

"Yes."

"Good," her sultry voice replied. "Maybe you'll have time for a little phone sex while you're gone."

His groin hardened painfully at the thought. He would most definitely have to rethink his position on technology. "You haven't forgotten what challenging me entails so soon, have you?"

"Apparently I'm a slow learner," she retorted, a sly smile turning up her mouth.

Groaning, he leaned his forehead against hers. "I must go."

"Okay," she whispered.

He rose and dressed while she watched. "I want you at Dev's until I return."

Again she nodded. Sarah's skills had been increasing at an astonishing rate. Only days after their bonding, she was already able to flash at will, which was something that took both Kate and Analise several weeks to master. He had no doubt his powerful blood had contributed to that.

"I want you there within the hour."

She mockingly saluted. "Sir, yes sir."

Leaning down, he locked lips with hers, pouring his every emotion into it. "You'll pay for that when I return."

"I look forward to it," she quipped.

He walked toward the bedroom door. Circo was waiting in the kitchen for him and he was already late. But he couldn't leave without saying one final thing.

He turned. "I love you, Sarah."

The grin she gifted him with was one of the brightest he'd seen yet. And he suddenly had a new goal in life. Topping one brilliant smile with an even better one.

Chapter 50

Rom

"It's fucking cold up here," Circo complained.

"Jesus, you pussy. Stop your whining already," Rom snapped. Yes, it was much colder than what his blood had warmed to in Washington, but this was the safest place for their rendezvous.

"Where is she?" Circo asked.

"She'll be here."

Rom had met with Ainsley three days back and she'd returned to Romania a day before yesterday, just as he had. She was taking a huge risk to herself, and her family's safety, by not only coming to the United States to warn him, but if Makare or Taiven discovered her sleuthing right underneath their noses, no doubt Makare would hold a public execution soiree. And Ainsley would be the guest of honor.

He had one last fruitless meeting before it was time to reunite with his brother in two hours. While he waited for Ainsley to arrive, he couldn't help but let his mind wander back to his Sarah and the amazing phone sex she'd instigated last night when he'd finally managed to get FaceTime to work. He may have exaggerated his ability to figure it out, but damn it all to hell, he hated changing technology. He eventually had to ask Circo for help and that bastard left his room laughing, knowing full well what he was up to.

All he could say now was, give the man or woman who'd invented such equipment a fucking prize, because ... *Hot Damn.* Not being able to touch his mate in the throes of rapture was torture, but the memory of watching her make herself come with such clarity had his cock hardening again. And the look in her hooded honey eyes when he'd gotten himself off to her dirty mouth had him wanting to flash home instantly, take her into his arms and bury himself to the hilt. He couldn't wait to return to her after he was done with his brother.

Twenty minutes later, he was getting slightly concerned that something had happened when Ainsley finally flashed into the densely wooded Carpathian Mountains where he now stood. It was a secret location that only himself and Ainsley were aware of, and he hadn't been here since he was about fifty-years young. The rickety cabin they'd built was long dilapidated, but it was a meeting place that would at least allow them some modicum of privacy.

"You're late," he snipped, not looking to Ainsley but the vampire she towed behind her. And he now had only ten minutes to get to his new meeting site, well before his brother.

"It couldn't be helped. Father was suspicious."

Christ. That's all he needed. It was already dangerous enough being in this godforsaken country longer than he needed to be, but he didn't need Azairah Amanar, Ainsley's father, sniffing around as well. At the time he'd left, Azairah was reluctantly conspiring with Makare on his illicit endeavors, but he didn't know what time had done to the elder vampire. Was he a friend or foe? In his experience, everyone had their own agenda and he didn't intend on discovering Azairah's. Next time he stepped foot in his homeland, it was likely to end his father's life, which would also end his mother's life, and that sat like bitter acid, rotting his gut from the inside out. He didn't need any more complications than he already had.

"Malachi, this is Romaric Dietrich. Romaric, meet Malachi Balcescu."

Rom nodded sternly and unleashed just enough power to let the other vampire know he wasn't to be toyed with. Since he'd slipped into Romania in the middle of the night two nights ago, he'd met with nearly a dozen high level, very powerful vampires in this exact spot.

And he was told the same thing by each and every one of them. None had any interest in rebellion. None thought Romaric powerful enough to win against Makare and they didn't want to put their lives, or that of their families', on the line to stand up to the tyrant. He couldn't blame them. That's how Makare self-proclaimed himself king all those years ago. Rom had also come to understand there had been many challengers for his position or who simply wanted him gone and all had been met with their demise. The confrontations were few and farther between now because Makare had acquired so much power that only the foolish or suicidal dared challenge him.

He'd also learned there were rumblings of a traitorous prodigal son that had returned. None of the vamps he'd met with were even aware Makare had another son until recently. And rumor was he was to be made an example of. All of them had only validated what Ainsley had shared with him. There was no happy family reunion planned. Only his death.

"I mean you no harm, vampire," Malachi smirked. Rom assessed the male. He was a couple inches shorter than his own six foot six frame and a little less bulky, but power and a commanding presence rolled off him in waves. But he needed a damned haircut. Rom purposely kept his hair shorn closely to his skull. It made him look more badass instead of like goddamned *GQ* model.

"What information can you offer me about my father?"

"Nothing, I'm afraid. Your father is demented and far too powerful for you to beat."

"So you say. Then what the fuck did you come here for?" His cool exterior was quickly shattering. These entire two days had been a complete and utter waste of time and he could have spent them with his precious Sarah instead.

"It's what I can offer about your brother that may interest you instead."

The shaggy-haired vampire was right. *That* did pique his interest.

Ten minutes later, and very enlightened, he'd arrived in the tower of the Reverie. Or what he and his brother used to call it when they were younger. It was really a church in southern

Romania built in the 1200s and was quite the fortress with bastions, drawbridges, secret underground passageways and a very high bell tower on top of the main building. They used to call it Reverie—Castle in the Air—and when he arrived he was surprised to discover how nostalgic it made him. He knew exactly why Taiven had selected it. It was their clandestine meeting place far from their father.

He and Taiven used to sneak away here when they were younger, to escape a mentally unstable Makare. Romaric tried shielding Taiven as much as possible, hoping Taiven wouldn't fall into Makare's elaborate web of lies and deceit, but he'd failed. He'd first failed his mother, then his brother and finally Seraphina. His life had been filled with so much failure and it weighed him down heavily for many years. But he would not fail Sarah. And if his brother aimed to get in the way of that, he would have no compunction in ending his life too.

Rom was almost two hours early, but just minutes after his own arrival, Taiven flashed in.

"I see we both had the same idea," Taiven smirked as he took the opposite corner of the cramped space.

Rom let a small smile upturn his lips. "Brother," he replied.

They both leaned against the opposite walls contemplating each other silently for several minutes. One may mistake their posture as aloof and nonchalant, but it was anything but. Each of them was coiled and ready to strike at the blink of an eye should they feel threatened. And this was Taiven's show, or so he'd let him think, and since he'd been the one to summon Rom, he wasn't about to speak first.

"So I heard you've been here for a couple of days already."

Fuck.

He didn't know why, but he was actually surprised Taiven knew as much. Maybe he had a far more dangerous opponent to be worried about than his father. And what kind of peril did that place Ainsley in? So far this meeting was not going as planned. "Your point?"

"Don't worry," he replied as if Rom hadn't spoken, "father doesn't have a fucking clue. His head is clouded with bloodlust and dementia." Vampires didn't get dementia, at least not in the human form, but Rom knew Taiven was right about both aspects. He could see the crazy in his father's eyes just a few short weeks ago. It had clearly escalated to explosive proportions.

"What am I doing here, Taiven?"

Eyes flitting to his mating mark, Taiven asked, "What did your Sarah tell you about me?"

He bristled, not liking the insinuating question, or the familiar tone that Taiven used when referring to Sarah. In fact, he didn't like him uttering her name at all. But he'd play this game, because he knew when someone was trying to bait him. His brother excelled at it.

"Clearly she told me to meet you here. Very mature of you to use my mate to get to me

337

when you could have simply tracked me down yourself."

Not rising to the bait, he continued with his questioning. "Did she tell you anything else?"

Taiven was now succeeding as pissing him the fuck off. "What else *should* she have told me?" he gritted.

A smug smirk curled his lips. "I think you should ask your mate that question. Brother."

Pushing off the wall, he drew the long curved silver Kilij sword he favored, picked especially for this little tête–à–tête. The curvature at the end of the blade was perfect for severing a head quickly, cleanly and fortunately for the bearer of his blade, painlessly. "It would be in your best interest, *brother*, to leave my mate out of this discussion and get to the point. Right. Fucking. Now."

Rom thought back to his brief conversation with Malachi and had a difficult time believing what the vampire said held true, as he now conversed with his brother. Taiven seemed as smug and conceited and taunting as ever.

Taiven remained unmoved by Rom's now aggressive stance. "Jesus, Romaric. You were always were so fucking dramatic and stuffy. Put your damn skull separator away."

When Rom didn't move, he added, "Relax and get comfortable, brother, because we have *much* to discuss."

Chapter 51

Sarah

She tried to stay awake. She really did. But three espressos and two Cokes later, all she managed to feel was exhausted, now with a sour, churning stomach. She'd tried calling Rom around 2:00 a.m. and he'd messaged her that he was fine but would be a while yet, so she gave up the fight sometime after 2:30, letting sleep take her. And what happened after that surprised her so much, she almost didn't believe it was true.

"Hi Sawa," sang a small boyish voice.

"Jack ..." she whispered unbelievingly. Her eyes were so blurry with moisture she could barely make out his small frame.

"Wanna play?" he asked, as he turned and skipped into the flowery, fragrant open field in front of them. He broke into a run, his little legs going so fast she almost couldn't keep up, terrified all the while he'd disappear into mist and scatter to the wind any second. When they got to a large oak tree, the only one she could see for miles, he stopped and hopped onto the wooden swing hanging from one thick branch.

"Push me," he giggled. "I like to go weally high, wememba?"

Yes, yes she remembered well. She would push him so high on their swing in the back yard, mom would yell at her to stop. Once he'd gone so high he fell off the back, knocking the wind out of him. Mom wasn't home that day and neither of them said a word, pinky swearing to take it to their graves. She knew he did.

Silently, tears streaming unbidden down her face, she stood in front of Jack, pushing him higher and faster on the tree swing. Throwing his head back in sheer joy, he laughed. It was that carefree, lyrical noise she remembered from when he was alive, and it both soothed her soul and broke it at the same time. He laughed so hard and so long, she couldn't help but join in. They giggled until their sides were sore.

There were so many questions she wanted to ask him, but she didn't want to ruin the moment so she stayed silent, content to just drink in the sight of the brother taken too early. He'd be fourteen now, if he still lived, but he was still the same eight-year-old boy that she remembered from six years ago.

She had no idea how long they'd been there, but the light in the sky, which wasn't the sun, started to fade and she knew consciousness was calling her name. No, please. She wanted to stay.

"I've missed you, Jack," she said on a choked breath as she let the swing slow.

The smile he gave her nearly broke her heart into a million pieces. "I've missed you too, but I made a fwiend. She's nice." The happy-go-lucky way he acted, like they were on an outing to the park, was hard to wrap her head around. But at the same time it warmed her heart that he seemed genuinely happy.

Looking around, she spotted no one. "That—that's great, Jack. What's her name?"

"It's hard to say. I always mess it up. Sewa, Sewa ..."

Oh God. *She could hardly breathe.*

"Seraphina?" *she supplied quietly.*

"Yes! Sewaphina. She takes cawe of me. I like hew. She said she knows you, Sawa! Hey, youw names awe alike!" *He hopped off and flung his arms around her waist.*

She swallowed hard, a thick lump now threatening to choke off her precious air supply.

"Where is she?"

"She said she wanted just us to play fow a while."

Just then Jack let go of her waist, got the biggest smile on his face and started running back toward the tree. She was just about to yell at him to be careful when Seraphina stepped out from behind. The sight of Jack running straight into her arms, like he'd done it a hundred times before, was one she would never forget as long as she lived. Pain and joy equally threatened to suffocate her.

Seraphina wrapped her arms around Sarah's brother and smiled at her as she held him tight. Sarah could see the love flowing between these two and for the first time in six years, she wasn't worried about Jack.

"Take care of him." *The words came out strangled and pained.*

"And you take care of him," *she replied. Seraphina didn't have to say which him, she was referring to.*

"I won't see you again, will I?"

"There is no need, Sarah. I've done what I was meant to do."

"Who were you to Romaric?" She desperately needed to know. There would be no closure unless she did.

She smiled gently. "All of our lives are intertwined, as the Fates directed. Who I was to Romaric matters not any longer. He is yours, as it should be." She gestured to her mating bond.

They turned to go and Sarah called after them. "Wait! How am I supposed to save him?"

"You already have, my dear. You reunited him with his brother. Taiven could not make himself known to you until you completed your bonding with Romaric. Two brothers united cannot be defeated."

Seraphina turned again, this time with Jack, and wrapped a delicate arm around his small shoulder.

"Bye Sawa. Love you to the moon and back!" Jack waived as he spun his head, a goofy smile plastered on his beautiful face, blue eyes shining bright.

Sarah stifled a sob with the back of her hand. They'd said that to each other every night before he went to bed. "Love you to the moon and back, baby brother."

They'd gone a few steps before Seraphina turned around one last time. "I'm proud of you for all you've endured and the strong woman that's made you. This is the life you were always meant to live. You'll make a great mother, Sarah Dietrich."

As she watched them walk away, taking another piece of her heart with every step, the words Seraphina spoke churned over and over. And a sudden peacefulness washed over her like a warm, fluffy blanket.

She knew she'd see Jack again someday. Maybe not often, but he'd visit her when she needed it. And in the meantime, Seraphina would take care of him.

She'd made the right choice bonding with Rom. She was his Moira and they were meant to be.

And as she slowly came awake, for the first time in months, she knew with one-hundred percent certainty everything would be okay. Rom would defeat both of their fathers and they would go on to live a long, happy life, blessed with children and grandchildren.

She felt light and happy and almost ... *free.*

Chapter 52

Rom

Nothing sounded better than to be in *their* bed, in *their* house, making love to his mate, but she slept so soundly, he couldn't bear to disturb her. Instead, he climbed into bed in what was quickly becoming their part of Devon's mansion and gathered his mate into his arms, settling her in the crook of his shoulder.

Feeling a huge weight lift, he sighed. Sarah had been safe these past two days, he knew, but he still couldn't breathe easy until he held her once more. He'd been loath to shut one eye in the last two days and he was exhausted, so he shouldn't have been surprised that sleep quickly pulled him under.

Coiled and ready to fight, he came awake with a start when he felt someone watching him.

"Back it down, buddy. It's just me."

Sarah sat cross-legged at the foot of the bed in a hideous nightgown of some sort that looked to be two sizes too big. He'd been none too happy to feel clothing covering her body when he slid into bed, but was too tired to care at that moment. "What the hell are you wearing?"

She looked down at the white polyester fabric covered with tiny yellow birds. "Clearly it's pajamas."

"And why, pray tell, are you wearing them? You should be in your birthday suit, beauty, not covered in some dreadful garb like that."

Crossing her arms with a frown on her face, she said, "I used to wear a nightgown like this when I was little and it reminded me of home."

Well shit.

Sitting up against the headboard, he replied contritely, "I'm sorry, Sarah. I didn't know."

For several seconds, he couldn't decipher the stoic look on her face. Then she burst out laughing, falling onto her side and cackling so hard tears leaked out of her closed eyes.

He'd been punked.

"Why you little brat."

Seconds later she was under him, his mouth greedily upon hers. Her laughter quickly softened to moans as their lips and tongues and hands were all over every square inch of each other. The hideous nightgown was quickly torn clean down the middle and discarded.

Her moans changed to pants when he ripped off her lace panties and plunged deeply into her wet pussy. Intertwining their hands, he raised them above their heads and looked upon the delicate, beautiful face he'd missed so much. He was so whipped for this woman, he could hardly think straight.

"Look at me." His body had a mind of its own, hips thrusting of their own accord. Her lids cracked, but he could tell it was difficult for her to keep them open and his ego swelled at the hazy pleasure he saw swirling in their depths. "You're a very bad girl," he punctuated between rough prods.

Her lips turned up slightly. "I guess I need punished then," she uttered with a breathy sigh.

"No, my beauty. You clearly need to be pleasured." Her blood called his name loudly, begging to be taken by its mate. Not able to wait a second longer, he slowly sunk his incisors into her supple flesh, drawing her essence into his body, which set off her climax and subsequently his. Their joining had been hurried and rough and exactly what they'd both needed.

Christ, he'd missed her.

Several minutes later, still naked, inside her and ready for round two, she asked, "How did the meeting with your brother go?"

The meeting with his brother had been … *interesting* and he daresay they'd even formed a loose alliance. At minimum, they had the same objective. But what he was more interested in right now was Taiven's comment alluding to his familiarity with Sarah beyond her one dream. He was not used to such feelings of jealousy. And he never did get a straight answer on why Taiven had been able to talk to Sarah in her dreams either, which still bothered him, more than he wanted to admit. It was an unheard of skill and his brother did a very good job on hedging.

Rolling over and never separating their bodies, he pulled her astride him. "It went well."

A broad smile spread across her face, reaching her brilliant eyes. "I'm glad."

"Tell me about your dreams of Taiven."

Her smile fell quickly, brows drawing in feigned confusion. "I don't know what you mean. I already told you about it."

His jaw ticked, that knot of jealousy growing bigger by the minute. "I mean the others."

She tried moving, but he grabbed her hips, holding her firmly in place.

"Did I happen to mention that one of my skills is the ability to detect a lie, Sarah?"

Lips pursed, she asked, "What did Taiven tell you?"

"Not a fucking thing. So you can imagine the shit I'm conjuring up about now. Next time I see the fucker, I may just kill him on principal alone."

She looked away and the pain in his heart couldn't have been any greater than if she'd stabbed him with his own Kilij. Looking back, instead of answering his question, she asked one of her own that took his breath away.

"Who is Seraphina?"

"What?" he muttered softly.

"Seraphina? Who is she? Or *was* she?"

Picking her up, he set her down on the bed and strode into the bathroom. Of course, her stubborn ass was right on his heels.

"I don't know a Seraphina."

She barked a laugh. "Did I tell you that one of *my* newly acquired skills is detecting a lie, mate?"

Touché.

"I can't talk about it, Sarah." Walking to the shower, he turned on the water and stepped under, not waiting for it to warm. Right now he needed the shock of the freezing cold water to clear his clouded mind. How the fuck did Sarah know about Seraphina? No one, outside of himself, knew of her. Not one single human or vampire alive.

And why wouldn't she tell him about what happened with Taiven? Could it have been that bad? Or that *good*? The thought literally made him fucking murderous and truce or not, if Taiven laid a finger on her, even in a dream, he was as good as fucking dead.

"Can't or won't?" she asked, standing in all her naked glory outside the black marble walls of the shower.

How dare she give him the third degree when she wouldn't answer *his* goddamned questions? Grabbing the soap, he scrubbed his body in short, angry motions.

"Won't," he bit out, daring her to challenge him.

Pain stabbed his soul. It was hers. Why was he so loath to talk about Seraphina when she was his past? Everyone had a past, including Sarah. Would she understand? Or would it just unnecessarily hurt her? *No.* The past was the past for a reason. And that's exactly where it should remain. It was done and over with and couldn't be changed.

Turning on her heels, she retreated to the bedroom. Shutting off the water before he'd even rinsed, and not bothering with a towel, he chased after her. "Tell me about Taiven. Now."

"Wow." She laughed sardonically. "You must be delusional. Tit for tat, vampire." She hastily dressed, minus her shredded panties, and sat on a chair to buckle her sandals.

"That's not the way this works, Sarah," he gritted.

She stopped to pin him with a hard glare, but softened as she began speaking, the hurt clearly reflected in her teary eyes and her broken voice. "It *is* the way it works, Rom. We are a team, you and I, and now we're tied together for all of eternity, however long that may be. We'll never make it if we don't trust each other. And once again we are back to you not trusting me, and it's beyond devastating." Her strained voice cracked on the last few words and he'd never felt more like shit than he did at this moment.

Finishing her task, she stood and walked to the bedroom door, pausing before she opened it, but not turning back. "In my dreams, Taiven watched over me, protected me, my whole life. I don't know why and I didn't know it was him until after we'd bonded and he appeared to me in that last dream."

"Did you fuck him?" He didn't miss the tensing of her shoulders at his crass and, frankly, uncalled for words. But they were out of his mouth before he could pull them back, his calm demeanor completely and totally blown to smithereens.

"No."

"Did he *want* to?" Sarah was a beautiful, desirable and irresistible female and Taiven was simply a male. Of course he'd want her. He didn't know why or how Taiven had been tied to Sarah and jealousy burned hot like acid through his veins at the thought of *him* watching her grow, of *him* protecting her when it should have been Rom and especially of *him* putting his hands anywhere near what was his.

"Maybe. I don't know. Since the morning you returned for me he's been absent, except for this last dream." He could feel how difficult it was to speak the truth because she knew it would hurt and anger him.

"Did he kiss you?"

Please, for the love of Christ, say no. Taiven was so dead if his lips had touched hers.

"No."

She cocked her head slightly. "I always thought it was you," she whispered. He and Taiven could pass as twins, so it's understandable how she could think that, but he wasn't sure if that made him feel better or worse.

Worse, definitely.

She opened the door, taking two steps before swinging back around, eyes locked with his. The water streaming down her face gutted him, but he couldn't make himself go to her and provide the comfort she both craved and deserved. She hadn't invited Taiven into her dreams. None of this was her fault, her doing, but it didn't make the sting of the situation lessen any.

"She told me to tell you she's sorry. That it was always meant to be me. And even if I'm in the dark, I'm sure you'll know what that message means."

Seraphina came to Sarah in a dream*? Why?*

She said the next part so softly, and with such hurt, it stripped him raw. "You may not have locked me in a room this time, Rom, but this is so much worse. You've locked me out of *you*. And that ... that is completely soul-shattering."

The soft click of the door shutting was the last sound he heard as he stood frozen in shock and agony. His past and future had collided. And he'd just let his future walk out the door, leaving behind a visible, tangible trail of hurt and betrayal.

God, he was a bastard.

His heart wept. He *wanted* to move beyond this. He *wanted* to share every last shred about himself with Sarah, good and bad.

He just didn't know *how*.

Chapter 53

Sarah

Lost. That's how she felt. She should be happy. In a fricken wedded state of bliss. But all she felt right now was numb ... and incredibly sad.

She'd missed her mate terribly these past two days and within minutes of seeing each other, they were already in an argument, because, once again, he refused to share something with her. Would it always be like this? Would he always shut her out? Would she ever be allowed into the deep recesses of his mind and soul?

Wandering around the large estate, she didn't dare go outside, but it was almost unbearable to be in the same vicinity as Rom. She should flash home, but she also didn't want to be too far away from him either. It was a conundrum that confused the hell out of her.

The minute she'd stepped foot downstairs, Jareth and Elliott had followed her around like the good little guard dogs they were. That was mean and, yes, she was being a royal bitch. They were just doing what their *Commander in Chief* had demanded. What she wouldn't give to run into Giselle right now so she could go a couple of rounds with someone who could take it. God knows she wouldn't be good company to anyone else less snarly than her.

As usual, she found herself in the library. This felt like a sanctuary to her. She'd spent an untold amount of time here over the last several months.

Walking along the expansive shelves chucked full of books, she ran her fingers along their spines, both old and new. It never failed to marvel her at how many books Devon had acquired over the course of his lifetime. And this wasn't even all of them. His office was also stuffed to the brim.

Unable to focus on reading, she flopped on the couch, gazing out the large window. The view wasn't much, since they were in the middle of nowhere, but it was peaceful. It was still early and birds chirped, unencumbered by anything other than finding food for the day or building their nests in anticipation of their new arrivals. She found herself slightly jealous of their easy-going and carefree existences.

Jealous of birds now? She'd sunk to a new low.

Was 7:00 a.m. too early for a glass of wine? It was five o'clock somewhere, right?

So many things had happened over the last couple of weeks. Things that she wanted to share with Rom, but for one reason or another, never seemed to get a chance. They were either fighting or fucking.

Sigh.

She wanted to tell him about Jack and how they'd played. She wanted to talk about her biological mom and share that she had an aunt and grandfather that she'd love to meet. She had a gut-wrenching *need* to understand who Seraphina was and how she connected with them both. She'd tried, but she just couldn't let that go. And she wasn't sure she'd be able to until she knew the truth.

As if on cue, Giselle suddenly appeared with a folder in her hand. And she looked ... *excited.* And dare she say ... *happy?*

"Trouble in paradise?"

Or not.

Well ... bring it bitch because Sarah was *not* in the mood to be fucked with.

"Nope. Just taking a break. My pussy's sore."

Giselle howled with laughter. "Oh my God, Sarah," she wailed. "Who knew you were a mini me?"

Uh ... what? Sarah was *nothing* like Giselle. Oh God ... *was* she? Right now she felt like it.

"That's just plain offensive, Giselle."

"Wow ... that bad, huh?" Giselle threw the folder she held on the table between them before taking a seat opposite her.

"You do listen to the words that come out of your own mouth, right?"

Giselle shrugged. "I suppose I could try a tiny bit harder to be less bitchy."

Her brows drew together in confusion. "Are you getting laid?" That's the only thing that made sense. Sarah had long thought Giselle needed her lady bits oiled a little, or a *lot*, and perhaps that would help her sour demeanor.

Giselle didn't respond, but a slight smile curved her lips.

"Oh my God! You are!" Sarah leaned forward, arms on her knees, her own troubles all but forgotten. "Who?"

This was surreal. She was sitting here, practically gossiping with Giselle. *Giselle*. The hardest, most jaded, frigid woman she'd ever met.

"Let's not push it. I'm new at this ... *shit*."

"Okay. Fair enough." Leaning back, she couldn't help but say, "You look happy."

A genuine smile graced Giselle's face and the only word that came to mind was *wow*. She'd thought Giselle beautiful before, but when she *really* smiled, she was simply breathtakingly stunning. "I am," she said finally.

"Did you just come by to chitchat and bond or was there another reason you stopped by?"

"I like the cheeky side of you better. I have a meeting with the lords in a few minutes, but I have something for you." Picking up the folder, Giselle pulled out several papers, spreading them on the coffee table in front of them. "We have a pretty good family tree put together that I wanted to give you."

"You what?" Shock almost stunned her speechless. "How?" Sarah hadn't missed the use of the word *"we"* but was too dumbfounded to care.

"Well, turns out your grandmother was quite the genealogist herself and had done a lot of research already. My ... *source* managed to take photos of the information when your grandfather spent twenty minutes taking a bathroom break."

Oohh. She probably could have gone without knowing that little tidbit.

"There are pictures in there too. Some pretty old. The quality isn't perfect and a few are grainy because they were printed from a camera phone, but I put everything in here we had."

Sarah could hardly believe her ears. Or her eyes. Which were now blurry. Swallowing hard, she tried twice before she could speak. "Thank you," she finally managed to utter.

Giselle clasped her hand over Sarah's. "You're welcome."

Giselle was leaving the room when she called back, "And Sarah ... just lock him out of heaven for a while. Whatever he's done, he'll be begging for forgiveness soon enough."

Sarah sat there, stunned. Not only did she have her maternal family's life spread in front of her, but she may have just made a new friend. *With Giselle.*

Huh? Who would have thunk it?

Chapter 54

Rom

It was another day spent filled with regret. After Sarah had walked out on him, he'd finished getting ready and found her in the library looking at pictures and papers. She'd quickly hidden them, but not before he'd gotten a good look. *A family tree? Where on Earth did she get that?*

"What are you doing?"

"Nothing," she replied curtly.

Apparently she was neither in the mood to share nor forgive. And he still couldn't bring himself to discuss the elephant in the room … Seraphina. The words sat on the tip of his tongue, like poison he needed to expel in order to prevent it from spreading and rotting and ruining his relationship with the one woman he cared about above all others.

But he just couldn't do it. So instead he'd told her he'd be in meetings all day and he'd find her later.

He was a goddamned coward.

And he hated himself for it.

So now, hours later, he sat once again around Dev's conference table, unable to fully engage in their final strategy session because he couldn't stop thinking about Sarah and Taiven and Seraphina. And what it all meant because there was no way in hell this was all coincidence. He was royally fucked if he went into the field without his head in the game and by the sounds of it they needed to make the hit on Xavier tonight because Geoffrey had a planned meeting with him. Who knew when they'd get another opportunity if they didn't take this one?

"Rom, you with us?" Damian asked.

It was painfully obvious to everyone in the room his body was present, but his mind was absent. "You're looking at me, aren't you?"

Damian smirked but was smart enough to keep his mouth shut for once.

"Geoffrey, have you uncovered anything new in the last couple of days?" Dev asked, diverting their attention back to the issue at hand.

The blond vampire looked grim. Shit ... this was going to be bad.

"Unfortunately yes. There is a very small compound that I happened to discover in the foothills of Nebraska, and only one vampire that I've run across is aware of this location. If the situation weren't so dire, it would be incredible, really. I don't know how or when he did it, but Xavier has managed to whisk away a very specialized group of biological scientists who have not only been able to successfully enhance existing vampiric skills, but they've also developed *new* vampiric powers that we've never seen. Invisibility, time travel, merging completely with another being to create a completely new one."

Geoffrey looked gravely around the room. "And even dreamwalking."

Holy fuck. This was so much worse than he could have imagined.

Suddenly it made sense. Vampires could not dreamwalk. That was only a human female skill. And yet somehow Taiven had reaped that power and was able to enter Sarah's dreams. *But why?* Why would he pick her and more importantly, how exactly did he come to obtain this power himself? He was an entire continent away. Was Taiven in cahoots somehow with Xavier? And how long had Xavier been experimenting with this? For more than twenty years, if what Sarah said was true. *"In my dreams, Taiven watched over me, protected me, my whole life."*

"Like with everything else he's developed, the formulas are hit and miss and have a very low success rate. In many instances it kills the vampire it's given to. It appears to have much higher success in enhancing an existing power than fully creating a new one, so they don't inject it until the vampire is at least fully blooded, at age twenty."

"That's just fucking great. And how many of these amped up rogues are running loose?" Damian spat.

"I simply don't know." Geoffrey shook his head, clearly distressed like everyone else. "I, myself, haven't come across a vamp with a previously non-existent skill, but I have seen a few that have incredibly magnified powers. I thought it was just a result of the other chemicals that are being pumped into them from the time they were born, and maybe it's a combination of the two. Who the hell knows at this point? But there were not any vamps or females kept in this facility, other than the human scientists."

"We need everyone one of those humans alive, along with every computer, every flash drive, every vial, every piece of equipment and every shred of paper, down to a Post-It note," Dev retorted.

Geoffrey nodded.

A firm plan in place, they ended the meeting late afternoon. All told, they had over one-hundred warriors that would make the various raids tonight, at 11:30 p.m. sharp, when Geoffrey was expected to meet with Xavier. Rom, Circo and six others would accompany Geoffrey. Damian and the other lieutenants would also lead teams, but Dev would stay back with their mates. After almost losing Kate, he refused to leave her alone again, especially since she was pregnant. It was a good plan. They all had too much at stake on the home front with their mates here.

They were to gather a mile to the west outside Devon's estate in a wooded clearing at 10:30 p.m. The goal was to hit fast and hard and be back in no more than an hour with the humans.

And while they argued about this for well over an hour, they finally agreed to save any child under the age of fifteen, that hadn't had their second blooding, but destroy any older than that. According to Geoffrey, once they had their second blooding, they were to be kept in another area of the compound and they were significantly more dangerous as they started heavy training then and a vampire became drastically more powerful after their second blooding. It absolutely gutted him to have to destroy ones so young, but they couldn't take the chance these rogues would grow into monsters, trying to emulate their sick and twisted leader.

Devon and Kate had worked tirelessly these last few days to prep and staff an empty area of the shelter for the dozens of women they expected to bring back. Dev had others diligently working at another location to prepare for the children to be taken there. Like him, Dev didn't want these unknowns anywhere near something as precious as his mate.

"Rom," Damian called as he tried to make a hasty exit. With only a few hours before the battle, he needed to see Sarah and if she was willing, spend it buried inside of her.

"What?" he barked, moving quickly. He needed to shake his friend like a bad habit right now.

"What the fuck is wrong with you, man?" Damian put a hand on his shoulder and his powers instinctively flared to life.

Whipping around, he pinned Damian to the wall behind him. Everyone else had disbursed except for Dev, Circo and Geoffrey, who now stood frozen, watching the ugly scene unfold in front of their eyes.

"Put your hands on me again, *friend*, and it will be your last," Rom sneered.

Damian's jaw ticked and Rom felt his hands and forearms warm where he held Damian tightly to the Sheetrock. Realizing what he'd done, he quickly let him go and turned, grabbing his head between his hands.

"Fuck!" he yelled.

"Rom, you'd better pull your shit together before tonight or you'll single-handedly jeopardize the entire operation," Dev said harshly, scolding him like a child.

Hell, he was *acting* like a child. He deserved every caustic word.

"Circo, accompany our *guest* to his quarters," Dev commanded, never taking his eyes from Rom. Until this evening, they weren't letting Geoffrey out of their sight, so he'd reluctantly agreed to be strapped down in one of the rogue rooms Devon had in the lower quarters.

"Yes, my lord."

As soon as they were gone, Damian was actually the one to speak first. "You're acting very out of character, my friend. What's going on?"

"None of your goddamned business," he snapped, sitting his large frame into one of the comfortable leather chairs.

"I beg to differ. You fuck this up because things aren't right at home, then you put all of our lives in even more danger and I will *not* allow you to do that to me, or my mate. Cut off the head, remember? And as the dragon slayer, *you* are on point to decapitate our foe. You fail, we all fail."

"No fucking pressure," he grumbled. He wanted this stupid conversation over with so he could find Sarah. Why he was even indulging them, he had no clue.

Damian laughed sarcastically. "Oh, there's plenty of fucking pressure, all right."

"Spill it," Dev said.

Rom glared at the both of them. "What is this, the girls' club? Jesus, did you two embrace your feminine side since becoming bonded or what? We are *males*. We don't sit around and talk about our feelings—boo hoo—for fuck's sake."

Dev chuckled, shaking his head. "Have you heard the human phrase *a happy wife, a happy life?*"

Rom rolled his eyes.

"Every time I've seen you like this, you're in a tiff with Sarah. Probably over something *you* did. You don't want to tell us, fine. But before ten thirty tonight, you'd better have smoothed things over with your mate, so you can concentrate on the battle and the confrontation with your father. Because you can't afford any distractions. None of us can."

They all sat silently for several minutes, Dev's words hanging heavily in the air.

"My first Moira died," Rom said gruffly. *Wow.* The relief at saying those words out loud was too great to put into words.

Damian and Dev exchanged confused looks.

"Uh ... you can only have one Moira, Rom. You must be mistaken," Damian said disbelievingly.

Rom grunted. "I assure you, Damian. I am not mistaken. That's why I'm in this fucking mess with my father. I didn't believe it could be true either, but the second I laid eyes on Sarah, I knew. I knew she was my Moira, but I wouldn't let myself believe it, so instead of trusting my instincts, I went to see my mother. If anyone had heard of such a thing before, it would be she. And to get to my mother, I had to go through my father."

He paused a few moments, wanting to spew the rest of his story to his friends, but suddenly it felt like a betrayal to not tell Sarah the entire sordid tale of Seraphina first. He should have given her the benefit of the doubt weeks ago and foolishly, he hadn't.

Dev and Damian were right. He needed to mend fences with his mate and to do that, he had to unburden himself of this heavy weight once and for all and trust that she could handle it as just part of who he was.

Standing, he made his way to the door. "See you at ten thirty. I need to see my mate."

As he left, he heard Damian say, "A top-secret father and now a dead Moira? What the hell else hasn't he told us?"

God, he was such a whiny bitch.

Chapter 55

Sarah

Wanting privacy, she'd spent the entire day in what she now referred to as their bedroom in Dev and Kate's house. She'd spent the first half hour this morning just staring at the pictures of her mother before spending hours more scouring the Internet for any more pieces of information she could get her hands on.

Not taking no for an answer, Kate had managed to drag her out of the room for lunch, but she'd hastily returned, devouring every piece of information and picture that was in the folder Giselle had left behind. Kate knew Sarah was keeping something from her, peppering her with dozens of questions, but until she'd had a chance to digest everything, she didn't want to tell anyone else about her covert operation.

And she didn't want to discuss her fight with Rom this morning either. It was still too painful and somehow talking about it with her sister would make it more so. From everything she could see, Kate and Dev had a very open relationship and he didn't keep things from Kate like Rom did from Sarah.

Neither Rosie nor Nancy had been particularly helpful either and both had been warring with each other all day. Rosie told her to give him time and Nancy's advice was a swift kick to the balls. Given her spitefulness at the moment, she was leaning heavily toward Nancy's method.

By mid-afternoon, her eyes were crossing and she thought it was time to stop for the day. She began scooping all of the photos and papers together and was straightening them when a small picture she hadn't seen before fluttered to the bedspread. She picked it up and noticed it was a very old drawing of a family as the earliest photos were.

As her eyes ran over the faces, chills ran down her spine. She frantically grabbed the family tree again, which had gone back all the way to the late 1300s, and scanned quickly.

Looking for one name in particular.

She hadn't spent much time on the oldest members of her family because, well, they were all dead. Just as she was ready to chalk it up to coincidence, she spotted it.

Seraphina Glynn. Born 1436. Died 1452.

Oh God. It *was* her.

An hour later she sat on the balcony, third glass of wine in hand. She couldn't stop thinking about what she'd just learned.

There were nine children in the picture. Three girls and six boys. And according to the family tree, all but three children died in 1452. There must have been some sort of pandemic or something, for it just wasn't possible that all would have died so closely together otherwise. It made sense too, with what she'd witnessed in her dream. Only two boys and one girl lived beyond that year. How tragic for their parents.

But what floored Sarah the most was that she was the direct descendent of Willa Flynn, Seraphina's sister, only living daughter of the Flynns. That certainly explained their striking similarities.

So now she finally knew who Seraphina finally was, but the one question that refused to leave her was, *who was she to Rom*? With his reaction at the mention of her name, she wasn't sure she'd ever find out.

As usual, she felt him before she saw him. And déjà vu hit, being in nearly this same position a couple of weeks ago after he'd locked her in the bedroom here. How fitting, given he'd locked her out in other, far more important, ways. At least this time she had alcohol to dull the ache.

Very mature, Sarah.

"I've messed up once again." The velvet timbre of his voice feathered over every nerve ending, bringing a calm she'd needed all day. She was mad and hurt, but she wasn't sure it mattered what Rom did. She would *always* forgive him because she loved him so damn much. But what kind of a cycle would that create? He would keep things from her. They would fight. She would forgive. And they'd never resolve anything. After years of that, she'd become a bitter, resentful, hateful woman.

"You could never be hateful, Sarah," he sighed, sitting on the couch next to her, grabbing hold of her free hand. "We're going into battle tonight. It's time to kill Xavier once and for all."

Anger turned to fear, spreading like fire ants under her skin and she turned toward him.

"I—"

"No. Let me talk. Please." Releasing her hand, he stood, walking toward the banister, his back to her. She felt the anxiety eating holes in his stomach.

"You don't have to tell me." And she meant it. If it caused him such angst, she didn't need to know.

"I was young, only eighty, and Seraphina was only sixteen. I saw her walking along a dirt road and I thought she would be easy prey. But the moment I looked into her eyes ... I knew."

He turned around and held her gaze. "I knew she was my Moira."

Sarah tried not to, but she gasped anyway. *His Moira? How could that be?*

"She was young and the eldest of nine children. She didn't want to leave her family, so she refused me at first. After two long weeks, I finally got her to agree to bond, but she insisted I first meet her father and on that night when I arrived ... the stench of death wafted from the shack like a thick fog."

Sarah couldn't breathe and could hardly see him through watery eyes. He continued as if he had to unburden himself now or he wouldn't be able. But he didn't need to, for she knew how this tragic story ended. She saw it with her own eyes.

"By the time I arrived, she'd already passed, as had two of her siblings. Two others were ill and died a short time later, I heard. Influenza."

Suddenly it all made sense.

His irrational fear of losing her.

His absurd, overprotective behavior.

His difficulty letting people get close to him.

And his secrecy.

He turned, his back to her and held the railing so tightly she was sure it would crack. His next words dug like a sharp knife in her chest and if she looked down, she was sure she'd see blood seeping from the wound in her chest.

"If I'd only forced her to bond, she wouldn't have died." His voice was filled with pain and totally unfounded guilt.

"And she'd be with you now. Instead of me," she murmured, barely able to utter the bitter tasting words that rose like bile from the depths of her gut.

Twirling he knelt before her, holding her face. "No, Sarah. No. *You* are my Destiny. I can't even find the words to tell you how much I love you. And yes, I won't lie. It was agony losing Seraphina, but now I know there was a purpose to my suffering. It was you. It was *always* you. It will only *ever* be you."

His lips crashed to hers and he swept her up in his arms, never breaking contact as he strode to the bed and quickly shed their clothes. This time there was no prelude, no foreplay, no sweet talk or dirty words. Just slow, sensual lovemaking. Linking their hands, his heated, adoring eyes never left hers, deliberately and painstakingly gliding his thick shaft leisurely in and out until they both shattered, calling out the other's name.

Their sweat-cooled bodies were pressed silently together and he never stopped touching her. Her hair. Her face. Her neck.

"I'm sorry," fell repeatedly from his lips.

"Enough."

He stopped his ministrations and rolled off her so they were facing each other on their sides. She feathered a finger down his scruffy, sexy jaw.

"I'm sorry. I shouldn't have pushed you. I was foolishly jealous and I pressed you on something that wasn't my business."

"Sarah, I—"

"No. It's my turn to talk. I've been dreaming about Seraphina since right after I met you. I called her mystery girl at first because she would come to me and tell me things, but she wouldn't tell me *who* she was. Or who she was to *you*."

He swallowed thickly and she knew this was still hard for him to talk about, but between his words that put her shattered heart back together, what Seraphina had repeatedly told her and what she'd discovered in her family tree, she was convinced this was where she was supposed to be. With Romaric Dietrich.

"What did she tell you?"

"Well, some of it I already told you. She said you'd suffered greatly. That you were in danger. And in order to save you we needed to bond. At the time she wouldn't tell me exactly what that meant."

He sucked in a quick, sharp breath. "That's not—"

"Stop. I bonded with you because for some reason I'm madly in love with your pain in the ass and I want to be with you forever." Smiling, he visibly relaxed. "I don't know what your brother has to do with this whole thing, but she said he couldn't make himself known to me until we'd bonded, but that reuniting you both was the key to saving you. So I don't care how or why Taiven has been with me, but if it means you'll be safe because of it, then you need to put that behind you."

His brows were furrowed, deep in thought, but he simply nodded.

"And last night I saw Jack. I pushed him on a tree swing. Seraphina takes care of him."

"She does?" he asked softly. His fingers interlocked with hers.

"Yes. He loves her very much," she said wistfully.

She wanted to tell him that she was a descendent of Seraphina's family somehow, but now didn't feel like the right time. One weight was off her chest, but too many still sat heavy and encumbering. "What time are you leaving?"

His lips pursed together. "We meet at ten thirty. We'll strike at eleven thirty."

She looked at the clock. It was already past 6:00 p.m. "Well then, I guess we'd better spend the next few hours making sure you're in tip top shape for kicking ass and taking names. Or heads."

Chuckling, he dipped his head until his hot mouth found her aching, wanting flesh, teeth scraping and teasing. "I think that sounds like the best plan you've had yet, beauty."

Chapter 56

Geoffrey

It was nearly time. T-minus five and counting. He'd be a liar if he said he wasn't nervous. This could either be the end or the beginning. They were outside the Kentucky complex, deep inside the Shawnee National Forest. Xavier's compounds were always in very remote locations and always underground. It served two purposes. Keep away wandering eyes and nosy humans, but also to lock away the screams and cries of the kidnapped women who were regularly tortured at his direction. And countless by Xavier's own hand.

Geoffrey may have racked up untold sins, but maliciously killing innocents wasn't one of them.

"He's inside," said Circo.

He'd come to learn that Circo's special talent was to detect another vampire's skill. He'd also learned that the night of the last raid, they knew Xavier wasn't in the compound before they'd struck. That simply reaffirmed what he'd known to be true about the lords. They were selfless and benevolent. Without Xavier present, they could have easily retreated after they'd rescued Damian's mate, leaving the females there to suffer and likely die, but they hadn't.

Circo ran down the list of skills he'd vetted in the compound and if they could kill Xavier, this should be a piece of cake. It was *almost* too easy, he thought. He'd fully expected Xavier to stand him up as he'd done many times before. He was about as unreliable as a candle in the wind.

Geoffrey would flash inside, meet with Xavier, and Rom would be just minutes behind. The less time they gave him to figure things out, the better. And Rom would be the first one in the compound. As soon as Circo could place the proximity of his skill, Rom would follow in short order.

Sounded easy enough, right?

"It's time," Rom said, clasping him on the shoulder like they were comrades. It felt oddly ... *good*. "Stick to the plan and I'll see you at the rendezvous point. And keep your fucking ass alive. I need you for another mission."

Yes, the *it's-time-to-kill-Rom's-father* mission. Rom had mentioned that he was taking Geoffrey up on his offer to assist him. Should he live, that is.

Not wasting another second, Geoffrey flashed inside the steel reinforced complex and was immediately met by two vampires, guarding the door. He recognized both and breathed a small sigh of relief when he was allowed to pass without issue or question. He had to believe that if Xavier was onto him that the guards at the door would be one of his first lines of defense. Xavier did like to play with his food, however.

Quickly making his way to Xavier's office, he knocked on the door, waiting for his cue.

"Enter," his slimy voice seeped through the fortified door.

When he opened the door, his steps faltered. Sitting in front of him, naked and tied to a chair, was the young vampire who'd provided the information on the secret compound. And he'd been worked over pretty good.

Fuck.

"Troubles, my lord?" he said nonchalantly, as he walked in and closed them in.

The vampire was already covered in blood and wounds, and it appeared he'd been here quite some time. Behind the gag, he whimpered, his eyes alight with fear. That was something Xavier never did. He thrived on the screams of his victims. He never gagged them.

They were fucked. He was so onto them. Rom couldn't get here fast enough.

"Good of you to join us, my *loyal* servant," he purred.

Yep, he was dead.

Xavier picked up a long knife and tested its sharpness. Geoffrey fully expected him to use it on the vampire currently immobilized in the chair, but faster than he could react, Xavier had unleashed the knife in a vicious throw directly at him, pinning him through the throat to the door behind him. In quick succession, he threw several more. Fire and agony erupted in nearly every part of his body. He was being used as a fucking dartboard, and because of Xavier's stasis power, there was nothing he could do to fight back. This is why he'd never been able to escape. Xavier was simply too powerful.

This was the end for him. Rom would never reach him in time before Xavier severed his head where he was now restrained.

Xavier picked up his favorite weapon. The sword of Damascus. One of the sharpest swords in the world.

"Do you know what I do with traitors, Geoffrey?"

He panted, almost unable to breathe through the throbbing anguish. Where the fuck was Rom?

"You know good and fucking well I do," he spat, blood pouring from his neck with each and every syllable. He cut them up like fish food. And he enjoyed every single second of dismembering his prey, like the sick motherfucker he was.

Xavier smiled, but it was full of evil and malevolence. Like his soul.

"Disloyal *and* disrespectful. Well ... at least you don't go half-assed," he said wickedly, slowly plunging the sword into Geoffrey's gut. He sliced upward, continuing to babble. "I raised you like a *son*. I trusted you, yet you go behind my back and climb into bed with my greatest enemy. *Our* greatest enemy! I'm going to enjoy cutting you apart, Geoffrey. I'm going to enjoy peeling the flesh from your bones and watching your duplicitous blood coat the floor."

A lung now punctured, he couldn't speak. He couldn't even think through the pain viciously ripping its way through every nerve ending.

Decapitation would be too easy. Xavier would make his death slow and painful.

Geoffrey would like to say he remained stoic and silent in his last minutes as his insides were being cleaved apart, but he didn't. He *couldn't.* The agony was simply too unbearable and he bellowed his misery and sorrow for failing in his mission.

For failing the lords.

For failing himself.

For failing his *Moira.*

As the darkness engulfed him, he began to hallucinate.

He thought he saw Romaric Dietrich.

He thought he saw a brief battle.

And he thought he saw Xavier's head leaving his body.

But that would be too good to be true. There was no doubt Geoffrey was headed to hell, but only in his wildest dreams could he ever hope to spend eternity in the fiery pits alongside the monster who'd sent *him* there. Because while his body would spend perpetuity in utter agony, at least his mind could rest in peace knowing the spawn of the devil would be suffering right alongside him.

As he fucking deserved.

Chapter 57

Rom

He almost felt gipped. How they'd spend a half a millennia chasing after Xavier's sorry ass, only to end his life in less than sixty seconds was, well ... anticlimactic. He'd hoped to at least break a sweat. No matter. The threat had finally been eliminated and a twisted empire dismantled, so at least there was that.

One menace down. One to go.

They'd wiped out the enemy, but sustained three severe and two mortal injuries on their side. Most everyone else returned with at least a few wounds, but all had been accounted for and the dead returned for proper interment by their families.

The second he was within distance to the estate to speak telepathically with Sarah, he did, letting her know he was safe and that he would still be quite a while, taking care of the injured and debriefing for hours. Her relief was palpable, as was her anxiety when he'd left. The need to go to her was almost too much to ignore, but he knew if he did, he wouldn't be leaving her side anytime soon.

Like every time he'd reaped a new skill, it hummed like a thousand volts of electricity in his arteries and veins and capillaries. It would take a few days to control and master it. And, as it always did, it created such an adrenaline rush, he could barely think of anything else besides fucking his mate.

Repeatedly. For days.

"How is he?"

"Touch and go, my lord. We're keeping him sedated until his internal organs heal," replied Big D.

"Keep me updated."

Rom left the infirmary and made his way to debrief. The meeting room was filled to capacity with loud, smelly, bloody vampires, every one of them hyped up on the adrenaline from battle. Renaldo, Dev's lieutenant, had been charged with running this meeting and he looked concerned, his face tight with anxiety.

"Quiet!" Ren finally yelled. After the noise had died down, he continued. "First order of business ... ding dong, the fucking witch is dead!" The quiet was obliterated by a loud, bloodthirsty roar, which took several more minutes to contain.

After calming the melee down again, he continued. "Pay attention so we can get the hell out of here. I, for one, need to get laid," Ren growled. "The mission was a success. We captured a few rogues for interrogation, but the rest were destroyed and the females and children rescued and placed in the shelters. However ..." Ren paused, staring directly at Rom, "the special compound in Nebraska that Geoffrey talked about was empty. Everything was gone, like it never existed."

Fucking hell. Outside of killing Xavier, that was the top priority.

It was clear when Rom arrived and Geoffrey was being sliced up like a Thanksgiving turkey that Xavier knew of his treachery. So ... he'd managed to move this location before they struck and now that everyone else was dead, they had no fucking idea where to find it. *Great*.

Rom nodded. He had no doubt Geoffrey would pull through his grave injuries, so as soon as he was conscious, Rom hoped he'd be able to provide some insight. If he'd had arrived much later, he was sure there would have been a completely different outcome for the vampire.

After two hours, showered and redressed, he stood in the corner of the shelter's kitchen, which was in total and utter chaos. Vampires and humans swarmed the place like bees. The medical staff tended to the physical health of the females while others tended to their mental health, including Sarah. He would never be able to keep her out of the fray. This was where she belonged. Through her own experiences, she had something invaluable to provide these tortured females.

Solidarity.

Sarah was a survivor and as he watched her, his chest swelled with pride. When she spotted him, she patted the female's hand she'd been talking to and made a beeline straight for him, wrapped her arms and legs around him and kissed him squarely on the lips. He turned them, sitting her on the counter.

"Thank God you're okay. I love you," she whispered between pecks.

"I love you, my beauty." He held her tightly; not wanting to ever let her go.

"I'm going to be quite a while yet. I just don't feel like I can leave until we get everyone settled."

"Anything I can do to help?" he murmured, not quite sure why he'd offered, but unable to take it back now.

She drew back and smiled. Ah ... *that's* why he offered. God, he loved this female beyond all reason.

"No offense, but I think you may be a little too scary for some of these women to handle. But thank you for offering. I know being here makes you uncomfortable."

He reluctantly let her pull back, desperately wanting to flash them home instead, but understanding her need to help. Leaning forward, he whispered against the shell of her ear, "Try to hurry. I need to be buried balls deep in your sweet heat something fierce." A shiver caused a small smile to turn his lips. "You have no idea how much I ache for you right now."

"I think I do," she muttered against his neck before nipping lightly.

Grabbing her hips, he pulled her forward so her core was flush with his throbbing cock. "Be very careful, Sarah. I'm about ten seconds away from shredding your clothes and taking you right here in front of everyone."

Her eyes flared, but she quickly recovered. *Damn.* His sweet Sarah wasn't an exhibitionist, was she?

381

"No," she yelped, slugging him in the arm.

"Good. Because I'm not sharing you." His voice hardened. "With anyone." They both knew exactly to whom he was referring.

"I need to go," she sighed. "You'll stay at the mansion until I'm done?"

"I wouldn't be anywhere else, beauty. Let me know if you need anything."

He took a step back, letting her ease off the counter. She gave him another peck before walking back to the female she'd earlier abandoned.

As he watched her go, he steeled himself for the next battle to come. The most important fight of his life. And he only hoped what Taiven said was true.

Had his brother really found a way to save their mother's life, while ending their father's?

Chapter 58

Sarah

A week later, things were finally slowing down at the shelter. Most of the women had returned home, but sixteen still remained. She and Rom had spent their days at Dev's, but their nights back at their home in Washington. She had to admit it was certainly advantageous to be bonded to a vampire, what with their speedy mode of transportation and all.

It was lunchtime and she had a sudden desire to spend a few stolen moments with Rom. Analise had told her the lords were in a meeting in Dev's office, so she headed that way, hoping he wouldn't be too upset with her for interrupting.

She had to admit that she felt immense relief that her crazy-assed biological father was dead. She wished there was a place worse than hell because that was far kinder than he deserved. As none of them had been allowed out for what seemed like an eternity, her sisters were planning a little shopping trip in a few days. She had yet to mention that one to Rom because she was sure he'd freak and try putting his foot down.

He could try.

Reaching Dev's office, she was just raising her hand to knock when she heard loud voices arguing. And Rom's was the noisiest.

"There is no fucking way we are doing that, vampire," Rom bellowed.

She didn't recognize the voice that replied, but in the back of her mind, it sounded vaguely familiar. "It's the only way."

"The fuck it is. We'll find another one."

"This is the best plan, Rom. And you know it," Damian replied.

"And if it were your mate we're talking about, Damian? What would you say then?"

Silence.

"That's what I thought," Rom said mockingly.

Not bothering to knock, she opened the door. Damian and Rom stood on opposite sides of the room and Dev sat behind his desk. But the person that had her full attention was the beautiful blond vampire casually sitting in a chair across from Dev, who now had his head turned her way. And by the looks of it, he was just as surprised to see her, as she was him.

"What the fuck, Sarah?" Rom thundered as he walked up to her and tried pushing her out of the room.

"Stop," she yelled, side-stepping him, never taking her gaze from blondie. "It's you," she whispered, barely able to believe her eyes.

His jaw ticked as he stood, fully facing her. Rom had stopped trying to shove her out of the room and now stood protectively by her side, arm wrapped firmly around her waist.

"Sarah? You *know* him?" he asked incredulously.

"Yes." With effort, she broke free of Rom's tight grip and walked up to the vampire that had essentially saved her life. Holding out her hand, she said, "Thank you."

He looked at her offering before throwing a nervous glance over her shoulder at Rom. She felt rage and confusion radiating from her mate, but she didn't care. Had it not been for this vampire, she would have been gang raped, repeatedly. And Moira or not, she wasn't sure she could have moved passed that to bond with Rom.

Clearing his throat, but not moving to shake her hand, he simply said, "No thanks necessary."

"You'd better tell me what the *fuck* is going on and right now, Geoffrey, or I swear by all that's holy, you will only *wish* you would have died at Xavier's hands, because I will make your death far more torturous and painful," her mate growled.

Spinning, she walked into Rom's arms, hugging him. "Rein it in, King Henry the Eighth. Geoffrey saved me when I was kidnapped. He didn't let the other vampires hurt me, at least not in *that* way." Rom's arms tightened around her and he buried his head in her long mane of hair. His anger at the mention of her kidnapping was tangible.

"Yah, but he was probably responsible for her being there in the first place," Damian jeered. Rom's head whipped up and, once again, she felt his fury, but this time it was like a living, breathing entity. Turning to look at Geoffrey, she could see the guilt written all over his face.

Professor Bailey. She knew it wasn't him all along ...

385

"Mother. *Fucker.* You were!" Damian yelled, starting across the room toward Geoffrey.

"I didn't know," he snapped. "She was identified as a dreamwalker in the professor's study. It was my *mission* to retrieve her. As soon as I discovered she was a Moira, I kept her safe until I could get Devon to raid the compound."

Damian was almost upon Geoffrey when Sarah rushed to his side. Foolish move, that. If these powerful vampires wanted Geoffrey dead, he would be.

"Stop." She should be angry that Geoffrey put her in that situation to begin with, and in truth, she was. It still gave her nightmares. But had he not, she never would have come *here*. She never would have known this life existed. Or that she had sisters.

And she would never have met, and bonded with, Rom. She would have unknowingly floated through life always feeling like she was missing the other half of her soul, but not understanding why.

"No one is going to touch him. He saved me," she declared.

"He put your life in peril!" Rom roared loud enough to shake the walls.

"Romaric," she pleaded. "Don't you see? It was meant to be. I wouldn't be here right now, *with you*, if it weren't for what he did."

"Sarah, I can't believe you're defending him." Her mate sounded tormented.

"And I can't believe you aren't."

"Come here," he croaked, holding out his hand for hers, which she took without hesitation.

"It's hard to admit when you're wrong, isn't it?"

"I want to kill him."

"Stop," she chided.

"If I could change things, believe me, I would," Geoffrey said softly.

"Don't say another fucking word or I'll cut out your tongue," Rom grated. Geoffrey winced, his face contorting in pain.

"Rom, please. Stop it," she begged, knowing her mate was the deliverer of Geoffrey's agony. Pulling his gaze to hers, she said, "Come. Let's get something to eat." After all, that's the reason she came, plus she needed to separate Geoffrey and Rom before Rom's anger made him do something that couldn't be undone.

"We'll continue this discussion later," Rom announced. Scooping her into his arms before she could protest, he flashed them to their bedroom in Washington, but she barely had a chance to register it because his mouth was everywhere, divesting her of all thought.

"What are you doing?" she breathed, heat pooling between her thighs.

"Fuck, Sarah. I need to be inside you," he rasped, backing her up against the closest wall. Reaching under her sundress, he ripped away the lace that covered her sex. Two fingers plunged roughly into her pussy as his mouth descended hard on hers. She rode his hand with complete abandon, quickly nearing the edge of bliss. Rom knew her body intimately, inside and out, and he expertly played it every single time he laid a finger on her. Which luckily, for her, was often.

"Don't stop," she panted.

He reached between them and unbuckled his pants. Wrapping her legs around him, his cock quickly replaced his fingers. She actually *whimpered* in ecstasy, head falling heavily against the wall. She would never tire of the raw masculinity that her mate exuded.

"Christ, you feel good. Ride my cock, beauty," his rough voice commanded. In the bedroom was the only place she willingly followed his bossy demands. And she was eager to follow this one.

The world narrowed to a tiny pinpoint of pleasure as they both chased the release they craved. They didn't exchange blood every time they had sex, but she had a ferocious desire to take his now. Without preamble, she struck swiftly and a curse fell from his lips. Heady power flashed like lightening through her bloodstream and with every suckle of his vein, she felt one with him.

His hot release set off hers and they exploded violently, riding the wave of rapture together. Panting, he pressed a lingering kiss to her swollen lips.

"Wow," she muttered as he trailed kisses to her ear. "That's the definition of a nooner. A girl could get used to that."

He barked a laugh. "You're an incredibly amazing woman, Sarah. I'm lucky to have found you."

"Yes. Yes, you are. And I'll remind you. Daily."

"Yes, I'm sure you will."

When he withdrew, she felt bereft, as she always did. If it was possible to make love to her mate every minute of every day, she would. She felt complete and whole when they were joined together.

He left and quickly returned with a hot cloth. Kneeling, he wiped gently between her legs. Pressing a soft kiss to her inner thigh, he lingered so long her arousal spiked again.

"You'll not hurt Geoffrey, right?"

Standing, he touched his lips to her forehead. "I hate that he put you in that place with those monsters. The thought of them touching you, touching what's *mine*, makes me homicidal, Sarah."

"I know. But I'm fine and I'm here with you now. And I wouldn't be without Geoffrey. Please, Rom. Everyone deserves a second chance."

He sighed. "If that's what you wish."

"It is."

He nodded sharply. "Okay."

"Thank you, Rom."

"I'd do anything for you, beauty. Anything."

"Do you want to grab a bite to eat before I have to head back?" she asked.

A devilish smile curved his lips. "Oh yes."

She laughed, trying to push him away. "I was talking about food, vampire."

Pinning her arms to the wall above her head, he answered in a low, rough and downright sexy voice. "Then perhaps you should have been clearer on that request from the get-go."

"I have a meeting at one o'clock," she sighed breathlessly, his talented tongue now doing wicked things to her body, steeling her ability to protest like she really meant it.

"I'm afraid you might just be late," he responded, nipping the hollow at the base of her throat.

Unable to deny her mate or her body, which was now writhing underneath his fevered touch, she had no choice but to acquiesce. And so while she *was* late, she had to admit, that was the best lunch she'd had in a very long time.

And she hoped to do it again tomorrow.

Chapter 59

Rom

Rom wanted to fucking *murder* him. Now he knew exactly how Dev and Damian felt. His head on a stake was sounding like a better idea with each passing moment. Maybe they could pass it around, like a trophy. Each lord keeping it four months out of the year.

Geoffrey had put *every* one of their mates' lives in jeopardy.

But he'd saved them too. Multiple times.

Fuck me. The logical side of his brain knew this to be true. Sarah would not be his had she not ended up with Xavier. Hell, Sarah would not be his had Geoffrey not saved her as a baby instead of destroying her as Xavier directed. But the sheer animal in him had a visceral need to end Geoffrey. He'd put Rom's mate in harm's way and while Sarah had assured him no rape happened, it could have ended very differently, in which case, no amount of pleading by his mate would have saved Geoffrey's soul.

Sarah had walked in on another strategy session. He'd gotten the text from his brother this morning that it was time. He was to return to Romania tomorrow evening. Much to his chagrin, Rom had to admit what Geoffrey had suggested was a brilliant plan. And Geoffrey was willing to do it, even though it put his own life in grave danger. Maybe he'd get lucky and the fucker would get killed. Then at least Sarah couldn't be mad at *him* because he would have honored his word.

Geoffrey's only condition was that if they made it through this alive, he was no longer indebted to Romaric or the other lords and he would be allowed to live his days free of any retribution by any of them.

They'd all agreed.

"Do you trust him?" his brother asked.

"About as much as I do you," he retorted.

The people, that Rom implicitly trusted, could be counted on one hand and his brother and Geoffrey didn't make the cut. Far from it.

Taiven's laughter carried through the burner phone. "Then tonight we'll set our plan into motion. I'll see you tomorrow night, brother."

"If you fuck me over, there will be retribution," Rom warned. Devon and Damian would be unstoppable until both Taiven and Makare were dead. The silence extended for so long, he thought Taiven had hung up.

"I understand you have no reason to believe me, Romaric, but there is only one vampire I wish to fuck over. And it isn't you."

Rom felt a twinge of guilt but quickly pushed it aside. Anger and distrust were the predominant feelings he had for his brother. Guilt had no place in the mix.

"Why her?" Rom asked. He didn't need to further explain his question, for Taiven knew exactly to what he was referring.

"That's a discussion for another day, brother. Should we both live to see another sunrise after tomorrow that is."

"Hear me well. She's mine and I'm not big on sharing what's mine. Do it again and, brother or not, I'll take immense pleasure in slowly killing you myself."

"So noted."

"Until tomorrow." He hung up without waiting for a reply and threw the phone on the couch.

Rom looked around the room at his comrades. His friends. Hell, his *in-laws*. "It's done."

"Have you changed your mind about letting us help?" asked Damian.

"No. This is my battle. Not yours."

"We'll protect her with our lives, Rom," Damian responded.

He nodded. If he died, then that wasn't really necessary, for Sarah would perish within several days after him, a week tops. Now that they were bonded, she needed his blood for survival. At least she'd have her family by her side if it came to that.

Which it wouldn't. He'd be victorious. He had no other choice.

Just then the door opened and Ren walked in with Geoffrey in tow.

Rom stood, walking toward Geoffrey until they were toe to toe. Geoffrey was very well matched with the lords in bulk and height and he had to admit, intelligence and skill as well. "It's time," he stated simply.

Geoffrey dipped his head in agreement.

"Your injuries were severe. Are you certain you're one-hundred percent healed?" They needed all their faculties and wits about them to come out the other side of this alive and the last thing Rom needed was to drag an injured vampire on his coattails.

"I'm sure, my lord."

Rom smirked. That's the first time Geoffrey had gifted him with the respect his position deserved. Sarah's earlier words echoed around, *"Everyone deserves a second chance",* and his fury at the vampire abated some. "We'll stick to the plan we originally discussed and I'll see you there."

"And Geoffrey," he called after the retreating vampire. "Good luck."

"And to you, my lord."

He'd take it because they sure as fuck were gonna need it.

Chapter 60

Sarah

She'd stayed home from the shelter today to spend it with Rom and they'd had a simply magical day. She felt giddy, like a kid at Disney World. They lounged in bed much of the morning, making love and talking. At his insistence, she'd given him some of the sordid details about her month in captivity and then soothed his anger, very thoroughly, with her mouth and lips and tongue. Tracing every line, every muscle, every dip, especially the sexy V that she loved so much.

Then they'd eaten a light lunch and spent hours in the afternoon horseback riding. She loved the freedom and power being on a horse wielded. Having a wild beast under her control, which outweighed her by almost ten times, was intoxicating.

Ha! Kind of like her mate.

But as wonderful as the day had been, the time was drawing near for him to leave. She'd pushed aside Rom's coming confrontation with his father tonight all day, trying desperately to avoid thinking about it so she could make new memories without tainting them with sadness and fear, but with only two hours before he left, she'd finally lost that battle.

There were things she wanted to tell him before he left. In case this was the last time they laid eyes on each other in this lifetime.

"What are you thinking about, beauty?" Rom asked quietly, as his hand found her naked breast under the warm water, gently tweaking her pebbled nipple.

"Mmmm ... so many things," she replied, sighing at his ministrations.

"Tell me," he whispered against the shell of her ear. She wished they could stay like this forever. The deep tub had quickly become one of her favorite spots in the house and when they sat there like they did this evening, watching the stars sparkle like diamonds in the sky, her back pressed firmly against his chest, it was like a fairytale. Only this was an *erotic* fairytale, because it always ended in mind-melting sex.

"I found out my mother's name."

His hand stilled. "You did? How?"

"I, um, asked Giselle to help me."

Laughing, he linked their hands and placed them across her belly. "I would have liked to have been a fly on the wall during that conversation."

Sarah had a weird urge to defend Giselle. "She's not so bad."

"Outside of me, she's the coldest vampire I've ever met."

Twisting her head and capturing his gaze, she said, "You're not cold. Just ... misunderstood. And I think she is too."

Leaning forward, he kissed the tip of her nose. "You see the good in everybody, Sarah. I so love that about you."

Turning back around to look out at the night sky, she continued, "Her name was Marna Clark. And I have an aunt and a grandfather alive. My grandmother died last year. They live in Illinois."

"Would you like to meet them?"

"Yes," she answered, no hesitation. "Someday."

"Then we shall make that happen."

This next part was a little harder, because she hated to ruin the moment by talking about his past. About Seraphina. But she wanted him to know.

"And my grandmother had a very extensive family tree that Giselle managed to get me as well, along with quite a few pictures. It goes all the way back to the late thirteen hundreds."

"Mmm, really?" he asked, hips gently thrusting behind her, his erection digging into her back. Clearly other ways to fill their remaining time together was on his mind. But she wasn't through.

"Yes. And I saw a name and an old picture that caught my eye."

"Sarah, I need to fuck you before I leave," he mumbled against her neck, her stomach fluttering in anticipation.

Oh my. His wandering hands and naughty words made it *very* difficult to form sentences.

"It appears I'm a descendent of Willa Glynn." When he didn't react, she added, "Seraphina's sister."

He turned her around to face him, sloshing water over the sides of the tub. "What did you say?"

Crooking her eyebrows, she shrugged. "Pretty incredible, huh?"

"Are you sure?" he asked doubtfully.

"Positive." Hating that she felt so insecure that she wasn't his first, she decided to ask the question that had plagued her since Rom finally divulged who Seraphina was. "I thought vampires could only have one Moira? Are you sure I'm yours, if Seraphina was?"

"Yes, Sarah. I'm sure. I never bonded with Seraphina, as I told you, so apparently the Fates granted me another chance of finding my one true mate. I don't think Seraphina was ever intended to be my mate and I should have listened to my gut the second I saw you, instead of spending days questioning fate. And because I didn't, we're now both in danger from my father."

"What do you mean?"

His smile was thin and didn't reach his eyes. And that made her slightly sick. He looked away before capturing her gaze again. "I've been alive a very long time, Sarah, and I'd never heard of a vampire having two Moiras, but there was no denying in my gut and in my blood that you were mine. And so I sought answers from the only person I knew would have heard of such a thing. My mother. But to get to her, I had to go through my father first. If I had just trusted my instinct, I wouldn't have to confront him tonight. I wouldn't have to kill him. I wouldn't have put us in danger."

Her brows furrowed. "But if you kill your father, doesn't your mother also die?"

"Taiven claims to have found a way to prevent that. I'm not convinced."

"And you're willing to take a chance?"

His face turned impassive. "I'm not willing to risk losing you. Period."

"I'm sorry," she muttered, laying her head on his shoulder.

Strong arms wrapped around her. "I'm the one that's sorry, beauty. I'm the one that's sorry."

Chapter 61

Rom

Standing on the steps once again of his father's house, he was half surprised there wasn't an ambush waiting for him. When he was growing up, that was a tactic his father regularly used with unsuspecting visitors called to his home under false pretenses. Makare much more preferred to trick and play with his enemies than battle them fairly and squarely.

As they'd all agreed having cell phones was too risky, Rom was going on blind faith that Taiven, Ainsley and Geoffrey had everything in place for his arrival. If they ran into any glitches, he wouldn't know until it was too late.

Sarah had told him before he left that in a dream, Seraphina said that reuniting him and Taiven was the key to saving Rom's life. He still wasn't sure what to make of that and he wasn't at all sure what to make of what the vampire on the mountain had told him of Taiven.

"He's a good vampire. Trustworthy."

Rom snorted. "Good and trustworthy aren't adjectives I'd use to describe my brother. Cocky, self-centered, and sadistic? Yes. Good? Hardly."

"You haven't seen your brother in over five hundred years. A lot can change in that time. Your father is the sadistic one. Taiven has saved hundreds of women from a fate worse than death. A fate

imposed upon them by your father. He's even saved many of your American women's lives."

"How so?"

"That's a longer discussion than we have time for, I'm afraid. What you need to know now is that Taiven's objectives and yours align. Taiven is respected and benevolent and fair. And our true leader. Everything Makare is not. It's only a matter of time before Makare discovers Taiven's subterfuge and when that happens, he will be publicly executed and our people cannot allow that to happen. Together, I believe you'll be powerful enough to finally rid the world of your father."

The sound of the castle door opening yanked him back to the present. Dammit, he could not afford any distractions, no matter how momentary.

"Sire, this way, please."

Showtime.

The servant took him on the same path that he'd taken just a few short weeks ago, winding through the castle directly to the throne room. Upon entering, his steps wavered. As expected, perched high on his throne was his father. But this time, instead of a naked whore on his lap, his unclothed mother sat instead.

There was a collar around her neck and attached to it was a leash, which Makare held in one hand while stroking her hair with the other, much like one would do with a lap pet. Even from this far away, she visibly shivered, but it wasn't from a chill or in anticipation. It was from *fear*.

When he entered the room, his mother's eye caught his briefly but quickly looked away. He could almost feel her embarrassment at being put on such vulgar display.

Mother. Fucker. He wanted to rip Makare's fucking head off this very instant. How *dare* he debase his mother in front of her children? And how dare Taiven let this happen? Where the fuck was this supposedly honorable vampire that Malachi had spoken of? He was supposed to be here. Sixty seconds in the door and their plans were already shot to shit.

"Romaric," his father greeted. "I'm surprised you actually came."

Taiven and Ainsley were to tell his father that Rom had been found and had reluctantly agreed to come listen to his father's *request* to rejoin the family. He wouldn't be able to hide it now, should his father look, but at least Makare hadn't known of his mating to Sarah since he wasn't bonded last time he was here. That is unless Taiven or Ainsley betrayed him. Which, at this point, since they were both notably absent, was very fucking likely.

Inclining his head, Rom let his power flare slightly, stating evenly, "You shouldn't be. *I'm* an honorable vampire."

He didn't miss the quick nostril flare at his unspoken insinuation that his father wasn't.

"You know why you're here?" his father clipped.

So you can try to kill me, asshole.

402

"I have a pretty good idea."

"You really should learn better manners, Romaric. Let's start with bowing to your King."

"I said I was honorable. Not respectful."

His father stood abruptly, causing his mother to fall with a thud to the floor and down a few stairs. Makare still had a tight hold on the leash and from her angle on the ground she was clearly choking, clawing at the collar for relief.

Rom gritted his teeth and barely held his fury in check. He should end this now, but he didn't know what had become of Taiven, Geoffrey or Ainsley. Not that he should give a fuck about the first two, but he didn't wish any harm to come to Ainsley.

"Do you know what happens to traitors, Romaric?"

"I'm sure you plan on telling me, Makare."

Malevolent eyes never leaving his, his father snapped his fingers. Seconds later, two men walked in, dragging a severely beaten and tortured vampire between them. He didn't recognize the vampire until they got closer.

Taiven.

They were royally fucked.

This was absolutely not *part of the plan.*

"I don't think I can describe how gut wrenching it is to have not only one, but *two*, sons betray you," his father continued, still brutally holding his mother's life in his hands.

The vampires viciously threw Taiven on the cold floor at his feet, taking only a few steps back. They crossed their arms, pinning Rom with a hard, cold glare, clearly ready to do their master's bidding. Taiven wasn't even moving. Where the *fuck* were Geoffrey and Ainsley?

Makare began walking slowly down the stairs; finally abandoning his mother, who now gulped lungsful of air.

"You could have had everything."

"Freedom was preferable to living under a tyrant's rule."

Makare's jaw clenched and Rom felt the first inklings of his father's power. Instead of throwing up his shields and negating his father's control, he welcomed it. He reaped it. Took it as his own.

"You *will* return to your rightful place or you will die. Today."

Rom's eyes flitted to Taiven's still form. He could hear the vampire's breaths. They were shallow and uneven, but even for the short time he'd been unceremoniously dumped there he was rapidly improving. He wondered if his father was aware.

"Cut the shit. You'd sooner have my head than have me rule by your side."

An evil smile curled his father's mouth. "Not true. You may have left, but I've decided that's a betrayal I can forgive. Your brother's betrayal, however, I cannot."

Makare didn't know they were working together to kill him? What other betrayal could he possibly be referring to?

"My plate's kind of full at the moment. I'll check back with you in another six hundred years."

"Hmmm. I think I have something that may change your mind. *Son.*" Makare's eyes slowly made their way to Rom's mating mark and his blood ran ice cold. "Ah, yes. I *am* aware of your recent mating status."

As if waiting for her cue, Ainsley walked in. And she wasn't alone.

"Sarah ..." Rom uttered.

He could hardly breathe. Unbridled rage boiled his blood to the breaking point and his gut burned at Ainsley's betrayal.

How the fuck did they find Sarah? He'd only left her a couple hours ago and she was supposed to be at Dev's. Was Geoffrey in on the ruse as well, pretending all along to help him? Of course he was. How could he not be?

He couldn't work out the fucking mess he now saw in front of him.

"Come here, pet," his father called to his mate.

"Don't. You. Fucking. Touch. Her," he gritted. The one advantage he'd had over his father he'd given away as part of their elaborate scheme to take him down. He'd not liked the idea from the beginning, but his father would expect something unexpected from Rom. He wouldn't from Taiven.

And now ... now he had nothing to best his father with. Taiven lay in a broken pile on the ground and his father had his mate. His father had him firmly by the balls and by the smirk on his face he knew it.

This was a clusterfuck of epic proportions.

This was the end.

"It's okay, Romaric. Your mate and I have been getting to know each other."

Sarah shook, but didn't say a word as Ainsley walked her straight to his father. Makare's pulled her in front of him and wrapped an arm around his mate's neck, pinning her tightly to his body. It was a clear threat.

"Sarah, are you okay?"

No response.

Fuck!

His mind completely shut down. Whatever his father asked of him, he'd gladly do. He now had the upper hand, holding the only thing that mattered to Rom in his dirty, slimy hands.

"Whatever you want, I'll do it. Just let her go."

"Good. I'm glad we're finally seeing eye-to-eye. First, what I want is for you to kill your traitorous brother. Right now. And if it's all the same to you, I'll hang onto your lovely Sarah until you comply."

Makare looked to the two vampires standing just a few feet away and one produced a long, sharp sword, similar to the Kilij that he favored. He was handed the steel, which now hung heavy and offending in his hand.

Rom may not trust Taiven, or even like him at this point, but he certainly did *not* want to kill him. And not when he was unable to defend himself. But what other choice did he have? He would not put Sarah's life in jeopardy.

"Give me your word you will not harm her if I comply."

"You have my word." Makare's word meant *nothing*. He was completely backed into a fucking corner with no way out.

With his foot, Rom pushed Taiven so that he lay on his back. His heart rate and pulse sounded stronger than before and his injuries had even lessened in the few minutes he'd been lying there, but his eyes were still closed and unmoving.

Rom's stomach felt like undiluted acid had been poured directly into it and it was eating his innards from the inside out. His father knew exactly what he was doing. Protecting his own head, he'd put his mate directly in front of him. Rom couldn't flash behind him in an attempt to sever it, because Sarah would get hurt at any angle.

"It will be okay, Sarah." He tried to sound reassuring when he felt anything but. Looking into her eyes, he expected fear, but instead he saw steely resolve.

"Do it. Now," his father thundered.

"Forgive me, brother," he whispered.

As he unwillingly raised the weighty blade to strike his brother dead, the events that unfolded happened so fast his addled brain could hardly keep up. Out of the corner of his eye, he caught a glint of steel being raised and plunged into the heart of his mate so fast he couldn't react. His father's face then twisted in pain and he let out a roar so loud, it shook the stone walls as he loosened his death grip on Sarah and she fell forward, clutching her chest, but not making a sound.

But then Sarah's form dissolved and changed right before his very eyes. And standing in her place was Geoffrey. Makare was twisted around, eyes behind him, taking his attention from Geoffrey, who now brandished a sword matching the one he held which was whizzing through the air.

Rom watched with apathy and confusion as his father's head fell slowly from his body, his eyes frozen in surprise. Already unleashing his power, he immediately prepared himself for a battle with Ainsley and the other two vampires, but they calmly stood by watching the events unfold as if it had all been orchestrated.

What.

The.

Fuck?

It all *had* been orchestrated. Or *re*-orchestrated. *Without* his knowledge.

A plethora of emotions hit him at once, threatening to bring him to his knees. The biggest of them being relief.

Relief that Sarah wasn't actually here with a dagger through her heart.

Relief that he hadn't been double-crossed.

And relief that the threat to his current and future happiness was lying in a pile of now rotting flesh and blood on the floor at his feet.

Chapter 62

Sarah
Two weeks later...

She was so nervous she could throw up. She hadn't even been this nervous to talk to her parents the first time after she'd been rescued.

"How are you doing, my beauty?"

"Good. Good. I'm really ... good."

Laughing, he pulled her onto his lap. They were, once again, sitting in a stretch limousine and the memories of what they'd done last time raced through her head, but she was too damned jittery to re-enact them. And besides ... this time they weren't alone.

"You're not a very good liar," Rom whispered in her ear. "Would you like me to take your mind off it?"

Would she ever.

He chuckled. *"Oh, the pleasures I'm going to lavish on your body later, Sarah."*

"Do tell."

"First, I'm going to—"

"Would you guys knock it off? I can see the flush of her skin from here, for Christ's sake," Giselle jibed.

"Tell me again why we brought them along?" Rom grumbled.

Sighing, she wrapped her arms around his neck. "Romaric, I can't just show up on his doorstep, popping up out of thin air. Be nice," she scolded.

"I can't believe you let your woman talk to you like that," Mike joked, pulling Giselle so close to him she was sure no air circulated between them. The love she saw arching between the two was palpable and the raw possessiveness in the way Mike touched her was reminiscent of how the lords handled their mates.

Hmmm?

Rom glared his way. "Like you're one to talk, human."

The vehicle slowed and finally stopped in front of a small, but decent looking ranch house. The gray paint was faded and peeling and the driveway, with weeds growing through the cracks, had seen better days, but this was it.

Her grandfather's house.

"I think I'm going to throw up," she muttered.

Rom grabbed her face, turning her toward him. "He will love you as much as I do, beauty. How can he not?"

He always knew what to say to make her feel better. A smile tugged the corner of her mouth. "I love you, Rom."

"I think *I'm* going to throw up," Giselle complained, stepping out the car.

"You got this, Sarah," Mike said, patting her knee upon his exit, earning him a vicious glare from her mate.

Rom stepped out first, holding out his hand for hers. Then they were standing at the door, ringing the doorbell, waiting for it to be answered. Rom supported her wobbly legs with an arm wrapped tightly around her waist.

Bud Clark was expecting them. Well, he was at least expecting Detective Mike Thatcher, Giselle's unexpected boyfriend or lover or whatever he was to her. He was the one savvy enough to find Bud Clark in the first place. He was the one that had the foresight to take snapshots of the family tree, her mother and Seraphina. And he was the one responsible for reuniting a long lost family.

The door opened and standing there was not only her grandfather, but who she assumed was her aunt Brynne. She hadn't seen pictures of her before. Two sets of eyes latched immediately onto hers. The resemblance to her aunt Brynne was unbelievable.

Mike cleared his throat. "Bud, Brynne, I'd like to introduce you to Marna's daughter. Sarah Dietrich."

———

They walked into the great room, hand in hand, one of the last to arrive. Quickly scanning the room, however, she didn't see the one vampire that she'd hoped would be there.

"Sarah!" Kate and Analise called to her at the same time from across the room and rushed to her side, pulling her away from her mate. "How did it go?" Analise excitedly asked.

411

She couldn't help the broad smile that hadn't left her face all day. They'd spent several hours this morning and early afternoon with her grandfather and aunt. Even her mother and father had been genuinely excited that they were going to meet.

"It was great. My grandpa Bud couldn't stop hugging me. And I really liked Brynne. She's not that much older than I am. We're going to have dinner sometime next week."

"And Rom was okay with that?" Analise probed.

She shrugged one shoulder. "He suggested it."

"Huh?"

"Analise, stop. He's not that bad," Sarah scolded. Her sisters had her back, but they were unnecessarily hard on Rom. She was tired of everyone thinking her mate was emotionless and mean. He *wasn't*.

"You're right, Sarah. I'm sorry. I can see that he's changed." Analise pulled into a quick hug. "It won't happen again."

"Say, don't you start classes next week?" Kate asked.

With all that had happened in the last few weeks, she'd waffled on whether to continue with the two classes she'd signed up for, but after some gentle coaxing from Rom, she decided to finish her degree.

"Yes. I'm excited." And she genuinely was.

Changing the topic, she asked, "Is Geoffrey coming?"

"I don't know. I haven't heard," Kate replied.

She hoped so. She wanted to thank the vampire who had single-handedly been responsible for saving not only her own life, but her mate's.

Chapter 63

Rom

"What the fuck are you wearing?" Damian quipped, handing him a beer. Rom had a hard time taking his eyes off Sarah, who now stood with her sisters, talking excitedly about her little family reunion. In fact, he had a hard time being away from her for any length of time these days.

Rom looked down at his black t-shirt and dark denims. He had to admit, they were more comfortable than he thought they would be. And the lust he'd seen in Sarah's eyes as she raked over him slowly when he'd walked out of the closet was worth every minute he spent in them. In fact, he had a dozen more pairs on order.

"I believe they're called jeans."

"I know what they're called, asshole. I've never seen you wear a pair. In your life."

"I'm turning over a new leaf. Where's Taiven?" The fuck if he was going to stand here and discuss his wardrobe with Damian. It was bad enough him and Dev were already so far up his business, he felt like all his privacy had been stripped. Practically nothing was sacred between Sarah and her sisters. He knew things about both Damian and Dev that he simply wanted to scour out of his brain.

Damian jerked his head toward the opposite end of the room. "He and Dev have been huddled in the corner for quite some time."

"And Geoffrey?"

"I haven't seen him yet."

Rom hadn't spoken to Geoffrey since that night. He owed the vampire his and Taiven's life. And that of Sarah's. *Once again.* He wouldn't be standing here today, with his mate, if it weren't for Geoffrey.

None of them would. Time and again over the last several weeks Geoffrey had proven himself trustworthy. And it was time all past indiscretions were put behind them, so he could start anew with a clean slate.

"What the hell happened that night?" Damian inquired.

Rom hadn't talked about it, other than with Sarah. The only thing he'd told the lords was that things hadn't gone quite as planned, but his father was dead by Geoffrey's hand. But it was time they knew, because he expected them to all be on board with letting Geoffrey move on with his life. He deserved their forgiveness and like it or not, *they* owed *him*. Not the other way around.

But he was going to play with Damian a bit before he told him. Yes, he'd lightened up considerably since he'd met Sarah, her playfulness quickly rubbing off.

"Are you going to whine like a bitch baby if I don't tell you?"

"Fuck off. I'm not sure I like this new you," Damian retorted, walking away.

He laughed and it felt good. *Really* good. With Xavier and his father dead, and especially with Sarah at his side, he felt like a completely new vampire.

He felt liberated.

Alive.

Like he was *really* living for the first time in his long life.

And it felt fucking phenomenal.

Sarah had singlehandedly reawakened things in him that he'd long buried and thought dead. Things he wasn't even sure ever existed before. She owned every part of him. Now and forever.

Taiven caught his eye and ended his conversation with Dev, striding toward him. Rom had seen his brother only once since that night, but they had been too preoccupied burying their mother to make small talk. At that time, Taiven still had a few more serious injuries that hadn't quite healed and it was a strange relief to lay eyes on his brother's healthy form once again.

"Brother," Taiven greeted.

"Brother." He bowed his head slightly in acknowledgement. After a few silent beats, he added, "You look well."

"I should be fucking pissed at you for almost chopping off my head, but … curiously I'm not. Even though I haven't found my Moira yet, I find that in the same situation, I would likely have done the same thing." He would have. Without a second thought.

Rom couldn't respond. Given the chance to redo that night, he wouldn't have made a different decision, but guilt ate at him nonetheless that he was willing to take his brother's life.

"Geoffrey's plan was brilliant, I'll give him that. I owe him my life."

"As do I," he responded quietly.

"Listen, about Sarah ..." Taiven started.

"Forget it. It's done and over with and so long as you stay out of her goddamned dreams, it shall stay in the past." The last thing he wanted to do was talk about his mate with Taiven. He was still plenty pissed, but not wanting to carry around another burden, he was willing to put it behind him.

Taiven nodded sharply.

At that moment, Sarah walked up, wrapping her arms around him. He didn't miss the *interested* look his brother gave her.

Fucker was walking a mighty tight rope.

"Why are you guys so serious over here? This is a party." Turning toward Taiven, she extended her hand. "Hi, we haven't officially met. I'm Sarah and you must be Taiven."

Without hesitation, Taiven accepted and brought her hand to his mouth, feathering a kiss over her knuckles.

Rom growled, his vision going blood red. Sarah's throaty laugh pulled him back from the brink of a full-blown attack on his brother.

"I can practically see the testosterone dueling in the air. Dial it back, boys."

"I was just welcoming my new sister-in-law into the family, brother. Nothing nefarious intended."

"Touch her again and you won't have a family. Or a head," he warned.

Taiven walked away, laughing. And not a second too soon.

"I'm going to—"

Sarah broke away before he could finish and rushed across the room, throwing herself into yet another vampire's arms.

Geoffrey.

Fuck him.

At this rate, his raging jealousy was going to cause more than one vampire's death before the night was over.

And he'd been doing so well.

Chapter 64

Sarah

"Thank you," she whispered. "Thank you for saving my mate."

"Ah ... you're welcome." He patted her back lightly; clearly uncomfortable that she had her arms wrapped around his neck.

"Geoffrey," a low voice rumbled behind her. Or growled. "Take your hands off my mate."

Oh shit, that was definitely a growl.

Well screw Rom. He should be nicer to Geoffrey. Neither of them would be here had it not been for him.

"I'm trying," Geoffrey muttered. Sarah finally let go, sensing her mate's ire rapidly increasing. Spinning around, she latched onto him, burying her head in his firm chest, his strong arms enfolded her possessively. She was about to scold Rom when he spoke words that couldn't have shocked her more.

"Thank you." She extracted herself from Rom in time to see him extend his hand, which Geoffrey took, shaking firmly.

"My pleasure, my lord."

Well, this was quite a contradiction to the last time she'd seen these two together. A couple weeks ago in Dev's office, Rom looked like he'd sooner Geoffrey be dead than standing in front of him.

Geoffrey inclined his head in respect and strode across the room, toward Taiven.

"I'm proud of you." She didn't want to sound condescending, but she knew it was uncomfortable for Rom to express his feelings with anyone else but her, and those two simple words he'd spoken to Geoffrey were full of heartfelt emotion.

For the second time since they walked in the room, she heard her mate laugh. It was such a glorious sound and she'd heard it more in the last two weeks than she ever had. Looking down at her, he smiled gently, the pure love radiating from his eyes enthralling her as always.

"It's because of you."

"I know," she joked.

"Are you always going to be so cheeky and difficult?"

"You love it."

"Hmmm ... I wouldn't use the word *love*."

She stood on her tiptoes, brushing her lips across his. "This is sounding oddly familiar," she murmured against his mouth, nipping his lower lip, wishing they were alone so she could rip his clothes off and spend hours riding him.

Cupping her cheeks, his intense gaze colliding with hers. Lust and passion engulfed her and his eyes shone bright, full of desire and love. "I love you. So fucking much, Sarah. You've brought me back to life."

Sarah's heart swelled. She never really understood the true definition of happiness until she'd met Rom. Her cheeks hurt many days because she couldn't stop smiling. "And you *gave* me mine."

Uncaring about the PDA, she captured his lips in a heated kiss.

Damian's loud complaining and everyone's laughter broke them out of their sensual spell. "Okay, I want to know what the fuck happened that night. *Somebody* tell me *something*, for the love of Christ."

Hardly able to tear their eyes from each other, she was anxious to get back home to be alone with her mate, but at the same time was content to know that they had many days and nights ahead of them to live and love. She wasn't naïve enough to think another threat wouldn't surface, but until it did, she would live each day of her new life to the fullest with her Vampire Lord mate.

And, good or bad, she looked forward to every single one.

Epilogue

Geoffrey

"I think that's Geoffrey's story to tell," Romaric said, after breaking the lip lock with his mate, who was now sitting on his lap on one of the three couches in the room. Jealousy spiked. *He* wanted to sit on the couch with his Moira, happy and relaxed and content, but he pushed that aside for the moment. His immediate objectives had been to make it out of these last two missions alive. So he could be free.

And he had. *Barely.* He was finally at full strength again and his next mission would not involve weapons, unless one counted the relentless emotional pursuit he would yield with expert precision to acquire the one thing he now wanted most in the world.

Elizabeth Armstrong. *Beth.* His Moira.

"Um, that's kind of you, but I believe it's your story to tell," he replied, feeling a bit uncomfortable being in the spotlight in a room of vamps that clearly didn't welcome him with open arms.

"I would be honored if you would tell it," Rom said, respectfully.

Geoffrey had developed immense respect for Romaric Dietrich over these past few weeks, not only for saving his life, but because he was fair and honorable. There was a reason he was a lord, beyond his immeasurable power. Romaric was the epitome of a leader. And as such, it didn't chafe him to call him by the title he'd earned.

"As you wish, my lord."

Taiven graciously handed him a beer. Over the last two weeks, he'd gotten to know Romaric's brother quite well and had come to find they'd had a common altruistic mission over the last few decades. Color him surprised to find out that Taiven was the head of the European ring to whom he filtered some of the females he'd saved over the years. It was far safer to get them out of the country than to return them to their homes. For all of them.

Except for Taiven, when his father found out. Which was quite inconvenient timing. He was not going to share this with the group, because he wasn't sure how much Romaric knew and he wasn't about to spill any secrets. God knows with his skill, he had plenty of them.

"The original plan was for myself to mimic Taiven. As such, I would expect to be armed. Taiven would hide in the wings and use Xavier's power of stasis to immobilize his father and I could easily behead him. However, when I arrived, Taiven didn't show at our rendezvous point. Ainsley arrived instead. Taiven had been detained by his father, labeled as a traitor and beaten severely for the twenty-four hours leading up to Romaric's arrival.

"So Ainsley and I had to come up with a new plan on the fly. And we had no way to warn Romaric what he was walking into. It was better that we didn't anyway, because the genuine surprise on his face played perfectly into our ruse.

"I took Sarah's form and Ainsley pretended that she was able to kidnap me to keep Romaric in line. The guards were also in on the coup. What I didn't expect was to be stabbed in the heart, but the bigger surprise was Taiven and Romaric's mother. Had it not been for her, it's likely none of us would be standing here today. Just as I was stabbed, she stabbed Makare in the back, distracting him, so I was able to execute him."

Everyone gaped at him. The room eerily quiet. It was really quite an unbelievable story. Had he not been there, he wouldn't have believed it himself. And had he not seen Sarah that day in Dev's office little more than two weeks ago, they would have been fucked ten ways to Sunday. Geoffrey couldn't mimic someone he hadn't seen before and that's what she'd walked in on that day. Geoffrey had suggested it and Rom threw a shit fit.

"I have so many questions, I don't even know where to begin," Damian groaned. The quiet turned to chaos as everyone started talking at once, volleying questions like rapid gunfire to Romaric and Taiven.

The one that he caught was whether their mother still lived.

Not every story had a happy ending. Because Taiven had been detained by his father, he never had a chance to give her the potion he'd procured from a witch. By distracting her mate, she selflessly gave of her life so her children could live. Taiven and Romaric buried her just a few days ago. Both were pretty broken up about it, but at least Geoffrey made the killing blow. He wasn't sure either could, or should, have to live with the guilt that bringing down a monster had caused an innocent to perish as well.

Geoffrey wasn't sure what to expect when he'd walked into the room several hours ago, but to be *welcomed* and *thanked* even *respected* by the great Romaric wasn't at the top of the list. In fact, he'd fully expected to be met with little more than barely contained disdain by the lords. Granted, Dev and Damian had been much cooler to him when he'd arrived, but by the time he'd left, they each offered a handshake and their thanks as well, although it was a little tougher for Damian, who was rightfully still holding onto a lot of resentment toward him.

That was a bridge that quickly needed repaired, because to get to Beth, he would need to go through Damian and his mate, who he'd come to discover was best friends with his Moira. Beth was still living at the shelter and there was no way in hell he'd be allowed anywhere near her without getting Analise DiStephano on his side.

So he'd been wracking his brain over the last two weeks on how he was going to accomplish that and had come up with a loose plan of sorts. It would require working closely with the lords, and now that he'd spent time with them this evening, it felt more plausible than it did before he'd arrived. The last thing he wanted to do was go to war with the almighty powerful lords because he knew he would never win.

But he would also do absolutely *anything* and *everything* it took to get his Moira. If the roles were reversed, he knew each and every one of the lords would move heaven and earth to get to their Moiras, killing anyone that stood in their way. Hell, Romaric was ready to behead his own brother to save Sarah.

The fact that Beth was here, in this estate, so close, yet so far away, was an agonizing and bitter pill to swallow. She was *his,* goddammit.

It was only a matter of time before he made her so.

"Soon, my sweet. Very soon."

~ The End ~

My musical inspiration for this book was simply two songs. The first represents Romaric pre-Sarah. The second is Romaric post-Sarah.

Give them a listen. I think you'll agree ...

"I Am Machine" by Three Days Grace
"Alive" by Adelita's Way.

Acknowledgements and Thanks!

It's a little surreal to be writing the acknowledgements for my third novel. When I started this journey, I didn't even know if I could finish one full-length book, let alone three.

When I created the Regent Vampire Lords and their world in my mind, I envisioned sexy, alpha males who passionately fall in love with their Fated, their world now revolving around their beloved. It's what we all want, right? I mean...that's why we read romance novels to begin with.

In Surrendering, book 1 of the series, Romaric was a definite enigma. Even to me. But writing Romaric was probably the most rewarding of all the Lords so far. It took him a while to reveal his himself to me throughout this book, but in the end, he may be my favorite lord so far and I don't think I could have found a better mate for him than Sarah. I'm absolutely in love with their story!

First and foremost, to my readers: **Thank you** for purchasing my book!! The number of people who have reached out to me to offer support and praise for this series is humbling and a little mind-blowing. If you like my book, please tell your friends! Please write a review, please support your favorite authors. The best thing you can do to support an author you love is word of mouth and reviews.

My list of "girls" is expanding and I have met some amazing people throughout this process. Tara, Kaitlyn, Beth, Sherri, Emma, Diane and Sabrina...a million thanks will never be enough for your honesty and your valued opinions. I'm so blessed to have each and every one of you in my life! (Sniffle, sniffle, get the tissue...)

To my husband: Babe, you are my everything, my inspiration, my very heart. I can write about romance because I live it every day with you. Thanks for your undying support when I am literally consumed with my writing, even when I don't always get dinner on the table or I forgot to call the table guy or I couldn't tear myself away from the story to order the new sheets we so desperately needed for our bed! You are my rock and I'm so very glad that you're proud of what I've been able to accomplish, because none of it would have been possible without you.

Thanks to my editor, Amanda, for all of your collaboration, support and guidance. I have learned so much about this world thanks to you and I'm lucky to have met you so many months ago. And finally a special thanks to Yocla Designs for the absolutely *A MA Z I N G* job you did on the book cover art once again! You brought my vision of the story to life and a picture really does say a thousand words through your work!

Lastly, I want to shout out to all of the amazing romance authors, of whom there are too many to name, who inspire me daily.

About the Author

Most authors will tell you that writing is all they've ever wanted to do. I guess I'm one of the few that don't fit in that bucket. Writing a book was never on my bucket list until three years ago. On my list was: Climb the Corporate ladder. *Check*. Go to Europe. *Check*. Complete a half marathon. *Check*. Eat chocolate daily. *Double check*. *Isn't this on everyone's bucket list?* Catch up on two seasons of Games of Thrones in one day. *Painful, but check*. And finally, devouring romance books at an alarming pace like the unashamed book addict I am...*Over a thousand checks!*

Living in Nebraska with my soul-mate hubby, I pen my magic world at night, while paying the bills with an actual paying job in the corporate world during the day. Writing is just an all-consuming passion for now, but boy, if I could dream...

My other loves include my simply amazing, incredible and talented children, a steamy novel, great friends and family, and a warm ocean breeze gliding over my sun drenched skin with a cocktail in hand.

If you enjoyed this book, <u>please</u> consider leaving a review where you purchased the book or on Goodreads. Even one or two sentences or simply rating the book is helpful. If you're anything like me, you rely on reader reviews to help make your determination on purchasing a great book in the vast sea of many available. Many THANKS!

Finally, if you would like to stalk about me, please visit me at the following places:

Facebook:
https://www.facebook.com/pages/KL-Kreig/808927362462053?ref=hl

Website:
http://www.klkreig.com

Goodreads:
https://www.goodreads.com/author/show/9845429.K_L_Kreig

TSU:
http://www.tsu.co/klkreig

Twitter:
https://twitter.com/klkreig

Made in the USA
Las Vegas, NV
17 November 2023